A Time for Courage

Margaret Graham has been writing for thirty years. Her first novel was published in 1986 and since then she has written fourteen novels, and is currently working on her fifteenth. As a bestselling author her novels have been published in the UK, Europe and the USA. *A Time for Courage* was previously published as *A Measure of Peace*.

Margaret has written two plays, co-researched a television documentary – which grew out of *Canopy of Silence* – and has written numerous short stories and features. She is a writing tutor and speaker and has written regularly for Writers' Forum. She founded and administered the Yeovil Literary Prize to raise funds for the creative arts of the Yeovil area and it continues to thrive under the stewardship of one of her ex-students. Margaret now lives near High Wycombe and has launched Words for the Wounded which raises funds for the rehabilitation of wounded troops by donations and writing prizes.

She has 'him indoors', four children and three grand-children who think OAP stands for Old Ancient Person. They have yet to understand the politics of pocket money. Margaret is a member of the Rock Choir, the WI and a Chair of her local U3A. She does Pilates and Tai Chi and travels as often as she can.

For more information about Margaret Graham visit her website at www.margaret-graham.com

D0367890

Margaret GRAHAM

A Time for Courage

arrow books

Published by Arrow Books 2014

2 4 6 8 10 9 7 5 3 1

First published in Great Britain in 1989 by
William Heinemann Ltd as *A Measure of Peace*

Arrow Books
Random House, 20 Vauxhall Bridge Road,
London SW1V 2SA

www.randomhouse.co.uk

Addresses for companies within The Random House Group Limited can
be found at: www.randomhouse.co.uk/offices.htm

The Random House Group Limited Reg. No. 954009

A CIP catalogue record for this book
is available from the British Library

ISBN 9780099585831

Printed and bound by CPI Group (UK) Ltd, Croydon, CR0 4YY

Penguin Random House is committed to a sustainable future
for our business, our readers and our planet. This book is made
from Forest Stewardship Council® certified paper.

For Ian, Roger and David

A Time for Courage

1 The room was dark as it always was. The drapes were half-drawn to keep out the sunlight which beat down on the newly mown lawn; her father didn't like the sunlight, did he? It faded the carpets and was unhealthy.

Hannah heard the ticking of the grandfather clock in the corner and waited for the chime which would run on for what seemed like for ever, but would only be thirty seconds at the most.

There it was; the big hand at twelve, the small at three. On and on it went. She jabbed the needle hard down through the fine linen cloth held taut in the wooden frame which was screwed tight; her well-boned face drawn with concentration, her brown eyes seeing beyond her work, her slim body tense.

Antimacassars wouldn't be necessary, she had mouthed silently as Mrs Brennan had passed this one to her last night, wouldn't be necessary if he didn't wear hair oil. Why did men wear hair oil? The needle dug hard into her finger as she pressed it right through, but she preferred that to a thimble which was tight and heavy. She brought the needle back up and smoothed the satin stitch down with the forefinger of her other hand, liking the sleek feel of silk against the matt linen. But her hands were sticky in the summer heat and she feared they would mark the sheer white of the work, so she wiped them on her handkerchief and sat with them open in her lap.

Mrs Brennan the housekeeper had said her mother had given instructions that if the needlework was soiled Hannah was to work for a further hour. She mimicked the twitching shoulders and pursed mouth of Beaky Brennan, remembering how Harry had laughed when she had decided that they must call the housekeeper that. But that was before he had gone away to school. Hannah returned to her task. Well, the woman did have round, owl-like eyes with short sparse eyelashes and a sharp nose, didn't she? Without lifting her head she could hear the call of the knife grinder in the street and the rattle of the cart and carriage wheels as they ground along the crescent at the front of the house. Her father had forbidden straw to be laid in the road to deaden the noise as was usual in the case of sickness. Because, she had overheard him telling the nurse, it was unseemly that the neighbours should know that his wife had failed again in her duty.

It was fortunate, therefore, that her mother's bedroom was at the back, overlooking the quiet of the garden as this room did, but her mother would not be looking out, would she?

The sofa was uncomfortable against her back. The buttons which drew the satin deep into the hair padding made awkward hillocks, but her mother always said that it was as well that they did, since girls of fifteen should learn to sit up without support. Queen Victoria might have passed away, her mother had said on their return from viewing the funeral procession when winter was at its height, but it should not be forgotten that our Queen could sit for hours with a straight back.

Hannah tugged at the black dress she wore. A straight back and a face that looked as though it had sucked an unripe gooseberry, she thought. Prince Albert was wise to leave when he did. She stabbed her needle through the linen, drawing the stitch too tight; loosening it with the point; seeing the black of her dress against the white of the antimacassar; feeling the anger rise. Exhibiting good posture is not all the Queen managed to achieve, is it, but they don't think of that, she ground out. She heard her own voice but she didn't care. She wanted to shout it so that the whole of London could hear, so that some of the pain would go.

That old black widow had wanted the Transvaal War; the war that was still not ended. The war that was intended to slap down the Boers who were challenging the Empire. The war which had killed Uncle Simon, her mother's older brother. Hannah snapped her thread in her anger.

It was not fair that her uncle's laughter would never again be heard, his blond hair and grey eyes never again catch the light. It was not fair that his firm arms would no longer hug her when he first arrived from leave or from the Cornish house, Penhallon, which he had shared with her mother's elder sister, Eliza. The house which Hannah loved and which had been in her mother's family for generations.

It was not fair because it left her no one who would hold her now, for her parents did not care for displays of affection. Her hand was suddenly wet from the heat, wet from the sound of his laughing, and her eyes could not see the stitching any longer. So she listened for the rattle of wheels, for the chatter of birds in the garden, for the sounds of life and, finally, she heard them, edging and pushing past the sound of Uncle Simon. First it was the blackbird, who always rested in the horse-chestnut, then the finches from the terrace, the muted cries of the rag-and-bone man, the distant rumble of the wheels until even the echoes of his laughter were gone; for now.

Her neck ached from being so still, listening so hard, and she flung her embroidery to one side, wiping her hands down the darkness of her day dress. The bodice was tight and the stays dug into her flesh. She rose to ease her discomfort, to release herself from the restraint of needlework, of her mind.

She walked first to the mantelshelf, her stride clipped but fast. The mirror above the mantelshelf was at last free of the black crêpe drape which had cloaked it for six months after the announcement of Victoria's death. There had been black everywhere, but why, she had wanted to ask, since the old Queen herself had decided on a white funeral. That must have been a shock to everyone, she thought, picking up a filigree framed miniature of her grandfather. Had the rest of Victorian society considered discarding black and hanging white instead like her parents had?

What had they all thought of the coffin covered with white and golden pall, and lamp-posts hung with purple drapes set off with white bows instead of an all-pervading black? What a to-do that had caused, and she smiled faintly, pleased that she could do so again. She replaced the miniature, smelling her hands, which were pungent now with the dark smell of silver. Her father had not thought it necessary to hang drapes for Uncle Simon and she had been glad because there had been no darkness in that man.

She turned, leaning her shoulders back against the mantel-shelf, seeing the crimson silk sofa with its nearby tables waiting to be drawn close should they be needed. The whatnots with their four-tiered stands crammed full of ornaments; their pillars looking like the twisted barley sugar which she often bought from the Emporium on the way to Miss Fletcher's School for Girls. One piece for her and one for her cousin Esther, who would wait in the entrance hall for her until she arrived; though Esther was not really her cousin, but the daughter of her father's cousin, Thomas Mann, that rich and prominent lawyer who drove her father puce with envy, though nobody knew that she had realised this. She moved across to her father's chair, the one nearest to the fireplace, and ran her fingers above but not on the glistening antimacassar. She could smell his smell; stale smoke and hair oil, and her dress seemed tighter still.

There was so much clutter; how could people breathe amongst it. She moved, wanting to sweep her hand across the surface of the mantelshelf to create some space. Her dress brushed the dark red and black of the Indian carpet as she hurried past the two occasional tables holding glass-domed shell flowers until she reached the heavy drapes. They too smelt of stale smoke. Why didn't that man smoke in his study? He knew it made her mother cough. She reached up and pulled the left curtain back, watching the light fall into the room, touching the green glass vase which held dyed pampas-grass. She must have brushed too close as she passed because some of its seeds floated high in the light and a few, she now saw, clung, deep blue, deep red, to her dress. She did not brush them off but looked instead at each of the dark oil paintings that hung on their long wires from the picture rails; at the tables that clustered about the room.

Against the bottom of the wood-panelled door was the velvet snake, solid and heavy from its stuffing of sand, well able to perform its task of excluding the winter draught, which otherwise froze your feet and back; unless, of course, you were sitting by the fire. She looked again at her father's chair. She understood why he had decreed that black should not be

4

draped for Uncle Simon; why should he mourn when he spoke of her mother's family in a voice filled with contempt. She shook her head, wanting to be free of thoughts such as these.

Esther had called this morning. She seemed to find it as hard as Hannah to be apart for too long, and during the holidays they called on one another, leaving cards in silver trays then darting up to old nurseries or into empty drawing-rooms to laugh and talk. This morning though they had not laughed but tried to talk of Miss Fletcher and the grey dresses she always wore, of the new desks which had arrived in the middle of the Bishop's visit, of the Monitor's badges they would wear next term. But the footsteps of the doctor and the nurse had driven through their words and the murmur of lowered voices had smothered their own.

Esther had soon risen, saying that she would come again tomorrow, and had left flowers which Mrs Brennan had later placed in water. Hannah had wanted to stop her, make her sit again with her because she couldn't bear to be alone, but she had not.

She had moved quickly now to the other curtain and pulled that back too then walked out into the sun, feeling its heat on her face, on her hands, seeping through her clothes and knew that she would redden and therefore be discovered, but just for now, this minute, it didn't matter somehow.

The terracotta pots were brilliant with roses and their fragrance was in the air, filling it. She walked down the steps, out on to the lawn, seeing the dead black patches that had been the daisies that she loved but which were now salted and destroyed. How could anyone object to their summer beauty? But her father did, insisting a garden should be ordered, should be as their neighbours would wish, as society would expect.

She lifted her skirt as she walked along the paths to the borders of lavender, lemon, thyme and mint. This was the area that she loved, fragrantly tucked away on the west side of the garden, away from the geometrical shapes that her father and the gardener had devised and edged with miniature box hedges, clipped exactly, enclosing marigolds, alyssum and tight-headed neat flowers that did not stray beyond their allotted space.

Over here though, behind the herbs, were the remains of the guinea-pig hutches where she and her brother Harry had fed, watered and cleaned the soft, furred creatures; holding their warmth in their hands, rubbing their cheeks against the rosettes of coats, feeling the busyness of their bodies.

Further up, by the old horse-chestnut was the thick looped rope which hung empty now. She moved along and pushed it in the windless air. It was warm to the touch and frayed, bristling with small hairs for as high as she could reach. Here, before Harry had been sent to school when he was eight and she was six, he had spun her as she leant back with both hands clutching the rope, her foot wedged in the loop; spun her until the blue and green above merged and laughter filled the space around them both.

Here he had bowled her stumps clean out of the ground, and tried to teach her Ring-goal, but catching and throwing a ring with two sticks proved too difficult for her. Here he had chased her until she was hot in her combinations and heavy dress, until there was no breath left in her body and she had flung herself down and begged for mercy and he had lain beside her, his breath warm in her face. He had picked daisies and threaded them but left the dandelions, since they made you wet the bed and what a fuss there would then have been from Beaky, he had groaned. And then, at the end of that last summer, he had waved goodbye from the window of the train and nothing had been the same again.

She dropped the rope. Harry would be home for the holidays soon but that would barely change the pattern of her days. For, he had told her when he returned after his first term, after he had written the letter, you are a girl, and boys don't play with girls, especially their sisters.

Now she didn't run because it was not permitted; girls did not run or jump or put their arms above their head. Hannah swept her hair back off her face, where it had strayed from the pins which gathered it into the pleat on the back of her head, and stretched her arms high, her fists clenched.

She looked back towards the house. Her mother's windows were shut, the curtains drawn. Above her, on the second floor, her own were also shut and she tightened her lips. Beaky had done it again.

She swung away, down to the bottom of the garden, her stride long now, her shoulders back, her skirt dragging on the grass. Down to the fernery, to the stream which ran along the back of the gardens in this suburb of London. Here there was no noise from the street, just the sound of the water and at last a slight breeze. She bent and grasped a fern, dragging her hands up the spine, tearing the fronds so that they curled into her hands, feeling the stinging on her palm. She opened her hand, it was stained green and scored red from the friction. It stung and she was glad. She tossed the curled leaves on to the water, watching as they passed on down, away from her and from the house. Where did the stream go, she wondered. Perhaps to the river and then out to the sea, the wide, wind-swept sea. She looked back again and knew that it must be time.

She walked towards the house, pausing by the shrubbed lavender, running her hand in amongst the bush, feeling for a large sprig. There was one near the centre but the woody stem was moist and green and she had to bend it backwards and forwards, backwards and forwards until finally the stringy fibre gave way. She rubbed the leaves, the oily flowers, and smelt the fragrance on her fingers, but the bitterness of the filigree silver still broke through so she stooped and crunched lemon thyme in her hands as well, rubbing the small leaves and their thin stems but leaving the shrub still intact. Now, at last the bitterness was gone.

'Miss Hannah!' The voice was shrill and Hannah turned to face Mrs Brennan who stood on the top step, her black dress stark in the sunlight, her small white apron startling in its contrast. She was shading her eyes.

Hannah looked up at the window. She moved quickly over to the housekeeper. 'Mother might be sleeping, Mrs Brennan,' she said quietly, wanting to clap a hand over the tight mouth which could shout so loudly through those thin wet lips.

'Your poor dear mother is lying awake waiting to see you, Miss Hannah, and it's a sorry tale I'll have to be telling her.' She stepped to one side and waited for Hannah to walk before her into the drawing-room. 'There's your embroidery lying undone on the sofa in spite of those young men that give their lives just so that you can learn the arts that young ladies should.'

Hannah stepped from the flagstones of the terrace on to the wood flooring, her feet in their patent boots clicking until they reached the carpet. All was dark again and she twisted the lavender in her hands. 'What young men?' she asked.

Mrs Brennan did not answer but said, 'And these curtains should not be drawn back like this, Miss Hannah, you know that very well, now what would your father be saying if he could see this?'

Hannah turned and watched Mrs Brennan as she shook the curtains along the rails until the light no longer fell on the pampas-grass or the carpet. Until there was only shadow again.

'How is mother now?' She didn't want to ask, didn't want to know in case, this time, she was not going to get better.

Mrs Brennan turned; she was breathless now and her face was shiny. She was too fat, Hannah thought, and walked like the ships that wallowed in the harbour near her aunt's home in Cornwall. Her grey hair was immaculately tidy, though, and Hannah tucked back the brown strands of her own hair that had shaken free from her pleat again.

'Your mother is over the worst,' Mrs Brennan said, her hands smoothing down the drapes, 'and it's a shame I shall have to tell her of your behaviour. It doesn't encourage her recovery, you know.'

'But perhaps if I just sewed for an hour when I have seen her there would be no need to say anything.' She looked at the lavender in her hand, at her dress, crumpled where she had clutched it as she walked up the steps, into Beaky Brennan's face and thought again how like an owl's it really was. Did Harry still think so too?

Why was he always away when this happened with their mother? It was so much worse to be here, to see her and hear the comings and goings of the nurse, to try and shut out the noise from the bedroom. But Beaky was talking again.

'That's not the height of it, though, is it, Miss Hannah? Out in the sun without a parasol and you knowing how much your mother is trying to do her best for you. A pale skin is important, you know.'

Hannah nodded, feeling the sun still hot on her cheeks. 'I'll go up then, Mrs Brennan.' Her voice sounded dead now, the sun far away through the narrowed gap. How far would the fronds have gone, she wondered. It was better to think of that than her mother's disappointment, which was made worse as there was no defence. She had known at the time what the end result would be and wished, as she so often did, that there was not this urge within her to push against rules which seemed too tight and petty to be endured but were deeply ingrained in society and, therefore, in her family.

She stepped back as Beaky waited to be allowed to pass before her through the door, and walk heavily up the stairs, clutching the banisters as she always did; the only servant allowed to use the front stairs.

Hannah stood with her back against the door jamb watching the housekeeper pause for breath on the half-landing before hauling herself up the remainder and then into the bedroom with her mouth full of words which would bring that creasing of her mother's forehead, that tightening of her lips.

She ran her finger round the high collar, now damp from the hot afternoon. The hall was dark with just two shafts of light, stained red by the coloured segments set into the small side windows either side of the door.

There were no visiting cards in the bowl set on top of the carved rug-chest for there would be no 'At Home' today or for some time to come. There were two letters, though, in the wire cage which jutted out on this side of the letter-box. She moved across and lifted the lid. One was from Harry to her parents, the other for her father, and she placed them on the silver tray, neatly butting up the edges so that they were exactly in line; but Harry's was too long. She bent over, her breath clouding the silver; an inch either side and . . . there, they were exact. Still Beaky had not called. Hannah moved over to the foot of the stairs. The nurse would be there too. She would hear about the daughter who had . . .

9

'Miss Hannah, your mother would like to see you now.' Hannah heard the voice before the closing of the door and the sound of Beaky's bulk on the stairs. As she came down the last flight Hannah looked up at her.

'What did you mean about men dying so that I could sew antimacassars, Mrs Brennan?' The banister was cool under her hand.

She could hear the loud breath of the housekeeper as she reached the bottom and, standing next to her, could smell the peppermint that she sucked so much of the time.

'It's those young men, Miss Hannah. The needle grinders of the Midlands. They sharpen the points, see, and the metal sticks in their lungs and they never see more than twenty-five years in all.'

Beaky Brennan moved past Hannah, dabbing her face with her handkerchief.

'But why do they do it?' Hannah asked, swallowing as she wondered whether the filings cut the throat too.

'Because it's a job, and at least it gives the families enough for a while after they've gone.'

'But that's dreadful, Mrs Brennan, it's so wrong, so unfair. It would be better if everything was plain, surely, nothing was embroidered.'

Mrs Brennan stopped and looked. 'We all know what you would like, Miss Hannah, less work for you.' She smiled coldly and Hannah felt the heat rush to her face.

'No I didn't mean that, not that,' she protested.

'Go and see your mother now,' Mrs Brennan was already at the end of the hall, opening the door on to the servants' quarters.

Hannah grasped her skirt in her hands but the lavender caught and snagged a thread; gently she released it, pulling the material until it was no longer noticeable, and mounted the stairs. The nurse was outside the closed door, her white apron starched and clean.

'Not too long now,' she instructed. 'Your mother is very weak.'

It was the smell Hannah hated. Hot darkness that smelt of

illness. Would it be the same this year? She turned to the nurse as she opened the door.

'Couldn't we open the windows? I'm sure it would be more pleasant for Mother.'

'Just go in please, Miss.' The nurse's face had closed against Hannah.

And it was dark and it did smell; that same smell but she wouldn't think of it; she would breathe through her mouth, walk over to the bed, avoiding the small easy chair, she told herself; the one which was pulled out of place to make room for the empty white-draped cradle. Why did they leave it here to upset her mother? Why did she go on having babies and where did they come from anyway? No one would explain. Her mother had just told her that she must wait until her wedding night. But why did she keep having them?

Hannah dug her nails into the hard stem of the lavender. Had she spoken the words? She couldn't tell but her anger had returned. Why did she keep having them? They only died. Wasn't she enough, and Harry? After all, one day her mother might die too and that would leave her all alone with Father. Fear filled her chest but did not remove the rage which she was afraid would spill out all over that small figure when she opened her mouth to speak.

'Hallo, Mother.' And so it had not.

There was enough light filtering through the curtains where they did not quite meet for her to see her mother's face, and it was not beautiful as it usually was, with calm grey eyes and pale smooth skin, but drawn and sunken and sallow and the mouth was tight, the forehead creased.

'I'm so sorry, Mother.' I will improve, she thought, knowing that to say so would irritate. And now guilt had taken the place of anger, though fear remained. Her mother turned towards her, her voice slow and tired.

'It won't do, Hannah. It really won't do. You have wasted an afternoon, neglected your duty. Now that you have reached fifteen, you must learn to drive from your thoughts all but those designed to please others. There can be no room for selfishness in a woman's life. Your priorities will soon be the care of a husband and children; it is wrong to think in any other way. You must develop the skills which will bring happiness and contentment to those about you; attract the right sort of husband.'

'But I don't think it makes men happy to have embroidered antimacassars. After all, Father never smiles, does he? And it kills the grinders, did you know that? Isn't it a greater selfishness to continue to sew once we realise the real cost?' She watched as her mother lifted her hand for silence. It was white and the veins stood out and it looked so small. Hannah moved her own hand towards it but stopped, for her mother did not like to touch, or be touched.

'Hannah, can it be that Miss Fletcher is not teaching the right attitude? Should we take you away? This storm of words, this preoccupation with things that are nothing whatsoever to do with you. How can you expect your father to look happy when there is this attitude in his home? How can we hope for a good marriage if you allow your tongue to run away with you? And how do you expect Harry to cope with a sister who refuses to obey the rules of society, especially when he enters the Household Cavalry as your father intends? You simply have to remember who you are and your obligations. Your duties may seem trivial to you but they are essential to developing a respectable attitude, to becoming a lady.' Her breathing was rapid now but she raised her head, holding up her hand to still Hannah's protests.

'Father so wishes that you should raise yourself to the level of his cousins, and the only way to do that is through a good marriage and for that you must be brought to a peak of suitability.' She paused. 'Should we be thinking in terms of a governess, Hannah?' Her eyes were half shut and her voice was still gentle but there was a real question in it.

Hannah felt her cheeks stiffen with the stirrings of panic. 'Oh no, it's not the school, I promise you it's not the school.' She sought for words that would push away the threat of separation from Miss Fletcher and her knowledge and understanding, the threat of separation from Esther. 'It's just that I forget sometimes what I should be aiming for and I don't find sewing easy, Mother. I'm better at my work and . . . I would like to teach, you see. And many women do, ladies I mean. Look at Miss Fletcher.'

Hannah interlaced her fingers, squeezing them tightly together. 'But I will try,' she continued. 'I promise I'll try, with my sewing and my attitude.' She must stay there at all costs and so her obedience must improve, her thoughts must stay deep down, hidden from sight, though surely deceit was a sin. She shook her head. Why did her head fill with endless questions when it should all be so simple; just needles and threads, rules and antimacassars. She smiled now at her mother. 'I'll try so hard, Mother,' she said.

She saw the crease in her mother's forehead fade and her mouth soften.

'Yes, you must try, and as for teaching, we'll see, Hannah, dear, but you must remember that there is no virtue in being clever. In fact, in the eyes of the society that your father adheres to it is almost a sin. Cleverness is reserved for the men of the family, for your father and Harry. I know that there are some very strange ideas coming in now with King Edward but those are not for people in our position.' She paused. 'Women have no position other than that within the family, Hannah. It is our pleasure, our duty to serve, nurture and to care, and you must at all times take your lead from your father who, quite rightly, dictates our standards. There is no room in our home for the attitudes which some say should sweep aside the old rules along with the old Queen; that is tantamount to sacrilege, my dear. As your father says, there is security and dignity in tradition but none in new ideas. Women do have a role and it is your duty to aspire to that role; you must always remember that.' She paused, drawing in a deep breath gathering strength to finish. 'I was wondering if a finishing school would help you to achieve the degree of sensibility that your father requires. It would after all groom you in all the graces, help you to meet the brothers of nice girls and you might enjoy seeing a foreign land. I do believe Esther will be going to one when she leaves Miss Fletcher.'

Hannah dug her nails into the leaves of the lavender and

tried to smile. Not a finishing school, not even with Esther. It had to be a university; somewhere which would educate and broaden her mind, make some sense of the confusion which was churning inside her head. 'But they're so expensive, Mother. Miss Fletcher feels there might be a chance of a University Scholarship to ease the financial burden. After all, Lady St John's daughter left Miss Fletcher's last year and is now at Newnham in Cambridge and already engaged to Lord Scarsdale's son.'

She had no desire to marry a Lord but her father would approve. She watched her mother's face.

'Well, the money would certainly have to be considered in whatever decision your father chooses to make and I agree with you that it does not appear to have spoilt dear Harriet's chances in any way. We'll say no more about it at the moment.' Her mother's lips were dry and her voice seemed faint; she was looking at the lavender so Hannah held it up, glad to move away from the discussion which was tiring this fragile woman.

'I've brought some of the flowers to burn. I thought it might make you feel more comfortable.' Her shoulders relaxed as her mother smiled; there were deep lines round her mouth as she did so which hadn't been there before today. I love you so much, Mother, Hannah thought, and I want you to love me too. I can't bear it when you're like this so I'll push this restlessness as far from me as I can and maybe it'll stay away and I'll forget it was ever there. Hannah traced her finger along the back of the pale hand, across the raised veins, and her mother did not pull her hand away but lifted it and held Hannah's for just a moment, then turned her face as tears seeped on to the pillow.

'I'm so sorry about the baby, Mother,' said Hannah, her own voice thick. 'But why do you keep having them when they make you so ill?' And this time she had spoken it because she couldn't bear to see her mother cry. Mothers shouldn't cry, because everything became so unsafe.

'Just go and burn the lavender, Hannah.' Her mother's voice did not sound like her own.

The silk-quilted dressing-table held a candlestick and matches, and the smell of sulphur was sharp as the new wick took a while to light, but then Hannah held the lavender in its flame and slowly its smell took the place of the acrid atmosphere of the room. She would not look back at her mother's tears but at things which were the same yesterday and would be tomorrow. She would look at her mother's hairpin boxes, the china ring-stand with her betrothal ring glowing in the light from the candle. Her hat-pins which caught the light in their holders and the pincushions which were stabbed with bead-topped pins.

In the mirror Hannah could see that her hair had come away from the bun again, that her cheekbones were sharp in the flickering light and that her mouth was still too big; and she could also see that the reflection of her mother showed her resting quietly now with no glint on her cheeks and no destroyed composure. Only then did she feel better and able to love this room as she usually did, for it was the only one that was comfortable and seemed like her mother. But most of all she loved the mirror. She was only allowed one that would fit into a handbag in her own room since vanity was a sin. Bodily flesh might be explored, Mrs Brennan had explained, since her mother did not discuss these things with her.

She turned again to the bed. 'Shall I open a window, Mother? It is so lovely outside.' But there was no reply so she laid the lavender on the plate next to the candle, snuffed out the flame, and walked quietly to the window. She pulled the top sash window down, just an inch so that it would not be obvious. She wanted her mother to breathe in some of the early summer.

Edith Watson watched through heavy-lidded eyes as her daughter left the room. Her body ached and where the baby had been was yet another wrenching emptiness. The Vicar had leant from the pulpit, his eyes boring into those of his congregation, and warned of this; of warped babies born to those who lusted. Was that why John would not lay straw in the street? Did he not want the world to know that again his wife had failed in her ordained task? Or was it a punishment for the sin she had committed? She knew that it was a sin because the Vicar had called it such, though he had not known that he was talking just to her.

She picked at the sheet, wishing that she could throw off the blanket. It was too heavy, too hot, but a mere sheet was not decent. She felt the slight breeze and was grateful to Hannah and remembered the feel of her daughter's hand in hers, warm and strong. It was good to have had someone's strength, even if it was only for a moment. The room was dark now that the candle had been snuffed but the scent of lavender still lingered.

Would Hannah cry when John told her she would never go to university? Because that is what he intended to do of course when he was ready. It was as though he enjoyed playing these cruel games but that could not be the case; she could not let herself believe that this was the case for that would be a further disloyalty, a further fall from grace. She brushed her hair from her face.

It would seem hard for the child but perhaps John was right when he said that suffering cleansed the soul; that is what so many seemed to think and who was she to argue? It was certainly correct that Hannah worked better feeling that there might be a chance of her dream and he did so want her to compete with Esther and triumph over her and therefore Thomas. And that was his dream; but did he really think it would make him appear the equal of that side of the family? How sad for him, for Hannah.

She stirred. Could it be cruelty? But no, it was John's attempt to save his daughter. Yes, that was what it was. To save her from the sin of selfishness, but I do hope she doesn't cry, Edith thought, and the words seemed to have a rhythm of their own as she mouthed them through dry, parched lips. The sheet was starched and rubbed her neck where it was folded over so she pushed it down, and the breeze which swept across her shoulders soothed the panic which was gathering in her body and calmed her, although she thought of the spirit she could see growing in Hannah and which John might also see. A spirit which would cause the child pain, as it had done with her, unless it was suppressed.

There was a wilfulness which had all too clearly passed from mother to daughter and she wanted to weep with the pain of guilt. My beloved Hannah has too much of me in her. She must be led down the proper path so that John does not realise that in his daughter is the likeness of her mother. For then there would be no redemption. Not for Hannah in the future or for herself, because now her own survival was at stake. Would he cast her out without her children, without his name? Without her money, because he had it all?

She must instruct Mrs Brennan not to divulge Hannah's lack of endeavour, her selfishness of today which was so reminiscent of her own and might renew his shock and repugnance at the lapse in her morality seven months ago which had never again been mentioned in words, only in looks full of distaste and hatred. Deservedly so because she had broken the rules by which they lived.

He had not come to see her last night or today. Would he come up this evening? She glanced at the empty cot. She knew the answer and that he was correct to blame her. She was tossing and turning now.

The door opened and the nurse came to the bed. 'You must sleep now, Mrs Watson. You need to regain your strength.'

Her hands pulled the bedclothes straight and the breeze from the window ruffled the curtains; Edith willed the nurse to look at her, not at the gently lifting drapes. It was so hot, so very hot. But the stocky woman in her purple dress straightened, her lips pursed. She looked down but Edith closed her eyes and she walked to the window and heaved it shut before leaving the room.

Breathing in the heat was difficult, she could feel the dampness where her head touched the pillow, she was wet all over her body. She moved her legs slightly apart, stretched her arms out to the side. The noise of the carriages and the raucous call of the muffin boys as they passed the front of the house jabbed through her head.

Had it been this hot for poor Simon, out there in that country and had he remembered Cornwall before he died? Had he remembered her and Eliza and the days when the three of them walked the cliffs as children and could see, in the distance, the tin mine which their father owned? She would never know, but Eliza swore that he would have remembered and perhaps she was right. It was such a distant war, not even one that protected England.

She turned her head. The water jug was covered with a beaded net and small bubbles clung to the sides. It would not be cool. She would ask John if they could go down to Cornwall, to Eliza, to go walking along that cliff, looking down at the harbour, feeling the wind cooling them, pressing them away from the edge. If Harry came too he would agree to the visit. He would take his son fishing, and smile, and perhaps forgive her for this dead baby and for that October night seven months ago when she had writhed beneath him, laying aside restraint and clutching him to her, moving herself to his rhythm, groaning. She flushed as she remembered how he had frozen and lifted himself from her and looked with repugnance on her face.

You forget yourself, my dear, he had said, and now she passed her hands over her eyes as she remembered how she had cried and clung to him because she wanted him to come back into her, not to leave her while she was swollen and full of need for love, for his body. She groaned now. The sexual act, which she had known nothing of before the night of their marriage, had touched something in her and she knew she enjoyed what no decent woman should, though, until that dreadful night, she had always taken such care to hide her lust.

She still did not know what had possessed her to allow heedless words to come, as, appalled, he had torn her hands away. Please, she had said, we can just have each other to love and to hold and to feel tonight; does there have to be a baby? Her hair had been loose and had caught in her mouth as she clung to him, her night-dress, which he would never remove, clinging and hampering her. He had struck her face and called her a whore, a Godless whore, and had left her room and not visited it since. But there had been a baby anyway, from his visit to her bed the month before.

Her hands were throbbing now, and her legs. Her head was hurting even more. Yes, lust was wicked. The Vicar was right. Another baby dead and the guilt was hers. Yes, she must control Hannah, must make her understand that to submit is a virtue and leads to less pain, less guilt, for she couldn't bear that her daughter should go through all that she had suffered.

Procreation, John had said as he left the room that night, is your reason to live. To desire anything else is to assume the nature of a harlot, an animal. Have you taken leave of your senses?

Yes, she must go to Cornwall again, go home, and perhaps he would come and fish in the trout stream with Harry, the son she had given him, and perhaps he would visit her room again and if she was good perhaps the baby would live. But Hannah must not be there, must not produce a tension that could affect a reconciliation. She must stay in the marriage at all costs to remain near to Hannah, to keep her position as a married woman.

The nurse came back into the room, walked to the bed and lifted the net cover from the water. 'A little sip then, Mrs Watson.' Edith pushed herself up, just a few inches and the water was warm as she had known it would be.

The dining-room table was laid with a white cloth, and her father sat in his mahogany carver chair at the end of the table. Mrs Brennan had placed her in the usual place, halfway down. The steamed fish looked small on the gold-edged plate, its flesh almost indistinguishable from the white bone china. There was no vegetable other than a small potato because it was Friday and the Vicar favoured fasting. Her father had salmon steak as usual. He was reading, his book lying on the bookrest that stood by his chair. It only needed an eagle to turn into a lectern, thought Hannah.

The light from the hissing gas lamps caught the elaborate mouldings of the sideboard, the dark shadows hiding the grey dust which Polly the maid could never clean from the sharpened carvings. The huge picture of the stag at bay hung as always on the wall above, looking in the dim light even more as though it was going to snap its wires and plunge onto the tantalus which held her father's decanters of whisky and brandy. That would make him lose his place, she thought, and ate a small mouthful of fish slowly to make it seem more substantial.

Venison would be nice, she thought, looking at the stag. Her father had bought it because it seemed a lot of picture for a small amount of money and he liked to think he had picked up a bargain; or so she had heard him tell Grandfather before he died. She was glad her grandfather had been 'gathered', as the Vicar would say, because he smelt unpleasant and had hardly any teeth left so that he spat when he talked.

She took another mouthful. Mother obviously had not told Father about her behaviour because he had said nothing and she had not been banished to her room with no food. Not that this meal would fill her up.

Her father turned from his book and poured more champagne. He never allowed the cork to pop but eased it from the angled bottle, his lower lip protruding, watching the vapour before pouring. Her fish was almost finished now.

She watched as he took a sip and then some food before returning to his book. As he chewed his jaw clicked; it always did and as she watched she found her breathing was in time with it. She took another mouthful and then some of the potato but now she was chewing in time too.

'Remember that we do not finish our meals, Hannah. One must never even suggest that we could be hungry. That is a state we do not recognise.' His eyes flicked towards her and then back to his book.

'Yes, Father,' she replied, and laid her knife and fork down. But I am hungry, she wanted to say, but knew that it was a different sort of hunger, a poor hunger, that he meant. Did the needle sharpeners eat well before they died, she wondered.

He had finished his champagne and was leaning back in his chair now, wiping his drooping moustache first with his napkin and then with his finger, smoothing it back into shape so that it fell brown and glistening almost to his chin. She hated his nails; they were long and like those of the witch who had haunted her childhood and brought people poisoned apples. Harry had said that their father kept his nails long to show he didn't have to do any rough work. Grandfather's had been the same, he said. She couldn't remember that, but she could imagine the two men together poring over their clients' cases, pointing to the important items before advising them to buy property or sue a tradesman.

Did he know about the needle sharpeners? Perhaps he didn't, and if she told him he just might think it wrong and forbid the use of needles in his home which would save a few lives; but she knew it was unlikely. She looked down the table at him. His brows were heavy, shading his eyes so that there was never any life in them or, when he looked at her, any love. They frightened her, and made her feel alone. She looked back at her plate.

'Mrs Brennan says that needle sharpeners die by twenty-five. It's not right, is it?' It came out in a rush because of those eyes and she wished she had not felt as though she must challenge him with her sense of injustice. Her father sat quite still and she wondered if he had heard her.

'Mrs Brennan talks a great deal too much,' he replied, his voice as cold as usual.

He took a cigarette from his case and lit it, sucking the smoke right down before drawing back his lips and letting the smoke stream through his widely spaced teeth in strips. Hannah looked away; his teeth were like old park railings. They'd probably drop out like Grandfather's and he'd chew his gums. She shuddered. He had returned to his book and she felt a flush of anger. He didn't read when Harry was home or her mother was well enough to eat downstairs. He made no pretence at liking her. She was a girl, wasn't she?

Hannah persisted. 'But it doesn't seem right that they choose work which kills them just so that they can make sure their families eat.' Her heart was beating very fast now and it seemed to have moved up into her throat from her chest.

He put his leather bookmark in place before snapping the covers shut. She flinched at his violence. 'This subject should not arise in a girl's mind. Suffice it to say that society is not in any way responsible for these people. Every man starts with quite sufficient opportunities, as you would know if you paid attention at all to the Vicar in Matins. Therefore it is solely the fault of the people concerned if they do not rise to our station; they deserve their poverty and I wish to hear no more about this. You may leave the table and prepare for bed.'

It was still so hot in her room, up on the floor above her mother, but she had opened the windows so there was at least a breeze. She hoped that air still circulated in the room below. Hannah leant back against the pillows. Yes, her father had certainly taken opportunities when they presented themselves. After all she had overheard Eliza once saying to Simon that he had married mother along with one-third of the tin mine profits. But how could a needle grinder ever meet a rich woman? Or his daughter have enough money to attend Miss Fletcher's? There never seemed to be an answer to these questions and it still wasn't acceptable that they should die, or for that matter that Simon should die. If her mother had another baby would she then finally die? She felt the fear return, the anger. Why keep having the babies? She lay, looking at the play of light on the ceiling. Did the heart just stop beating, she wondered, or did it slow down so that you had time to call for help? She put her hand on her left breast, even though it was a sin to touch, but yes, there it was, thud, thud, thud.

She would lie each night like this so that there was no danger of being gathered while she slept and then, if it began to stop, the doctor could be fetched. She felt easier now, though what if her left breast grew more slowly than the other one because it was having to push against her hand?

Hannah leant forward, her arms round her knees, listening to the carriages as they passed until she found the answer. She would open her fingers so that the breast would grow through the gap and drag the rest along behind, then no one would know that she had touched herself. Only God, and if she was feeling her heart she would have time to ask for forgiveness should it stop.

The moon was high now, casting its light into the room. Harry would be home soon and perhaps, just perhaps, they would go to Cornwall again.

2 The dogcart looked new although Aunt Eliza had bought it last year; the leather seats were the colour of the sweet sherry in the decanter on Penhallon's dining-room sideboard and still smelt of the polish the groom had used. Harry shook out the reins and the pony broke into a trot along the broadening track which led up to the junction where they would turn left away from the house and out into the high-banked Cornish lanes. He smiled. Yes, it was as comfortable as he had thought it would be. His father stirred beside him and craned his neck round the down.

'Good idea, these rubber tyres, aren't they, my boy?'

Harry nodded. The early morning mist still lay over the harbour and cliffs which they would soon leave behind as they travelled inland. Their fishing rods rattled as they rested almost upright in the back of the cart and he wondered whether he should wedge the picnic basket against them. He looked but the rods had not moved so he did nothing.

He loved the early morning but not the fishing. In fact he had forgotten all that he had been taught by his father when they were here two years ago but a repeat of the lesson might jolly the old man along a bit. He seemed even more taciturn than at Christmas, more preoccupied if that was possible. But bloody hell, fishing was so boring. Standing about waiting for the trout to bite, trying to think of things to say to the old boy. Feeling on edge all the time in case that tension which was never far below the surface of this dark man would snarl out from those eyes, that mouth, and make his stomach churn and his hands tremble. Was it fear his father aroused in him, he wondered, and knew that it was.

Perhaps Hannah was having the best of it after all, tucked up in a warm cottage; her feet weren't going to get wet and her hands numb with cold. Women were lucky; looked after and cosseted as they were.

'Move him on a bit, boy, we've a fair way to go this morning, you know.' The pony had slowed to an amble and his father's elbow dug hard into his ribs.

Damnation, he'd want to take the reins soon and that would mean a sweated pony and shaken wine. He edged further along the seat, away from the pressure of his father's arm. 'Yes, Father,' he replied, but quietly, since the mist silenced the countryside, turning its atmosphere into that of the school chapel. To speak in more than a whisper seemed somehow vulgar. His father had shouted, of course. But now, all was quiet again except for the quickening hoofs, the creaking of the harness and the rattle of the bit as the pony mouthed the metal, tossing its head as it did so. Harry eased his shoulders. It was strange to come down so early in the school holiday but his father said that his mother had been ill again. He lifted his tweed cap briefly from his head and wiped the droplets of mist from his forehead with the back of his hand. The mist clung also to his sleeve, caught on the hairs of the tweed. The reins felt damp in his hand so he caught the leathers between his knees, shaking his head as his father leant over to take them, while he drew his gloves from his pocket. Then the pony shied at a magpie breaking cover from the hedge that seemed to loom higher than it really was in the uncertain light, and he breathed, 'whoa, boy', as he took up the reins again, pulling the glove over his wrist with his teeth.

A breeze was setting up, gentle but definite, which meant that the sun would soon break through the dim mist and the pony would settle.

His father was sitting with arms crossed, his chin on his chest, his eyes closed, and only now did Harry feel able to relax and think about why his mother had arranged for Hannah to stay with a friend of Aunt Eliza's further inland and not with them. She had explained that Eliza had enough with three of them, especially after poor Simon's death, but Beaky had said that Hannah had been difficult. Just that, nothing more, but she had clasped her hands as she said it and rolled her shoulders and though her face hadn't smirked, her body had. He was glad that the old bat had not come down here with them and that Father had left the staff at home on board wages. That would wipe the smile off her face but it was hard on Polly and the gardener, he supposed.

What was wrong with Hannah, he mused. She was so quiet with him now and when he had asked what the problem was she had just looked at him. I don't know, she had said, I wish I did, and had turned from him and walked from the room, over the terrace and into the old play garden.

He had noticed that she dressed in long clothes now and her hair was up; it had surprised him. Suddenly she looked quite grown-up, so that explained a lot. Girls were different when they were growing up; they couldn't run or catch a ball, something to do with the way they changed shape, Benton Minor had said. Exercise made them ill. Yes, even her face was different – longer – and you could see that there were bones in it. This change had only happened recently though, because at Christmas her face was still similar to the one that had cried on the platform as she waved him away when he first joined the school. He had thought how round she was then, a round face and round body on top of frilled combinations, the blue sash of her white dress making her look like an Easter egg.

And then she'd sent him a drawing of the guinea-pigs with tears running from their eyes, and next to them, a girl in a dress with a blue sash with tears too. I love you, she'd scrawled in big joined writing, come home. There were kisses too. He had felt such a longing, a missing as he sat on his bed in the dormitory which was always dreary because the windows were so small and so high and his own tears had begun.

But then the paper had been snatched from his hand and a prefect had held it up to the dormitory and had gripped his hair, turned his wet face to the dormitory, shouting that cissies would not be tolerated. Harry could still feel that hand tearing the hair from his head and he pulled his cap on harder.

He remembered how the bugger had made the other boys form two rows after they had collected wet towels from the latrines, forcing him to run down between the rows while he was beaten. He shrugged his shoulders and clicked his tongue at the pony. His father was still asleep. He remembered the first stinging pains even now. At first it seemed as though his new friends were reluctant but the prefect called in his study chums to stand in the row too. One to every four of the younger boys and he was made to run back through the rows again. When he wouldn't tear Hannah's paper up he was made to run again and again. It was the noise he could never forget, it was like the baying of hounds after a fox. When the prefect grabbed him by the neck at the end of the fifth run and held the picture up in front of his face he did not see guinea-pigs but instead there was the swing rope and the horse-chestnut tree with Hannah whirling round and round as he pushed her faster and faster, hearing her laughter go on and on. When he still would not shred the picture into pieces he was taken to the latrines and his face was pushed into the water closet and he was sluiced in flushing water until his heart pumped for lack of air. It was this which made him do as they said.

He looked up. The sun was shining through the thinning mist, not hot yet but bright. Don't write to me again, ever, he had told her in his next letter home.

The hedge dipped and Harry could see the fields widening out into moorland; it wouldn't be long now. Yes, life was easier with just his friends. But sometimes, in the strangest of places, he would still remember that laugh as he had swung her round beneath the tree.

The sun had a glimmering of warmth at last and the hedge was clearly visible growing out of the high-banked stone; full of grass with honeysuckle climbing all over the hawthorn. When the sun was high the honeysuckle's scent would begin to fill the lane and by the time they returned it would be at its strongest. The track dwindled to a narrow strip of baked earth which wound round the flattened granite boulders lying amongst the heather. There were trees over to the right, about half a mile away.

'Head for that, m'boy.' His father was awake now and pointing. 'We'll follow the stream until we come to the pool. You remember it, don't you?'

Harry nodded but he didn't. The pony was sweating now but at the scent of water his stride sharpened and soon they were alongside the coursing stream which frothed white as it mounted and swerved round the jutting rocks. The pony pulled against the rein, eager to drink, but Harry urged him onwards until they reached the pool, oily in its stillness. And then he remembered how his father had beaten Hannah when he had heard of the incident in the dormitory. She must learn not to be a nuisance, he had told Harry when he had asked why.

It was cold standing up to his knees in the pool but so far his waders had kept out the water. The only wetness came from the dripping line as he drew it back to cast again. His father had given him a fly line that would float throughout its entire length saying that later he would graduate to one with a sinking tip, but privately Harry had cringed at the thought of more days like this. 'Let's try it again then, Harry.' His father stood with his legs apart, his tweed hat pulled down over his eyes. 'Remember, it's all a matter of timing. A good forward cast is entirely dependent on a good back cast. I want to see you straighten out fully behind and bend the rod tip backwards.'

Harry gripped the rod and moved it up. The sun was playing on the water and ripples ran out from his legs.

'No, no. Start horizontally over the water, boy. Don't you remember a thing I say? Use only the forearm until you reach about eleven o'clock, then a final flick of the wrist and back the line goes.'

Harry did as his father said, wishing that it was lunch-time. They had already been in the water nearly an hour; the sun was high and hot.

'Right, pause there to let the line straighten out. Go on, turn and watch the line.' His voice was impatient, his hat pulled down over his eyes to keep out the glare as he turned to his son. Harry did so but felt his feet shift on the bottom of the pool and for a moment thought he was going over. He hated water; he could barely swim and the thought of those boots filling and holding him under so that water gushed into his mouth and nose made him sweat.

His father's voice was sharp, his hand outstretched. 'Keep still, you fool. You'll see off the trout with all this confounded disturbance.'

Harry took deep breaths and wiped his forehead with his arm. Oh Christ, the old man was getting angry. There was a high bank on the other side with ferns and stunted trees stretching away. It looked cool and dark and quiet. All around, the moor stretched endlessly beneath the heat-hazed sky. To the north the Atlantic would be crashing against the coast bringing a cold wind to the shore; but it wasn't reaching inland today, damn it. He watched his father looking out anxiously over the pool, checking for ripples, for signs of disturbance from Harry's boots. Come on, for heaven's sake, Harry breathed, through lips tightened with tension. His father held up his own rod and turned back to Harry.

'Flex the tip backwards and then forwards again down and through to the original position.'

Harry heard the irritation and the more he was told the more mistakes he made. His father sighed and Harry's face set.

'But you didn't hold the line behind the butt ring like I told you, you stupid boy. Bring it down here.' His voice was hard, a muscle tightened in his cheek and Harry watched as his father brought his own rod back and then forwards again, grasping the line with his left hand and pulling it down towards his trouser pocket. His movements were so controlled, so vicious. 'Speeding up the back cast allows the line to shoot back behind more quickly. You took the rod too far back – the line wasn't damn well straight. Now let's do that again.'

The muscle still twitched, the voice grated and Harry held his breath. This time he did it in tune with his father and the noise of the reel and the birds as they wheeled high above them sounded too loud in the midday heat. He knew the trembling had begun but it was not yet visible and for that he was grateful. Water ran down Harry's hand, soaking his cuff and sleeve as far as his elbow. He worked the rod forward then back again and his wrist was chafed with each movement but he did not dare to stop. Again and again he cast until he saw the muscle relax. He heard the voice loosen and knew that at last he had satisfied his father who was looking over the pool again.

'Won't get many trout rising today, Harry, so we'll use the wet flies. The nymph will do nicely.' He waded from the water and Harry started to follow, his boots grating on the stones, his line reeled in and caught in his hand close to the rod.

'Stay there, boy. You'll only stir up the water.' His father's voice was harsh again, and Harry flushed.

God, he wished he'd waited and gone up to Scotland with Arthur. He'd never been shooting but at least it wasn't like being on parade. His father had said he could not afford to send him. He clenched his hands hard on the rod and watched as his father brought out two flies from his bag and eased himself back into the water coming close up to Harry.

'The nymph is usually reliable. The trout will think it's natural food if you work it in the water and make it seem alive.' His father's voice was relaxed now as though there had never been anger or tension. His breathing was heavy, his head bent over the end of the line, and Harry could smell the stale smoke on his breath. He moved and watched as a water-boatman skimmed across the surface. There was a ripple on the water and the boatman was gone. Was that a trout, he thought, but said nothing because it would mean changing to a dry fly and the morning would be endless. His stomach was empty. Breakfast had been early so that they could have the whole day on the moor. He was hungry now that the trembling had gone.

'There you go then. I'm moving a bit downstream to get out of your way. Want to go back with both my eyes, don't I?' His father laughed and Harry did too, dutifully. He cast again and there was a faint plop as the fly hit the surface and sank. He moved the rod occasionally; it was made from split cane brought from China and was his father's second best.

'So how is school these days, Harry?' His father was speaking quietly, though whether fish had ears was doubtful, Harry thought, and all the earlier shouting would have alerted them anyway.

'Fine, thank you, Father.' He was casting again. So far there had been no tug on his line, thank God. He dreaded a catch, the lashing fish at the end of the line, the hook which tore from the mouth of the fish. And then the gasping limpness.

He did not move the rod, just let the line lie as it was, tugged only by the water but not like food the fish would enjoy.

'Been doing much sport then?' His father was half-turned from him, his shoulders rounded as he handled his rod. His strength was evident from the broadness of his back, the bulge of muscle either side of his spine.

Harry replied, 'Cricket this term and we've been doing a lot of paper chases. I was the hare, you know, and beat the lot of them. First time it's been done this year.'

His father laughed. 'Not bad at all.'

It had been bloody good, thought Harry. The bag which dug into his shoulder as he set off at the edge of the copse had scarcely held him up at all, and by the time he was over by the meadows fringing the village much of the paper had gone. There'd been no wind so it had lain where it had fallen.

'Everything was against me,' he called across to his father. 'No wind, you see. They could get a good track on me.' He saw his father nod.

He'd finally skirted round the bottom wood and then he'd heard them as they sighted him and he'd run until he thought he could breathe no more. The air was pumping in and out like a knife and the ground was uneven so, once, he fell. He had thought they would be on him then but somehow he had risen, looking behind as he did so, and, although they'd been close, there was still a chance. Something like terror had gripped him then. Terror and excitement combined. They were so many and so nearly on him. He turned and ran, not seeing the woods or the bridge that he pounded over. Not seeing the boys grouped at the edge of the school playing fields cheering him in. Not stopping until he reached the finishing post and the sports master had caught him by the arm and slapped him on the back.

'Has young Arthur been notching up the runs again then?' his father called across.

Harry nodded. 'Rather. He's deadly with a bat, you know, Father.' He was with all sports but had not been able to catch Harry on that chase even though he'd been one of the front runners. The golden boy had been beaten, just for once. How blond he was, Harry thought as he shifted his grip on the rod – a kite was wheeling on an air current high above the pool – almost as blond as Uncle Simon.

30

'It was a shame about Uncle Simon, wasn't it, Father?'

His father turned and looked at him, his brown eyes narrowed against the sun. 'Yes, but it's a marvellous thing to lay down your life for your country, isn't it? Why, just think. If it lasts a few more years you will be in it, Harry.'

'But it won't, surely? It's nearly over, isn't it?' Harry reeled in slightly. All the papers said that it was over. The Boers were on the run.

His father cast once again, then reeled in his line. 'Be a while yet, so there's a chance.' He looked at his son. 'Bring your line in now, Harry, and let's have some lunch.' They waded carefully to the bank, then drew their galoshes off. Cook had packed up hard-boiled eggs, ham pie and sandwiches, and Harry went down to the water and pulled up the bottle of wine which he had wedged in shallow water to cool.

His father sat back against a stunted oak, its dry lichen brushing off on to his jacket. 'I can remember the day war was declared.' He wiped his mouth with the corner of the napkin which he had tucked into his collar. 'I was walking back from the office to the Underground.' He paused. 'It was cold, you know, I had my coat on and it was only mid-October. Anyway you could hear the paper sellers shouting it out from the corners. Ultimatum by Kruger. Declaration of war. Damned cheek. A bunch of ruffians turning against us. They don't know what's good for them, that's the trouble.' He ate more of the ham pie, then took a sip of wine.

'But they beat us for a while, didn't they, Father, and I can remember the Headmaster telling us it would be over in three months. That week in December was a shock. Everything seemed to stop. Methuen, Gatacre and even Buller were defeated in that week. Those Boers must have known how to fight.'

The pie was rather dry, he thought, but the egg was moist. He poured himself some wine and looked across at his father. They had been drilled harder in the school Rifle Volunteer Corps during that week, the one called Black Week.

'Dirty fighters though, skulking about in those velds in their tatty clothes. They're not gentlemen, you know, Harry, and we've got them on the run now, my boy; thank God, because the buses are never on time with these old nags drawing them. The army took the best ones for the war, you know, but we shouldn't complain, it's all in a good cause. These ruffians have to learn they can't just toss the British to one side because they feel like being independent. They need us to civilise them, you know. Give 'em a few of our laws, a bit of our discipline. They need to know their place.' He paused as he searched in his jacket pocket, finally finding his cigarette case. 'Mark you, so do these damn Liberals shouting their support. It's treason, boy. They deserve to be shot. Like that fool Gladstone forever rambling on about Home Rule for Ireland. He tried to give away parts of the Empire. It was a disgrace. Freedom, my foot, the man was an idiot, and it's a great relief to me that he's finally dead.'

He tossed over his cigarette case to Harry who was surprised. His father had never offered him one before. He undid the catch. It was silver and was engraved inside the lid. John Watson, from his father. He took one and leant forward as his father lit it. He drew in his breath and he felt the heat on his tongue but he did not choke on the smoke because he and Arthur had tried behind the cricket pavilion several times.

'Throw them back then,' his father said, but he was smiling. He lit his own and removed his cap. 'Hot now, eh?' He took off his jacket, the black armband puckered where it was stitched to the tweed, and removed his tie, rolling up his sleeves, leaving his cigarette in his mouth while he did so, squinting his eyes half-shut against the smoke which was rising in an upright stream in the windless air. In this clear light Harry could see that the right side of his moustache and hair was stained yellow from the nicotine.

'I had a word with my cousin at the Club when he came down to London last week,' his father said, flicking his ash to one side, and Harry waited, feeling his shoulders tense. He took a sip of wine, then balanced the glass on his knee and removed his jacket, also with its armband, while he listened. 'He's going to speak to the adjutant of the Household Cavalry and after that there'll be no doubt about your future.'

Harry smiled and nodded. 'Thank you, Father,' he murmured, but he thought of the Volunteer Rifles, thought how tedious he found it all, and wondered how he could bear the Army for every minute of every day. But on the other hand how could he not, for he knew that it was all his father had ever considered a suitable career for his eldest son, his only son.

Arthur was going to university, Oxford of course, but Classics held no appeal for him either. It was mining that did, but he dared not tell his father that for he knew the answer. It would be, 'To work in a tin mine is not what you've been educated for.' He could imagine the fuss it would cause, and it wouldn't help that it was his mother's family mine.

Damn the tin slump. He'd be willing to bet that if there'd been the chance of money it would be a different story. He ground out the stub of his cigarette in the grass, close-cropped by the sheep which grazed on the thin scrub. He could smell the charred earth, the blackened tobacco as he looked at his father whose cap was tipped over his face as he breathed evenly, his head down on his chest. He was asleep. Harry loosened the knot on his black tie, undid the top stud and lay back with his hands beneath his head, glad that the mourning period for Simon would not last for ever. He had a grand tweed tie he wanted to try. He watched a bird circling high above him. Sam, Eliza's husband, had promised a trip to the mine for tomorrow. Hannah would be coming too. He looked at the bird again, breathing in the warm air. There was something about the mine which made him feel alive. Was it the scale of it, the smallness of men against the earth? Or was it in the blood, like his grey eyes which were those of his mother's family, mine-owners for generations? He laughed quietly at himself. What did it matter what it was? It would never happen. He'd be prancing about in fancy dress and polished boots for the rest of his life and the mine would just fade away.

The sun was flickering through the branches of the tree, the bird was gone, and it was quiet in the midday heat. He sat, his eyes heavy, and it was some while before he heard his father stir.

'Come on then, Harry. We haven't caught anything yet.

Stuff the plates back in the basket and let's get back to it. There are clouds coming in from the north.'

There was a breeze and the water seemed colder as Harry waded back in and, although he again stood with a still rod, there was, after all, a jerk on Harry's line and his father gripped his arm. 'Play it in, boy.'

And so he did, the rod alive in his hands, but he could not see the fish and he would not think of it either. His father stood close, his own rod still out, the water still snatching at the line as the wind freshened further and then his line, too, jerked. In they came, and Harry could see them now, the two small fish twitching and drowning in the air.

'Get the basket, Harry,' roared his father, his pale, long-nailed hand reaching for the thrashing body, and Harry backed up to the bank and pulled the fish basket over to the edge, nearer to his father.

He grasped his small brown trout, feeling the cold, wet, struggling life, dragging it off the hook, not looking as he did so and then he threw it towards the basket. He wiped his hand down his shirt. 'Damned messy business,' he muttered to himself and his voice was shaking. His father was wading towards him, his face lit with a smile.

'Mine is half a pound at least. How about yours?' Harry looked down. His had missed the basket and lay gasping and flaccid on the bank and he could not move to touch it. His father answered for him looking towards the fish. 'Not bad, quarter of a pound, I should say, but they're small down here so that's a good catch.'

Harry stood aside wanting him to reach the bank first. The pony was cropping grass nearby and he could hear the tearing of the grass and the clink of the bit as it chewed around it. A string of green slime hung from the corner of his mouth. He would not look at the fish but from the corner of his eye he saw his father lift a rock which he had levered from the bank and bring it down, crushing the fish's head before he threw it in the basket. He saw the leather strap being pulled tight, heard the creak of the wicker as it was buckled, and then watched the tilt of his father's head as he looked out over the moor towards the north. Saw him check his watch, cupping it in his hand, pulling his face into a frown. Harry breathed deeply; he would look at all this and forget the thrashing body he had felt in his hand. He wiped cold water on his face and felt the wind, fresher still. The branches were moving and the pony's mane was lifting.

He looked at his father with a question in his face. Don't say we'll fish on through the storm, he groaned silently, for he knew from the sky and the wind that one was coming, and soon. His father leant over and picked up the jackets, handing the smaller one to Harry.

'Perhaps we should be getting back, you know. It's getting fresh, Harry, and the clouds are moving up. It won't start just yet, mark you, but if it does the waterproofs are in the back anyway. Get the pony hitched up while I get all this together.' He pointed to the fish and tackle. 'I'll take the reins on the way back,' he added.

Harry pulled off his waders, they were wet and cold but they did not thrash and gasp.

John Watson held the reins loosely enough to be able to lift his hands and light another cigarette. He inhaled deeply. The wind was coming in harder from the north but the dark clouds, low and full of rain, still had some way to come. The fish would have come up nicely when the rain beat on the surface. He looked around him, at the moors studded with boulders, at the fields he could see in front of them. It was good to have a son, a companion; someone to share his pursuits.

Cornwall wasn't his part of the country but it was pleasant. As a boy he had lived the other side of the Tamar and he remembered his father telling him about the building of the bridge by Brunel. It had changed his father's fortunes. While practising as a solicitor he had already dabbled in property investment in Plymouth and when the bridge was begun he had seen the opportunity and had invested in country properties over in Cornwall, selling them at a healthy profit when people realised that, with the bridge, holiday homes were a viable possibility. It had given him enough backing to start up the office in London. Just the two of them, not her, not his mother. He shook himself to remove her memory and looked across at his son. Thank God the boy was a true Watson in spite of those eyes. He was devoid of the flaws which had been run deep into his father's wife, a woman he refused to call Mother. And what about Edith, his own wife?

He sucked heavily on the cigarette. He did not relish returning to Eliza's home now that Edith was considerably better and able to join them downstairs. He could hardly bear to look at her; at the woman who hid such sordid lusts behind that sickly exterior.

He grimaced. Was it too much to ask that a man should be able to think of his wife as beyond reproach, nurturer of his home and children? Good God, was it any wonder the wretched woman was unable to bear a living child? Each year they had tried, each year they had failed since Hannah was born. Her lack of decency had brought its own punishment but this afflicted him also and for that she was doubly to be condemned. Such selfishness did not bear thinking of and there was no point in her tears at the side of the empty cradle, no point unless it was to rue her own wickedness, her own sin.

For men, of course, it was different; they needed an outlet for their natural instincts and the correct place to practise these was with the women who were outside the code of chivalry, the harlots who roamed the streets. It was only with these that contraception should be considered, and then solely for protection against disease. How could that woman have even conceived the thought let alone mentioned it as she had done when he had swept from the room that night. A damned tube of sheep gut for use with a wife, he had roared. And what had she said? Only that rubber was available now.

He removed a piece of tobacco from his tongue. Carnal activity without procreation was a sin, everyone knew that. It would mean that a respectable woman was admitting to enjoyment and that, of course, was impossible. He shook his head in despair. Didn't she understand that by that attitude she debased her value in his eyes, quite apart from repelling him as a companion and provider. She was, first and foremost, the breeder of children. That was her sole purpose, to breed and nurture the family. What would she do with herself if she was not producing children, for God's sake, and no, he would not think of his own mother.

The wind was strengthening now. He pinched the stub of his cigarette and tossed it over the side of the cart. The pony was labouring, tired from the journey. He lashed the whip, glad that the end caught its hindquarters, pleased to see it start and rear its head. 'Pass over the waterproofs, Harry.' His voice was sharp and Harry obeyed quickly. His father did not thank him, he had too much outrage in his head.

What was to be done though, for he needed another son? A man should have more than one, it was too risky. But perhaps his wife had learnt her lesson now; she had been obedient and dutiful since that day. Yes, there was only one thing to do and that was to overcome his repugnance for long enough to produce another child. Please God, not another daughter though. They were nothing but an inconvenience, a burden.

He noticed that the wind had sprung up harshly and that the sky was black. He lifted his head as the lightning came. Then the thunder clapped loudly overhead and the pony shied. They were off the moor and heading down the lane which led eventually to the junction when the pony's frightened movement brushed the cart against the high-earthed hedge.

Harry called, 'Steady, Father.'

The pony tried to back in its shafts as the rain came, in what seemed like a solid dark sheet.

'Over the side, boy, grab his head,' John Watson shouted, reining in sharply. Through the deluge he could see Harry as he gripped the halter of the pony, near to the bit. Saw him as he put his hand on its nose, dragging him forward, talking, not shouting, to the beast and then watched as the pony walked on, ears back but steady. Watched as his son came back, jumping up over the side of the cart and grinning at him.

'He's fine now, Father.'

Yes, he would need another son.

3   Hannah lay in the bed. There was red behind her lids which meant the sun was up. The blankets were light on her body, the sheet was tangled about her arm which lay above her head. She stretched, and her fingers touched the cool wood of the headboard, feeling the carved surface that had not been noticeable last night in the dim glow from the oil lamp. She rolled over and only then opened her eyes; the sky was blue and high above were white clouds quite still and separate. Quite quiet. Oh yes, the birds were there, chattering and fluttering beneath the eaves but the sky was quiet.

She missed her mother but she wouldn't think of that, of leaving the rest of the family together in Eliza's house, of seeing the lights fading as she was driven away yesterday in the cart to this unfamiliar cottage on the edge of the village of Penbridge, stopping at Eliza's house only long enough to have a swift supper and separate her luggage from the rest. She would look instead at the window, at the patchwork curtains that splashed colour into the room.

She would have behaved though and she realised now that the thoughts would have to come or there would be no peace. She had told her Aunt Eliza that she would behave but the dogcart had been brought round anyway. It will make a change, Eliza had said. Mr and Mrs Arness have a son just a little older than you and Mr Arness might improve your water-colour technique; he is a very fine artist, well respected here and in America. He comes from one of the best East Coast families; Mrs Arness is Cornish, of course, though you would never know. It's the voice, Eliza had said, it changes, you see. She's a lovely woman and your mother would like you to improve your painting. Hannah had not wanted to hear about painting. She had wanted to stay, to cling to her mother. Hannah shut her eyes and saw the red behind her lids again.

No, she must not cry, here in this strange house, because her eyes would be red and everyone would know and her mother might be told. She pushed away the sheet and slipped on to the floor. The well-polished boards were cool and she felt better, more in control. Aunt Eliza looked more like Uncle Simon than her mother, Hannah thought. Her hair was yellow, not brown with streaks of grey. But she must not even think of that because it would bring the tears too.

There was no carpet at all, just brightly coloured rugs, and her feet left imprints as she walked across to the wardrobe. Again control returned.

A jug was in the bowl on the marble washstand, blue and white with just one chip on the handle and the water was cold but fresh when she splashed it on her face. The towel was thick and soft.

There was a picture of marigolds hanging on the white wall above the washstand with petals painted so thick that they stood out from the canvas, generous and warm. She touched them with her fingers, tracing the line of the palette knife, for that was what had been used she now saw. Dried flowers hung from the black beams and, faintly, Hannah caught their scent.

As she dressed she wished that she did not have to wear the liberty bodice in this heat. Her fingers were clumsy on the suspenders and her stockings slipped over and away from the button so she had to start again. There was a large mirror hanging on the back of the door and in it she could see the whole of herself. The white thigh against the black stocking, her dark hair rich in curls which still hung loose from the night. She saw and felt the blush which rose to her cheeks and turned away, twining her hair up and into a knot, securing it with pins, then looking into the mirror again, quickly, before she left the room. The stairs leading down were narrow and dark and creaked with every step and she tugged at her tight bodice, pulling it well down, tucking it into her skirt. There had been no breakfast gong and she could hear no voices as she reached the bottom of the thinly carpeted stairs, but there was a door to the left which stood ajar. She knocked and then entered. It was the dining-room but the table was not laid and the sideboard held no covered silver dishes. The room felt damp and was dark though the curtains which hung at the small window were open. She stood, unsure now, wanting to be with someone she knew, somewhere that was familiar. 'We eat in the kitchen, Hannah. You'll prefer it.' It was the son, Joe, standing behind her in the doorway, rolling the words in his strange drawl and he made her start because she had been lost deep in her longings.

He had met the cart last night, down at the gate about a hundred yards from the cottage and had leapt up into it once he had latched the gate behind him and shaken her hand while he talked and laughed with Eliza. His hand had been hard and rough and in the fading light he had looked brown and strong. Eliza had told her that he was seventeen.

He held the door wide now, sweeping his hand in a mock bow. 'It's damp and gloomy in here, don't you think?'

She paused, not knowing whether to nod. It seemed rude somehow to criticise the house and she must practise being polite or she might never return to her mother.

They walked past the bottom of the stairs, but this time she saw the passage which ran alongside and ended in a white-painted door.

Joe edged past her and opened it, pressing back for her to go before him. She shook her head and looked first at him and then back into the room. The light was vivid after the dark and she could see the corner of a deal table and the open garden door. She had never been in a kitchen before. 'Do please go first,' she said, keeping her voice to a whisper.

Joe smiled. 'It's difficult the first time in a new place, ain't it,' he whispered. 'Follow me, but remember that Mother doesn't eat girls, not on Thursdays anyway.'

She felt the smile begin as she walked in behind him. His voice was gentle and his smile was so wide that it seemed to take up half his face. His fair hair was tinged with red and he had freckles on the bridge of his nose. Her shoulders began to relax as she followed his broad back.

Joe's mother was standing by the sink, wringing out some washing. She turned. 'Come in, my dear. There's bread on the table, butter and marmalade. Joe, you help Hannah find her way around and I'll make some tea.'

Her smile was also broad and her voice drawled like Joe's. She was dressed much as last night in clothes that flowed about her body instead of pinning everything up inside like a suit of armour. Hannah pulled at her bodice again. Mrs Arness wore her hair in a long loose plait which hung down her back, not coiled round her head as it had been when she had stood at the doorway with the oil lamp blowing in the evening breeze. Now, in daylight, Hannah saw that it was the same russet colour as the blouse she was wearing, a blouse that was undone at the neck. Her skirt was red and full. Hannah felt her collar. Yes, it was safely buttoned. She hardly dared look at Mrs Arness again, at her open neck which her parents would recoil from and claim was indecent.

'Sit down then,' Joe said, pulling out a chair from the table. He sat opposite in his tweed suit, the jacket of which had leather patches on the elbows, and pushed the wooden board that held the round cottage loaf over to her.

Hannah took a piece, covering her confusion with action, intrigued by the newness of this way of life. Was this how all Americans lived? Where was the silver toast rack and the servants who quietly served them? Where was the tension of correct behaviour? Beads of water pushed to the surface as she spread some butter, still ridged from the wooden platters. Joe pushed marmalade towards her.

'Quince marmalade,' he said. 'Mother has made it every year since we've been here.' He looked over his shoulder towards his mother who was hanging ironed sheets on the wooden slats of the airer, which she had lowered in front of the black leaded stove. Hannah liked the bitter taste, liked the warm soft neck of Mrs Arness which she now glanced at again and again as she stooped and stretched with the clean linen. Joe turned to her.

'Excuse me, Hannah.' He pushed himself up from the table with his hands and again she saw how rough they were, how big. His eyes were blue, like his mother's, she noticed, as she watched Joe take the rope to raise the now laden airer. He was as big as Harry but not as big as her father and he had only a faint moustache, fair like his hair. She hoped he would not grow a beard because too much hair would hide his smile. She sat back in the chair, feeling its spokes against her back. The sun was pouring in through the door and windows and the room felt warm and dry; her back loosened and her shoulders drooped with the pleasure of just being.

Joe was talking to his mother as he carried out the washing she had just finished. Did people in Cornwall always talk to one another, she wondered, talk and laugh and eat in the kitchen? But she knew that was not so because at Eliza's it was just like being at home.

There was a washing-line running along the path which led from the door and Joe was handing his mother the clothes. How very strange. She had never seen a man do that before and it pleased her, made her feel complete. Polly sent their washing to the woman who lived in the back streets. Hannah took more marmalade. It was good, very good. She watched as Mrs Arness came back towards the door.

'Put a kettle on, would you, Hannah. I meant to but forgot.' She smiled and returned to the garden, her skirt swirling out and the plait catching the sun.

Hannah felt uncertain again as she looked around the kitchen. Where was the kettle? What was a kettle? She wiped her hands, sticky from the quince, on her serviette and rose, looking through the door at Joe and his mother. They were talking again, not looking at this visitor of theirs who was so ignorant, so unworldly. She wanted to groan aloud but there wasn't time. She hurried to the sink but there was nothing there. Perhaps it would be in the cupboards underneath – but there were only black pans like the old one that the gardener used to shell the peas into sitting on the glasshouse step. Would it do? Her skirt was dragging on the flagstoned floor. She moved one of the pans; it was heavy and black. She wanted to cry or to run away. Would Mrs Arness tell her father of her stupidity?

Then she heard footsteps behind and stood up, turning towards the sound. Would they stop smiling now that there was no kettle, no boiling water? But Joe did not; neither did his mother who said, 'The kettle's over on the side hob, Hannah. It'll need filling, I'm afraid.' She was pointing to the fire and Hannah nodded, brushing the dust from her skirt before she walked past the table and grasped the kettle. It too was heavy and she began to understand why Mrs Brennan insisted on employing only a good strong girl to help Cook in the kitchen.

At the sink the water splashed red-flecked from the tap into the kettle's dark insides, and as it grew heavier in her hand her arms began to shake. She tightened her grip. The geranium on the windowsill was splashed from the force of the water and its smell was acrid. She turned to Mrs Arness.

'Is it all right?' she asked, pointing to the strange water, but suddenly the kettle was full and water began spilling over. She heaved, feeling the strain in her shoulders, and as she lifted it the gushing flow caught the edge of the kettle and sprayed her. It was cold and sank through to her skin but she held on to the kettle, heaving it on to the scrubbed drainer.

'Oh, Hannah, not quite so much next time.'

Hannah flushed. 'I'm sorry.' She brushed at her soaked bodice and took the towel that Joe offered but at least Mrs Arness had said there would be a next time and it gave her a feeling of pleasure.

'Rub yourself down with that,' Joe said. 'We'll go out soon and the sun will sort it out for you.' He tipped some of the water out into the sink and again she saw the red flecks.

'That's what I meant really.' Hannah pointed to the red flakes which now lay on the bottom of the deep white sink. 'Are they all right?'

'Oh yes, they're iron. They'll make you good and strong, bring some colour to your cheeks.' He turned and put the kettle on the hob and Hannah thought she would only have one cup because colour was something her mother did not like. She had a boiled egg too, while she waited for the tea.

'If you don't mind having things the wrong way round,' Joe's mother said, and Hannah did not mind; she loved the ease of this woman, this boy.

The egg had been collected that morning and it oozed thick

43

and orange on to her spoon. The tea was strong and served in thick ceramic mugs that Mrs Arness had thrown on her potter's wheel, Joe said, and Hannah thought that she would like to try that one day as he explained how the clay was worked when it was soft and malleable, then fired and painted. Hannah looked at Mrs Arness's hands, they were wide and capable; safe hands. She liked to think of a woman creating something useful, something solid. It was strange but good. This whole world was good, it was full of words and useful work, not stitches and antimacassars.

Mrs Arness put the milk in first. Esther would have called her a miffer, and sniffed as she said that milk-in-firsts don't know what's what; but it was nice and tasted no different to Mother's so why should it matter? She felt the question waiting to burst out of her but she pushed it down. No, she was going to behave, to do as Mother wanted, wasn't she. She mustn't make her worse than she had done already. Father had said that to her as she left and Hannah had felt pain that she had never known before twist inside her at the thought that she was at least part of the cause of her mother's decline.

'I think it would be nice to go across the moor today.' Mrs Arness spoke as she folded up some dry washing. 'Take Hannah in the jingle as far as Old Bernie's and then have a walk, Joe. I have the books to sort out from last term. I've packed up the lunch.'

She put the folded washing on to a side table, passed Joe a half-full string bag which had been sitting on the pantry shelf and filled a flask with tea from the pot. The picnic bulged through the gaps in the bag and Joe slung it over his shoulder. Mrs Arness looked at Hannah and raised her eyes. 'Careful, that's Hannah's pasty. It will be crumbs in a moment.' Hannah laughed. The pain subsided. 'Out you go now but take these round to the compost first, please.' Mrs Arness swept the egg into a bucket which held potato peelings and lettuce.

The light and heat hit Hannah as though it had taken its hand to her. There was so much sky here above the garden and the fields and the distant moor. There were no other houses between them and the horizon. No wonder Mr Arness lived here. Wouldn't Miss Fletcher love it, though the roofs of the village would have been better. She loved to insist that the girls drew roofs. The angles, the colour, the shadows, she would say. Her face would light up and her eyebrows rise as they did when she was absorbed and enthusiastic, which she was for most of the lessons, especially with Hannah. You, my dear, she would say, have so much to offer the world. Inside your head there is a brain and it should be exercised; a scholarship for you should be quite possible, I think. And she had passed some of the younger children over to Hannah for some coaching, to improve her confidence, she had said, but in addition it had unlocked a passion to teach which neither had known was there until then. Miss Fletcher had been pleased.

Hannah felt Joe's hand on her arm. 'Round here then.' She followed him round the corner of the house, past a conservatory with a half-open door. There was a vine curling up the windows and out through two broken panes on the roof. Beyond was a narrow-shaped pile covered by an old carpet. At the bottom, dark earth, egg shells and cabbage stalks spilled on to the ground. Joe lifted a corner of the carpet and a heavy smell wafted out into the air. Hannah stepped back.

'Why do you put them here?' she asked, breathing at first through her mouth but then again through her nose because disease could rush in past the teeth, Mrs Brennan had told her, and surely smell was better than illness.

Joe finished with the bucket and clanged it down on the hard earth. It was rusted round the rim. 'Well, we haven't a pig at the moment so the peelings can go on the compost with the rest. It feeds the ground when we come to spring planting. Senseless to waste anything, isn't it?' He looked up at her, squinting in the sun. 'Don't you do the same in London then?'

She shook her head. 'Men come and take it, I suppose. The maids see to it.'

He put his head to one side and there was a faint smile on his face.

Hannah felt a rush of anger. 'Well, don't you have a maid?'

'Only one and she's on holiday. Her sister helps if necessary in term time, when Mother runs the school.'

Hannah's interest was immediate. 'Oh, a school. I didn't know your mother was a teacher. How wonderful. How many boys do you have? Does she teach them Classics? What about German? I'd like to learn German.'

'Steady,' he interrupted her, leaning over to pick up the bucket. 'Yes, she does teach Classics, no, she doesn't teach German. And we have six boys and five girls.' He was walking ahead of her now back to the kitchen, the bucket swinging from his hand, the string basket still over his shoulder.

'Girls and boys,' she called, shocked.

'Of course,' he called back. 'It's crazy otherwise, isn't it? What's different about girls and boys. They've got arms, legs and a brain, haven't they? And they've got to learn to live together, haven't they? That's what Mother and Father say anyway.' His voice faded as he entered the kitchen.

Hannah stood. A school with boys and girls, and Joe had said that his mother and father thought girls had a brain. His mother taught them together, in the same room, which was sinful in London, in her world. A world that seemed increasingly dark, set against the one which surrounded her here. Her confusion, her thoughts were returning. Her questions about life were stirring again. She explored her shock as though she were a tongue probing a sore tooth but found no answer.

She walked down the red-brick path leading to the dried stone wall which surrounded the garden. On either side of the path were marigolds mingling with lettuce. Lavender and rosemary were set further back and were already busy with bees. Geraniums were in pots, some tilted as they had settled half on the path, half on the earth. Lemon verbena grew amongst some red full-blown roses. Sin was difficult, she thought, as she knelt by the strawberry beds beyond the flowers. They came right up to the path which was warm beneath her knees. Who decided what sin was? God, she supposed, but men were the ones who passed it on. Surely, though, it was a sin to waste goodness as they did in London when here it was put back into the ground and new things grown? Why didn't the Vicar concern himself with that instead of shouting about damnation each Sunday? And why was it a sin to teach boys and girls together? Joe was right. That could not be wrong, surely? She sighed, grateful for the hardness of the brick through her skirt. That at least was something definite and so were the plants before her.

She parted the leaves and saw large late strawberries clustered in their shade. She slipped her hand beneath the largest and felt the straw which lay on the soil digging into her skin. She let the fruit lie heavy in her palm. It was round and red and shiny, with each seed embedded in it like the buttons on the back of the chair in her mother's bedroom. Sin seemed so dark and frightening, not laughing and strong and full of sun like this family.

The heat was striking up from the path into her face now and she rose at the sound of Joe's boots on the bricks. He held a straw hat and Mrs Arness called from the doorway, 'Take the hat, Hannah. It will save you getting too much sun. Your mother might prefer it.' She smiled and waved and Hannah was grateful.

'The jingle's over here.' Joe led the way along the wall past a shiny, dark-leaved bush. Hannah stopped and touched the shrub. 'That's myrtle,' he said. 'Father painted that, it's above the bed in your room.'

Hannah hadn't noticed but she said how nice it was.

Joe laughed. 'I don't know what Father would think of the word nice. He'd want to know what effect it had on you, the design, the colour.'

'I see.' Hannah thought for a moment wondering if this family would do nothing but surprise her. Could they really want to know the effect of a painting on a girl; a girl who was not supposed to consider herself or her feelings, only those of others. She turned to look at Joe as they walked; he was smiling at her and she sought words to talk of her private responses and it made her feel full of shyness but of excitement too. A clean excitement.

'Well, the marigolds above the washstand made me feel warm, made me feel as though I wanted to stretch and grasp in all the heat of the sun.'

'Now, that's a good deal better, isn't it?' he replied. They were at the stables now and Joe harnessed up a moorland pony, backing him into the shafts of a cart.

'Where's the jingle?' Hannah asked.

Joe swung the string bag over the side of the cart and Hannah thought of all the crumbs.

'This is it. Carrying your cornish pasty, or crumbs,' he grinned. 'It's a Cornish cart. Up you get then.'

The floor was covered in dried mud and there was straw and loose cabbage stalks as well. She lifted her skirt and sat on the seat and looked around. 'Are we going on our own?' She felt the heat rise in her cheeks.

Joe stopped and stared at her. 'Did you want someone else to come? Who, your brother?' Then he paused, a frown beginning. 'Do you mean a chaperon; with me?' Surprise was in his voice.

Hannah looked from him back at the house. There was a metal stork on the roof, to ward off evil spirits, Aunt Eliza had said when they had driven up last night. To stop the birds from messing more like, Joe had laughed. Eliza had too and Hannah had blushed. She was blushing now. Eliza seemed changed somehow. 'Well, I always do have a chaperon. If I were to be alone with anyone like you I think my mother would expect it.' By anyone like you she meant a man; and Joe was very nearly a man, wasn't he? Her hands were gripped tightly together and the freedom of the last minutes was forgotten. She looked up at him as he sat next to her. His eyebrows had drawn together now and he had a deep line between them. He shifted in his brown jacket. His tie was also a tweed, but green with a light blue check. She would look at that, not into his face.

'Oh, Hannah, I'm sorry. Mother has to sort out the term's work and Father is painting. Shall we stay here instead?' And then she did look at him. His eyes were a darker blue somehow. Was it because he was frowning, Hannah wondered, unable to think of an answer that would satisfy her mother but still enable her to go, for that was what she wanted. But if she did her mother would say she was spoilt for ever and her distress would be too hard to endure. She knew she would because they had said the same of the daughter of her father's late partner, the one her father had insisted should resign.

'I know. We're dropping off the jingle at Old Bernie's. He'll sit on the step and watch us. He can see right the way across the moor so that's all right, isn't it?'

He did not start the trap yet but waited and she realised that it was her decision. It was a strange feeling. She set the hat more securely on her head and looked across the moor; you could see a long way, she realised and nodded to herself and then to Joe.

The cart jolted down the track and she held the reins as Joe leapt out and opened the gate. 'Go on then, drive him through.'

She flapped the reins; the pony's tail swished and he began to walk.

'Keep him going,' called Joe as he threw the rope which secured the gate over the post and ran alongside, leaping up beside her. His arm touched hers and it felt good. Like Uncle Simon again. The cottage she could see at the foot of the track was small and an old man sat on a wooden seat at the front door. He rose to his feet, leaning heavily on his walking-stick. His hands were gnarled and his face was scarred down one side. 'Morning, Master Joe,' he called and lifted his hat towards Hannah.

She climbed down by herself, shaking her head at Joe's proffered hand. 'I can manage, thank you.' And she could.

They set off across the field, keeping near the walls. 'It's drier here,' Joe said. 'Out there in the middle it's still wet from the last night's rain and the morning mist.'

Hannah nodded, looking ahead at the wall which cut across the bottom of the field. Between the stones she could see daylight. 'Who is that old man? Does he work for you?'

Joe moved the bag on to his other shoulder. 'Not really. He's from the Penhallon Mine. You know, the one your family run. He's too old now and Father gave him the use of the cottage and pays him for a bit of gardening.'

'Hasn't he done enough work?' Hannah said indignantly, turning to Joe, holding her hat on her head. It dug into her bun and hurt.

'That's what we thought, so you can stop glaring,' Joe said, his smile less broad now. 'But he should be in the workhouse now because he's too old for the mine, him in one and his wife in another. Just like your sort of schools. No sort of life for him, is it, and he wouldn't come to the cottage when we offered it because it smacked of charity. So we asked him to do some work, just enough gardening to make him feel of use, that's all.' He shouldered past her, striding on up to the gate.

'It's hard working in the mines, you know,' he called back. 'You take a look round when you go tomorrow.'

Hannah stood still and watched as he pushed through the small gap at the end of the wall.

'Come on then,' he called and was gone.

She hurried on, frightened of losing him out here where there was no familiar landmark. The moor was spongy under her feet. They had been walking for what seemed like hours now and Joe had removed his jacket and tie, and undone his top button. He spoke of the land where he had been born, of its space, its growth, how there was a chance for everyone. He explained how there was no set pattern of class and privilege as there was in this nation, how a poor man could make good, and to Hannah it was a revelation, a story which could not be true, but he laughed and said it was.

Here there were fewer wild flowers. There was none of the clover which had darkened the fields they had tramped through or any smell of late violets, but there was still some bird's foot and lady's slipper though these were becoming more infrequent. There were lichen-covered, stunted oaks standing alone. Close to them were a few moorland mares, nuzzled from time to time by their foals.

'The river's not far off now,' Joe said.

At the thought of the cool wetness she lengthened her stride. But still she could not see the glint of sun on water which she remembered from the days she had come with Uncle Simon. 'Where is it?' she asked Joe. 'I can usually see it further off.'

'You're coming from the other direction, remember. There's a steep bank this side, almost a cliff so you won't see it until you almost fall in. But we'll go off down to the right.' He pointed to where stunted trees were clustering. 'It's a more gentle slope there.'

It took at least twenty minutes though Joe had promised only fifteen. They sat down facing the water which was quite gentle here, though as it sank down to the lower moor it gushed and tore over the boulders. Not far away a mare was cropping the grass, tearing it up so that roots hung from the side of her mouth. Hannah leant back against a moss-covered boulder. She was so hot, her bodice was too tight, and the stays so hard. She used her handkerchief to wipe her face which felt swollen with heat.

The foal was stretching her neck, sucking at the mare. Hannah looked away, over to the water. Joe was searching through the picnic. He handed her a pasty.

'I wonder if she wanted that baby,' Hannah said quietly, picking at the crust which was folded over and ridged with fork marks. She should not be talking about babies to anyone, but under this high blue sky the words were there in her mouth and tumbling out before she could suck them back. Would he pretend not to have heard, to save her pride?

'Animals do, helps to keep the species alive.' Joe was talking with food in his mouth and his words were slurred. He was lying back, as unconcerned as though she had asked him about the weather. Joe was too easy to talk to and more words came. Words which had long wanted to break out but which had never found the right time or place, words which would have signalled her wickedness to the world; but here, things were different. Thoughts were brimming in her head and had been since the morning had stirred them. Thoughts could become words, she felt, out here under the high sky under all this light, so now she let them flow.

'They just come anyway, poor things, don't they? Whether they want them or not.'

'Animals maybe but not humans. Shouldn't anyway.'

She bit into the meat and potato. It was peppery. There was swede as well.

'My mother does. She can't seem to help it and they die.'

Far, far away the old man would be watching from the house. But not listening.

'Your father should prevent it then.'

Hannah saw that he had reached the jam end of the pasty.

'What have fathers got to do with it?'

Joe caught a piece of pastry that was falling to his lap and scooped it back into his mouth. 'They give them the babies of course.'

Hannah did not understand. She had seen the swelling body of her mother of course but no one would ever discuss the matter. Esther did not know either. Her mother would not talk to her about such things, she had said, in case it made her unwell.

So Joe took a stick and, while the birds flew low over the stream and then rustled in the tree that threatened to tip over into the water like a man with a great thirst, he drew pictures and talked in his quiet voice and then Hannah felt as though she would be sick; as though she wanted to run from here, pulling her hair from her bun until it covered her face and her mind, shutting out the thought of her mother and father. Yes, she could see why Esther's mother might fear it would make her unwell. She felt hot and sick and angry. She did not want to imagine this sort of behaviour from her parents; those two bodies close together, her mother allowing that man into her.

Joe was unscrewing the flask. He poured the tea which she had helped to make this morning into the metal cup and handed it to her. 'Drink this,' he said quietly and she watched him as he knelt and passed it across but could not take it. Her hands were heavy. Her pasty lay on the dry grass. An ant was crawling on the crust, quickly, darting in a zig-zag.

Joe moved nearer. 'Here take it.' His voice was louder now, 'But just by the rim. It's hot, you see.'

Yes, she did see. And yes, the cup was hot. She could feel it as she took it from him. The cup was hot and the air was hot and the thought of the two bodies rose again.

The tea was sweet. She did not usually have sugar. Joe must like it. So *he* was to blame for her mother's illness; her father was to blame, and not his daughter, and not her mother either, for how could she force a man as strong and powerful as her father away from her or, for that matter, to take measures to prevent children if he did not choose to do so. There was no relief in the knowledge that the guilt was not hers just anger that the blame had been laid on her at all and revulsion at the thought of his body on her mother.

She finished the tea. It tasted strange. It must be because of the milk Joe had poured from the brown medicine bottle. Yellow blobs of cream had floated on the top of the tea. She had tried to catch them with her lips as she drank but they had melted before she could. And still there was anger and it was growing. Anger at her father. Pity for her mother. Anger at them both for blaming her for the illness and still the dull ache of her new knowledge.

Joe was taking his boots off. 'I'm going for a paddle,' he said and drew his socks from his feet. She looked away. His feet had hairs on the toes. She had not seen a man's foot before and it shocked her. It was ugly and big and powerful. So different from hers. Men were very different, weren't they? Was her father hairy like that, were his joints large, his bones thick?

'Come on,' he called as he turned towards the water.

She shook her head. 'No, I'm not allowed.' Not wanting to be too close to his maleness.

He walked carefully over the grass and stones, down to the sloping bank and over, stepping in, pulling his trouser legs up. 'It's lovely,' he called as though he had not heard. 'Come on in.'

But she wanted to think, to try and hold the facts. To push the images away.

It's wrong, she thought, for Mother to have to go through all this illness when it's not necessary. It is wrong of him. She was making herself think the words slowly and clearly or they would run away too fast, letting the pictures of the two of them together take over. But it is also wrong of Mother to let him. But she had no power, had she? She had no power. Oh Mother! And pity was mixed with rage again.

She looked at Joe, at the coolness of the water and her mouth felt hard, as though it was in a straight line, as though her lips had disappeared completely. She wanted to hurt them both, to break their rules as, in her mind, they didn't deserve her obedience. She took off her boots and stockings, rolled up her sleeves and undid her button. She would be brown tomorrow when she went to the mine, but what did it matter?

She walked on the grass, her skirt held up with her hand and she felt a freedom that was quite new. The earth crumpled beneath her feet as she slipped down the bank and it moved between her toes. Her feet were grey with dirt. Joe spun round and laughed. 'Good girl,' he said and turned back as she slid her feet into the water.

It was cold, so cold, and her toes gripped the bottom. Stones slipped over and round her feet, carried onwards by the water. 'Are you all right?' Joe asked. And she knew he did not mean the water.

She looked across at the bank opposite as the water dragged at the earth and swept some away. 'Yes, I'm quite all right, thank you.' She stooped and let her hand fall in the water. She caught some and let it trickle through her fingers. She stooped again and cupped some. It was quite clear.

'I'll teach you to tickle some trout if you like,' Joe offered, watching as she stood so quietly.

'Do they like it then?' she queried.

Joe laughed. 'You do me good, Hannah Watson,' he said. 'No, it means we'll catch some for our meal this evening. In our hands.'

Hannah thought of her father and brother. They would be fishing somewhere together, without her. With rods, with wine, with smiles on their faces; on their powerful faces. 'Yes, I'd like that,' she replied firmly though still, at the back of her mind, there were those pictures that shocked.

They lay on the bank, leaning far out over the shallow pool. Hannah's hand had been below the surface in the shadow of the rock for so long that it was almost numb. The trout was basking easily now, just above her fingers and she felt the pressure of Joe's hand on her arm. She closed her hand around the fish slowly because she was so numb and thought she had lost it but then she felt the firmness of flesh and held on even as it thrashed. Her hat was off now because it cast a shadow and her hair had loosened and strands dangled in the water. Her face was sore from the sun, and red. She was glad.

'Hang on now, Hannah,' Joe called, his voice full with excitement. She did. She hung on and as the afternoon wore on there were four fish on the bank beside them and inside her head the pictures were fading as she made herself concentrate on the trout, the water, the cold. There were two fish from her and two from Joe; enough for supper. Would her father and Harry catch as many with their rods and tackle? She hoped not.

But by now the air was heavy and the bank of cloud they had first seen an hour ago had moved, borne along on a wind that flicked at her hair and sent the birds from the tree. The foals were sheltering beside their mothers and Joe quickly put the fish in the string bag.

'Come on, Hannah. We shouldn't have stayed so long.'

He took her hand and pulled her up. She held her hat in the other and they collected their boots. Hannah's feet felt warm in her stockings but cramped in the shoes. They walked quickly, the wind pushing their clothes around them. The mares stood with their backs to the weather, their tails whipping close against their haunches.

Hannah held the flask, empty now, and pulled at her skirt with the other hand, edging round a flattened boulder.

'How do women stand up against men then? How can we become people, not belongings, because that is what we are, what mother is, isn't it?' she shouted at him, the wind snatching at the words as she spoke. Had he heard?

She saw him shrug. 'You need economic independence, my mother says. That's partly why she runs the school. She and father are equal, you see.'

'Yes, I see,' said Hannah. She had stopped now and he turned and pulled her on. 'I want to teach and to go to university. I just feel I must teach, you see.' She was shouting hard against the wind.

'Then you will, if you really want to.' He turned and looked at the clouds which now had a plum-coloured base. Hannah had never seen that before and then the sky was split by a dagger of light, and thunder followed so loud that she held her

head and screamed. It rolled on and on and Joe took her arm
and dragged her but she dropped the flask as the rains came.
Where was it? She couldn't see. Her hair was in her eyes, the
wind was driving the rain into her face and mouth.

'Where's the flask?' she was screaming at Joe as he tried to
pull her on. 'No, I must get the flask.' It had been in her
keeping and she was taking it back with her; that was her job.
And she struggled back until she was near the boulder again
and felt with her hands around the base. Mud rose up round
her shoes and all she could feel was cropped turf but then, just
to the right she felt its hardness. Clutching it to her she
struggled back, quicker now because the wind was behind
her.

'Yes,' he shouted, 'you'll do what you want, Hannah. I've no
fear of that, now stay with me; whatever you do, stay with me.'
His voice was firm and so was his hand.

'Why are your hands so hard?' she asked, but this time her
words were tossed away by the wind.

The bath was waiting for them in the room off the kitchen. Mrs
Arness left a towel and told Joe to go and drip in front of the fire
until it was his turn. The water was hot and dirt floated from
her feet and her legs; it had never done that before and Hannah
smiled. The dressing-gown, which belonged to Mrs Arness,
was too large so Hannah rolled up the sleeves and waited in the
chair in front of the kitchen fire while the fish were gutted and
cooked. Her skin still felt damp and her hair too and the smell
of cooking fish was thick in the room.

Mr Arness came from the studio when he was called. He was
large and wore a navy smock, marked with paint. He smelt of
turpentine and linseed oil.

He smiled and they sat down when Joe was ready. She felt so
hot. Dry and hot. Her head, her limbs, but the fish was good.
They were eating fish that she had caught – she and Joe had
caught. It felt good to have served a purpose. Her throat was
sore. Ginger beer was on the table in a squat brown bottle. It
was like the ginger beer that Uncle Simon had bought them.

'It's a shame that Uncle Simon died,' she said. And her voice sounded a long way off. 'But Father says it is a good thing to die like that.'

Mr Arness looked at her, a long look, and then at his wife. He had a nice face. It was lined but he only had a small moustache. It didn't dip into his food.

'People see things differently,' Mr Arness said. He sounded almost English and they talked of the weather and the painting on which he was working; a view from the studio window. He had captured the clouds this evening, he told them. The kitchen was bright with the patchwork curtains drawn; the airer was free of washing now.

'Miss Fletcher says that the Boers have a right to their independence. Father says they taxed foreign miners then wouldn't let them vote. He said the Boers have always wanted to break from Britain. He says they need crushing. There are concentration camps, the newspapers say, that sound dreadful.' She wondered how poor Uncle Simon had felt about dying. Had he thought it was a good thing? She doubted it somehow.

Mr Arness said carefully. 'Yes, perhaps you should listen to Miss Fletcher.'

'Yes, perhaps I should. She's my teacher, you know.' She was hotter still and her head was cracking like the lightning.

Mrs Arness spoke. 'They have concentrated the Boer women and children together behind fences. Many have died. It seems hardly a good example for Britain to set.'

Hannah smiled eagerly. 'Yes, that's what Miss Fletcher says.. But Father says we are a civilising influence on the world.' Her voice dropped now. Her father was wrong, she thought; about that and other things. How strange. To think so clearly suddenly when so much recently had been confused. What was the matter with her? Her knife felt heavy. She knew now that she was unwell. She saw Mrs Arness rise, putting her hand out to stop Joe coming round the table to her. Her soft clothes floated.

'Come with me, Hannah. You've taken a chill. It's time we got you into bed.'

Her legs felt heavy, very heavy, but the fish had been nice. It

57

was so good to have been useful. To have achieved something. She stopped at the door and turned.

'What I don't understand,' she mumbled, 'is that South Africa belongs to the black men, doesn't it, so what are the Boers and the British doing fighting over it anyway? It isn't either of ours, is it? I mean, where have the natives gone?' Mrs Arness led her through but she heard Mr Arness say, 'That is a very important question, Hannah. One I'm afraid we'd all forgotten to ask – except for you.'

The bed was soft and cool. The rain was still drumming outside. Mrs Arness blew on her hands and then tipped camphor into her cupped palm and rubbed it gently on Hannah's chest. Her breath had not warmed her hand but its coolness soothed. Could Joe's mother see if one breast was smaller than the other, she wondered, but was too tired to care. The camphor made her eyes sting. She closed them. It was nice to have Mrs Arness here, to have an arm around her shoulders, to have someone touching her. It was good, so good to be in a household where rules were not hard and unyielding, where warmth was everywhere.

Now she was pulling up the sheet and natives were dancing round her father's white body. How many fish had he and Harry caught? She turned as Mrs Arness moved from the bed, the oil lamp in her hand lighting her face.

'Why did Aunt Eliza send me here?' she queried, but the words were too quiet for anyone to hear.

4 Sam met Hannah and Harry as they drove the trap into the mine yard which was pitted with deep ruts still water-logged from the rain.

'Drive on further, Harry,' he instructed, pointing to a curved track which ran up to the front of the brick-built office standing to the left of the workings. Behind the low building which ran into sheds and store-rooms were the chimneys which cast long shadows. Around them the moor seemed undisturbed by this man-made intrusion, and set against the pale blue sky and distant white clouds the seagulls wheeled and called while below them kites silently hovered over their prey.

Sam had never allowed Hannah down into the mine but now as he helped her from the trap she asked him again. He shook his head, his hand tipped far back and his ginger hair, clean and free from oil, fell down on to his forehead.

'Your father would not approve,' he repeated, 'and besides, it's bad luck for women to go down amongst the darkness. The men would object.'

So it would just be Harry and he was pleased because they were already one day late. Serve her right to stand there with a face down to her boots, he thought. Damn the girl. Caught some sort of chill, his father had said when the message had arrived during a late dinner after that appalling storm. 'So you'll have to delay your trip, though why you want to go and delve in that filthy mess I cannot imagine. Hardly a gentlemanly activity.'

Harry had not attempted to explain but merely finished his port and wondered whether Sam took exception to his father's attitude. It was hard to tell as he sat across the table sipping his port from the crystal glass. Samuel Polgus was a man whose face showed little.

Now Harry stood with his hands in his pockets looking over the buildings, drinking in the smell of the place, seeing the gorse which grew out of thin earth wherever it could find a footing.

As Hannah kicked at the dried dirt of the track which dusted her skirt with grey, he looked at Sam giving orders to two men waiting outside the mine office. Sam was stocky in his brown suit and stood solidly on his feet. In fact everything looked solid about the man, as though he could block a punch from the boxing teacher at school with just a movement of his hand.

His marriage to Eliza had been a late one, Harry thought, and one that had not brought approval from his father, for Sam was the manager of the mine and that made him very little better than 'trade'. A downward move for Eliza and utter nonsense in his father's eyes since she had, to his certain knowledge, rejected far more suitable offers. It was a situation which would not be permissible in his family, he had said to his wife specifically for the ears of his son and daughter who were riding in the same carriage back to the wedding breakfast.

Harry remembered that when his mother had demurred and talked of love, his father had snorted that love had nothing to do with marriage. Marriage was the consolidation of property, and Harry thought then, and again now, that in that case Eliza had probably married well, since she no longer had to pay out a salary to Sam. It would be all in the family from now on. He looked around with satisfaction at the site. They were here at last and the rain had cleared, though the ride over had been slow because there was so much mud on the lanes.

Harry moved closer to Sam who was watching the men as they moved a trolley nearer to the shaft. The chimneys towered above them, all their shadows jagged as they fell over the square buildings. He turned to Hannah who was stroking the nose of the bay mare that was still in harness, letting it nuzzle her hand. 'Have you noticed that the chimney nearest to us has had a good few feet built on since we were last here?'

He watched as she stepped back and shaded her eyes, then shook her head saying, 'Well seen, Harry. Why was that, Sam?' Her face was puzzled. 'It looks so enormous.'

Harry was irritated that she had not asked him but Sam

smiled. His face was broad and his voice slow like that of most Cornishmen.

'We need a good up-draught to produce enough head of steam to drive the engine and, believe it or not, that extra height has made a good bit of difference, Hannah.' He was looking at her as he spoke, expecting her to understand, and she was pleased. Harry's nose was in the air and she knew he was annoyed that Sam was talking directly to her. Harry's mouth began to open so she continued in a rush.

'I know that one of the engines raises the skips but what about the others?' She watched Harry flush and it made her feel a little better about not going down the shaft. She saw that Sam had noticed too, but he just smiled and touched her arm lightly, drawing her to one side of a gorse bush which was sporting yellow flowers.

'The middle one works the pumps and that is invaluable since we're so near the sea and water is always a problem. The furthest is the stamp's engine-house.' He paused and looked around, his face clouding. 'It's a shame to see things so much quieter now. We're down to half the work-force we had just fifteen years ago. Cornwall provided a good part of the world's tin in the middle of Victoria's century, you know, but each year, Hannah, things get worse. Australia and Malaysia are the culprits, coming up steadily and taking over our markets, especially those in the East. Things are slow now and getting slower; your father's profits will show him that.'

Hannah looked at the mine; its stacks, the sea in the distance, the granite crags which loomed grey out of the purple of the heather. 'Mother's profits, you mean.' She spoke quietly but firmly.

'Hannah!' Harry's voice was loud and angry.

Hannah turned to him, her shoulders back. He was taller than her. Taller than Joe had been, though he had looked enormous in all that rain. She remembered the claps of thunder, the lightning which lit up the sky.

'How dare you speak like that.' Harry's face was quite red, she noticed, and his nose had come down in a hurry, hadn't it? She looked at him, not backing down because it was the truth.

'Come now, Harry, let's get down the mine.' Sam's voice was soothing, his hand on Harry's arm. 'Hannah, you stay up here. Go on over to the office and take a seat. Read a copy of the *Strand*. Conan Doyle's brought out a new Sherlock Holmes, and it's set in the West Country. *The Hound of the Baskervilles*, your aunt called it.' He shook Harry's arm, making him turn. Her brother's mouth had gone rather white around the edges now, Hannah saw with interest.

Sam was pointing over to the small shed. 'Get yourself into some clothes over there, lad. I'll fetch Hannah some clay and she can fix the candles for us before she makes herself comfortable. Remember the hats, there'll be a bit of blasting down there, I expect.' Sam followed on behind Harry, waving at the men with the trolley to hurry up. They nodded and bent over the trolley, manhandling it into the blacksmith's lean-to.

Sam was back soon, dressed in the canvas jacket and trousers and felt hat that all the miners wore. 'Here you are then, Hannah.' He gave her two lumps of clay to mould into balls. Her gloves were already off and lying on the seat of the trap and she stood by the wheel working the clay until it was warm and soft and squeezed up between her fingers. It felt good, like the clay Mrs Arness had allowed her to use yesterday. She pressed the candles in firmly and when Harry came from the shed Sam fixed one in each hat. Harry did not speak to her but Sam smiled and shook his head, winking as he turned and she felt warm, here in the sun, thinking of that kindly face.

She walked over to the grass-covered bank, climbing above the dust-sprayed edge to the flattened boulders which were strewn amongst gorse, the sheep-cropped pasture and the wind-blown heather. She turned, sitting on the flattest rock, and watched as they walked across to the shaft. They seemed so much smaller. The wind was snatching at her hat so she removed it, holding the hat-pin in her teeth, feeling the loose hair whipping about her face. The clay was drying now and she rubbed her hands together. It was good to see dirt on them as it had been on her feet at Joe's. She stuck the pin through the brim of the hat, pegging it hard into the earth, watching as Sam and Harry disappeared. They would use ladders to reach the workings and the climb would be hard and dark since they would not light the candles until they reached the bottom. Sitting here above the seams she was excluded, again. She pressed the hat-pin further into the ground until the jet bead caught against the felt of the hat. The ground was so solid, so heavy.

Harry felt the familiar surge of excitement as the darkness clamped around him and he gripped the rungs of the ladder. He wore no gloves because he liked the feel of the wood against his skin. Here, as he climbed down into the mine, his family's mine, was the taste of grit, the smell of ore, the heat that welled up from the depths. In the blackness he could hear men passing upwards on the man-engine as the shift finished, but his only tangible reality was the ladder he felt beneath his feet, beneath his hands. He counted with each downward step. Fifty-one, fifty-two, fifty-three. Dust fell on to his shoulder and, pausing, he looked quickly up beneath the shelter of his hand. He could see the glow from his uncle's pipe and grinned; it broke the spell. What would Sam do if this was a coal mine and methane gas threatened to blow his head off? Probably go and sit behind a desk, he thought, give up all this which is something he would find hard to do.

There was still hundreds of feet to go and his breathing was becoming laboured now as he felt for each rung carefully, wishing that he had the speed of the miners who came down regularly. Four hundred and ten, four hundred and eleven, he counted silently, not able to spare breath for words.

They had an instinct that he had not developed, but perhaps that was because speed to them was of the essence. Tributing made the men work fast because they earned a fixed percentage of the value of the ore they raised in a given time. Out of their wage at the end of the period the men would be charged for all their materials such as tools, candles and powder, so no wonder they needed every minute they could find. It was a good, economic way of working, his father had said, and he agreed.

'Do you still charge the men for their tools, Uncle?' he called out to the figure above, but he did not look up again because dust would be kicked into his eyes. His arms were aching, and his legs trembling. Five hundred and eighty, five hundred and eighty-one.

'No we don't, thank God. Damned bad way to treat people. We adjust the profits accordingly but don't tell your father. It's only a small percentage anyway.' His voice was thin because his pipe was still between his teeth.

It was too dark to see anything at all; the candles would only be lit when they reached the bottom and it was always at this stage that Harry felt scared. It was the dark. He didn't like the dark and at the count of seven hundred and fifty rungs he always felt lost, felt that he was climbing down into endless space, felt that he would never reach the end, never stop climbing. His hands were blistered now from gripping the rungs. He chewed the inside of his mouth and shut his eyes. It made him feel safer somehow. He clutched on to Sam's words turning them into letters in his mind. White letters against black pages. Words into sentences. Eight hundred and fifty.

Maybe if Sam still deducted for the materials he would have been able to go shooting, but he could not tell Father, that would be a betrayal of Sam; even though, in his opinion, he and Aunt Eliza were wrong. And what business did his aunt have to interfere anyway? Women knew nothing of business, and profit was all-important.

Nine hundred and forty. The blister stretched across the whole of his hand now, he was sure of it. Hannah had no right to make such a stupid remark about Mother's money and in public too. What was Mother's was Father's; she should know that by now. Women could not possibly manage their own affairs, there would be all sorts of mess. He let his left hand take more of his weight. The noise of drilling was reaching them now, so they were almost there, thank God.

At the base of the ladder they caught their breath, relieved to be in the dull glow of the lamps, seeing shapes for the first time for what seemed like hours. Men and machinery, rock walls, cut and carved, the well-propped lode. Their candles lit their way only dimly as they left the foot of the shaft and entered the dense darkness of the seams. The square-pitched pine props were set every three feet and groaned from the weight but he was not frightened. He was at home at last. They passed yawning black holes and heard in their depths the noise of miners as they shovelled and drilled. These mechanical drills had water fed through the centre, Harry saw, as one miner, working in a bulge in the main seam, levered a drill and cut out some of the ore. He pointed and Sam nodded.

'Lays the dust, improves the cutting.' Harry could not hear but in the light from the candles he could read Sam's mouth.

Fumes grew stronger with each step they took. Blasting had been going on this morning, he thought. The accumulated dust was making his eyes smart. His hand throbbed.

'I still think we should do our own smelting,' he shouted at his uncle, but Sam was talking to a miner. Harry waited until he had finished and then repeated his remark. Sam took a suck on his pipe, holding his hand over the bowl. How could he smoke when there was already so much dust and so many smells, Harry wondered and shook his head.

Sam took his arm. They stood to one side of the main seam watching the activity which flowed and ebbed before them. 'No, Harry. It's too much capital outlay and Malaysia is taking over smelting as well as mining. There's no future in English tin any more.' His mouth was against Harry's ear and he could just make out the words.

Harry reached out and ran his hands down the prop. Bloody hell. Why did tin have to be so common? Their usual customers were finding supplies nearer home now but it was in his blood, he knew that, and every time he came down here it was the same. He ground his boot in the dust. He knew his hair and the pores of his skin would be full of dirt and he would smell of the mine for days, but to him it was a good smell, an honest one. They leant back as a trolley was pushed past. He watched as the miner leant into the load, shoving the trolley with the whole of his body weight. He was small, a boy. A miner walked past him, a piece of wood in the corner of his mouth, he was chewing then spitting as he moved on down. Harry stayed where he was, resting against a blackened prop while Sam moved amongst the men, talking to the team leaders, checking with the supervisors, until eventually he turned back towards Harry and beckoned, nodding towards the shaft.

Harry pushed himself upright, reluctant to leave the scene so soon but knowing that it was time. He caught up with Sam who was relighting his pipe in a hacked-out bay of the main seam. They walked on together, their arms knocking, their feet kicking up dust which caught in their throats. Though he would have liked to stay for longer, Harry knew it put the men on edge to have the boss and the owner's son standing behind them as they worked, and besides, Eliza was preparing one of her cream teas for them.

And then he stopped, every muscle tense. He knew before he heard the creak, knew from the feeling which made his hands go cold; but nothing had happened, yet. It was not a feeling that had been growing as they walked – it was a sudden knowledge, a certainty which stopped him in his tracks and made the hair rise on the back of his neck. He half-turned, oblivious to everything else, not knowing whether Sam had also stopped, only knowing that he must listen to the next sound, listen hard for it above the noise of the mine; knowing that in a moment his world had changed from normality to crisis, from contentment to animal instinct. It would come and his world had ended, his life forced from his body if he couldn't place the next small sound.

He held quite still, his eyes straining into the darkness which lay beyond the candle's glow and there it was again, a creak; above him of course but to the left or to the right? He couldn't decide. He breathed through his mouth to hear just that fraction better. The dust made him want to cough but he did not, he could not afford to miss the next warning but where was it coming from, God damn it? Where?

There was a creak again, but faint, and he wanted to call for silence but that would distract him for perhaps a vital moment. If only it wasn't so dark. Then there was a crack. A noise which was taken up again and again. He strained to hear above the drilling, the rumbling of the trolleys, the shouts of the men. He strained to see into the thick darkness.

He held his breath and looked for Sam who was also standing quite still, waiting with his head cocked, his face tense and strained in the flicker of the candle-light. Christ, which way to move? To the left, or to the right or to stay here? Where was safety? There was too much darkness outside the flicker of his candle, too much darkness all around, pressing down on them, a thousand feet of heavy darkness pressing and cracking and coming to suck the breath from him. He was panting now, breathing up in his throat, trying to think, trying to hear because he had to guess right. Now there was no more time though how did he know that? He just did.

He moved then, to the right, gripping Sam, pulling him with him, feeling the canvas of his jacket, feeling the weight of the man resisting his slowness, but he did not let go. The cracking was louder but still the ceiling held though the dust was coming down now, dousing his candle, Sam's candle – but not before he had seen the man's face in the last flicker of the light, seen the fear which must have mirrored his own.

He hauled hard, sweating with effort, bracing his feet and taking Sam as though in a rugby tackle, letting his own weight take them across the main seam. Christ, let me be right, he groaned, and knew that he spoke aloud because he could taste the grit in his open mouth. Then it came, the roar that Harry had known would come in that first moment, which was probably only a few seconds ago. A grinding roar which exploded into bursting air, knocking them hard into the rock wall, blowing the breath from his body, hurling him down, on to the ground so hard that he thought his ribs were broken. And then he waited for the crushing weight of the tumbling ore to bear down and finish him, finish Sam. He reached out for the man, finding his arm and gripping it, not wanting to be alone when it came; and all the time there was a roaring.

But he had guessed right and no great weight came cutting into him or Sam. There was only pressure that hurt his ears, dust that whirled and choked until at last the noise ceased. Then there was just dust and darkness but no drilling, no rumbling of trolleys, and miners running to them and shielding their candles with their hands against the draught. He had never heard such quiet in the mine before.

The man-engine was a godsend. His ribs still ached and his limbs trembled as he stepped on to the moving rod on its up-stroke, fitting his hands and feet into the holds cut into it, stepping off at each platform as the rod went down again, then catching the other as it came down from above and then moved up again. Sam was coming up slowly behind, his pipe broken and in his pocket now. Harry's head ached and he shook it but his ears still felt strange. He didn't yet feel part of the world. He was still back there, tensed and waiting, and now the joy came flooding through him because, God damn it, he had guessed right. He stepped off the rod on to the platform. Damnation – he had guessed right and he wanted to shout but he remembered the feel of Sam's hand on his shoulder as he had dusted himself off, taking his hat from the outstretched hand of a wizened miner.

I owe you, lad, Sam had said. I'd not have been quick enough. He looked at him closely, a thoughtful expression in his eyes. You're blooded now, Harry. Harry set his shoulders back. By God, and so he was. He'd beaten the mine, he'd known it was coming for him and he'd bloody beaten it. Wait until he told Arthur. He jumped on to the upward rod and called down to Sam.

'Don't tell Hannah, or the family.' He listened, leaping on to the rod, straining to hear Sam's reply.

'She'll have to be told, Harry. She'll have heard the noise, seen the dust and even if she hasn't, the men who came down to help will have told her.'

Harry shook his head. 'God, I hope she keeps quiet about it.'

'She's bound to, isn't she?' Sam called up. 'She'll have to if you want to be allowed down the mine again.'

Harry did want to, now more than ever.

Hannah had moved from the bank soon after Sam and Harry had disappeared. The wind had grown cooler up there with no shelter and she had walked about Penhallon, seeing the piles of ore, the sheds, the stables which housed the ponies. Watching the shift that changed while her uncle and Harry were below.

68

She had seen the grimed men walk unsteadily from the moving rod, their faces drawn with tiredness, black blood from a cut ran down the cheek of one and she wondered where they would go when age took their livelihood away from them. To the workhouse too, to be separated from their wives for the rest of their lives? It was too dreadful to think about but she must. Joe had said she must.

She had taken baskets with Mother one Harvest Festival to the workhouse which served the area lying to the back of the Crescents. When they had entered the green-tiled room which lay at the end of a cold stone corridor she had thought it was empty, but then the small grey-clothed women sitting in chairs set against the walls had moved to see what the disturbance was before settling back again into their stillness. There had been a smell, not of dirt but of age and carbolic soap, and as she passed the Michaelmas daisies the hands that reached for them were gnarled and big-veined. But she hadn't felt sad; she hadn't wondered then where these people had come from, hadn't felt this confusion that was tearing at her now.

Then as she stood there, she had heard the noise, a muted roaring, and felt the earth shudder; had seen the men so tired and bowed turn and run back to the shaft. Dust had wafted up from the blackness and she knew what had happened. But who was hurt? Was it Harry? Or Sam?

She called to the men. 'What is it?' Wanting to clutch their arms.

'A fall,' one called, his tiredness gone, his voice urgent. He had not turned to speak to her but waited impatiently in the queue which was moving quickly back down the ladder. There had been no panic, just determination. The clerk from the office had come and stood with her. He was an old man and used to this, he told her. It happened frequently. But that did not help the feeling of fear and helplessness that gripped her. I'm not used to it, she had wanted to scream, wanting him to go and find out if her brother was safe, not stand there with a resigned expression on his face. Do something, she wanted to shout into his face, or let me do something, but by clasping her hands together she was able to hold herself back; was able to tell herself that the men climbing down the ladder were the only ones who could help. But Harry was her brother.

The wait was so long. The clerk wanted her to move over to the office but she couldn't. Not until she knew.

And then at last she saw him climb from the ladder, his face dirty and streaked with sweat, his smile wide. She did not run to him, though she wanted to, but walked across.

'Are you all right, Harry?' her voice was steady but her nails dug into her palms as she clenched her fists, fighting to appear calm.

'Not a scratch, Hannah. No one was hurt. It was just one of those little things that happen.'

Hannah saw Sam climb up now. He looked tired but he also smiled, and slowly she allowed herself to believe that her brother was still here, still whole, and she wanted to weep and clutch him to her, feel his breath on her face again as though it was a sunny day in the old garden.

Instead she said, 'So you're a real miner now, Harry.' Her voice sounded firm and strong but as he smiled at her she gripped his hand and held it to her mouth.

'Thank God you're safe,' she whispered, her eyes holding his.

Harry felt the warmth of her lips, the strength of her hand, and for an instant wanted to hold her close as he had once been able to do when they were very young. But men were climbing out, pushing past them, and he squeezed her hand. 'Don't tell Father,' he said. 'Please, Hannah.'

She held his gaze, then looked past him to Sam and nodded. 'I promise, Harry.' She wanted to wipe his face, to gently bathe the dirt away. 'If Beaky saw you now, she'd scrub you raw,' was all she said.

Sam brought them back to the big house for tea. She still thought of it as Eliza's house, though it had been her mother's as a girl too. Ivy covered the walls, and in the autumn this went a deep red and looked warm when all around the chill was settling on the ground. The gravel crunched beneath the wheels of the trap and beneath her feet as she walked over and on to the grass. She reached forward and took a leaf in her

70

hand. It was warm and limp from the sun and was summer-green.

'Come on then, Hannah, we're going up to the loft. Tea won't be for a while.'

She turned. For the men it was as though nothing had happened and she steeled herself to follow suit, for after all she had a promise to keep.

She liked the apple loft. It had been where Uncle Simon had always taken them. He would choose for each of them a green apple streaked with red, a leaf still on the stalk. That way, he had said, it smelt of the fresh air. The wooden stairs which led to the loft ran up from the stable-yard.

Simon had said that the lofts had once held the hay when his father kept a full stable of hunters, but that had been long ago, in the heyday of the mine and so this one had been fitted with slatted benches and put to better use. Hannah ran her hand up the green-mossed banister. It was slimy from yesterday's rain and marked her gloves. She removed them. The last time she had been up with Uncle Simon was when she was eleven. She remembered now that he had lifted her up on to a hunter he had borrowed and it had seemed a million miles from the ground. It was not possible that he would never come again.

Sam was holding the door open for her and she felt her lips smile as though they were not part of her. Sam said, 'Eliza will be along soon. She said she'd come down and collect us when the tea was set up. It's to be on the terrace today. The fresh air will do your mother good. Your father has gone to see the Vicar about tomorrow's sermon.'

Hannah stepped into the room and smelt the fruit. Harry had already reached the bench and was spacing out the few apples that remained. Some were wrinkled and drying, some as lush as when they were first picked, though there were not many of either left because the harvest would soon be in.

She leant back against the old dresser which had been moved out of the kitchen and now held twine and old flowerpots. Beyond her brother she could see through the open window across the fields and to the sea. It was blue today and ships were plying eastwards to the harbour. She felt very tired now and ran her hands along the surface of the dresser. Its grain had risen with age and she could smell the twine.

It would do her mother good to walk up on the cliffs or, if she hadn't the strength, perhaps they could use a bath chair. She would ask Eliza if they could arrange it. Yes, that is what she would think about today and later, in the quiet of the cottage when the lamps were out, she would think of other things, of Uncle Simon as he held her hand and ran with her in the orchard.

Harry rubbed a firm apple on his sleeve and took a bite. It was firm and the juice ran on to his chin. It tasted better than any other apple he had tasted and he grinned to himself. Perhaps life is sweet, he thought, never having considered death before. He wiped his chin with his handkerchief and then felt Sam's hand on his arm.

'I've something I want to show you, now more than ever,' Sam murmured and walked across to the old desk. Harry followed and waited as Sam opened the top right-hand drawer. Its knob was of brass and was dull and scratched. He withdrew a bundle of letters wrapped in a red ribbon. 'These are from Simon. I feel this last one is of particular interest to you but take them all. You'll bring them back of course before you leave for London. Your aunt likes to feel that they are here, where he spent so much of his time.'

Harry nodded, though he did not understand. Simon wasn't here so what did it matter where the letters were? Once you were dead, you were dead. He took the top one; the one that Sam was pointing to and read it.

Dear Eliza,
It is so very hot still and many of the men are sick with enteric, but this month we have not engaged the enemy. The Boers can hide anywhere. They are quite amazing and will be the death of some of us. But enough of that maudlin talk. Sam would love it here at any other time. The mines, Eliza! Gold and diamonds just spilling out of the earth. I know that a few big names hold the monopoly on the mines but

there is still room for the small set up. Cornish miners are already here and more hard-rock men are needed, especially for the gold-fields, which make Penhallon look very small. But, my dear, I can't write any more. We have to set out again. Take care and my love to you and regards to Sam. Tell him to show this to Harry. Perhaps he would like to come back with me. I've bought a smallholding as a base.

The paper was stained and the ink faint. Harry looked up at Sam. 'Yes, I thought you might be interested.'

Harry read through the letter again. God, why did Simon have to go and get himself killed, the stupid fool? He could have got round the old man, persuaded him that this was a better idea than stewing in some God-forsaken cavalry. Look at the money the South African mines had brought to London, the new rich who were buying up the big houses. He threw the letter on the table.

'It sounds good, doesn't it, Sam. Will you go?'

'Good Lord, it's not for a man my age, but maybe it's right for you. Anyway you have plenty of time to decide. You're still at school. But have a look at the rest of the letters. Poor Simon. He had such plans.' He reached over and took one himself. At least the war looked as though it would soon be over, he thought, but it would be too late for Eliza, who still mourned Simon's loss so much – a loss which seemed to have made her think that life was very short. He had been grateful to Mrs Arness for encouraging Eliza to help a little with her school; it had helped with the grief but she still cried at night and Simon's room was just as he had left it.

Hannah heard Eliza's steps on the stairs and her heavy breathing as she entered. She looked fatter, better somehow, Hannah thought, even in black. She watched as Eliza waved to Harry and came across to her. Her face was softer since she had married Sam, but there were dark marks under her eyes and they were shaded as her mother's were when a baby had failed to live.

'Well, Hannah.' Eliza spoke softly, trying to collect her

breath. 'Dear me, what a climb. I'm not as fit as I used to be. Or is it too much cream?' She laughed. 'Sam does like his cream, you know.'

Sam turned at the mention of his name. He was leaning with Harry over the letters on the desk. 'Don't go blaming everything on me,' he called, putting his arm round Harry's shoulder. Harry caught Hannah's eye and she saw that he was embarrassed by the gesture. Perhaps he too thought Sam was not quite good enough for Eliza, thought Hannah, but she had decided he was just right. He had changed Eliza into someone easy to be with.

'So, Hannah, how are you enjoying yourself at the Arness's? Mr Arness is hung in all the best galleries, you know.'

Hannah remembered the marigolds in her room and was not surprised. There was a vigour to his paintings that pleased her.

'It's very different there,' she replied quietly, looking towards Harry and Sam, but they were bending over the papers again.

Eliza nodded. 'But are you enjoying it?' Her grey eyes were questioning; her wide mouth was still slightly open while she waited for Hannah's answer.

Hannah watched the motes in the light from the window as she picked out her words. 'Yes,' she replied finally, 'more than I could have dreamed I would ever enjoy anything. Being with the Arness family has shown me how people can live and think and feel – if they want to. But I want to ask if you knew what it would be like.'

She had never spoken openly to her aunt before and wondered whether it was safe or if she would be admonished.

'Yes, I did know, Hannah.'

'But why did you do it? You know what Father would say and Mother. You knew that I would have to act at the Arness's in a way which, if discovered, would bring disaster on me.'

Eliza flushed. The child was direct, as Edith had once been, and that was the key of course. Hannah was very like her mother with the same spirit that had once been present in that shadow of a person whom she barely recognised as her sister. And that was partly why she had sent her to the Americans' cottage. Her spirit was being stifled by that man, by the tenets of the society he so heartily endorsed. He had crushed Edith and was now doing the same to his daughter in spite of the fact that the world was changing, and for the better. Mrs Arness had shown Eliza and Sam. Now she wanted Edith's daughter to flourish, not to wither as her poor mother was doing. That, though, was only part of the reason but it was the only one she was prepared to admit to herself for the moment, so she said, 'Because I felt you needed to see another kind of life and it might give you cause to think and consider. Might show you that to enjoy the benefit of some things it is sometimes necessary to engage in a little subterfuge, if that is the only way that it can be brought about.' She smiled and patted Hannah's hand. 'But of course you must plan your advancement in the context of your mother's health.'

She was looking hard at Hannah now. 'She is a very tired woman, Hannah. We won't discuss the whys and wherefores but she must try to achieve a measure of peace. And you must do the same.' She had turned now, back to the door, and Hannah had to strain to hear her last words. 'You owe that to yourself and that is where the problems will arise.'

'Aunt Eliza,' she called after her but Eliza had stopped on the top step.

'Come on now, all of you, tea is in the garden and the wasps will be having a splendid time with the strawberry jam.'

She would sit Sam next to her and hope that Mr Watson, for she could never think of him as John, would not be back for a while. And Mr Watson was, of course, the other reason for sending Hannah to the cottage, she admitted to herself at last as she crossed the stable-yard. She hated Hannah's father for the way he treated Sam, hated his arrogance, his hypocrisy. Let him try to restrain his daughter now, let him try to suck every spark from her. He would be beaten in the end, and that thought gave her great satisfaction.

And as Hannah followed her down the loft stairs she looked back at Harry and wondered whether Eliza would have told him to plan his advancement in the context of his mother's health and knew that she would not. It was to be her burden alone.

5 In the hall of her uncle's house on New Year's
Eve a great fire blazed; holly hung on top of the
portrait of Esther's grandfather, flopping down
and half covering his face. Hannah wondered if
she had instructed the maids to do that. Esther
had not liked the old man – his nose dripped. But
Hannah had thought he had been kind, drawing barley sugar
from the inside pocket of his frock coat, pulling her to his side
and saying Happy New Year, Hannah. The fire had always
stung her with its heat because he stood just there, in front of
the mantelshelf, to welcome them. She looked at the stone
mantel, at the stag's head which was above it attached to a
wooden shield. It had blue glassy eyes and looked like Harry
had done when he had drunk too much champagne on
Christmas Eve. Aunt Camilla would only allow it to be dusted
with an owl's wing because the barbs were excellent, she
always said, for preventing moths, fleas and a shiny nose. The
wooden panelling looked more welcoming than usual because
of the Chinese lanterns hung at intervals around the room, but
that was the extent of the greeting, for there was no one else
except for the butler who took Father's hat and Harry's too.

'I'll announce you, sir,' he said before turning towards the
drawing-room door.

'I miss the old man,' whispered Hannah, 'he always had a
smile along with the dew-drop.'

Harry grinned. He seemed happier since the holiday in
Cornwall. More approachable. She felt in her coat pocket. Yes,
it was still there – the musical box that Joe had sent for
Christmas. It didn't seem like four months since he had taken
her into his father's studio, rich with colour and the smell of oil
paint and turpentine, and then on into his own. She had seen
his carpenter's bench; the chisel, the small knives that he
would have used to carve the box. It played Tchaikovsky's *1812*
but didn't have the cannon, he had written in the note which

had accompanied the Christmas present, but at least it would remind her of the day the storm came.

She ran her gloved fingers over the indented surface of the box, thankful for deep pockets, thankful for her father's preoccupation at his cousin's absence for it would prevent him noticing the bulge. She had been forbidden to bring her presents to show Esther; it was vain and self-indulgent, Father had said. But this was so beautiful and made especially for her – it had to be displayed.

When Joe had taken her to his workshop before the end of the holiday the wood shavings were heaped into one corner. Some, though, still lay curled like ringlets on his bench and she had put her finger through the middle of one then taken an end and pulled it out full length. It was so long and fine and smooth and all around there was the clean smell of wood in the room.

It all takes time, he had said, when he had shown her the objects he had made. Boxes, animals, and a half-finished chair in one corner. It was plain, in light wood. I don't like clutter, he had continued. I like clean lines in a room. He had told her how he taught the other pupils some of his skills for one hour each day. He said that his mother felt it important that horizons should be broadened, and when the Vicar had said that he felt it was diverging from the bare necessities of instruction, she had answered that if woodwork was good enough for his Jesus Christ, surely it was good enough for his flock. The Vicar had choked on his cake, Joe told her, and his father had slapped his back so hard that his tea had spilt.

Hannah looked at Harry's hands as he withdrew his watch yet again to check the time; he had been doing it since they left the house. The snow had held up the carriage and the road sweeper had slipped and fallen as they passed, his broom skidding over the hard-packed ice and frightening the horses. The gardener had been driving the horses and had had difficulty restarting them until sand from the roadside had been heaped under the wheels and on the ground beneath their hooves. That's taken ten minutes, Harry called, and she had seen her father's mouth tighten. To be late for the rich cousins was like forgetting to curtsy before royalty.

Hannah had looked from the window and checked that the sweeper was unhurt. That is none of our business, her father had replied when she told them.

Now, waiting for the appearance of Uncle Thomas, she watched Harry click the watch case shut with long, tapered, white hands. Were Christ's hands like Joe's then? They must be, she thought, so why were they always portrayed in paintings as hands like Harry's? In all the heat of Jerusalem he must be brown anyway. In fact he must be a Jew. Her father hated Jews. Swarthy creatures, he would say. Did he not know Christ was a Jew? The Vicar's Christ had looked all pink and white in the crib for the Christmas service. Perhaps she should tell the Vicar that Christ was not an Englishman. Perhaps he would also choke and she wanted to laugh out loud.

Her father was tapping his leg with the silver-tipped walking-stick her mother had given him for Christmas. It would be New Year's Day tomorrow – perhaps his cousin Thomas was seeing to some last-minute affairs. He seemed to have a lot, mostly of the unmentionable variety, or so Mrs Brennan had told Cook – whatever that might mean.

Harry had brought out the watch again. It was ridiculous, she wanted to tell him, when there was a perfectly good grandfather clock in the corner over by the dining-room door. It had a gold face too, just like his watch.

She knew why he did it, of course, and thought of the embroidery set which was all she had been given for Christmas from her parents. But would her father allow Harry to keep the watch when he announced to them all the decision he had made? Would he tell them today, when he had the support of Thomas, for her uncle did support the boy, she knew that. Father would blame it all on Eliza of course, and Cornwall – try and talk him round, forbid him perhaps – but it must be right for there was a light in Harry's eyes now, a looseness that made him want to talk to her, made her enjoy him again. He had even brought her a painting for Christmas, one of Newlyn, full of light and children, and she sighed with pleasure.

Miss Fletcher had said that she should pass the entrance examination with no difficulty and King's College London

78

were accepting more and more women now. Her father had not yet mentioned university to her and her mother would not allow her to ask, but she was full of hope. Would Esther come too or would it be finishing school for her? And where was she anyway? Hannah tugged at the white scarf which was wound round her neck and fastened at the back with a safety pin. Her mother sat down on the old leather chair by the fire; it was the grandfather's chair which had pipe burns on the arms and no antimacassars. Mother looked tired again and was unwell in the mornings. Hannah walked across and touched her shoulder.

'Are you all right?'

The blue was there again under her mother's eyes and Hannah felt a churning in her stomach. She could not bear to look at her father, his great weight and height. Had he done it again? Had she, her mother, allowed him to again? Hannah squeezed her mother's shoulder.

'It will be all right, Mother. I'll look after you.' She felt her mother lean against her, just for a moment, but then her father hissed from his place near the Chippendale table, which had no letters on its silver plate, 'For goodness sake sit up, woman. Thomas could be here at any moment.' His voice was low and vicious and Hannah could see the reflection of his back in the gilt mirror which hung over the table, she felt the stiffening of her mother's shoulder and tried to keep her close but her mother forced herself upright as the door from the drawing-room opened.

'My dear John, how lovely to see you.' Thomas was in evening dress too, his white waistcoat creased into folds across his stomach. Camilla was behind him, her hair caught back in combs at the sides, then allowed to fall down in loose curls at the back.

She called out to them all, 'So very sorry to keep you all waiting. We were just sorting out a few details. Cook seems to have become confused about the numbers again.' Camilla came across to Hannah. 'Pop upstairs, dear. Esther is waiting in the nursery. She has such plans for this evening.'

Camilla held a mother-of-pearl fan in one hand and Hannah

could feel the draught from it as she waved it briskly in front of her face. Edith Watson rose from the chair and Hannah was quick to grasp her elbow and steady her. Camilla looked elegant in her pale pink dress which glittered with sequins, whilst her mother was subdued in black, cut high on her neck. She wore a jet necklace, which was permissible when one was in mourning, she had told Hannah. Hannah wished that she did not have to wear black also.

Camilla's neckline was cut away a little but not as much as the ladies in Prince Edward's set. Her necklace of pearls had gained another string since last year, Hannah noticed. 'Thank you, Aunt Camilla. Will you be all right, Mother?' Hannah looked into her mother's face.

'Off you go now, Hannah. We will see you in time for dinner, remember.' Her mother's voice was strained and high-pitched. She was tired; Hannah knew she was tired. She turned to catch Harry's eye but he and her father were already being ushered by Thomas into the drawing-room.

The wide stairs swept round on to the first landing and then the second, carpeted thickly in dark red so that her patent boots made no noise. Heavy oil paintings of Esther's forebears hung at regular intervals, though they ceased when the stairs narrowed on the next flight. Now there was only a covering of linoleum to walk on and her boots tapped with each step.

Hannah looked above her and saw that the wicker gate that had ensured Esther did not fall as a small child was shut outside the nursery landing. She opened it and the tin bell which was attached jangled, the door ahead of her was flung open, and Esther held out her arms.

'Oh Hannah, where have you been?' Her face with its eyes the colour of violets was flushed and her blonde hair was dishevelled.

'Climbing these stairs on my own.' Hannah answered. 'I suppose you just happened to have something pressing which required your attention and, coincidentally, saved you a long climb.'

She was panting a little and grinned as Esther pulled a face and drew Hannah into the room, which was lit by gas lights burning yellow at the fringe and blue at the heart. The fire was crackling in the blue-tiled grate, tinsel was draped all around and Chinese lanterns hung from cotton strung across the ceiling so the impression was one of light.

Hannah eased out of her coat, feeling dark and dull against the vivid blue of Esther's dress. She wore dancing slippers of bronze kid with crossed over elastic. 'You look far too nice,' she said to Esther, who laughed and bent forward, kissing her on the cheek.

'The blue is to match my eyes. I chose it. Your dress hardly looks like mourning, you know, with that black embroidery.' She pulled Hannah over to the long mirror.

The dark of Hannah's dress seemed to swallow what light there was around her whilst Esther's flung it back into the room. 'Father's in a rage because we're late.' It sounded trivial spoken aloud. Hannah sat down opposite Esther in one of the wicker chairs near the fire. There was a wire guard set up, and on the table where she and Esther had eaten nursery teas when they were younger was a pile of chiffon; pale green, blue and orange. The rugs were the same frayed ones that had always been there but there was a new puzzle set out on the card table in the corner. The outside edges were complete and a pile of pieces waited to be sorted in the centre. Esther sat down opposite.

'Tell me what dear old Santa Claus put in your stocking then?' Esther asked, smiling. Her teeth were even and white. She pulled a face when she heard. 'It's not good enough, you know, Hannah.' Her voice was indignant. 'You should have more than that.'

Hannah laughed. 'I don't want a large pocket watch, thank you.' Esther threw a cushion at her and Hannah caught it, then placed it behind her. 'How kind of you, dear,' she mocked. The fire was hot on her face and she pushed the chair back.

'And were you and George pleased with your presents?'

George was older than Esther, much older. He was twenty-five and Esther was fifteen, as Hannah was. Hannah did not look at Esther while she waited for the answer. She did not really want to know because it would hurt. And then she remembered. 'But look at this, Esther,' she said when Esther had run through her list. She stood and picked up her coat from the back of a wooden chair, delving deep into the pocket before returning to her seat. She passed the musical box over to Esther who opened it, laughing at the music and at the thought of Hannah caught in the rain with an American boy while the chaperon was in the cover of his porch, miles away.

Esther closed the lid when the music finished, putting it back into Hannah's coat pocket then calling her across to the table where the chiffon lay.

'Do look at this, Hannah, isn't it glorious?'

Hannah picked up a piece and let it drift down through the air back on to the table. It was so light she could hardly feel it. She looked at Esther who explained.

'Mother said we should do an entertainment tonight. George did one on Boxing Day. Something light and airy, Mother says, something which is fun. They've been to a soirée with King Edward, you know, and think he is a vast improvement on the old lady so these things are permissible now.' She paused. 'Well, it was a very big soirée and I doubt if he knew they were there but they certainly knew. Such excitement, Hannah. Anyway, George thinks we should do a dance, the one about the autumn leaves that we learnt at the classes. Mother will play the music.'

Hannah watched as she performed a few steps, her arms languid, her toes pointing in those beautiful pumps. Esther stopped and gripped Hannah's arm. 'Do you remember that dreadful ballet teacher last term; how she slapped one of the girls and Miss Fletcher sent her from the school, there and then.'

They returned to the chairs, Hannah laughing as Esther lay back, her arms clasped above her head, her legs relaxed in a sprawl. Esther was very beautiful, Hannah knew. But knew also that as quickly as she drew people to her she would also discard them. Much like the way she talked; here, there and everywhere. She was enchanting but how deep did it all go? Hannah didn't know, hadn't yet had to know.

They had been friends for years, since Thomas had sent Esther to what was now Miss Fletcher's school and, not to be outdone, John Watson had entered his daughter. It had been wonderful from the start; especially as Harry had already turned away from her. Relation and friend, how very fortunate. Hannah smiled again.

'And then we had that lady who walked like a duck, do you remember, Esther? We called her Quack and Sonia made glorious duck noises. She had a faint moustache.'

They laughed again and the heat from the fire was pleasant on her face. There was a box of bon-bons topped with crystallised violets on top of the bookcase at Esther's right hand. She picked one out and threw it to Hannah.

'Spoil your meal with that, Hannah. At least you'll be able to leave a bit on your plate without your father rapping your knuckles this year. Do you remember last year how he leant over and tapped you with his knife?'

Hannah did remember and though she laughed, no vestige touched beneath the surface, where there was only coldness at the memory. 'He'll have more to make him angry than that this year. Has your father told you about Harry?'

Esther held her bon-bon between her thumb and finger, eating it with small bites. Chocolate stuck to her teeth and she ran her tongue over them. She nodded. 'I was rather looking forward to seeing Harry in a uniform, he would have made a good escort. He's a fearful spoilsport.'

Hannah grinned and shook her head. 'You know what he's like with girls. He doesn't like us.'

'Doesn't like you, you mean. Sisters are different.'

'I mean he doesn't like girls. He and this friend Arthur seem to spend all their time playing cricket or running round chasing pieces of paper, as far as I can see.'

Esther was licking her fingers; the chocolate was gone. 'I could get him to like me,' she murmured. 'After all, he could be very rich one day.' She half smiled at her friend, her eyes thoughtful.

This time Hannah threw the cushion. 'You're just a gold-digger.'

Esther grinned. 'Hardly me, dear. That's what you should be calling Harry. With a bit of luck anyway.'

Harry was sitting back from the fire. His uncle had broken with tradition and opened a bottle of champagne before the meal. The glasses were cold and a fine mist settled on the outside. He held his by the stem, knowing that his uncle had tried to make it easier for him and for his father, but it would not be easy to cross him. Ever.

'Really, John,' his uncle was saying. 'Think about it a bit. The lad could end up like the big-timers out there, Rhodes, Barnato and Beit. The South African mines have given them fortunes and power. Think of the power, man.'

Harry looked at his father. He sat back in the chair smoking, not looking at Thomas but across at the window where the tassels of the valance shone deep red in the light from the electric lights. It was a quiet form of lighting, Harry thought, and bright but his uncle had only installed it downstairs until he was sure that this new-fangled idea was safe. He looked back again at his father who still gazed at the window.

'Jews, you mean,' he said.

'For God's sake, John,' his uncle said, his voice rising. Harry's hand tightened on the stem. He made himself sit quite still, his legs crossed, his left arm resting on the arm of the settee. If his uncle allowed himself to anger, his father would simply shut his mind.

'What I mean is, old man' – Thomas was speaking in a deliberate and slow voice now – 'there are opportunities out there that we will never see the likes of over here. Think of the money he could make in gold or diamond mining. With his family background he could return in a few years well set up to become a man of property, of standing in the community.'

Thomas stood up and leant against the mantelshelf, one arm draped along its length. His grey hair made him look much older than Harry's father, older, wiser and kinder. But then, as Harry's father had said to him on more than one occasion, that side of the family had had things easy. He had sounded full of bitterness.

At last his father turned to Thomas, but still not to Harry. 'What if it were George wanting to throw up his law practice and sail out to some idea he had pulled out of the air?' His lips were barely moving and smoke puffed out of his mouth and through his teeth as he spoke.

Thomas pushed back a log which had fallen to one side of the grate. Sparks spun around his polished boot until, with one final thrust, he turned to John, his eye catching Harry's as he did so. There was a smile in it now.

'Why, of course I'd be delighted. Give him my best toothbrush! Shows a bit of spirit, you know. Something to be proud of in a boy, John. Why, where would you be if you hadn't shown spirit and moved up to London?'

Harry took a sip of champagne. It was almost warm now and flat. His uncle was a clever man, no wonder he made an excellent barrister.

There was a pause while his father tapped his knee. The fire was crackling, the clock in the corner had a long slow tick and the brass pendulum shone as it swung. Shone like gold, Harry thought, and felt the excitement begin again. How much would he find, or would it be diamonds?

'Harold should really think of the status he will be throwing away.' His father's voice was quiet but icy.

The status *you* would be throwing away, thought Harry, suddenly afraid no longer but angry. Good God, I should hate to be a soldier. So tedious. So senseless. And what if he ever had to kill someone? He thought of the fish on the end of his line and shuddered. All so damned messy. And soldiering hadn't done Simon much good, had it, poor old chap, and just when he had made up his mind to get out too. Hannah had said that his death had made her realise how short life could be and that therefore it should not be wasted. She really was too intelligent for a girl, did too much thinking. She should be careful or she would make herself unmarriageable or contract brain fever.

He could hear his uncle's soft reply and silence fell again. His father was studying the fire through his glass. He took his watch from his pocket and checked the time, then turned it over and over in his hand. Harry flushed as he felt the weight of his Christmas present in his waistcoat pocket. Should he have told his father before? But it was so difficult. Arthur had told him to write but somehow the words would not come. Perhaps he should return the present but that would mean he couldn't show it to the chaps at school. God, why was life so difficult?

'Very well.' His father still did not look at him or speak to him directly. 'I shall allow the boy to forgo the army at this stage. He can attend to his mining exams but he must do the thing properly in a university situation, then if he still wants to explore the possibilities of South Africa we shall discuss it again.'

That was all. There was silence for a moment then Thomas looked across at Harry and smiled before turning again to John Watson.

'Well done, man,' he said to him, sweeping the champagne bottle from the ice-bucket and pouring more into both their glasses, beckoning Harry to come over. 'This calls for a toast.'

He pulled Harry over to stand beside him and they both watched as Harry's father rose slowly from his chair. His face was set but Thomas continued as though he had not noticed.

'To this young man; a son to be proud of. Good luck, my boy.'

His father drank to this along with Thomas but still said nothing.

Thomas put down his glass, it was half full. 'Do excuse me a moment, both of you. I must see where the ladies are. They seem to have been overseeing the dining-room preparations for far too long.' Before leaving he handed round the silver cigarette box. Harry refused but his father took one, tapping the cigarette on the back of his nail, watching Thomas as he left the room. Harry stood by the fire, uncertain whether to take his place again on the settee. He saw that his father's fingers were more heavily stained with nicotine than they had been in the summer and that the discoloration of his moustache and hair was more obvious too. There was no belly on him as there was with Thomas.

His father did not ask him to sit but sat gazing into the fire. It was a shock when he spoke; he had been silent for so long.

'I have acquiesced because your uncle seems to feel the idea has its merits but I have suffered a grave disappointment. For, as you know, I feel there is nothing finer than a man fighting to save the honour of his country.'

His voice shook and his hands were trembling, he could not go on and Harry knew that there was a great rage building and felt the tension rise in himself, tension and fear, but then the door opened. Thomas stood there with the girls, calling them all to dine and announcing that later the young ladies would be entertaining them with an amusing interlude.

Hannah loved the dining-room when it was decorated for this evening. There were garlands of holly, and tinsel hanging from the picture rails. A Christmas rose was placed in a crystal vase either side of the mantelshelf in front of the tall thin chimney mirrors so that their reflections were bathed in the glow of the candles set in candelabras down the length of the table. The table was laid with the finest porcelain, crystal wine glasses, silver cutlery and the epergne in the centre all on a crisp table-cloth. In the corner opposite the serving door was a forest tree decorated with shining balls of red, gold and silver, and alive with small candles glinting and lighting their corner. The electric lights were not on this evening and she was glad. George sat between her and Esther and after grace he made her pull a cracker but only the crêpe tore and left the brown paper strip with the gunpowder on. Esther laughed, calling Harry to turn and watch Hannah pull the end.

Hannah hated the bang, hated the smell and the flash but George said she must and Esther too so she gripped it, her body rigid and the smile set too fixedly on her face, and pulled. There it was, the bang and Esther shrieked and Hannah laughed, but not really.

Her father had a green paper hat on and he was drinking a great deal of wine as the soup, the fish and then the saddle of mutton came and went while the butler watched the servants and refilled the glasses.

George was kind and his deep voice talked to her of Cornwall and school but then he and Harry leant over the table as they drank their wine and Hannah and Esther sat back in their chairs and talked. Hannah had been given wine; it made her cheeks hot and laughter well in her throat. She was hot and wished that she was in a light dress like Esther and her mother. It would be nice to have her neck free of restraining heat.

'Of course the Liberals have been stabbing the government in the back with all this pro-Boer business. Independence for the Transvaal, I ask you,' Harry was saying. His eyes were very bright and she could tell from her father's face that he now knew about the mining.

'That damned Lloyd-George too, waffling on about the moans of the poor.' George was sweating all over his forehead and his collar was quite limp, Hannah saw. 'Good God, the poor have always been with us. What do he and those bounders, the Liberals, expect us to do about them?'

Her father broke in from further down the table. 'Now the war is closing they'll be bringing down the income tax again and about time too.'

Esther poked George in the ribs. 'What's income tax?'

He laughed and turned towards her, his back now to Hannah but she heard his reply before Harry cut in.

'It'll get worse if the Liberals bring in their reforms.'

Harry was drinking more wine. It was red and full to the brim. He slopped some on the table and the stain spread a deep pink. Why pink when the wine is red, thought Hannah and could feel a smile still on her face. She sipped at her wine again.

'That's true, they want to use our money to improve things for the poor. It's a disgrace. But they won't get the support they need,' George said.

Her tongue felt heavy and her words came out slowly as she turned to her cousin. 'Why won't they get support?' George hadn't heard so she tapped him on the shoulder and repeated her question, but her words were sounding strange; clumsy and slow and her head was full of air.

'Because, Hannah, the rules about voting mean that very few of the poor have the vote, so how can they get these trouble-makers into Parliament? It's a question of voting qualifications, you see. Rate payers and so on.'

He was signalling to the butler who brought water and

poured some for Hannah. George smiled. 'Drink some of this, my dear. You've had quite enough wine.'

She was thirsty and the room was hot. Heads were bent towards one another and Esther was leaning over the table, listening to Harry with her eyes as wide as she could make them. Harry, Hannah saw to her surprise, was talking to her now as though Esther was the only person in the room. There was chatter all around the table.

'I'll support them,' Hannah said. 'I'm not poor. I'll vote.'

George leant back and slapped his leg, laughing until he coughed. 'But you're a woman. You can't vote.' Wiping his face with his handkerchief.

Hannah sat back feeling hot, so hot. 'I forgot,' she murmured. 'Just for a moment I forgot. How could I have forgotten something like that?'

George shook his head and patted her hand which lay on the table. 'My dear Hannah, it is of no importance. We can't have women worrying their heads about serious matters, can we? You just let your husband do it, when the big day comes, because he will decide what is best. After all, women aren't really suited to thinking, are they? They're pretty little things that do a man's eye a power of good and look splendid in his sitting-room.'

Harry was calling him now and she watched them talking and Esther laughing up into Harry's face. We just need a bit of a dusting from time to time, do we, just like the other belongings in the home? She was still too hot as she watched the butler bring meringue with strawberry and brandy preserve, followed by cream in a large silver jug.

'We have a wonderful cook and a wonderful gardener. His strawberries are a taste of heaven,' Camilla said waving towards the dessert, and everyone nodded but Hannah.

She was remembering the feel and the heat of the fruit in her hand at Joe's. So, Mrs Arness is a thing too, is she? But she wasn't, was she? She had become a partner and if she had been a thing that would not have been possible. But was it enough just to improve your own life? Mrs Arness was changing the lives of the children she taught, wasn't she, so then they would do the same for their children. And it would all grow. Was education enough? She realised that she didn't think it was. Votes were important and could change the government of the country and therefore the conditions and attitudes in that country. Votes would give you a vestige of power, a certain importance, a sense of being a person. Votes for women had to come soon and she now wanted to see that they did.

'Nearly twenty thousand camp dead, I've heard.' It was George speaking again. 'Seems a strange way to run a war, scorching the earth and then locking the families up.'

Hannah spoke now and her voice felt almost like her own. She felt strong. 'Father says Britain has to civilise the Empire but how can England have any pride if this is how she goes about her business? How can anyone have given those orders and how could anyone have carried them out?'

There was silence round the table. She hadn't realised she was shouting. She looked at Harry, then at Esther who was grinning. Harry was not.

'One thing you have yet to learn, Hannah,' said her father, his green hat slipping over his left eye making him look absurd. Should she tell him? But it was too late, he was talking, pointing his finger at her as he spoke. 'Is that an order is an order and will be obeyed. What that order contains should hold no interest to the person who receives it. Obedience is all.' His eyes were cold and they fixed on hers though his mouth was smiling.

'Even if it's murder?' she replied and caught the movement of Harry's head as he turned to look at his father. Thomas and Camilla were frowning, George was embarrassed and making great play of eating his dessert. Just how long did he expect that one piece of meringue to last, she wondered. She did not look at her mother.

'There is no such thing as murder if one is obeying an order,' her father replied. 'In war, all death can be justified. Concentration camps included.' Her father was lifting his glass to his mouth now, drinking and then wiping his moustache with his napkin. It was pink where his moustache had drooped into the wine. Slowly a murmur of talk grew up around the table again but still Hannah looked at her father and still he looked at her and now the smile had gone.

'Eat your dessert, Hannah, but don't have any dessert wine,' Esther was calling past George. 'We must go and change soon.'

They waited outside the drawing-room door with cloaks over their shoulders. The chiffon was light and cool after the wool of her dress. Their arms were bare. Her mother had helped Camilla to pin the costumes, though Hannah knew she was worried about the effect of the performance on her husband.

Don't be silly, dear, Camilla had called out, pins still in her mouth as she moved Esther round to reach the hem. It's light-hearted fun. It's the Edwardian age now, you know. Prince Edward is setting all sorts of new fashions and ideas. Her mother had frowned and continued to adjust the chiffon layers.

When the women left to announce the entertainment Esther had brought down her red leather Bible from the bookcase and run her tongue over her lips. Go on, you too, she had said, we're actresses tonight; she rubbed the book against her lips and they became quite red as though they had been painted. Hannah took it, licking her lips again, grinding them into the cover. It tasted different to anything she had come across, bitter and sticky. How could her father speak of the deaths of those women and children as he had? He had no goodness in him, nothing for her to respect, just for her to fear and she was tired of fear. She had rubbed her lips on the Bible again.

Now, as she waited outside the door, she could still taste the dyed leather and knew very well what she had done, for the Vicar had said that only harlots painted their lips. She could feel the cool marble floor beneath feet stripped of shoes and stockings because painted lips had not been enough for her challenge to her father. Feet should never be without coverings, the legs never visible, should they?

Hannah's breathing was rapid because soon he would see her reply to his rules, his cold dark authority, his cruelty. Nothing else mattered at the moment, not even university. This was more important somehow.

Now Camilla was playing the entrance march and Esther

was opening the drawing-room door. The ballet was one they had learnt long ago but they remembered each step and Hannah tried not to look at her mother as she almost crouched in her chair while her father sat rigid with affront. Harry was watching only Esther. Harry and George clapped loudly at the end. Her father and Thomas did not and her mother rose and went to Camilla.

'How beautifully you played,' she said, and so she had not had to clap either. Hannah's lips felt large and sticky and still there was the bitter taste. Her feet were warm and she had danced as never before. Her bare legs and naked arms were what her father was looking at.

The journey home in the carriage was silent. Harry sat back, his face held in a small smile. Esther had hugged Hannah as they left. See, she said, I told you I could get him to like me and don't worry about the parents, it will all blow over. Father is a softie really. But Hannah's father was not and Hannah knew that her challenge would be answered and that she must bear the consequences.

Mrs Brennan had left the gas lights on low and as Hannah started to follow Harry up the stairs her father at last spoke.

'How dare you disgrace me this evening.' His voice was low but taut.

Hannah did not turn though she knew he spoke to her. She saw Harry pause on the lower landing.

'Turn and look at me when I speak to you, madam,' her father said. And she did so. 'There is evil in children that must be eradicated before they reach adulthood or death. As though it were not bad enough to venture an opinion during the meal you then paint your lips like a common harlot, bare your legs, lifting them into the air so that all may see.' He was shaking, not just his hands but his body. Her mother stood slightly behind him her face in the shadow of her bonnet.

Hannah put her hand in her pocket and felt the musical box, and heard the storm, the lightning, the thunder. Felt the grass under her feet, the water as it trickled through her hand and knew that there were parts of her he couldn't reach, couldn't hurt because he had no knowledge of them and this she hugged to herself for protection.

His face was dark and drawn up into gashes of hate. 'You are filled with an evil which I shall do my best to eradicate, according to my sense of duty,' he said. 'You will learn humility and obedience. You will accept your place as a woman. Therefore Harry is to go to university, not you. He will study for his mining degree. You will develop the attributes which will make you desirable as a wife, for that is your calling just as it is Esther's. Just as it was your mother's. You will develop humility. Now go and wash that filth off your face and cleanse your mind of its perpetual unrest.'

Hannah did not move. She could still feel the banister with her hand; she could still see him with her eyes as he turned and strode towards the door, brushing past her mother as he did so and snarling, 'It's your blood which has contaminated this family.'

The door banged as he left. Hannah heard it slam but inside there was nothing but his words which she had known would come because how else did he think he could destroy her?

The snow was falling again but his hat kept off the worst. It was not long past midnight and the revellers were still about seeing in the year of our Lord, 1902. John Watson walked on, waving away a cab with harsh movements. His walking-stick dug deep into the snow with every rapid stride seeing her red lips, her white legs. Dear God, what a nightmare it had all been. It was Edith's blood that had bred this wanton daughter, that had caused his son to turn from him and the path he had chosen for him, and the anger was so great at them all that he could not feel the cold. But it was better now than it had been. Now that he had vented some of his rage on her damnable daughter, for, after all, he had never intended that she should go to university and telling her so in this manner would force from her all false vanity.

A girl had no right to be as clever as she appeared to be from her school reports. Softness, malleability, subservience were the qualities she should be imbued with, not cleverness. It was

93

indecent in a woman, unnecessary. To deprive her of her ambition would cleanse her and would also set her against the boy. He would be truly his now.

No, he could not risk directing his anger against his son. God damn it, he loved the boy. There must be no humiliation for him, only for those that needed it. He brushed past the lamplighter who was warming himself round a brazier. Damn Thomas for speaking up for the boy, but there was no doubt he approved of the idea and that would mean there would be no recommendation for the Household Cavalry. So could it be that Thomas was right? Perhaps it would be the making of the family name.

He grunted as he turned the corner and the wind snatched at his hat. It was darker now, fewer lights lit this end of the area. Yes, perhaps the mining would work out well in the end, but by God, Hannah had needed some humiliation to drive her on to the path of decency. But would it be enough?

He clenched his teeth, breathing deeply, pleased that he had done his duty, but still anger raged because even though her dream was broken she was not; she had not cried. She had not broken beneath him; had not shown herself to be changed. Why would she never break? After all, her mother had finally done so.

There were plenty of women as he approached the footpath which ran along the canal leading eventually to the arches under the bridge. He had known there would be, there always were. He wanted the one he had found last month. Some were bare to their waists even in this cold but he pushed on past.

He saw her then, over there, loitering beneath the snow-laden trees just visible in the dim light of the gas lamp and she came to him as he stopped, pressing her body against his, and he nodded, giving her the money.

He led her out of the pool of light into the shelter of the bridge, away from the prying eyes of home-going revellers passing along the road above them. She was silent as they walked through the snow and he pulled her to him when they stopped. Her breath was putrid and her body smelt; her hair was greasy and tangled. He gripped it and pulled her head back, pressing his mouth to hers, his hand to her breast, tearing at the shawl that was knotted at the front.

So, Hannah thought to defy him, did she? Did she think she was an animal like this thing? He would show her, he would mould her into the daughter he required. The snow-laden tree hung low over them and the fog from the river swirled and caught in his throat. Further along fog horns were sounding, but the woman's breast was exposed now, dirty and goose-fleshed. He sucked the nipple, then kissed her foul mouth again, pushing her to the ground in the darkness of the bridge; for this was how it pleasured him. The snow was cold on his knees as he tore bare her other breast. He did not remove his gloves. He never did. His breath came quickly as he worked her skirt up, but not over her breasts because these he must hurt.

He liked this girl, he had used her several times. She was Hannah's age. Her flesh was firm and he ran his hands over her thighs and felt hers on him. So she remembered what he liked. She tightened her grip.

'Not yet,' he hissed.

She slowed and then he took her hands from him and held them above her head, lashed together in his one hand while he finally thrust into her, deep, hard, so that he heard her indrawn breath. Saw her face in the light tighten with pain.

'Move, damn you, move,' he ordered, and as he felt her legs clasp round him and her movements thrust in tune with his he kneaded her breast until he saw the look of pain that he sought and heard her screams. In that moment he bared his teeth and groaned as he thrust violently; filling her, hurting her, grinding her into the ground. Calling 'Mother!' as he did so.

Hannah had helped her mother to bed. I hope you don't cry, her mother had said in the bedroom, which was lit only by the landing light seeping in through the open door. I couldn't bear it if you cried. He means it for the best. I'm sure he means it for the best, my little girl, but why did you give him the opportunity? Her hand had been cold as she stroked Hannah's face and there was a trembling which ran through the whole of her body as Hannah helped her into her nightdress. Quiet now,

Mother, she had soothed, you must rest. And her mother had nodded, feeling like a child again. Hannah lit the oil lamp which she knew her mother liked because of its dim light and warm brass fittings and the smell which reminded her of Cornwall. She placed it on the dressing-table to burn throughout the night, seeing in the mirror that it cast deep shadows round her eyes and merely made her lips look dark, not red. There was no lavender here this time. She returned to the bed moving easily, for there was no cradle to displace the other furniture. She laid her mother's clothes on the ottoman at the foot of her bed for the maid to hang up in the morning, smoothing them out, seeing nothing familiar in their dark, flat, empty shapes. They were devoid of her mother, weren't they, so meant nothing to her as they were.

She kissed her mother, who was too tired to speak again but not too tired to stop thinking as her head lay on the pillow, which was soft and quiet. Yes, she must rest, for this time the baby must live because she had been good. She had been good and he had come back to her for one night, but that was all. Only the one night.

She did not hear Hannah leave the room; she was too busy wishing that she had, long ago, kept some of her own money so that she could have sent her daughter to university. But would she ever really have had the courage to go against her husband? Edith Watson cried as she realised the answer.

The gas fire was popping in Hannah's room casting deep shadows into the corners, blanking out the pictures of rural life into blind squares. She did not light the lamp but sat in the chair. Harry had tried to speak to her, taking her arm, gripping it tightly, but she had brushed him aside, not looking at his face. He could say nothing that she wanted to hear. She had brought it on herself, this she knew, but that he should go in her place made her flinch from him.

And no, she had replied to his tense question, she wouldn't break her promise and tell of the accident, but her voice had sounded cracked and dry, as dry as their voices when they came up from the mine that day.

She wouldn't cry, not where they could see but there was no

one here now, was there? Just the memory of the anger which had consumed her, driven her to challenge that man and for that she could not be sorry, but none the less, the pain was deep and strong as the tears fell. Her shoulders heaved and her chest too. And when all the tears were done the misery was still there. But so was something else. This would not be the end. She would not allow this to be the end. She stood and walked to the window.

She would ask Miss Fletcher to help her to become a teacher without going to university. She would ask for help in learning about her body so that she could not be like her mother, for she, Miss Hannah Watson, had decided on her future. And she would ask Miss Fletcher to tell her how she could become a person, not just a piece of property, and all the while her father would not know what she was doing.

Tonight all confusion was finally gone and hate had entered her life.

6 The brass knob of the heavy school door gleamed. Hannah could see the dent which lay just to the right of its centre. Miss Fletcher's maid had still not managed to rub the dirt from its depth. Hannah held out her gloved forefinger, the navy sharp against the yellow as she ran it over the cold surface, feeling the dip, seeing it, but hearing only her father's voice as he had spoken one week ago, harsh and grating and full of hate. She curled her hand around the brass knob, tighter and tighter, surprised that it did not fold beneath her fury. Miss Fletcher's study was at the end of a long, dark, wood-panelled corridor which sucked at any light. Hannah knew that she would be there. She always was half an hour before school was due to start and had probably been there far earlier on the first day of Spring Term. Her feet echoed on the black and white tiles of the entrance porch. She had not stopped for barley sugar from the Emporium this morning, there was no time for that any more. Childhood had gone, completely gone, and now something had to be put in its place.

She pushed open the swing-door into the assembly hall. Soon it would be filled with rows of girls, navy and white, hair pinned and hymn books open. Miss Fletcher would take her place on the stage to lead the prayers, and behind would range the five members of her staff. Would Mrs Kent be there, dark and swarthy with hair hanging lank either side of her face, torn as ever between her native French and her adopted English? Would she cry as she always did when *Eternal Father* was sung and her husband was alive again for a brief moment?

Hannah stood looking around the hall. It smelt the same, the whole school smelt the same but there was no sound and she had never known it like this before. No opening and shutting of doors, no music wafting from the music room, muted until an opening door snatched out the sound. No sound of feet walking, never running. No murmur from the classrooms which bordered the hall, their tall internal windows unable to open, placed high so that light could enter but sight could not leave.

She smiled and walked across the wood-blocked floor. She and Esther had been appointed window monitors for their class a few years ago and when the fire practice bell was rung they had been talking behind their hands in the back row of their classroom. They had rushed to close the windows, hauling at the thin ropes, as the others had filed out into the playground. At last, in long rows, they had stood facing Miss Fletcher. Behind her all windows were closed except for theirs. They had been so deep in their own private world that they had opened them as wide as was humanly possible, Miss Fletcher had said as they had reported to her during lunch break.

They had been relieved of their window duties publicly, and now Hannah's smile was rueful. Her hand ached from the hundred lines they had also had to do but it was the humiliation that had taught her more. It had never happened again. Now she pulled at her gloves, brushing at her skirt though there was nothing to mar its crisp navy. She took a deep breath and pushed open the door into the corridor. Why was it so dark? Miss Fletcher wasn't dark, wasn't forbidding, even when punishments were given.

She passed the side door which only parents could use and some light came in then, multicoloured through the green and blue stained glass. But the door was set into its own small lobby and the dim light did not reach beyond this.

At the end of the corridor outside Miss Fletcher's room there was a bench along the right-hand wall and above it was a photograph of Queen Victoria. She'll have to get that down soon, thought Hannah, and put Edward up there after the Coronation in June. Just imagine, a man in a girls' school. What will the parents say? She straightened her shoulders. But her father had said enough already, and now she knocked, hard and fast, and almost immediately she heard Miss Fletcher's voice, surprised but calm as it always was.

'Enter.' And she did, feeling the hardness which had so rapidly filled her giving way even as she opened the door.

Miss Fletcher sat behind the desk in grey, as always, her bored face inclined towards the door, tilted in query until she saw Hannah, and then she smiled and Hannah was warmed.

'Hannah, this is a surprise, but a pleasant one.' Miss Fletcher waved towards the hard wooden chair which was placed almost opposite her. 'I hope that you've come to me with good news and that we can be considering the Classical Tripos for you, but first, of course, there is the Cambridge Junior Examination.'

Hannah smoothed her skirt then interlocked her fingers and drove them hard down, pushing back the material of her gloves. Her throat hurt and she looked up, not at Miss Fletcher but through the window which was above the dark mahogany filing cabinets to the left of where they sat. Papers lay on top of the cabinets and exercise books were heaped on the floor beneath the sill, spilling against the bottom of the green curtains. Bottles of ink stood on the varnished shelf which hung between the corner and the window. Some had splashed against the pale green flock wallpaper and the blue had changed to black.

Outside, the shrubbery looked bleak and grey in its January setting and the fog, the ever-present London fog, was looming and blanking out the neighbouring streets and buildings; but not the street noises, which it magnified – the rattle of the carriages, the sound of horses and traders' cries. Still, there was too much of a tightness to speak, too much uncertainty of poise to attempt an answer.

She looked down at her hands again, then up but not at Miss Fletcher, not yet, she was not yet ready to tell her. On up to something, anything, which she could hang on to and gain composure and there it was. The painting above Miss Fletcher. Vivid and thick with paint. Sun on geraniums, warm and vigorous as the marigolds had been. Stay with me, Joe had said in the rain that drenched and froze, and she felt again his hand, his hard strong hand and somehow his strength was for a moment hers.

'No,' she answered and her voice was not high or broken but, perhaps, rather loud. 'No, I am not allowed to go to university.'

She saw the frown begin on Miss Fletcher's forehead, the darkening of her hazel eyes and the hand which darted to the pearl buttons on her high-necked dress.

'But why, my dear?' This time Miss Fletcher's voice was not calm but sharp and urgent. 'I must speak to your father. I will write to him today and ask if he will come and see me, or I could visit him.'

Hannah shook her head. 'No, please don't. There is no hope of ever changing his mind.' She looked from Miss Fletcher to her hands, pulling her gloves off now, finger by finger, laying them neatly one on top of the other, flattening her body shape from them. She would not think of him, his dark violence, his rigid form. She would not think of her mother's sickness and swelling belly, full of him. She would not think of Harry as he took her place.

'I want to teach, I want to learn how to look after myself and my mother and how not to have babies. I want to learn how to become a person, not a piece of property.'

And now she looked straight at Miss Fletcher, into her calm face framed by chestnut hair. 'Therefore I need you to employ me as your pupil teacher and I need to join the St John's organisation; I know you sometimes help them to raise funds and therefore you will have the name of someone I can go and see.' It sounded rude, abrupt, but that was not how she felt inside. Would Miss Fletcher realise that? Hannah sat back and said nothing more.

For many minutes there was silence. There was not even the ticking of a clock because Miss Fletcher had said long ago that she could do without every extremity of her body longing to twitch in time to its regular rhythm. The clock was now in the dining-hall and could not be heard above the rattle of knives and forks. Eventually Miss Fletcher picked up a pencil, first rolling it between her hands before using it to write what appeared to Hannah to be a list. All the time there was a frown between her eyes and now, as she finished, she looked briefly at the hunter watch that she kept on her desk to one side of the large blotter pad, and then up at Hannah.

'Would you care to tell me what has happened, Hannah?'

She straightened her pad of paper then nodded as Hannah said, 'No, if you don't mind, Miss Fletcher, I would prefer not to, at the moment anyway.'

Miss Fletcher nodded. 'Very well, my dear.' She smiled and briskly tapped the desk. 'Now, time is getting short. The girls will already be arriving. With regard to your requests, I have a few ideas I need to consider, to investigate, before I can give you an answer but,' and here she put up her hand as Hannah started to protest, her impatience for an answer insupportable, her fear that it would be negative drying her mouth, 'I can understand that it is probably advisable that you are not late home if, as I suspect, there has been a difficulty.' She smiled as Hannah flushed. 'My dear, I am thirty-three years of age and was not born yesterday. Now, perhaps you would join me here again at luncheon. I shall arrange to have a meal brought to us for we have a great deal to discuss.' She paused. 'It might be as well not to mention that fact to others, even that blonde shadow of yours.'

She smiled, and so did Hannah, who felt suddenly that it would be all right, that there was someone wiser alongside her. That her requests would be granted.

Miss Fletcher looked again at her watch, then clicked it shut. 'Off you go then, Hannah. I have to remind Miss Dobson that it is definitely not a good idea to start the rather dreary Spring Term with *Eternal Father*. It is somewhat more than one can bear, don't you think? Especially after the machinations of Christmas.'

Hannah rose, drawing on her gloves again. ' "Thank you" doesn't seem adequate somehow, Miss Fletcher,' she said, hesitating.

'Just wait until you see what I have in mind – you might not feel like thanking me. Teaching is not quite as idyllic as you perhaps think it is.' Miss Fletcher laughed and waved to the door.

As Hannah reached it she paused and looked back. 'Esther will be applying for university so you will have someone to groom,' she volunteered, for Esther had written to tell her this. It was Uncle Thomas's punishment.

Miss Fletcher laughed gently. 'Not quite what I had in mind for that young lady,' she said. 'Perhaps you are both being punished?' And she returned to the papers on her desk as Hannah closed the door, wondering if there was anything that escaped Miss Fletcher.

Esther was waiting for her in the cloakroom, by the pegs near the big square stone sinks with their gaping plug-holes. She was smart in the regulation high-collared white shirt and the navy serge skirt and thick cardigan.

'For heaven's sake, Hannah, darling. Where have you been and where are my sweets?'

She was pinning her hair up in the mirror which she always carried. It was propped up on the white-tiled window-ledge, which was not ideal because the light was too vivid in her eyes.

'Sorry, not today. I had to see Miss Fletcher about something,' Hannah said and reached for the mirror, holding it at a better angle for Esther.

'How are you?' she asked, looking closely at Esther. 'Is your father still angry?' They had not seen one another since New Year's Eve and she had missed her cousin.

Esther pouted taking the last pin from her mouth and sliding it into the roll of hair at the nape of her neck. She patted it and turned slightly sideways. 'How's that?'

Hannah grinned. 'Passable, I suppose.' She wouldn't think of Esther at university.

Esther pulled a face, putting the mirror back into the large leather bag that they all carried for their books. She linked her arm through Hannah's and they strolled back into their classroom, Esther sitting in the desk nearest to the fire and Hannah taking the one behind her to avoid the direct gaze of the teacher. The room was full now with girls talking and laughing, the blackboard was quite black, devoid of any trace of chalk. The windows were closed against the weather, and the wood-panelled walls gleamed from holiday polishing. There was a smell of wax. Girls greeted Hannah as they passed and she smiled but was trying all the time to hear Esther.

'Of course he's not too cross,' she heard. 'He's so busy sorting out that lovely brother of yours who's grown so much, so well.' She lifted her eyebrows and moved her shoulders and Hannah could have slapped her.

'What's he sorting out, for heaven's sake?' she asked, passing a ruler to Marjorie, who sat behind and wanted to draw up her margins.

'Oh, you know, his training for this romantic mining of his.'

Esther nodded as Mary Miller asked if she was warm enough. 'Thank you yes, Mary, dear, and there's no need to look like that, the swiftest wins the prize.' She swung back to Hannah.

'Well, where is he going?' Hannah asked, desperately wanting to know because she had not been able to bring herself to speak to Harry before he had left for school.

'Oh to the London School of Mines. It was a choice of that or Camborne but I pointed out to dear Papa that it would be so much easier all round if it was London, and surely London has that certain flair that perhaps Cornwall has not?'

Hannah sat back. 'Why on earth should you involve yourself in it at all?'

She felt Marjorie prod her and reached over her shoulder for her ruler as Esther put her pencils on her desk.

'Well, darling. If that lovely brother of yours is in London, then I shall see rather more of him. I know you love to disappear to the wilderness of the Cornish peninsula, but I don't and anyway, it's all far too far.'

Hannah was laughing now. 'Are you really serious? He's just a schoolboy. You know, like us.'

Esther grinned. 'Hardly like us, dear.'

Hannah blushed, knowing to what extent that was true. Did Esther know, really know? She wondered and doubted it. The school bell was ringing for the start of assembly and she took the hymn book from her desk. It was covered with green cardboard, but for a moment she could taste red leather. Rising with the others, she caught hold of Esther.

'But you'll be studying too hard for your Cambridge entrance. It needs hours of extra tuition,' she whispered.

'Certainly not. Somehow I will have to make the time and it's up to you to help me.'

They filed into the hall. Miss Dobson was already playing the opening bars to *Oh God Our Help In Ages Past* and Hannah wondered who it was that he had helped.

Luncheon in Miss Fletcher's study was served by one of the maids on trays covered with white linen embroidered with pink thread.

'A Christmas present from one of the leaving girls,' Miss Fletcher commented, smiling at Hannah. 'Just put Miss Hannah's on the other side of the desk, please, Beatrice,' she instructed, and unfolded her serviette, spreading it out on her lap while she waited for the maid to leave the room.

'Come along, Hannah.' Miss Fletcher pointed to the plate of roast pork and vegetables. 'Eat up, for goodness sake, we have much to discuss and a full stomach is better than an empty one, so the sooner we have dispatched the pork, the sooner the talking can begin.'

As they ate, little was said. The fire was burning in the grate, the blue and white tiles of the surround glinting in its light. Miss Fletcher's liver-and-white spaniel was now lolling in front of the fire on the small faded Turkish rug which toned in with the muted red of the Indian carpet. Two of the first-years had earlier taken it for a walk and the damp canine odour was heavy.

It was odd to be here, like this, but not uncomfortable somehow. She did not feel tension snapping at her back as she did when she ate with her father, but merely a companionable presence.

What was Esther thinking, she wondered. Her face had clouded when Hannah had explained that she had to speak to Miss Fletcher and would therefore miss lunch. Esther needed her, she knew that. She had few friends besides Hannah, perhaps because she was too quick to take and slow to give, but that was not because she was mean, Hannah had explained to Marjorie and Mary Miller last term. It was because her mind went from one thing to another so quickly that without meaning to she upset people sometimes. You become used to it, she had added, and Marjorie had tossed her head. You might have to because she's your cousin but I don't. Hannah had shaken her head. She's only my cousin once removed which is different. I don't have to like her, Marjorie, I just do. I've grown up with her and she's like my sister.

The pork was tender and it was hard to leave some as she had been schooled to do. She placed her knife and fork together, wiping her lips with her serviette, leaving it crumpled on the tray as proof that it had been used and would require washing.

Bookshelves set behind glass lined the wall opposite the window. Hannah could see that Shakespeare was amongst the leather-bound volumes. Further from her, near the fire, were H. G. Wells and Oscar Wilde. Her father would not permit Wilde's books to be discussed or read, and Hannah wondered why.

Miss Fletcher folded her napkin carefully and smiled at Hannah.

'I shall use mine again this evening. The maids have more than enough to do without extra work created by me.'

Hannah smiled in reply but wondered why the maids' workload had never occurred to her. They had always just been there.

Miss Fletcher rose and picked up her tray, and Hannah was quick to copy. She followed her over to the side table which stood near the window through which she saw that the fog had thickened, heavy, yellow and stinking.

'Just put it down next to mine. Beatrice can collect it when we've finished our discussion.' Miss Fletcher swept back to her chair, her straight skirt devoid of the statutory black bustle. Hannah watched as she drew a set of papers from the side of the desk and sorted them into three piles. She sat down in the seat opposite her Headmistress.

'Now, Hannah. The first request was to accept you as my pupil teacher.' Miss Fletcher patted the sheets of paper as she spoke. 'Though it is unfortunate that we should have to be holding this particular discussion, it is none the less a remarkable coincidence that you should be having to plan your career at this time.' Miss Fletcher sat back, her arms lying along the arms of her chair, her hands quite still. 'You may or may not know that there is a movement afoot to reform the way the education of the country is run. Last year the Board of Education was set up as the first step towards regulating the present system which is failing to produce sufficient numbers of adequately educated young people. As a result a new Education Bill has been formulated whereby secondary education is to be substantially improved, as is the elementary stage.'

Hannah frowned. 'Does this mean the government is beginning to care?' She thought of her father and the Vicar and how they despised the poor.

Miss Fletcher laughed. 'Certainly not. We have an Empire and an industrial revolution to maintain, a position of superiority to preserve in the world, and we cannot do so unless we have more people capable of working in it. It is expediency, that is all.' She paused. 'And it's clearly keeping a few people awake at night. After all, what might an educated "mass" lead to?' She laughed. 'So there is certainly a hot debate going on in Parliament but, none the less, the Bill will be carried. The local authorities will be given responsibility for secondary and technical education and money from the rates will be made available for improvements.'

'Does this mean public schools will go?' Hannah asked, thinking of Harry.

Miss Fletcher lifted her hands in mock horror. 'Good God,' and Hannah was startled by this profanity. 'Those bastions will be here until the end of time. They are the breeding ground for our leaders, my dear. It is there that Empire, Christianity and cricket are taught. It is there that the status quo is elevated to a religion, but I digress.'

Miss Fletcher broke off and looked into the fire, her face thoughtful, her fingers tapping on the desk. 'It's the development of the individual that I subscribe to, and perhaps this will be spread with this new system. There must be so much ability which never gets aired, and that is sacrilege. I shall be taking scholarship pupils, mixing them up with my girls. It will be exciting. Britain needs people who can think for themselves, break the mould of tradition.'

Hannah nodded, excited now. 'Yes, advancement should be on merit, shouldn't it, not privilege. We should unlock minds: teach, not instruct. We should make children explore, not just repeat and learn. That way they will question, that way rules will change.' She was leaning forward now, talking quickly, her hands shaping her thoughts and Miss Fletcher watched her carefully.

'Bravo, spoken like a true teacher.' Miss Fletcher laughed but reached for the oil lamp which stood at the corner of the desk. 'It really is too gloomy to be borne. I think a little light would be a good idea.'

The glass globe was tinged with green and Miss Fletcher moved to the fire and took a taper from the mantelshelf, shielding the flame that she lit from the glowing coals as she walked slowly back. The wick flared until she lowered it and placed the glass globe back in place. There was a smell of oil now, as there was in her mother's bedroom in the evenings when they sat together and Hannah prayed that this baby would not destroy the woman whom she was beginning to know.

Miss Fletcher was speaking again. 'Now, where were we? Oh yes. This new system will call for more qualified teachers and that is where you will benefit.' She leant forward and picked up one of the sheets of paper, tapping it with her finger. 'Pupil teachers have had to learn how to teach whilst actually in charge of a class. There have been attempts to give them some instruction at schools designed for that purpose but it has been totally inadequate and, since most of these pupil teachers start at thirteen following an elementary education limited to the three R's, there has been a great problem. This new scheme will be improving on this deplorable state of affairs. Already facilities have been established for training teachers and this includes London. Now,' and here she sat back, placing her hands on the desk, 'I suggest that, as you have requested, I take you on as a pupil teacher, pay you accordingly, say ten shillings a week, and in the afternoons you attend college to become a qualified teacher.'

Hannah watched as Miss Fletcher passed her the piece of

paper she had been holding. It seemed that her hand was slow to take it but somehow it was there, and she was reading the list of subjects she would have to study, the times she would have to attend, and the classes she would have to take at this, her own school, and knew that this was what she wanted; to teach and to be taught. What had been snatched from her by her father she was now taking back; or was it being given by this woman? She didn't know but either way it was happening. Before she could show her gratitude Miss Fletcher moved on to the second pile of papers.

'The St John's group give regular lectures, as I suspect you already know, since you have clearly done some investigating?' Miss Fletcher looked over the sheet of paper at Hannah who nodded. 'None the less it does no harm to reiterate the facts in case you have not fully understood. Hand in hand with the lectures go demonstrations on first aid, hygiene and so on. At the end of the year you receive a certificate if you pass. This means that you can then go on to show others, or before that, if you felt confident. I certainly have knowledge of the local leader and have already written to her, saying that you will be visiting her shortly. I suggest straight after school one afternoon; you may leave a little early. You will, of course, write beforehand to Mrs Glover at this address.' She was smiling as she pointed to the paper before looking up. 'I, of course, am available to help with other queries about health and well-being that the admirable St John's group might not feel equipped to deal with – like the prevention of children.'

Hannah took the second sheet of paper that Miss Fletcher handed her. Could it all really be this easy? But of course not, for she still had to gain permission from her father. She pushed that thought to the back of her head, because somehow she would make it happen. The fire was dying down now and Hannah rose, putting new coals on, watching as the red was hidden by the black. The tongs slid down when she tried to rest them against the fireplace but she caught and lodged them in between the wooden surround and the tiles. The dog lifted her head as she bent over her and she stroked her soft smooth coat before she walked back. Then she looked at Miss Fletcher and spoke.

'Thank you. I can't say how much this means to me.'

Miss Fletcher shrugged and shook her head, her smile quick but warm. 'Not at all. You should really be given the chance of a university education as I was, but perhaps this vocational training might suit you better. I have a feeling that you will always need a commitment, a cause, my dear.' Her voice died away and they both sat there, closed off in this study by the fog, by the crackling fire and the heavy oak door.

As Hannah eventually stirred, Miss Fletcher looked at her watch on the table.

'We are running out of time, my dear, but before you return to your classroom there is your last problem. How to become a person, not a piece of property.' Her sigh was long and her face looked tired suddenly, and dispirited. Hannah watched as Miss Fletcher rose from her chair and walked to the window. She stood with her hands loosely clasped before her, her face close to the glass, her breath misting the pane, but she did not seem to notice. Eventually she turned. She did not move back to the desk but stood against the curtain, which was dull green against her grey, like a person preparing to do battle. Her voice when she spoke was taut.

'Women are still property. It is not a state peculiar to you, Hannah, but to all females.' She was smiling but her eyes were distracted.

Hannah protested. 'But not to you, Miss Fletcher. After all, you are independent. You own this school, you have your own income.' She flushed. 'I'm sorry, one should not discuss money but . . .'

Miss Fletcher laughed, throwing back her head so that her hair caught on the curtain. She pulled her head away and smoothed down the strands which had been pulled from her bun. Far away there was the sound of a fog horn on the river.

'Nonsense, there is very little that one should not discuss if one is trying to get to the seat of a problem. Yes, I have money left to me by my parents.' Miss Fletcher moved now, not back to her seat behind the desk but to the dark maroon carpet chair with its varnished wooden frame. She pointed to a similar one in the far corner of the room, by the door beneath a picture of a country cottage.

'Draw that chair up, Hannah, we have only a few moments in which to explore the situation, though we will need to pursue it at greater length another time if you are to get a proper answer from me.'

The chair was not comfortable, the frame dug into Hannah's legs and the material had no give in it but she hardly noticed as she listened.

'My father was an exceptional man. He sent me to university, which I loved of course but women were still barred from obtaining a degree at the end of the course.'

'But why?' Hannah asked.

'For the same reason that we are denied the vote. We are not considered the equal of men. As you have so rightly discovered, though I don't know how or why, we are merely property. Firstly of the father, and secondly of the husband.'

Hannah ran her fingers along the edge of the wooden chair arm. It was scratched and she traced the indented lines with her fingers. Yes, this was what she knew, but how good to hear it from another woman. She paused in her thoughts. But surely Miss Fletcher had no husband and was therefore free, she queried.

'In that narrow sense yes, but still there is this need in some women, not all by any means, to be publicly recognised as people. To feel that they have a right to decide for themselves on matters which they deem important. I feel that equality before the law is essential for women and for that reason it is a matter of the gravest importance that women must achieve what two-thirds of men already have – the vote. Oh, not just to be able to say that we are equal, but to be able to use our vote to change injustices in society, to feel that we have a voice.' Now Miss Fletcher was drawing words and ideas with her hands and she looked somehow younger.

'I agree, so much,' Hannah said, leaning forward. The dog stirred, grunted and then fell silently back into sleep. She did not notice his smell now. 'How can it be done?' She felt eager and impatient.

'That is what we would all like to know. I became a suffragist, and we believe that by sensible lobbying of Members of Parliament to introduce private members' franchise bills we shall eventually win. We need to show everyone that we are capable and deserving of their support, so our members seek seats on parish councils, school boards, and the Boards of Guardians; sorting out the poor wretches condemned to workhouses; proving that we are capable of more than embroidery or endless childbearing.'

Hannah saw again the long corridor, the grey, still figures and the smell of carbolic old age; saw Bernie, Joe's old miner, and his cottage overlooking the moor, their moor. While she sat she listened as this woman, who was soon to be her employer, explained that her colleagues also joined organisations such as the Women's Liberal Federation to visibly canvass at election time, since paid help for prospective MPs was no longer permitted. Anything to draw attention to the fact that women were not mere 'angels of the hearth' but living, thinking people.

The ringing of the bell for the start of afternoon school startled them both. Hannah gripped her hands together in her lap. There was so much more she wanted to hear, to say, and there was now no time. She rose, confused, embarrassed, brought back into the present, wondering how she had come so easily to sit next to her Headmistress and forget the barriers of position.

Miss Fletcher had also risen. Again the dog stirred, yelping now but still asleep. Was she chasing rabbits? Hannah looked down at her and smiled.

Miss Fletcher moved to the door. 'We have more to talk about, you and I, but now your biggest problem is going to be taking this next step. Somehow you have to persuade your father to agree, Hannah. Without his permission I cannot proceed with any of these ideas.'

Her face was serious, a frown was growing.

Hannah nodded and felt the familiar tension knot her back. She looked about the room with its low light, its familiar smell of oil and dog. It should have been comforting but now she felt detached from it. The papers which Miss Fletcher had given her were still on the desk and she moved quickly to retrieve them. She looked again at the picture that brought the sun into her heart and then heard as though from a distance the sound of storm and wind and the slow drawled voice of Joe.

Stay with me, he had said, hadn't he, but something else also and she could hear it now, as though he was speaking while reaching for her hand. You'll do what you want, Hannah, he had said, I have no fear of that. And his hand had been hard and strong.

She turned now, the papers clutched so tightly that they crumpled where she held them.

'That picture is post-Impressionist. I'm glad that you seem to like it. These new artists are very brave, they are trying to change the mould.' Miss Fletcher's face was questioning, and Hannah smiled as she passed by her and then through the door.

'My father will give his permission, Miss Fletcher. I promise you that.'

She was glad that the corridor was dark and without distraction because an idea was emerging even as Miss Fletcher shut the door. It was an idea that required a bargain with Esther.

Hannah sat through afternoon lessons while Esther ignored her, sulking because she had been excluded but from what she didn't know. As the bell rang for the end of school Hannah ran to catch up with Esther, who was leaving the cloakroom without her. She tucked her arm through her cousin's but there was no response. Esther would not turn her head as they walked down the drive and through the gate into the fog, which was still thick and tasted and smelt as it looked, yellow and sulphurous.

'Put your scarf up over your nose,' Hannah ordered, knowing how Esther would cough throughout the night if she did not.

But Esther tipped her head up and strode on, not replying, stiff and unyielding. Hannah pulled her own scarf up and lengthened her stride, torn between irritation and anxiety. Irritation at her cousin's childishness and anxiety in case she was unable to persuade Esther to co-operate in the plan which she had devised during mathematics. But she must, that was all there was to it.

Hannah stopped, the air harsh in her eyes, pulling her cousin to a standstill, her arm still locked around Esther's. She could hear the sound of the hansom cabs, carts and carriages, but only saw them at the last minute as they loomed out of the swirling fog and passed alongside the pavement, their lamps useless but alight none the less.

Hannah was not frightened because the route was familiar; these iron railings to the right enclosed the park, the cutting that they had just passed ran round the rear of the school. The sound of fog horns echoed from the river where barges eased their way along. Fog was not strange, it was usual in this world of industry and blackened chimneys.

'Esther,' Hannah shouted. 'Don't be absurd. I have a plan to give you that time you spoke of earlier.' Esther walked forward again, not looking at Hannah, not speaking, and this time Hannah stood still, letting her hand fall from Esther's arm, waiting for her to stop, because she knew that she would if it was to her advantage. Hannah was surprised at her thoughts but realised with absolute clarity that she had found the key to her cousin but it didn't matter, she still loved her.

Esther did stop and slowly turn, her face set and her eyes cold, but they did not move towards one another and Hannah could see the fog drifting even in the short space that separated them. She hooked her scarf up over her face again as she felt the coughing begin but Esther still stood there with hers hanging loose. Hannah felt impatience flash again and she strode forward seizing and wrapping the scarf around the girl's face.

'You're worse than a baby,' she shouted, startling a horse as it passed and she flinched as the driver hauled on the reins, then bore down with his whip, cursing Hannah as he struggled to control the clattering, thrashing horse before disappearing into the swirling darkness.

The girls looked at one another and then laughed until the air rasped in their lungs and the coughing began.

'You see,' Hannah gasped, 'even the horses take notice

before you do.' They moved nearer to the railings, walking to the point where their paths diverged.

Hannah again linked her arm in Esther's and this time there was an answering pressure and so she explained and outlined her idea.

'If you really want to have time to see more of Harry and not study for Cambridge I will persuade Miss Fletcher to take you on as a pupil teacher because that is what she is doing with me.'

She put up her hand as Esther swung round. 'I'll go into it all later but you will need to approach Uncle Thomas properly. You will need to convince him that you want to teach, that you want to take life more seriously.' She shook her head at Esther's raised eyebrows and did not pause. 'That you find me a steadying influence. That you don't want to go away to Cambridge or to finishing school but that you want to make some use of your life before you marry.'

They were beneath the hissing gas lamp now which threw barely any light on to the pavement. Hannah's scarf was down again, warm and moist from her condensed breath. She wanted her words to be clear and firm.

Esther leant back against the lamppost and laughed. 'Father will think some miracle has occurred if I trot out all that.'

Hannah laughed too. 'Say what you like but it must succeed if you wish to achieve your aim.' She turned and walked on, too cold to stand still any longer.

'So,' Esther said, pulling her scarf tighter and walking beside her, her voice sounding muffled now, her eyes curious above the scarf, 'what is the bargain then, if you arrange this with Miss Fletcher?'

Hannah didn't turn but braced her shoulders. 'As I said, you will have to convince your father that you need me there with you. He will have to persuade my father to allow me to take up the position. You know, as a sort of chaperon.'

There, it was out now, and she pulled the scarf back over her nose and mouth. It was cold and damp. Miss Fletcher had already agreed to offer Esther a position but she would not tell her cousin that yet.

Esther sank her chin deep into her chest as she pondered.

'We get paid, don't we?' she asked eventually, and Hannah nodded. 'It all rather smacks of trade, you know. Not quite the thing.'

They had reached the corner where Hannah would turn off the main thoroughfare and begin the walk to the crescent. She felt the panic but fought to keep her voice even.

'Nonsense,' she answered. 'Miss Fletcher runs a good private school and you will be a qualified teacher, having attended a college in London. It is considered a profession with status, you know, and the college isn't far from Harry's.'

She paused, pushing her hands deep into her pockets, clenching them into fists before adding a piece of news that she had heard Beaky telling Cook. Her voice was loud as she fought to keep Esther's attention against the clatter of the traffic.

'I hear that Sir Armstrong's boy is back from the Rand where the gold mines are working well again after being shut down when the war was at its height. He's bought a house in Eaton Square and is only twenty-five. He made a lucky strike, I gather.'

She waited then but knew that she had played her best card and felt no remorse for using Harry, for hadn't he taken more from her?

It was during Sunday dinner three weeks later, when the Vicar was seated opposite and her mother had been forced to join them, that her father informed her that he was about to approach Miss Fletcher with a view to Hannah earning her own living in the capacity of a pupil teacher.

Hannah flushed with joy but, raising her eyes, saw a warning, quickly gone, in her mother's face and dropped her head to her plate, uncertain of its meaning.

Her father then said in his cold black voice. 'You do well to bow down in distress for you must learn that girls obey their fathers and cast aside all thoughts but those of humility. This is not university but work, hard work and you are also to act as chaperon to your cousin. You will remember your place.' She looked at him then and saw the triumph in his eyes and understood her mother's look. Permission had only been granted because he felt that he had asserted his power and caused her pain. How little he knew her; and she was glad that inside the shell of her body she was hidden from him.

7 The June sun was still warm even though it was early evening as Hannah stood by the window of her mother's bedroom and looked out, seeing the last remnants of the white pear blossom still faintly visible between the fresh green of the new leaves. The tree standing beyond the lawn was old; the bark gnarled and rough, though from here this could not be discerned.

'Is that tree older than the house, Mother? It must be, I suppose.'

She looked across at her mother, who sat in the chair that Hannah had moved to the window, and smiled.

Her mother glanced at her, her face fuller now with pregnancy, her body large with the child that had been conceived in 1901 but which would, if Hannah had anything to do with it, safely arrive in 1902 at the prescribed time.

Her mother nodded. 'Yes, long before this was built, I should think. The bark is thick and rucked, if you peel some back there is another layer underneath.' She hesitated. 'If you know what I mean.'

Hannah nodded, surprised. So her mother had done as she had done; rubbed her hands across that uneven surface, dug her fingers into a crack and prised at the warm flaking bark. Her hands would have been dirty as Hannah's had been and at this thought Hannah sat down in the wicker chair which she had made more comfortable with white linen cushions. But first she adjusted the carefully worked fine wool shawl around her mother's shoulders.

'It is cool under the tree in the height of summer, isn't it?' Hannah murmured. Contact had to be made with her mother through sleights and images because words of tenderness were still too bold, too personal in this household ruled by him; that man, her father. But she pushed the thought of his darkness from her and watched the smile appear and grow on her

118

mother's face and they nodded at one another. Both remembering a place neither knew the other had visited and enjoyed until this moment.

Hannah was glad that the St John's nursing was bringing an increasing intimacy between them, allowing her to touch and soothe as she had never been able to do before. And now her mother was stronger and Hannah dared to hope that all would be well. She turned again to the garden, relaxed now, her back easy against a cushion. There were daisies on the lawn, not blackened and destroyed yet, and their whiteness, together with the yellow of the buttercups in the old guinea-pig area, added a freshness to the garden which the formal rows of tulips, waxed and stiff, had not achieved. The gardener's besom, the broom which she and her mother had watched him make from gathered twigs, lay against the glasshouse where he had left it before leaving for home.

Hannah grinned. She must tell Beaky Brennan it was there in case she decided to go shopping, the old witch.

'Did you have a good afternoon, Hannah?' her mother asked as her hair lifted in the warm draught from the window, which was fully opened to admit the evening air.

Beaky had closed it when Hannah had left after lunch today and that would not happen again, Hannah determined. That woman would do as she was told. Her mother needed fresh air, fresh food and rest as her St John's instructor had explained.

'It went well,' she answered. 'We struggled with geometry this afternoon and English, which I find easier, I have to admit.' She laughed and her mother joined her.

Hannah reached across to the table and the bowl of fruit which stood at her mother's side. 'Do have a banana, Mother. Dinner is not for a while.' She took one out and peeled it, knowing that her mother's sense of waste would not now allow her to refuse, watching as the frail woman took the plate from her and cut and ate with the small knife and fork which Hannah insisted Beaky renewed throughout the day. Her mother's hands were white still but the blue veins were no longer as prominent as they had been last year. There was even a hint of colour in her cheeks which looked healthy against the

white of her cotton night-gown with its wide collar and full
sleeves and Hannah felt a sense of satisfaction. She had bought
the bananas herself from the high-class fruiterers which she
passed in London on her way to King's College. They were
firm and unblemished in their yellowness and had been
wrapped individually in cotton wool to travel all the way from
the West Indies, the shopkeeper had informed her. And sold at
an individual price too, she had thought as she paid him, but it
was worth forfeiting some of her wages to provide the essentials
that her father considered indulgences and would therefore not
provide for his wife. Hannah had wanted to scream at him that
it was a potential son, too, but had sat meekly as she always did
now because that was the price she had to pay for her new life.
The shadows were long in the garden but there were still many
hours of daylight left. Through the window they could hear the
sounds of the newspaper sellers calling the headlines, the rattle
of a child's metal hoop on cobbles, the ever-present rumble of
carriages and horses and in the distance, from this height, they
could see the distant smoke which belched continuously from
factory chimneys. Beyond them would be the docks which
transported the finished goods halfway round the world.

At least, thought Hannah, the industrial revolution had
made her future possible and for that she should be grateful;
and I am, I am, she thought, and sighed deeply, sitting with
her eyes closed, seeing the white flashes of sun beneath her lids,
smelling the lilac which her mother loved to have in her room
but which Beaky grumbled over, saying it was bad luck to have
it in the house. Hannah loved its small fragrant flowers
gathered in a plume, several to a stem. She loved the lush way
the blooms filled the vase, spilling and lolling so that some bent
and touched the dresser whilst others stood proud. So far bad
luck had not struck and she felt a coldness settle at the thought.
Should she remove them, she wondered; but turning to look at
them decided that it gave her mother pleasure, and since the
season was almost finished, there was a natural solution to the
problem. She sighed. But did they really bring bad luck as the
Romanies said?

She frowned and her mother looked concerned, so quickly

Hannah smiled instead, taking the plate from her. 'Are you tired, Mother? Would you like to rest in bed?'

'No, Hannah. That was lovely, my dear. I should like to stay here for a while longer but if you have work to do don't feel you must sit with me.'

'I'd better prepare for tomorrow's lesson soon but for now I'm enjoying the quiet.' She watched as her mother settled in her chair, resting her head back and slowly closing her eyes. It was good to say that, to think of her class tomorrow. This year had been so good. She was so busy, useful. College was hard and stimulating, pupil teaching filled her with excitement.

She breathed deeply and only now remembered the dress hanging up behind her on the wardrobe door, its crinoline bulging out into the room, the green shot silk dull and faded. She turned and looked at it and then at Arthur's invitation propped against the clock.

How dare Harry put her in this position. She turned again to the window and now heard her mother's voice.

'I'm sorry, my dear, that your father does not consider that there is enough money to provide you with a new dress, one more suitable for the ball.' Edith Watson's face was sad and her voice uncertain. Hannah rose and walked quickly to the dress, her back to her mother, her face hidden for a few important moments. She stood there, stroking the smooth silk of her mother's old dress and then turned, her smile broad.

'I love it, Mother. I shall be the belle of the ball.' And she knew that her voice sounded convincing and was glad.

The invitation had not been a surprise, for Harry had written to tell them that Arthur's family were having a ball on 26 June to celebrate the coronation of Edward VII on the same day. Esther would be receiving an invitation, he had said, and so would Hannah in order to release Aunt Camilla from chaperon duties.

How Hannah had laughed while wanting to cry. There seemed no end to her brother's ability to wound. Was that the sum total of her worth in his eyes too? Chaperon to the wonderful Esther?

She turned now and walked back to her mother who was

struggling up from her chair, her shawl slipping from her shoulders.

'I think I'll settle into bed now, Hannah, I'm tired again. I saw your father in the garden so dinner will soon be served.' Her mother's face was tense now, her arm in Hannah's hand was shaking. Hannah threw back the bed covers and eased her mother on to the bed, lifting her legs and drawing up the covers.

She brought over a pillow from the chair on the other side of the bed and then the hairbrush which her mother always asked for at this time of day. It seemed to calm her. Slowly she unpinned her mother's hair and it fell to her shoulders, thick now and shiny and Hannah wanted to take it in both her hands and bury her face in its loveliness, in its smell, and be taken back years to a time when the sun always shone and her brother loved her and her mother was strong. Her mother was coiling her hair up now in a loose pleat, holding hair pins in her mouth, her lip pulled down, her teeth white, her eyes nervous. Was it in case he came, or in case he did not come? Hannah was not sure.

Dinner was served in the dining-room as it always was. The soup tureen had been cleared from the table. Hannah sat upright in her chair looking at the candlestick, which shone from the maid's polishing. She did not look at her father who had been seated by the time she had reached the dining-room. He was wearing his new red corduroy smoking-jacket and that ridiculous fez with a tassel. Would he jump like a monkey on a stick if she pulled it?

Hannah pleated her napkin between her middle- and forefinger. Did the fez really keep the smoke from his hair? Would the lamb never come? But then why hurry it? This was the moment she savoured each day. The moment when she sat like a meek, dutiful daughter, crushed beneath the righteous father, and told the candlestick how much she hated its master with his coal-black heart which shadowed the lives within his orbit. She waited until she was sitting here, with him, to think of the discussions that she had with Miss Fletcher about the rights of women and the vote. This was her continuing rebellion, her reply to his power and she would think and absorb and consider the battle which had gone on in the past without her and would go on in the future but include her, his daughter. She would fight to make sure that women were freed from tyrants such as this man. She would work with Miss Fletcher and others to ensure that women not only became equal but, deep inside, felt equal. She had become a suffragist, posting letters through doors, painting posters, speaking at meetings which other suffragists attended, learning all the time.

Hannah looked up as her father carved the lamb. Steam was rising and blood oozed as he sliced and sliced again. He passed her plate without looking at her and she took it.

'Thank you, Father,' she said quietly. The room was growing darker now and soon Beaky would be in to light the gas lamps which ranged round the walls. The potatoes were crisp and the carrots cut into slim sticks. She ladled the gravy on to her plate and then passed it to within easy reach of her father. Eliza would approve of her demeanour, her subterfuge, for hadn't she said in Cornwall last year that sometimes such behaviour was necessary to achieve one's aims?

Hannah looked down the table. Her father still hadn't finished serving himself and by now the steam was no longer rising from her plate and her food would be cold, again, for she could not begin until he had lifted his knife and fork. Did he do it deliberately? But she did not care, because she could, with a flick of her mind, repay his actions.

Yes, she thought, the women will go on fighting for what is their right. We've been balked up to now, but soon people like you (and here she glanced at her father) will have to listen to us.

'You may begin, Hannah.' Her father's voice was cold.

Just like my food, she thought, but merely replied, 'Thank you, Father,' and was glad that her mother was upstairs and able to eat in peace.

It was a problem though, Hannah thought, reverting to the inside of her head again. Do we go for votes for all men and

123

women, irrespective of property, and frighten the middle class? People like you, dear Father, with your fear of the masses forgetting their place and forcing you to move over and make room for them. Or do we go for the present property limits and urge votes only for the better class women, which many of the suffragists think would be the best starting point? But, dear Father, is anyone out there listening to any of our polite requests? Did any politicians rush to push the 1897 Franchise Bill into being? I don't think so, do you? And have they listened to us since then? No. Are they deaf, or do they see us as irritating children who ask for attention and are placated with a pat on the head? But we're not irritating children, which is why some of the women are withholding tax, boycotting the census. But does it work?

The cold doors don't listen as we knock. The mean streets don't welcome us as we walk through the fog to our meetings, nor the hard chairs and cold halls, nor the men who loiter and heckle and laugh. Does anyone listen as we canvass to elect Frances to the Guardians' Board? Perhaps, Mr John Watson, upright and respectable, we need to shout a little louder, tug at jackets, kick at shins until you all listen.

She wondered who these Pankhursts were who worked in Manchester and shouted. She felt excited. Would they come down here? Would they make London listen? She hoped so, how she hoped so, and when her mother had borne the child she too would be free to leave here and make people listen.

'The Peace Treaty was signed last night,' her father said. Hannah dragged her attention back to the room, to the gas lights which were now spluttering. She must have missed Beaky coming in to light them.

'The Peace of Vereeniging?' she replied, glad that she had caught his words.

Her father frowned and Hannah knew that she had made a mistake to expose her knowledge.

'I had to explain it to the children today,' she added meekly and watched as he nodded and returned to his meal.

Hannah played with her cold potato. She could not put down her knife and fork before he did; it would lead to a lecture on good manners. But thank God the South African war was now finally over. It had been fought to promote the rights of the Uitlanders – those miners with no votes – and so perhaps now there would be more hope for the rights of the women of the country, but she doubted this somehow. The Uitlanders were men, weren't they?

'Perhaps now the income tax will go down,' her father grunted, his meal finished at last.

Hannah placed her knife and fork together neatly and sat quietly with her hands crossed in her lap.

'We showed them, didn't we, those little Boers. We showed them what happens to those who rebel.' He was sitting back in his seat now, drawing a cigarette from his case, his long nails tapping on the silver surface.

Hannah sat still, thinking how ugly her father was and how stupid, but she must say nothing. He must think of her as broken if she was to be left in peace to live her life. She thought of the shouting in Manchester. Yes, one day soon, when Mother was well enough, but only then, she would leave this house, she would be financially independent and nothing could stop her. How he would rage when it happened. Let him sit there talking of rebellion, breathing his smoke over my hair which does not have the protection of a silly hat. Yes, go on then, she thought, though her face was impassive. Go on and tell me about how rebels are crushed, the glory of war, for I know that you will, with your eyes glinting and your nose sweating.

'I said,' her father repeated in a louder voice, 'we showed them, didn't we, Hannah, that rebellion must be crushed. That obedience and respect will be forthcoming at all costs. They mistook their enemy, forgot he was the proud British soldier.' His eyes were clenched tight against the smoke which rose in a spiral past his face, but Hannah could see that they were looking straight at her. His mouth pursed and he exhaled smoke in streams through his teeth.

'Yes, Father,' she replied, fighting the surge of fear which his rantings still aroused, forcing her feelings into anger instead, waiting until it came. And here it was and now she wanted to grip his lapels and force him to look at the photograph she had of Uncle Simon in her room, at the photographs that other mothers must have; Boers and English. She wanted to force him to see, really see, pictures now being shown in newspapers of the concentration camps. The anger was too much now, soon it would show. She clenched her hands because it must stay within her, for now at least.

'Humility is everything, Hannah,' he said, waving Beaky away as she brought in dessert.

Hannah saw Beaky smirk as she came round the table and stood on her left, waiting for Hannah to serve herself.

Yes, she would just suit a broom, Hannah thought, breaking free from the pictures, the rage, the sadness, and returning to the glinting candlestick, the cigarette smoke which now hung above the table. Feeling glad that the fear had been diverted, that she had won again but knowing that the anger, though used as a weapon against her father, was one that was truly felt.

The apple pie had a thick crust and was dry. She bit on a clove and wanted to spit it out but swallowed it instead. She would write to Joe about the crinoline. Would he laugh? She knew he wouldn't. She would write and tell him that they couldn't come to Cornwall this year because of her mother's confinement, but was he still coming to London to work with a sculptor? And she would tell him that she was now a suffragist but an increasingly impatient one. How do we make these politicians listen? Gentle persuasion doesn't seem to be enough, she would say, but from the North we are hearing of another way.

Yes, she was calmer now and after dessert she rose.

'Good night, Father,' she said, and left the room, anxious to breathe freely but glad that she had spent time in his company thinking of her life lived in opposition to his.

Edith Watson lay back on her pillows, watching the moon through the window. It was late and Hannah had left her to work and write letters, leaving the curtains wide open as her mother wished. Edith smiled slightly at the new-found authority of her daughter over Mrs Brennan and how she drew on her St John's training to insist on her own way; how Mrs Brennan had been forced to acquiesce. Except for today when she had shut the window in spite of Hannah's instructions. But Hannah would rectify that tomorrow, Edith knew.

She had finished her meal tonight and Hannah had been pleased. She had smoothed the pillows and sheets and sat in the light of the oil lamp mending a stocking for school tomorrow. There was a strength in Hannah now, Edith thought. The rebellion and tension of last year seemed to have gone, though sometimes a shadow was there, deep in the back of her eyes, and this made Edith unhappy. That shadow had been there tonight before she had turned and walked over to the dress. Edith could still see its shape, though not its colour, and her heart broke for her daughter. Her first dance and only an invitation because of her cousin and not even a fashionable dress.

She felt angry with Harry for his tactlessness but knew that she should not be, for how could men change the way they were? If they were not strong and masterful, how would their families survive? Edith picked at the sheet, then lay her hands on the moving body that kicked within her. This baby felt strong and she breathed deeply as Hannah had taught her, trying to disperse the tension that had suddenly gripped her shoulders. Please, dear God, let it be strong, let me be forgiven for my lusts. For she knew now that they had gone for ever. She no longer desired her husband, no longer craved his touch. There was emptiness where that heat had been but she did not miss it for a warmth had taken over the rest of her life. A warmth that was the companionship of her daughter. A warmth which kept at a distance the fear which drew from her all her health and strength.

Edith looked again at the dress; its faded colour, its outmoded shape and heaved herself upright, reaching for the bell which hung behind her bed, determined as never before. Mrs Brennan must bring her husband to her. Money must be made available for Hannah's dress.

John Watson flung his tie on to his dressing-room chair. Damn and blast the woman, but yes, perhaps this time she was right. Arthur was after all the son of a Lord, the second son but still a valuable ladder in the order of things. Perhaps, as Edith said, there was a possibility of a match between Hannah and the boy. She was cowed now, biddable, and the season was well under way. It could be that those girls who 'came out' would snap him up first, but the advantage Hannah had was that Harry was the boy's friend. John Watson strode to the window past the heavy mahogany wardrobes which lined the room, hearing the last few birds in the trees which lined the avenue, seeing the hansom cab draw to a halt under the lamp further down the street. Would there be a match between Harry and Esther? He felt excitement begin to rise. They weren't first cousins after all and Thomas was worth a bit. It would bring the family up, but not as much as Hannah's marriage into the peerage.

He turned from the window, snatching up his tie again, knotting it rapidly before pulling on his black jacket. He was feeling a tension he had not experienced since Hannah had challenged him at Thomas's. If he was prepared to buy a new dress the least the girl could do was to bring the young cub Arthur to heel. He ground his teeth. God help the girl if she let him down. God help that interfering mother. He strode to the door. Yes, he would provide the money for a decent dress but Edith had better ensure that the girl repaid his generosity.

He felt in his pocket then turned back to the dresser and picked up his money. Anger was building now, anger and tension. She was meek now, he'd seen to that, he thought, as he slammed the door behind him and started down the stairs and out into the street. Meek but still too intelligent. Had he done the right thing by turning her into a teacher? What would a Lord's son think of a girl who was almost reduced to trade? The streets were darker now away from the wide avenues. Narrow alleys with stray dogs and rubbish piled high echoed his footsteps.

Anger was mounting as he pictured her at the dining-table. Treaty of Vereeniging indeed. How dare she attempt to display her knowledge. She must wear a dress which would attract the boy, but which showed nothing of her body. His breathing was rapid now. Hannah must keep her mouth shut; her mother must see to that, if she was capable of seeing to anything. Would this new child be a boy? Would it live? He doubted that his wife was capable of even that. Were women capable of anything except the ruination of all they touched? The dampness of the river was all around him now and feverishly he plunged on to the tow path. Was there no purity to be found at all? He quickened his stride. His relief was not far away now, and soon, from the depths of him, would come the word 'Mother', and tonight he would not dream of her.

8 The coronation had been postponed because King Edward had collapsed with appendicitis on 23 June but, or so the bulletins said, was recovering well. The dance was to proceed as arranged, Aunt Camilla had told her mother.

The day of the 26th seemed long, the hours difficult to fill, but at last it was nearly time and the new dress fitted perfectly. Polly had pulled and laced her stays before hooking the pearl buttons which were the same rich white as her heavy silk dress. Hannah stepped back from her mother's mirror, her arms held out from her sides. She turned slowly, watching her reflection in the mirror. Could this woman be her, graceful and poised, hair coiled and full? Could this woman really be her? She lifted her eyes to her mother who stood at the foot of the bed.

'You look quite beautiful, Hannah,' her mother began, but could not continue because her voice was full; and Hannah saw her turn and pick up the fan which Joe had sent and Hannah could not speak either because her own throat was too full of gratitude.

How had this dear woman persuaded her father to spend such a great deal of money on the best dressmaker in the area? Her mother would not say but had told Hannah to accept that the green crinoline would not be seen again and they had laughed together. Hannah lifted her skirt and walked across to her mother, helping her into bed, smoothing the sheets and seeing from the clock on the dressing-table that Aunt Camilla and Esther would be arriving with the carriage in fifteen minutes.

Her hands were shaking as she took the fan which her mother offered her, her grey eyes soft. It was beautiful, made from ivory and painted by Joe in the palest of creams, for he had not laughed at her letter but had worked without sleep for two days and nights, or so Eliza had written, to produce something unique for her to take to the dance. Eliza had sent a string of her own pearls which matched the cream exactly and now lay cool on her skin. Hannah felt them now, rolled them between her fingers before flicking open the fan and sweeping it backwards and forwards. The draught lifted strands of her mother's hair which was brushed but not yet pinned and disciplined. It cooled them both and neither spoke but listened to the late calls of the birds in the garden. Hannah looked at the clock again. There were ten minutes left now. Her legs were trembling. She wore silk stockings which Miss Fletcher and her suffragist friends had given her. Her hands were trembling now and she did not sit down in the chair at the side of her mother's bed for fear of creasing her dress and she saw her mother smile.

'You'll have to sit down in the carriage, my dear,' she said and Hannah nodded.

'I know, but I just feel so strange, Mother; so scared, I suppose. It's worse than facing a class of monsters.'

Her hands were damp and she wanted to run them down her dress but could not. She felt the carved ivory stems of Joe's fan, its edges smooth but definite in her hands and then even the thought of his face bent over his workbench, his hands so large and hard, could not calm her. She looked at her own hands and wished they were as delicate as Esther's and then she spun round, dropping the fan, her eyes seeking but not seeing her gloves; where were her gloves? She turned back to the dressing table where an oil lamp burned, to the mahogany side table where another was lit. Her hands were at her mouth now. Oh God, she couldn't go with bare arms.

'Oh, Mother, my gloves, my bare arms, my hands.'

She rushed to the chairs which were by the window, her dress, caught up by a small bustle at the back but hanging almost straight at the front, hampering her stride. Perhaps she had left them there when they had sat after her mother's meal but now in the clear evening light there was no sign of them and then she heard her mother's voice, calling, laughing.

'Hannah, listen to me. They're here. I have them safe.'

And then they heard the door bell and knew that it was time. Hannah ran to her mother.

'Walk, Hannah, walk, or you will be red and hot and your hair will be down around your shoulders.' Her mother held up the gloves telling Hannah to keep her fingers straight; rolling them on up to her elbows. And Hannah was, for a moment, a child again, and she did not want to move from this room with its pictures, its lace bedspread, its furniture which had not changed since her birth. She wanted to stay here, with her mother and not face the stares of Esther and Camilla who were expecting the crinoline, or meet her brother, for the first time since January, or that perfect friend of his, Arthur.

'Miss Hannah!' It was Polly and Hannah took one last look in the mirror before turning back to her mother.

'Will I do, Mother?' she asked.

Edith Watson nodded, taking her hands in hers, pulling Hannah towards her. 'You look beautiful, my dear, very beautiful and I love you so much.'

Hannah felt her mother's breath on her cheek, her cool lips as they brushed her skin and knew that she would remember this moment until she died.

'And I love you, Mother,' she replied, holding her mother in her arms now, her face deep in that loose thick hair knowing that sleights and images would now no longer be necessary to show their love.

'Miss Hannah,' called Polly again, and Hannah stood up now and smiled, easing her mother back on to her pillows.

She turned and walked towards the door, past the small table to the right of the blanket chest. The smell of fresh lilac was rich and full, the blooms losing colour in the fading light. They should not be there.

'I thought the tree was finished,' Hannah said, not turning to her mother, her voice carefully level.

'Mrs Brennan found just enough for one last vase, my dear,' she said and Hannah walked down the stairs, the fan loose in her gloved hand, unable to free herself from the smell of lilac.

Esther and her mother had left her the whole of the seat for her crinoline and were less than talkative on the journey to Lord Wilmot's house. Neither had commented on the dress but their eyes had said much. Hannah sat opposite them now, her mother's cloak hanging loosely from her shoulders, thinking already of how she would write to Joe to thank him, and tell him of the new dress; but soon he had said he would be here, in London, and so letters would no longer be necessary. Soon, he had said, they could sit and talk of her plans. Had she forgotten that she was going to teach women how to improve their lives? Was it enough just to fight for the vote? What about education? Hannah shook her head. Yes, there was a great deal to talk about, and no, she hadn't forgotten she would write to him. But there was plenty of time, wasn't there? The carriage swayed past windows still hung with flags which had not yet been removed. When would the King be crowned, she wondered. It seemed unfair to be dancing while he lay ill, but then again, it was not often that he and his Marlborough set had to miss their fun. Perhaps it would do them good.

She smiled slightly and looking up caught Esther's eye. She smiled again and laughed as Esther pulled a face.

'Crinoline indeed,' she said. 'You are a shady character, Hannah Watson, and no example to your pupils.'

They were still laughing as the carriage drew up and the door was opened by a liveried footman. As Camilla and Esther stepped out Hannah rocked with the movement of the carriage springs. She could see the crowds collected on the pavement and the policeman stationed to prevent them from pressing too far forward in their efforts to see the guests arriving. Esther was waiting for her, her blonde hair glistening in the light which flooded out from the great hall of the house, and Hannah gathered her dress and let her fan hang from the loop around her wrist as she stepped on to the red carpeted pavement.

'We'd better watch the clock,' she murmured to Esther as they followed Camilla up the porticoed steps. 'If we're not home by midnight we'll turn into pumpkins.'

'It is rather grand,' whispered Esther as they were admitted by another footman and their invitations taken from them and delivered to the butler.

'Be good girls,' whispered Camilla. 'I shall be playing bridge with Lady Wilmot in the library.'

They nodded.

'I gather a diamond mine investor lives next door,' Esther continued as they waited to be announced. 'Obviously a great deal of money in that business.'

Hannah looked at her as the butler announced their names to the waiting hosts who were lined up at the entrance to the ballroom. She really is very serious about all this, isn't she, Hannah thought, and wondered what it would be like to have Esther as a sister-in-law.

Lord Wilmot was elderly with white hair but a grey moustache. His faded blue eyes smiled politely but nothing more. His handshake was limp and bored. Lady Wilmot wore a diamond necklace and Esther squeezed Hannah's hand fiercely, her eyes wide. Was it Harry or his potential wealth she was after, Hannah mused, but was unaffected by the thought, for Harry no longer concerned her.

Arthur was standing next to his older brother. He shook hands with Camilla and Esther, saying how pleased he was to meet them and that they would find Harry over by the west door, and then turned to Hannah.

He was taller than Joe and his hair was the colour of the oats ripening in the field which lay on the approach to the moor.

'You are very much more beautiful than Harry,' he said and the hand which took hers was warm and strong and his voice was confident and sure.

He did not smile as he held her there but his eyes were violet with black flecks and Hannah knew why Harry was his friend. Hannah saw his brother, who was taller and darker nudge his arm and Arthur released her hand then and turned to greet the woman who smelt of eau de cologne and was too close to Hannah.

She walked on into the crowded ballroom, feeling a smile grow on her face.

'Rather a lovely young man,' Esther said as she held her arm. 'Are you impressed?'

Hannah laughed, pausing to allow a man with a monocle to precede them through the crowded ballroom to the west door where she could see Harry waiting, his face strained, his eyes anxious as he looked to either side and then in front but still he had not seen them.

Esther pinched her arm. 'Well, have you gone deaf? Are you impressed?'

Hannah flicked out her fan, waved it in front of Esther's face. 'Calm down, silly child. I can see why Harry likes him. He's sure of himself, he's . . .' she sought for the word that she wanted. 'He's easy somehow.'

'And very handsome,' Esther snapped.

'And very handsome,' Hannah agreed, though she would have used the word beautiful. She looked across at Harry again, who was moving towards them now, his face eager, but as he reached them and looked only at Esther she saw that he trembled as he took his cousin's hand and kissed it. He was tall and broad, all signs of boyhood gone. Her father would be proud, she thought, of this son who was an undoubted gentleman.

Hannah looked away, outside the feelings that were gripping her brother, outside the love that poured from him. She saw the brilliant crystal chandeliers, lit by electricity, hanging from the white-and-gold-painted ceiling. She felt the heat from the flickering candles held tight in the branches of the silver candelabras which stood on every side table, alongside displays of flowers which added their scent to the heavy air. And then she looked back again at Esther and her brother and still they stood with their eyes only for each other.

Yes, she thought, Arthur was beautiful, like this room, white and light and easy, and she wished that she had someone who looked at her with eyes suddenly dark, who held her with hands that trembled and stopped her feeling so alone.

The music whirled on, drawing dancers into its rhythm. Dresses shone and jewels glittered and nearby the candles fluttered in the draught from a newly opened window. Now Harry turned to her and smiled and said, 'How are you, Hannah?'

But although his eyes were looking at her they were not seeing. They were still filled with Esther and so she said, 'Quite well, thank you, Harry,' knowing as she spoke that he did not hear her, though he nodded and smiled.

135

He stopped a waiter and handed punch to Esther and then to her and it was cool on her lips. She watched the swirl of pink liquid as she waved the glass gently, the fruit collecting together against the rim. A grape and an apple segment. Apples for Uncle Simon, she chanted in time to the music. Apple lofts and wrinkled fruit. Joe on the moor, gold-red hair and strength. Arthur with hair the colour of oats. And she saw him coming now, weaving through the jostling guests, nodding and laughing and greeting but keeping his eyes for her, looking at her as Harry had not and she smiled as he came because now she would not be standing alone, on the outside of Harry's love.

He reached for her hand but his did not tremble; his eyes saw her and there was pleasure but not eagerness. He led her to the floor and they danced. The orchestra was raised on a platform edged with palms and played without a break, and his voice was low as he told her of Lady Banyon and her Pekinese which ran amok and bit the Bishop who screamed, Oh God, but it did no good. He leant back and laughed with her and told her how lovely she looked in white and how beautiful he found the embroidery about the neck. And all the time she thought how strange it was to have a man so close, to have his breath on her hair, her cheek, to have his arm around her and his hand holding hers. She was glad of her gloves lying between their two skins as she dipped and whirled. Supper was laid out in the ante-room off the ballroom and Arthur escorted her, though she saw his brother shake his head and nod towards a girl in a pale blue dress.

Hannah hesitated and said, 'Please, do go, Arthur, I shall be quite all right. I shall find Harry.'

He shook his head. 'Good Lord, my dear girl. My best friend's sister and the belle of the ball is entitled to the most handsome man in the room.'

They sat at one of the small tables, set in formal rows, and his arm lay around the back of the gilt chair that he was saving for Harry. A waiter brought pink champagne and it was cool and the bubbles splashed fine spray on her face. She drank it as Arthur laughed and handed her another. Heavy mirrors hung from white walls catching at men and women, reflecting their smiles, their gloss, before releasing them into the room again. Music still played, but quietly now.

The footman brought a silver bucket and pushed a champagne bottle deep into the crushed ice. The candelabra on their table made her hotter still. The music had swollen to fill the room, the murmur of voices crowded too close. She wanted to dip her hands into the ice, gather up crisp, cold, moist crystals and bury her face in it until the heat was gone. But then she felt the weight of her fan. She had forgotten it, its cream satin, its cool ivory, and now she held it so that its cool draught fanned her face, her shoulders, her body, and became the breeze of the moors and the music, the cry of the gulls.

'Here they are, at last,' Arthur said and his voice wrenched her back to Harry, to Esther and the room which seemed quieter now, cooler, and she noticed that all the windows had been opened and the long satin drapes were moving in the wind.

'The heat of the day is turning to rain,' Harry said as they sat down. 'Do you remember the storm last summer?' he said and looked across at Hannah, who nodded, surprised, and more than that, pleased that he had drawn her across to him.

Then Esther laid her hand on his arm, drawing his attention back to her and Hannah's reply, 'Yes, I shall never forget it,' went unnoticed by her brother.

But Arthur was there to lean forward and ask, 'Quite some storm then, was it, Hannah?'

She was grateful for the ease with which he caught the awkward moment and led her away from Harry's dismissal. She smiled at him and nodded.

'A great deal happened that day,' she murmured and did not respond to his look of enquiry because it was her memory alone, hers and Joe's and was clutched deep inside her mind.

Footmen brought lobster on silver trays held high above their shoulders until they swooped low to serve their table. Harry and Arthur cracked the claws with heavy silver crushers, leaning over to do so; brushing close so that Esther giggled and leant in, forward, closer still to Harry, whose colour rose and whose hands trembled again. Hannah sat quite still, watching as Arthur's pale fine hands neatly exerted just enough pressure to break the red glistening shells, but not enough to crush and spoil the white flecked meat. Jagged red now lay against white and Hannah smiled and lifted a segment to her mouth. It was moist and fresh.

'Brought up yesterday from the coast,' Arthur said, taking some himself. A piece fell from his fork but he caught it with his other hand before it could reach the table.

'Well caught, that man,' called Harry, lifting his champagne glass to his lips and smiling across.

Arthur bowed and Hannah laughed, the warmth of her gratitude still present, hearing, as though from a distance, the thud of willow on leather, seeing Harry on the school green so many years ago now. Had Arthur been there too, his whites sharp against the grounds, his hands pale against the red of the leather? She looked at him again as he sat back, beckoning the footman, asking for cherries to add to the champagne. There were beads of sweat on his forehead and the starch of his collar was not as stiff as it had been. And she felt a warmth rising in her body at his beauty. They ate strawberries with their cherries and champagne and she saw red against yellow; the yellow of the straw, the red of Joe's strawberries. Arthur picked one up in his fingers and ate it, and then there was red against white. The music was gentle now but the curtains were billowing in the wind and the candles were flickering and it was too cool for her fan which she now laid down on the table and its cream was the colour of Arthur's skin.

They danced again when they had poured the last of the champagne and the ice in the bucket was clouding and melting. Round and round they spun under the lights from the chandeliers, under the white and gold of the ceiling, past candelabras which wept white wax in streams against the silver. They passed mirrors and were caught together, white against black and she felt his leg against hers as he turned her and her hands were white against his for her gloves were on the table together with her fan, and her skin was against his, her dampness mingling with his, her laugh full and her body loose because this friend of Harry's was so beautiful, so kind, so easy.

It was as though the sun had found him and never left and Hannah wanted to stay here for ever, whirling round in the light and the music and the laughter which left no room for fear, or struggle, or pain, and which reminded her of something. But what? A white dress and blue bow hovered and was gone.

Harry stood on the steps as the carriage drew away, taking Esther from him and he waved again as her gloved hand disappeared. The storm was high now but he still stood under the portico, watching until he could no longer see the outline of the landau or hear the horses as they clattered out into the main thoroughfare. Arthur stood with him, a cigarette hanging from his mouth, the smoke snatched away by the wind, the tip glowing and burning fast, unaffected by the rain which could not reach them here but had caused the gutters to overrun and the cobbles to be lost under a film of water.

It was gone now, the carriage taking his love away, and he took the cigarette which Arthur offered from his gold case. He drew smoke deep into his lungs, feeling its heat before exhaling.

'Hannah is . . .' Arthur paused, dropping his cigarette and grinding it under his heel, his patent pumps gleaming in the light which still spilled from the wide glass doors. 'Interesting,' he continued. 'You are lucky to have a sister like that. A girl who is quiet but laughs. A girl who thinks before she speaks. One who looks as though she would leave a fellow to live his own life; not interfere in his pleasures.'

Harry looked at him. Yes, his sister seemed to be all those things and had indeed laughed, though not with him, and he was relieved to think that in accepting her true role in life, as his father had written in his monthly letter, Hannah was happier. He wished now that he had spoken to her, listened to her, but with Esther so close nothing else had mattered. He looked in the direction that the carriage had taken and thought of Hannah in her white dress, slim and elegant, and remembered the blue sash of that other one, so long ago. Blue on white remembered so clearly from a time which seemed a thousand years ago. How very strange that the memory still refused to go. His cigarette was finished and he tossed it into the rain, watching as the glow died under the weight of the rain, and then, as he turned, he heard her laugh as she whirled on the rope beneath the horse-chestnut tree and saw her head hang back and her hair fall about her face.

'Esther's a beauty, Harry,' Arthur said and Harry looked at him and nodded.

When he was with her there was warmth and laughter and excitement and he knew he could not bear to think of losing her too.

Arthur took his arm. 'Let's move back inside, shall we? We have to be back at school tomorrow, old boy.'

Harry nodded. 'You're lucky to be so bloody rich, Arthur, to be someone of consequence.'

They moved through the hall and climbed the sweeping stairs. Arthur punched him lightly on the arm. 'Gets a bit repressive though, you know. It's my parents, you see. They expect exemplary behaviour at all times and I'm not like that, as you know. How can a fellow sow wild oats or throw a few dice with them watching and hauling me in all the time? What I need is some sensible girl who'll leave me to run with the hounds, as it were, but who will be there for the parents to approve of as a steadying influence. Someone who doesn't care too much about me for I will never be able to put all my affections in just one area. D'you get my drift, old fellow?'

Harry nodded, though he was not really listening. He was still thinking of money and how it made things possible. 'You're still lucky,' he insisted, 'to have all of this around you and something to come your way in the end.'

At this Arthur laughed. 'You'll beat all of us, Harry, once you get out to the Rand. There'll be diamonds and gold coming out of your ears, old boy, before you know where you are.'

Harry nodded, looking at the oil paintings as they passed, knowing that in order to keep Esther he would have to supply her with all this.

'I just hope you're right, Arthur,' he replied.

Hannah and Esther spoke in whispers in the landau. Aunt

Camilla was asleep, her head moving in tune with the carriage as it rolled round corners and bounced on rough, mud-heaped roads.

'Such wealth, Hannah,' Esther said, her eyes bright, her hair flattened by the cloak which Harry had pulled up to protect her from the rain.

Hannah nodded, thinking of the music, the feel of Arthur so close to her, the strangeness of it all, the light, the glitter, the laughter.

'It's all from mining and railways, you know,' Esther continued. 'And property of course. Big landowners too. We must try and arrange an invitation to the family seat.' She gripped Hannah's arm. 'That is something you must encourage and I will organise Harry to do the same.'

Hannah sighed at the intrusion into her thoughts, then laughed. 'For heaven's sake, Esther, I might not see him again.'

'Oh yes you will.' Esther's voice was determined and Hannah looked at her, seeing the tilt of her chin and the set of her mouth.

'For my sake or for yours?' she asked, watching her friend carefully. 'If it's that important why not chase him yourself?' She felt the stirring of anger suddenly and wondered where it had leapt from and why.

Esther slumped back against the seat. 'I don't want to marry a second son, darling. There's no future in that.'

Hannah laughed, relieved that Esther was merely joking, for she was, wasn't she? Camilla stirred.

'Well, I'm not sure that Father would have much to leave Harry,' Hannah said, her eyes intent.

Esther looked round at her, her eyebrows raised. 'Arthur said Harry will do very well in South Africa. He introduced us to his neighbour, the gold mine owner. He has more money than Arthur's family will ever have.' And though she was smiling Hannah saw that the blue wide eyes were, for a moment, devoid of humour and a silence hung between them, disturbed only as the carriage turned into her crescent and lurched on mud, the horses losing their nerve and shying, throwing Hannah on to Esther and causing Camilla to wake and shout at the driver to be more careful, foolish man.

Hannah looked from the window and saw that the lights were on throughout her house. She could not understand why and turned to Esther and then back again to the house and now she saw the black of the doctor's trap standing stark outside the house, and there was nothing in her head now but her mother.

She leapt from the carriage before it had stopped; tearing from Camilla's hands, which tried to hold her back; running in through the door, which was unlocked, and up the stairs, her skirt grasped in her hand so that she could take two at a time. There was no one there at the top of the stairs and she was shouting now. 'Mother, Mother.' And the noise was so loud that she wondered if she would ever stop hearing it inside her head.

Across the landing it was dark and she rushed to her mother's door but it would not open. She turned the handle, hearing Camilla come up the stairs now, feeling her hands on her arms, pulling her back.

'Mother,' she called again and now the door opened and Beaky pushed her back and Hannah fought free from Camilla, hearing but not listening as she soothed and stroked, but Beaky still stood in front of the door, large and black and sour, saying nothing.

'Get away from that door,' Hannah said, suddenly quiet. 'Get away from that door at once.'

Beaky did not move.

'I said, get away from my mother's door.' And now she was not quiet but shouting.

'Stop that noise, you silly child,' Beaky said, her voice whiplike in its whisper.

But Hannah was tired of not shouting. 'I will shout until you open that door.' And her throat was sore and her hands were gripped into fists which beat the air. 'I want to be with my mother.' She would not ask if the baby was dead, if her mother was dead. She could not stand that pain. But now Beaky moved to one side and stood large with her arms crossed.

'The baby died. Your mother is still alive, but only just. You were not here.' With that she turned, walked to the chair under the high small window and sat, dark and brooding.

Camilla dropped her hands because Hannah stood still now and Esther, who was waiting at the head of the stairs, moved towards her, but she brushed her away and walked slowly into the room.

The nurse and the doctor were standing either side of the bed, not moving but just looking at the still form, which, in the lowered light of the oil lamp, was pale again, as pale as the sheets which were drawn up tight across her shoulders.

Hannah pushed past the white-draped cradle, knowing it was empty, ignoring the rocking which she had set in motion. It was heavy with heat in the room, heavy with the scent of lilac and illness. The curtains were drawn across the window, the fire was raging in the grate, the blankets were heavy on her mother's body. She undid her cloak with one hand and let it fall to the floor behind her.

She did not acknowledge the doctor as he stepped back to allow her passage, but looked only at her mother, taking her hot limp hand, talking all the time, gently, quietly.

'I'm sorry I wasn't here. I shall never leave you again.' The words kept coming, the same each time but there was no answer, no movement at all, only beads of sweat on her mother's white forehead and Hannah threw to the floor the beaded net which covered the jug of water on the bedside table and tore strips off the white linen sheet, so immaculate, so orderly, pushing aside the doctor's protests, tipping water over the linen which she now held, jagged with loose thread hanging.

As she placed it on her mother's forehead she turned. 'Open that window immediately.'

Neither nurse nor doctor moved. 'Open that window immediately. I am responsible now that my mother is ill. Open it at once.' She was not shouting. She would not shout in this room where her mother lay.

'If you value the custom of this road, of Uncle Thomas, of any of this neighbourhood you will open that window.'

She was stripping back the blankets now, hurling them to

143

the floor, and the doctor looked at her with eyes narrowed in affront. Hannah lifted the cloth from her mother's forehead. The coolness was gone from it. She poured more water from the jug, too much this time so that it soaked her gloves, fell on to the bed. She sponged her mother's hair, her neck, gently unbuttoning the heavy cotton bodice to the waist, sponging her breasts which were full and blue-veined with milk that would not be needed. There could be milk fever. She must keep them cool. And all the time she talked and soothed and nodded as she heard the curtains draw back.

'Now open that window and leave it open until I tell you to close it.' And the nurse looked at her, then at the doctor, who nodded. Hannah could hear the wind and the rain now, could feel the air dampen down the heat, and suck the lilac out into the dark night.

'I shall be speaking to your father, Miss Hannah.' The doctor's voice was crisp and hard.

She did not turn, her eyes too busy with her mother. 'No doubt you will but he is not here now, is he? At his club, is he? Away from all unpleasantness, all failure?'

She heard the gasp of the nurse, the rustle of offended cloth as the doctor turned sharply towards the door.

'I will be waiting outside,' he said, his voice cold.

'Yes. I think that would be best.' Hannah looked up, but not at him, at the nurse. 'And would you please go and fetch cool water from the scullery and thank my aunt and cousin. Tell them that I am grateful for their kindness but that I will send to their house if I need them.'

As the nurse turned, she called her back. 'And you are to allow the fire to die down, to go out. Do I make myself clear?' She smiled now, as the nurse nodded. 'And then perhaps you should sit in the chair over by the dresser and get some rest. There will be much for you to do tomorrow.'

For her mother was not going to die. She would not let that happen, would not allow all this love to be wasted. It couldn't be allowed to just disappear.

The night was long. The storm reached its height before dawn, the thunder cracking and slashing and then her mother moved her lips and Hannah squeezed water from a clean cloth and watched it trickle into that parched mouth. She watched the pale lids open and her mother turn her head slightly, looking first at the hand which held hers and then up into Hannah's face.

'He said it was a girl and so death was a blessing.' The words were a broken whisper, the eyes dark with grief and pain, and Hannah knew she spoke of her father.

When dawn had broken and her mother was asleep and the nurse sat where Hannah had been throughout the night, she took the vase which held the lush, heavy lilac, carried it down the stairs and into the sitting-room, where she lit the fire which Polly always laid, and burnt it, bloom by bloom.

She rose then, easing off her white kid dancing shoes, her silk stockings, before opening the French windows and walking on to the paved terrace which was still wet, out into the early morning sun. It was not dew which soaked her bare feet but the ravages of the night.

It was cool and she felt the grass between her toes and saw again the running stream and the trout that she had tickled and Joe's hand outstretched for hers.

She found the axe in the gardener's shed. It was heavy but not too heavy. She felled the lilac within the hour, its leaves showering her with water with every thudding stroke, her breath heaving in her chest, her arms aching with each swing. She dragged each branch, each leaf, each browned bloom past the blackened daisies to the back of the shed, stacking them into a pile, pouring paraffin over them, and throwing a lighted match into its heart. Soon the lilac was completely gone.

She picked lavender now, sprig after sprig, and carried it back through the sitting-room, up the stairs, feeling the carpet warm now beneath her feet, seeing her dress so soiled and creased.

But that did not matter now; the baby was dead but her mother must live. She dug her nails into the fragrant stems before entering the room. She knew that she had made a choice and that the shouting, the fighting must go on without her, for now. She stood outside the door. Hadn't Eliza said that everything must be done in the context of her mother's health? And so where did that leave her now? And she dug her nails into the fragrant stems again.

9 The wheels of the bath chair had dug furrows from the gravel path to the base of the pear tree. Hannah sat in her own wicker chair, which creaked as she removed a fallen leaf from the green-and-white checked wool blanket which lay around her mother's legs. Her mother did not stir; her hands lay limp and thin and translucent, their veins too easily seen, too blue.

'It's such a beautiful day, Mother, for September; it's usually such a changeable month but this time it's been kind to us. Joe says it is called an Indian Summer after the redskins who live on his great plains and have warm autumns too.'

'Is September autumn, Hannah? Is it soon to be the start of winter?'

Edith Watson's voice was light and frail and sank almost to a whisper as she finished. Her hands were still motionless, it was only her lips that had moved.

Hannah looked away, up into the tree, to the green leaves and the blue sky beyond. If she put her head right back that was all it was possible to see; just flickering leaves, the faded brown of the branches, the sky streaked with high thin cloud. The pears were few this year after the storm of that June night. Hannah sighed, pushing her hair back with her hand, lowering her head so that she could see her mother again, her head resting against the white cushion that Hannah had sewn and embroidered, stitch by stitch, as she sat day after day, night after night at the bedside. Beaky had smiled and said that her father would be pleased to see such industry. He had need of another antimacassar. Hannah had said nothing but drawn through another strand of silk, pale pink this time and seen a frown form and thicken on the housekeeper's brow. This is for my mother, Hannah had said at last, as she cut the strand. There had been no answer. Were the needle-grinders still dying, Hannah wondered now, but was too tired to care.

Since the June night when it had all happened the days had been full of sun; she knew, because Esther had told her. Ascot had been brilliant when her cousin had gone with Harry and Arthur and how it had shone at Cowes; and what gaiety there had been at the Coronation which had at last taken place in August. But there seemed to have been such darkness here, such struggle in forcing away the weakness which dragged greedily at her mother, such effort in breaching the cloak of despair which had wrapped tightly round Edith Watson and slowly but steadily drawn the breath from her body and the sense from her mind. It had taken all Hannah's strength, all her energy to pull her back.

She rose from her chair. Its legs had sunk into the ground and earth coated the bamboo. She walked to the trunk of the tree.

'Look, Mother, do you remember this?' And she dug her nails into the bark and peeled a layer back. It broke off in her fingers and she handed it to her mother, watching as the dulled eyes travelled to the bark, then up to Hannah's face. She was so drawn, this mother who was more like her child, but Hannah did not allow this thought to show but crouched down beside the bath chair, hearing it creak as she placed the bark in the limp hands, then, resting her arms on the side, her dark blue skirt trailing on the grass, 'Layer after layer, do you remember?' Hannah took her mother's hand in hers, the one which held the bark, and she smiled as her mother nodded. She ran her mother's other hand over the layers, seeing the dust leave its trail against the pale of her skin.

'Yes, my dear Hannah, I do remember but it seems so long ago.' And her voice trailed away but Hannah sat down again, pleased that today the improvements continued.

Miss Fletcher had been so kind. The new college year had begun of course and lectures must not be missed, though the work in the classroom, her Headmistress had insisted, could always be curtailed

Neither was she needed to canvass support for Mrs Jones, a suffragist fighting for a seat on the Parish Council and Hannah had wept as she was limited to writing letters to local dignatories.

But this had enabled her to stay for part of the morning with her mother, leaving her for the afternoon in the care of the much improved nurse, and so she should be grateful.

Harry had not been home except for lunch one Sunday. He had stayed with Arthur for the vacation. It was not the place for a young man to be, her father had said, his voice cold, but Hannah would not think of that. He had travelled to Biarritz in between day trips with Esther and Arthur.

He had begun at the School of Mines full time. Nothing must be put in the way of his pleasure or career, she thought, feeling the muscles in her neck tense, and she took the bark and threw it down towards the old hutches, which were now barely recognisable as such.

'Will you be long this afternoon?' her mother asked, her eyes filled with pleading, her face uplifted, her hand rising to touch Hannah's skirt.

Hannah shook her head, looking out across the garden at the neat hedges, the pruned roses, the horse-chestnut tree with crisp brown leaves. 'No, Mother, I won't be long and nurse will be here.'

Arthur's mother, Lady Wilmot, had called and left her card soon after the dance and her father had smiled at his daughter during dinner that evening. When this unfortunate episode with your mother is over I would be happy if you were to see more of the Honourable Arthur, he had said, and Hannah had been surprised to think of Arthur in that way.

Well, Father dear, she thought grimly as she took and held her mother's hand, you will be happy tonight because this afternoon Arthur and I are going with your son and his love to the Zoological Gardens to take tea in the conservatory, with all the other gentlefolk. But, Father dear, what would make you less happy is the thought that before that I am going to see a mere colonial, and on my own.

'But you won't be long, you won't leave me alone for long,' her mother persisted.

Hannah crouched down again, stroking her hand, burying the scream and saying gently, 'No, I won't leave you for long, Mother. I will never leave you again, you know that.' And love fought with anger and her mind whirled in circles of despair.

The horse-bus took her to the station and she breathed in the free air along with the hawkers' cries, the traffic's clatter and the conversation which nudged at her on either side of the seat. Straw had been laid on the floor to soak up mud but there was none today, and dust danced in the air and caught in throats. She hugged her thoughts to her, her joy, her relief because she was going to see Joe and he would give her succour; his strength would become her strength. How she had waited for him, all the long summer, and at last he was here, working in wood, carving, sanding as he had done last year. Had he changed? Would he think she had changed? She moved along the bench as the bus halted at the stop before the station to make more room. The men went upstairs on top of the bus, and the woman sat next to Hannah, her black coat straining across her breasts, her face red in the heat. It was too warm closed up inside the bus but women were not allowed upstairs. Hannah eased her collar and the bus jerked and moved forward again but only for a few minutes for then the station loomed.

The underground train was loud, and steam and sulphur filled the tunnels and the dark carriages and Hannah wondered how Joe could bear the noise, the grime, the smell of London after the Cornish air. He had only been here for two weeks working under the auspices of his father's friend and attending classes at the art school. Hannah had warmed at the thought that at last he was here but knew that her father would never allow a foreigner to visit his house, one without a pedigree. And so she had written to Joe and told him this, knowing that truth was the only course with him.

He had written again. Then come to me, he had said. I'm not fussy about foreigners in my home, even if it's one who goes on the moors without a chaperon. She laughed now as she climbed the stairs from the train into the light. Joe, oh Joe, how I need you. And the picture of Esther and Harry and Arthur laughing and talking, travelling and boating while her mother fought for life faded into nothingness.

His room was off the Fulham Road. She walked along,

buying a bunch of dahlias from a street trader, feeling the water soaking through the tissue paper into her glove, looking into shops as she passed, smelling the meat from the butcher's, the bread from the baker's, moving out of the way of a man carrying furniture to a van, dodging past an open cellar down which coal was being tipped from a sacking bag.

She turned right and right again and the noise of the street was left behind as the roads narrowed, sprouting alleys across which washing lines were strung, some heavy with clothes, others empty and drab.

Hannah looked at Joe's note again. It couldn't be far now. She had passed the second pub with its stench of beer reaching right out into the street. Women passed her, shawls over their heads instead of hats like hers, and one stared, then smiled, her blackened teeth ugly in her face.

Hannah quickened her stride. There seemed no daylight here, with the streets so close together but it was still warm. Why did Joe have to rent a room out here? Was this where his father's friend had his studio?

She looked around her. Endon Terrace, his letter said. She checked again and walked back the way she had come. Perhaps she had missed it but then she heard him.

'Hannah, Hannah, this way.' She turned and he stood at the entrance to a street, not an alley, just a bit further than she had walked, and he was taller and bigger but his smile was the same and his eyes too and the colour of his hair was as warm and red as she had remembered.

She walked towards him, a smile broad across her face, wanting to run to him, wanting him to hold her and to listen to her and make everything all right again. The walls she passed were stained black, the pavements broken and uneven and Hannah saw that Joe was a man now and she stopped as she reached him.

'Hello, Joe,' was all she said, because he wasn't the boy she had known and she was no longer a girl and the air was not easy between them.

'Well, hello again, Hannah,' Joe said. Hannah was glad that he had not come to her house, because in that cloaked and formal atmosphere it would not have been possible to recapture the friendship which filled the space where her brother had once been. Would it be possible here to break through the change which letters had masked?

The stairs up to his room were dark and the cart which belonged to the children who lived downstairs partially blocked their way. Joe took her arm as she stepped over it and for a moment she was frightened. There was a smell here of dirt and food and his hand was touching her, this boy who had become a man. Fear caught in her throat. She shouldn't be here. She would be compromised if it became known. His hand was still on her arm. They were climbing the stairs, side by side. It was dark; she wanted to go home. To write to Joe on white paper with the thought of him in her mind, not with the feel of this strange hand on her arm. And then he spoke and in the darkness the voice was Joe's, the drawl, the soft laugh, and now she barely felt the hand as he opened the door of his room and light fell out into the dark of the landing, and on the wall which she faced as she entered was the painting of marigolds which had been above the washstand of her room at the cottage. She stepped inside, and slowly, very slowly, the tension was leaving her and the cry of the gulls, the feel of the wind was here, but faint still, so faint.

'Shall I take your coat, your hat?' His eyes were on hers and his voice was hesitant in the daylight and Hannah was surprised – Joe was always so certain. But she shook her head. She needed them on; they were a protection, a barrier against this man who might not be the same boy she had known and written to and trusted.

Joe pointed to a chair, one of two which stood at a small kitchen table. His smile was tentative but it was there and Hannah sat, her lips stiff, her hands tight around the dahlias. Their fresh smell reached her suddenly and she held them out to him.

'To welcome you to your new home.' She watched as he took them, holding them to his face, the water dripping from the paper on to his hands, which seemed too large to be so gentle, and from them on to the floor.

'They're so lovely, Hannah.' He moved to the stone sink in the corner of the room and put them in an earthenware jug. He stood for a moment, looking at her, then around the room, and she could think of nothing to say.

'Would you like a cup of tea?' He spoke at last, the drawl so different from Arthur's clipped neat speech, the soft checked shirt so different to the starched white of Harry's.

He filled the kettle, his arms strong, his shirt sleeves rolled up to his elbows. There was no iron in the water this time. She looked past him at the bed which ran along the length of the wall. His sheets were pulled down and she could see where he had lain. She looked away quickly. Frightened again. This room was his bedroom too.

His letter was still in her hand, crumpled now, and she straightened it, then folded it again and again into neat exact lines, looking no further than the paper against her knee. She flicked the fan shape that she had made up and down against her skirt, hearing the kettle heating on the stove, remembering his fan, remembering his letters, remembering his hand in the storm; and now the kettle was singing. His hands, as they handed her the blue and white cup were the same, large and steady; were they as hard?

She looked only at her cup now, bringing it to her lips, feeling the tea too hot in her mouth but if she did not drink she would have to talk, to look, and there was nothing for her to grasp that was familiar now. The moors were vanishing with the cries of the gulls. The bed loomed large in the corner. Joe stood at the table, not drinking his tea but looking at her as she drank hers. He was too different, his world was not her world and she gripped the handle of the cup tightly. But he had been her support throughout the days and the months and she pictured his written words. He had been her strength, but now there was nothing but strangeness and she thought of Arthur waiting for her at the Zoological Gardens, of Harry and Esther, clipped voices and neat clothes, familiar manners and conventions.

She put down the cup; the tea was finished and her mouth was sore. She must go from here, and she started to rise, not looking at him, but he took her again by the arm, and she lifted her face to his. He was close now, his smile was there and his eyes were warm and blue.

'See what I've made for you,' he said. 'My Hannah, my Cornish girl.' And his teeth were white against his lips, his moustache was red-gold and hairs curled from the unbuttoned collar of his shirt. His smell was the same and he was close, so close, but he turned her from him and she saw, on the far side of the room, the work-bench, which she had not noticed before. It was the same one that he had shown her in Cornwall. Wood chips lay on the floor and there were brushmarks and sawdust where some shavings had been swept into a pile in the corner. The broom rested on the wall. She moved from him across to the bench, seeing motes rising and falling in the light which streamed in from the window set high in the sloping roof.

The jewellery box was made of mahogany, highly polished but devoid of intricate carving. The beauty was in its simplicity, its cool uncluttered lines. Hannah removed her gloves, and did not lift the box but ran her fingers along its surface, leaving a blurring of condensation. She looked along the bench, smelling the wood, and she picked up a curled shaving, pulling it out to its full length, then letting it roll up again, warm and marked with its grain.

'This one has no tune. It's just a straight box but I dare say now you've grown into a woman you'll be needing it.'

He was beside her now as he had been in his work-room in Cornwall and she watched as he turned and took up the broom and swept the floor quite clean beneath the bench. And then she laughed, picking up the box, holding it to her and laughing because he was the same boy, the same man, who had entered her life a year ago and she pushed the clean and clipped Arthur away from her again.

They talked of his tutor who had a studio near the Art School; of this room which he had chosen because of the light; of the dolly-pegs he made for women to stir their washing with in the dolly-tub; of the wringer-rollers which were made of sycamore for fitting into mangles. And Hannah had asked why, when he could make a box like this.

He laughed and she smiled to hear him and he told her that it

154

made him more money than all the fine furniture and boxes in the world because no one wanted simplicity yet, but they would. One day they would and she warmed to hear his certainty, his strength.

He told her how he had already felled his own trees with his tutor alongside, how he had ripped them into one-inch, two-inch or larger planks but he stopped when Hannah looked puzzled at the word 'ripped' and explained that he had sawn them along the grain. He told her how he had stored the planks, held apart by slats of wood to let the air through and would now let them lie until his course was finished – in three years.

'To season them of course, you London girl,' he laughed.

He pointed to the treadle lathe in the corner. 'That's my real beauty,' he boasted.

Hannah smiled at its size, at the height of the heavy wooden flywheel, and the gearing which transmitted the movement of the treadle up and down to turn the work continuously in the right direction. His hands as he showed how he was working some elm wagon-hubs were dextrous, and when he cut himself on some raw wood and she ran the tap hard into the wound she knew that they were as hard as they had always been.

He sat with her at the table and this time she left the tea he poured her until it was warm and she told him that her mother would live – but for how long? She told him that Harry had begun at the London School of Mines; that Esther was teaching too and was just the same, living for the fun which life could offer, and she laughed to think of her golden hair and the smile which danced across her face. But she didn't tell him of Arthur, of the dance, of Lady Wilmot's visit, of the Zoological Gardens, for now that seemed a great distance away; too far. It was better to stay here, with Joe.

She told him of Miss Fletcher, of the handbills they delivered, the letters they wrote to Members of Parliament, lobbying them to support female suffrage. Of the terrible emptiness inside her as she heard of the women campaigning loudly in the northern villages against the injustice of the female textile workers being asked by their unions to contribute sixpence a week toward the Labour candidate's election campaign though still barred from voting. Of the Pankhursts who were making their voices heard and who were shouting.

She stood up and walked to the sink, leaning on it, gripping the cold stone, seeing the green drip mark under the tap; turning from it and walking back again, past the marigolds, away from the bed, picking up the paper fan which lay on the table, remembering Joe's made of ivory.

She looked at him and he was sitting back, his arm along the table, his eyes on her.

'I can't shout, Joe. I can't do anything.' She could feel the tears wet on her face but her voice was steady. How strange. It was not as though she was crying at all; and why was she crying, because she did not cry in front of people, but Joe was not people, he was hers.

He was still looking at her, not speaking.

'Eliza said my mother must have a measure of peace, her health must take priority and so it must because I could not bear it if she died, but I want my freedom too, Joe. My plan was always to break free of that house, of its restraints, and fight for equality but now I can do nothing, though others are beginning. If I long for my freedom it means that I long for her death because that is the only way I shall ever be free now. I love her so, Joe, but I am being ground into nothingness. My life is empty, my plans are finished. I'm too tired, too helpless.' And now the tears were running into her mouth but still her voice had not crumpled.

She stood in front of him now, wanting the touch of his hand, wanting his arm about her, wanting his body close so that she could lean into him and not have to think or struggle any more. Stay with me, he had said, when the storm raged and that is what she wanted, for ever, and she knew that this was a very big word. Her eyes were closed and she waited for him to come to her and she felt him rise and his hands grip her arms and then his voice lashed out and caught her, slapping her eyes open, tightening her muscles.

'How dare you stand there and tell me your plans have been ruined! Your freedom spoilt just because you cannot fight for some future vote which you have just showed very clearly you don't deserve.'

His voice still drawled but it was deep and hard. He shook her, and his face was close to her, his eyes dark, his lips drawn back, thinned by his anger. Hannah felt him and heard him and could not understand. She saw the table, the treadle, her jewellery box. She felt her breath which had caught in her throat. What was he saying, why was he shouting like this? He should have been kind, strong. She wanted to stop his words but he kept on talking.

'I'm ashamed of you, Hannah Watson. What of your teaching?'

She tore from him then, her anger and her disappointment cutting too deep to be borne. This was not what she needed, not what she expected from Joe.

'Haven't you been listening, Joe? I do teach, I nurse too but that is not all that is needed. Women need to fight and I can't fight. Not until I leave home and that will only be when my mother is dead.'

'Sit down, Hannah.' He pushed her on to the chair but she struggled to rise, knocking the fan to the floor. 'Sit down, I said.' He was big over her and his eyes did not leave hers. She tried to look away but he held her head.

'Out there, in those streets you walked through, in the streets behind your grand and glorious crescent there are women who need knowledge, who need self-confidence. There are women like your mother, crippled by childbearing. Women who need to be told about birth control; pessaries, sponges. Women who need to be told not to use quinine or syringes. You of all people know that. Have you forgotten so much of what you said last year?'

Hannah pushed his hand from her, turned away. The kettle was bubbling on the stove. She would not listen to this. It was not what a man should speak of to a woman, even Joe to her. This was not why she had come. She had come for love, for support, not for this. All this which had come so quickly out of nowhere. Hadn't she been through enough?

And this is what she screamed at him, hearing her voice,

seeing him move back from the spittle which came from her mouth, but she didn't care. He had turned from her when she needed him. How could he hurt her in this way? He was hers and now he had turned from her.

'Haven't I been through enough?' And it was a scream.

'No, Hannah, you have not been through enough. You have been through very little.' He was pulling her to her feet now. 'There are women who need you, women who want the sort of help you can give. Look at your mother, Hannah. She is the one who has been through enough. Remember the moor, Hannah. Since then all that you have done has been for yourself, for your own satisfaction.'

He was turning her now, towards the door. How could he say that? What of the nursing, the hours of care?

'You are the daughter your father thinks you are, weak and frightened and feeble, and I won't have it. You are worth more than that, you can do more. Dutiful daughters nurse; you are more than a dutiful daughter, you have forgotten yourself.'

He was dragging her towards the door.

'Leave me alone, you're just a raw colonial with no breeding. You have no right to touch me. Leave me alone.'

She was hitting him now, wanting to hurt him as he was hurting her, wanting to smash the months of trust, the pictures she had held close of their time together, but he didn't turn and they were through the door.

'You want the vote, don't you? Well, my girl, until you can join in that particular struggle you should be teaching women to be able to cope with that sort of responsibility. You should be teaching them that life does not have to be one long pregnancy, that children do not have to die.' He was panting now, pulling her down each dark, dank step as she fought against him. 'You should be teaching women how to read, how to manage what little money they have. You should be preparing them for the vote, you stupid silly girl. Not sitting feeling sorry for yourself. You have the facilities at Miss Fletcher's. You have the time. Tell your mother. She might help, especially now after the last child. You won't have to leave her to do this; to work towards something just as important as chasing the vote. You have the talent but not the grit. You don't deserve the vote.'

'Let me alone. I want to go home.' She wrenched one hand free and hit his face, feeling his lip burst beneath the force of her blow and there was blood on his teeth, red against white and she wanted to cry because it had all gone so wrong. He was moving away from her, like Harry had done.

And suddenly they were both quiet, the struggle was finished, but he did not release her arm.

'So you want to go home or is it that you are really rushing to this Honourable Arthur that Eliza has told me so much about? Is it this man that has wiped so much of importance from your mind?' His smile was twisted now and he made no effort to wipe away the blood which ran down his chin. 'Well, before you go to wherever it is you are going you will see that there is much you can do, Miss Watson.' He inclined his head in a mock bow and forced her down the remaining stairs to the room on the landing below his. He knocked and pulled her after him as he entered.

There were three small children on the bed, which had rags sewn together to make sheets. The floor was covered with made and unmade and half-made matchboxes. There were no chairs and a young woman with a lined, drawn face sat on the floor. Her hair was unkempt and fell forward across her face. Her scraped patent leather boots, buttoned at the side, were visible beneath her torn skirt. She looked up at Joe and he smiled.

'I have a friend with me who would like to see just how the matchboxes that her dear father uses are made.'

Hannah tried to jerk her arm free but he held it like a vice. The woman nodded, not smiling, not showing anything on her face or in her dull eyes. They were like Mother's, Hannah thought. The children lay quiet on the bed but they were not asleep. Their eyes also watched her and were dull too. Dirt was everywhere and mingled with the light from the small cracked window and the brown streaked walls was a smell of sweat and cabbage.

Joe pulled her further into the room. Hannah wouldn't look but he squeezed her arm until the pain made her want to call out and then she watched as one motion of the woman's dirty hands with their cracked and blackened nails bent into shape the notched frame of the case. She watched as another strip with a ready-pasted printed wrapper was instantly fitted and then the sandpaper which had been ready pasted beforehand was applied and pressed, so that the woman's face strained with effort. She threw it on to the floor.

'To dry,' Joe said.

The woman then took the long narrow strip which formed the frame of the drawer and placed it on the ready-pasted paper which was the base. This she bent and stuck to the drawer frame and threw on the floor too.

'To dry,' Joe said again. His was the only voice in the room. 'All this has to be done one hundred and forty-four times for twopence-farthing. Then each drawer and case has to be fitted together and the packets tied up with hemp. Isn't that right, Mary?'

Hannah watched as Mary nodded. She looked at the children again. They had not moved. There was stale bread on the table cut into thick wedges.

'Mary is having another child soon, aren't you?' Joe did not look at Hannah, but at the woman, who nodded though she still did not speak.

Joe looked at the children. 'If it is damp a fire must be kept up or the paste will not dry. The fire, paste and hemp must all be paid for out of the worker's pocket. Her husband has no work; he drinks.'

Joe turned suddenly, jerking Hannah and then dropping his hand from her arm and when he did that, she felt alone. He walked towards the door, not looking to see if she was following. She smiled at the woman who looked down at the boxes, working again. The children had still not moved.

Joe was climbing the stairs when she left the room. 'Joe,' she called.

He stopped but did not turn to look at her. 'Go home, Hannah, or back to Arthur. I am ashamed of you.'

She looked at him, standing with his back to her, refusing even to look in her direction and it hurt too much.

'Well, I am going to see him,' she cried out, her hand at her throat, the air and the darkness stifling her. 'I'm going to the Zoological Gardens and taking tea with a gentleman.'

He turned then and she saw his face and it was white and his hair seemed dark against it. 'Yes, you do that, little English lady. Go and gawp at the creatures neatly behind bars where they cannot intrude and then return to your mannered empty life.' His voice was low, all anger gone and she turned from him, her own anger rising, hearing him call as she left.

'Remember that it was you who called it a terrible emptiness, my Hannah, my Cornish girl.'

He heard the door into the street slam. He had known that she would slam it and he wished he could have taken back the time which he had just spent with her, taken it back and shaped it differently, more gently; coaxed her into the life she should be living, bring her back close to him but it was too late, too sudden and too late.

She would be walking back to the Fulham Road now, hailing a hansom, turning her face and her life away from him to Arthur. Why had such cruel and clumsy words poured from his mouth? He thought of Cornwall, saw the sun and the trout they had caught and the storm. London was different, he knew that now.

He walked slowly up the stairs, into his room. Her gloves were still there and the jewellery box. He would send the box to her but not the gloves for they were all he had left of her now, along with his memories, and he lifted them to his lips, holding them hard to his mouth, wanting to feel the pain where she had struck him.

The tea was served in bone china as they sat on the terrace overlooking the rhododendrons of the gardens. In the distance Hannah could hear the animals as they roared or chattered or called. Children ran past them while their parents sat; the women under parasols, the men still in their top hats.

Esther was laughing. 'Go on, do tell us how your American is. Has he made you any quaint little boxes recently?' She turned to Arthur. 'Hannah has this little American who is frightfully good with his hands and sends her little gifts.'

Hannah stirred her tea. Arthur was smiling, his silk handkerchief dark green in his breast pocket, his hand lazily clasping his umbrella above the silk. Harry looked irritable.

'You're not going to see that Joe fellow, surely? Father would be most displeased.'

Hannah continued to stir her tea. No, she would not be seeing Joe again. He was changed, different. She sought for words to block out the memory of his words, his hand on her arm. He was too hard, too brash. She would never think of him again, never long to be near him again and she would not miss him. No, she must decide never to miss him and she shook her head. Pain and anger mingled; fighting, hurting.

She looked across at Harry. Friends and brothers had a nasty habit of hurting.

'No, I will not be seeing Joe, so don't fret, brother dear.' And she smiled as Arthur smiled, nodded as he nodded but as they all left the terrace and strolled back towards his carriage she could still feel Joe's grip on her arm and wondered if there was a bruise, and if so, how long it would remain, for when it was gone Joe was also gone and so too the Cornish summer sun. She could still hear his anger, his contempt, and her words which she had spat at him, a raw colonial with no breeding, and knew that a great deal had been lost today.

10 The train whistle shrieked and the dark of the tunnel gave way to light, though it was a grey cold light. It was 1907 and spring was late this year, Hannah thought, as she looked out on to freshly turned fields. There were not many primroses in the banks but then they were north of Oundle and Arthur had said it would be colder up here which was why he preferred the London house. She hoped that he would be there to meet the train when they arrived; the wind, which was jogging the hedgerows as they passed, was strong enough to be cold.

She settled back in the first-class compartment, letting the curtain fall back into place, watching Esther laughing into Harry's face, her hair coiled under the large grey hat, her well cut light wool suit matching perfectly the darker grey of the ribbon which decorated the brim. The girlish looks had gone and at twenty-one Esther was a beautiful woman.

Harry bent and kissed Esther's hand and Hannah turned back to the window. There were woods in the distance now, still brown. The pear tree at home was budding, though there was no blossom yet, and her mother was waiting for the pale green tinged flowers that meant the end of winter. She tried to breathe evenly, to push away the anxiety which came in a sudden wave of heat and pulled at the leather window strap which was hooked on to the brass knob. It was too hot in here, she thought, anger stirring; she wanted some air but if she opened the window the noise would be worse.

Would Mother be all right? Would Eliza keep Beaky under control? Would she keep the curtains drawn back to let the light in as her mother preferred? She ran her fingers over her lips. Would her father let her mother take her meals in her room? She ate so much better at the window which looked out on the pear tree. Hannah felt hotter still; she shouldn't have left her alone, not even for this weekend. And then she saw that

Harry was looking at her, at her fingers which were playing over her mouth, and she made herself smile.

'I hope Mother will be all right, that she'll not be too unhappy while I'm away,' she said and could hear that her voice was too high, too taut.

'For heaven's sake, Hannah, it's only two days and Eliza's her sister after all. She'll know better than you what keeps Mother content.'

Hannah said nothing. The train was labouring now up a slight incline which was leading to a small hamlet. No one knew her mother better than she did, she wanted to shout into his face, but he had turned again to Esther's. So she did not shout. She must not shout, must she? The last time she had shouted had been at Joe and he had been right, hadn't he? But how could she ever tell him, after speaking to him as she had. No, I must not shout. Say it ten times, Miss Watson, and she smelt the classroom and the chalk and the children who sat in rows. No, I must not shout. And now she was saying it in time with the wheels as they clicked over the joints in the track. And she must not think of Joe, not any more and she seldom did, except when marigolds bloomed and the wind roared or gulls called or . . . but now she clenched her mind shut, tugging at the tiredness which pulled at her, looking out of the carriage, out to where the air was buffeting and pushing at the clouds.

The churned fields were giving way to grey stone houses which lay on either side of the track. These threw back the noise which had until now rolled on and over the fields and helped to drive thoughts from her mind, but they could not remove the tiredness from the broken nights. She saw again the pale, frail hands but made herself look instead at the picture of London Bridge which hung in its gilt frame above the heads of Harry and Esther; at the brocade which covered the seats, at the rack which held their bags, and she felt calmer.

Mother was better than she had been, that was all she must think about, and with the coming of spring the improvement would be even greater.

Hannah sat with her hands loosely clasped in her lap now, forcing her shoulders down, her muscles to relax. The noise was less again, the houses were left behind and trees which crept up to the embankment took their place. It wouldn't be far to Arthur's junction now. He had said three hours out from London and it must be nearly that now. She pushed back the sleeve of her dark blue suit and looked at the wrist-watch which had been Arthur's Christmas gift; in fifteen minutes they should be arriving and she was curious to see his country seat.

He had spoken of it often during the past four years but her father had refused permission for such a visit until now, his face darkening at the mere suggestion, his tone cutting through the air as he forbade such indulgences. But this weekend was special; it was to be Harry's farewell and he had approached their father saying that Lord Wilmot wanted to introduce Hannah to his county set as the girl they favoured for their son. Hannah had swallowed when she saw the sweat that had appeared on her father's forehead, at the smile which began to play around his mouth, disgust churning her stomach. She knew that this was not the truth. Lord Wilmot had no intention of introducing anyone as his second son's potential wife, for Arthur was still far too young, and for that Hannah was grateful, she had too much to do to think of marriage. She was more than aware that the real reason Harry required her presence was, yet again, that Esther would be able to attend. As the train rattled on she looked at her brother. Would he like the hot parched land where Uncle Simon lay? Would it bring him the wealth he wanted? She sighed. Was it really so many years since they had laughed together in the garden, since that young boy had swung her on the rope, run with her on the grass, laughed into her neck as they fell face down and watched the ants climbing the stems? This was the boy who had become a man and climbed from the mine and had pressed her hand when she had held his to her lips. This was the man who had taken her education from her. But here she stopped. Had he taken it, or had it been given to him?

She looked at the neat moustache, the starched collar, the mouth which talked words of love to the girl in a grey suit and hat, with coiled hair. She looked at his eyes; eyes which had been nudged by the knowledge of departure for the last few days and weeks and months. She looked at his hands which had swung the rope and they were the same ones that she had pushed from her when he had tried to talk to her on the stairs as their father had stalked from the house. She wished now that she had not done so, for there was still an empty space where first he, and then Joe had been.

And now he was to go and it was all too late, wasn't it? The emptiness must stay hidden away as though it were not there. She looked again at her watch. Only ten minutes now. There were distant hills standing proud against the gathering grey clouds and birds were being blown off course. The train whistle shrieked as they passed under a bridge which Harry said held the road leading to the village this side of Alburton Manor, the Wilmots' home. Hannah craned round to watch as it curved into the distance. There was a trap shying away from an Austin car. Was it Arthur's automobile, she wondered, and smiled. If it was, he would be late.

'Hannah.' She turned as she felt the tap on her knee as Esther leant forward to attract her attention. 'How will your Sunday ladies manage without you?' Esther's face was tilted and her mouth struggled not to smile.

Hannah felt herself grow tense at the question.

'Yes, Father seems most awfully pleased with you, Hannah,' Harry said, looking at her curiously. 'Your good works seem to have made the old boy feel that at last he can relax. He seems to feel that you have grown into Mother's role quite nicely. Dutiful daughter at home and Bible study with the deserving poor.' His eyes were probing, his voice full of doubt. This was the sister who had fought and struggled against her father, against God knows what demons for so long, the child who had held her own against him before he went to school, and here she was taking Bible classes for the fifth year running. Had Father broken her after all? He looked at her again in a way that he had not done for many years and shook his head, surprised at the regret that the thought brought him.

She lowered her eyes before his gaze and he realised that she seldom met his eyes any more but said and did the right thing, demure and self-contained. Yes, during the five years the four of them had been laughing, talking and socialising it was suddenly clear to him that he did not know this adult Hannah at all. There was something private about her now, something hidden beneath the correct exterior. There was a hint of it with his mother too. A cloaking of the eyes, a preoccupation. Was it because of Arthur, he wondered. If so, they had no cause to worry, since that young man was very pleased with Hannah and so, it seemed, were the family; their reservations at Hannah's lack of pedigree overcome by her mature influence. This, they seemed to feel, or so Arthur had told him with a laugh, was calming their son's interest in the music-hall actresses who so enchanted him. Harry remembered the wet steps outside Arthur's London house on the night of the Coronation dance. What was it Arthur had said about needing a sensible woman? He looked out of the window. It was something about needing someone who would let him enjoy himself.

Harry shrugged. Did Hannah love Arthur? It was so hard to tell, for there seemed to be a distance between Hannah and everyone and everything. It was almost as though she were only half aware of everyday life, as though she were waiting, but for what? But now he felt the pressure of Esther's hand and his heart caught in his throat; she was so small, so delicate, so beautiful and soon he would be gone. But not for long. No, not for long because that he could not bear. Soon he would be back with money enough to approach her father for her hand in marriage. No, he must not be long because he could not be certain she would wait.

He laid his hand on hers and wanted to grip it, raise it to his lips, draw her to him and sink his mouth on to hers, feel her body against his, stroke her breasts as she had allowed him to do last week, but instead he moved his arm against hers and smiled at the answering pressure.

Hannah did not smile at Esther's question, at Harry's curiosity, but looked at her hands. They were no longer clasped loosely but squeezed tightly. Yes, the women would manage just this once but Esther must not stir curiosity again. It was too important to be treated as a mere game but that seemed to be what life was to Esther and always had been.

When Hannah had approached Miss Fletcher the week after she had left Joe's, the Headmistress had thought it was a splendid idea to hold classes for adults. Hannah had not mentioned that it was not hers alone. They had used the front room in Miss Fletcher's private quarters so that parents of the schoolchildren could never have cause to complain that the school premises were being used for purposes they would undoubtedly disapprove of.

As they had handed out suffrage handbills during that week they spoke to the women on the doorsteps, urging, cajoling, and some had come. They had arrived on Sunday morning, some with children because their husbands would not baby-mind. Against the murmured protests of infants that were as dirty and lethargic as the matchmaker's had been, Hannah had begun to teach. Buns and apples had appeared from Miss Fletcher's kitchen and the children had eaten them sitting on the floor, forcing more and more into their mouths, scrabbling for the crumbs, fighting and screaming, refusing to sit on chairs, which were something they had not seen before. The next week more had come to listen and to learn and to eat, for meat sandwiches were included now. In the first few weeks they had concentrated on hygiene lessons before moving in due course to first aid. As the weeks progressed they had explained birth control and then more came and asked for reading and writing. Hannah and Miss Fletcher had worked around the tables, showing the women how to hold pens, how to form letters; showing the children how to sit still long enough to build bricks, to paint shapes. As they leant over them their smell was strong and so, as part of the course, they ran hot water and encouraged baths.

One day a husband had come, forcing his way in, pushing aside Miss Fletcher, grabbing his wife, dragging her from the room until Hannah had barred the door, feeling the wood solid behind her back, seeing the faces of those who remained; fearful, excited. She had asked him quietly amidst the furore why he would not allow his wife to stay and he had shouted at her, his breath rancid in her face, that why should she be able to read when he could not?

And so now they taught reading in a mixed class but saved hygiene and birth control and discussions about equality for the women alone, fearing that the men would forbid the knowledge. The children laughed now and played with toys made by Hannah's mother, who sewed in her room and nodded to Hannah to sit and tell her of the progress the Sunday school was making and they would laugh softly together, aware that this was a secret that they shared. Her mother's eyes would grow brighter as Hannah talked and her hands would grip the sides of her chair and she said that she was glad that some women would not have their life sapped from them.

Hannah had not been able to bear that and had knelt and laid her head on her mother's knee and her mother had stroked her hair and had, for a moment, felt the impatience which still tore at her subside for a moment, but only a moment for Mrs Pankhurst's suffragettes were fighting loudly now while the suffragists were still writing letters, and Hannah knew that this and her Sunday mornings were not enough.

'I play the piano, you know, Harry dear, at Hannah's fundraising teas.'

Esther's voice startled Hannah who was full with memories but she listened to Harry as he smiled and patted Esther's hand.

'And quite beautifully too, my dear,' he said.

Hannah nodded. Oh yes, quite beautifully, but that was all she would do because Esther had caught fleas the first time she had come to help with the children. Hannah and Miss Fletcher had left the room and laughed until their stomachs ached and had then had to splash their faces with cold water before they re-entered and sympathised and sent her home to bathe.

'We buy bricks for the children, don't we, Hannah, and pay for the refreshments?' Esther said. Hannah scratched her arm and then her hand. Esther's face grew red and Hannah laughed, and after a long moment, so did Esther.

Hannah relaxed. Esther would be more careful now because she would not want Harry or the Wilmots to know that she had once had fleas. There must be no suspicions about the Sunday classes or her father would insist on their termination, which would be a senseless waste, and the repercussions of his fury on her mother would be too dangerous. She felt anger again. Why did that girl take so long to grow up? Esther knew that it was imperative to keep the Sunday school subterfuge intact but it was as though she became bored and threw pebbles in the pond, just to see how far the ripples would go.

Hannah shook the thought from her head. The classes must not stop. They were important for the women and perhaps Joe would be proud of her, and then she paused. But of course he wouldn't, not now, not after that afternoon, and besides, Eliza had told her that he was busy with commissions for furniture now that his course was finished and how strange, Eliza had said, that he never mentions you, Hannah. Hannah felt the train slowing now, the brakes squealing as they drew into the station past the buff-painted roof of the station master's house and the lattice windows of the waiting-room. So Joe would not want to hear of her Sunday class, would he?

The porter held open the door while they stepped down on to the platform. Hannah drew her coat around her, guiding Esther towards the waiting-room. They stood by the fire, the brass scuttle glinting in the light, and Hannah watched from the window as the guard walked up and down with a green flag under his arm. The flower beds on the platform were edged with whitewashed stones and blue crocuses with tissue sheathed stems struggled in the wind. Across the tracks were carts with lowered backs into which boys were lifting goods brought by the train.

The wind caught at the cap of one and he ran stamping with his feet but he did not catch it until it was brought up sharp against the drystone wall which bordered the track. Hannah laughed, the sound bursting from her, and she turned towards Esther, who was rubbing her hands, her kid gloves shining as she did so.

'It's so splendid to be away. Far away from it all,' Hannah said and Esther looked up and smiled.

'Yes, it is, darling. You look tired. You need the rest.'

Hannah nodded and turned again to the window, watching as Harry walked along the white palings at the end of the platform, looking for Arthur. Yes, it was good to be away, to see great stretches of country, great swathes of sky. To be able to breathe in sharp clean air and have time to think.

She ran her finger along the small panes, down one and then another as her breath condensed and blurred. But thoughts had a habit of coming back to the same face, or the same fight. But she would not think of the face, only the fight, for perhaps that could still be won despite the failure of the 1905 Franchise Bill which had been talked out by anti-suffrage members.

The suffragists had expected success but Campbell-Bannerman, the sympathetic Prime Minister, had said that his Cabinet was opposed. She ran her hand across the pane of glass, wiping out the patterns she had made. And what had been the reaction from Mrs Fawcett's National Union of Women's Suffrage Societies? Patience, ladies, patience, because the Liberals were in power after the Conservatives had split over whether trade should be free or protected. And Liberals were reformers; gentle persuasion would bring results now. But couldn't they see that Asquith was in the Cabinet and that he had a great deal of support against women's suffrage?

Hannah stared out at the crocuses which were being blown and battered. Patience, for God's sake! There had been enough of that particular virtue to last a lifetime.

Arthur drove them in his car. His goggles were mud-splashed but the three of them sat protected in the covered back seat and Hannah laughed as his scarf streamed in the wind and his song soared above the roar of the engine. Their luggage was strapped into the boot and the maids unpacked for them as Lady Wilmot told Arthur to take his guests into the grounds to shake the travelling cramp from their legs.

Hannah walked with her hand in his arm and the gravel of the paths did not crunch beneath their feet because frost still froze it hard, and icicles hung down from the eaves as they passed by the stables where hot breath from stamping hunters could be heard as well as seen.

'You did bring your riding clothes, didn't you, dear?' Arthur asked and she nodded, looking up into his face which was pinched by the cold. She must look at him, only at him, and ignore the contrast with the poverty, the hardship which she saw each week. She was tired, too tired, and must leave it behind just for these few hours. Was that too much to ask?

His eyes were alive and eager and his lips drew back from his teeth as he moved his arm from her hand and put it around her shoulders and hugged her to him, and she liked the feel of his warmth seeping through his clothes and into her. She must forget.

They walked on past the end of the stables. Harry and Esther were ahead and waiting for them at the end of the path, standing under a clump of overhanging trees which admitted no light. The gravel changed to an old red-brick yard here and Harry was pointing to a slightly raised mound off to the left. Hannah looked at Arthur, a query in her eyes, glad to feel a question rising concerning the mound, glad that other thoughts did not intrude.

He bent to kiss her again lightly, but Hannah did not want such intimacies to be viewed and she stiffened and moved away. Arthur smiled quickly at her and nodded, following as she walked towards the other couple.

Hannah called, 'What is it, Harry? It's so dreadfully cold here, so dark. Arthur doesn't bury the victims of his crimes of passion here, does he?' And now she was really interested in what she could see, really forgetting those dark streets, and it felt good.

Arthur laughed and ran to catch up with her. 'Absolutely,' he said. 'Particularly when they thwart my kisses, spurn my heartfelt advances.' He stood with his hand on his heart and his mouth turned down.

'Well, you'd better open it up and get ready to fit another one in,' retorted Hannah, pushing him away, hearing the laughter and enjoying it.

She watched as Arthur moved to Harry. 'Remember when you came up last, old lad, that the grooms were too busy to sort out the horses so we missed our hunt?'

Harry nodded and Hannah wondered at the guarded look which came over his face.

'Well, no fears of that this time. We shall be following the fox tomorrow all right, all of us.' Arthur laughed and so did Harry but the laugh did not reach his eyes. 'It'll be your first time, Harry, so we'd better get the fox or you'll not be blooded.'

Again Hannah wondered at the set mouth of her brother, at the way he looked at the ground, then the trees. Was it fear she saw? Arthur moved nearer to the mound, looking back at Hannah and Esther.

'The reason poor Harry missed out on the hunt was because of the heavy fall of snow.' He raised his hand as Esther began to speak. 'No, dear girl, thou with the light and airy fingers which strum out tunes at ham teas. No, not because the poor little horses don't like it but because the grooms were too busy here. This wonderful creation is an ice-house.'

Hannah watched as he reached forward and broke off a hazel twig, ripping the young wood from the branch so that it left a jagged tear of white wood against the brown bark. Arthur motioned towards the slightly raised shape and she was reminded of Miss Fletcher as she pointed out some of the intricacies of algebra, which Hannah could still not abide even though she had been fully qualified for well over a year now.

'Are you listening, Hannah? Can't have inattention at the back of the class, you know.' Esther laughed and Hannah joined her. Harry was still off to one side, still looking at the trees. She walked across and tugged at his sleeve; it was damp where the drips from the overhead branches had soaked in. He turned and his face was pale, his eyes looking at some distant thought. She shook his arm.

'Teacher's begun,' she said, and drew him with her, back into the group, seeing his eyes lose their blankness as they focused on Esther. She realised again that Esther was his world and she felt inexplicable fear for him and a sense of exclusion for herself.

'Please may I have the attention of the class or there will be no dancing tonight after dinner.' Arthur put back his head and laughed as Esther grabbed Harry's arm.

'Dancing,' she whooped. 'I just love dancing. But, Arthur, how good of you. How splendid of your parents. Just for us?'

'Certainly not, my dear. We have asked just a few young

notables, those that Harry already knows, and it is all in honour of this dear boy who will soon be leaving us to cover himself in gold-dust and hang diamonds from his ears, or rather your ears, dear Esther.'

Arthur bowed towards her, his stick dug into the ground now and bending beneath his weight. His polished boots were encrusted with mud and his nose was red. 'We're having Mother's cousin to dinner beforehand, though, and her husband, the Master of the hunt.'

'Come on, Arthur,' Hannah called. 'Please can we have this lesson and then rush back for some tea or no one will be fit for dancing; we'll all be frozen to the spot and they'll have to break off our legs to move us at all.'

Arthur raised his eyebrows. 'I shall begin. You talk of being frozen, well, in this deep cavern is about four tons of ice.' Hannah moved forward, her cold hands forgotten. 'The grooms rush out along with the gardeners at the first heavy fall of snow and gather up stacks of the stuff then bring it here.' He banged with his foot on the ground. 'There is a brick-built chamber below that slightly raised roof but you can see that all of it is underground really. They trample it down until it is hard ice and then seal it. And so you shall have your champagne cooled in ice tonight as usual.'

'How long does it last?' asked Esther, and Hannah nodded.

'Surely when the summer comes it all melts,' Hannah said.

Arthur shook his head. 'You can see for yourself.' He pointed with the hazel twig to the stable walls. 'It's north-facing here and besides the trees act as a barrier to any sun.'

Harry nodded. 'He's quite right. Last summer there was still more ice than we could use. Do you remember, Arthur, we had that tennis party?'

Arthur nodded. 'But come along. I think I can hear Mother. We'll get back for tea.'

Arthur smiled and moved to take Hannah's arm, flicking at his leg with the stick as they walked back towards the gothic house through the yew hedges, leaving the stables far behind them.

The dining-room was warm and large. A fire burned in the grate, the marble surround reflecting the leaping flames, the brass fire irons alive in their glow. Hannah sat back against the embroidered satin dining-chair, her body vibrant from the afternoon air. She felt loose, relaxed, and smiled across the table at Arthur. He was talking lazily to his mother, his mouth half-smiling as it usually was, his wrists strong against the starched white cuffs of his dinner shirt, the black of his jacket smooth and well fitting. She knew he had seen her because his fingers waved discreetly in her direction and he nodded slightly. Lady Wilmot's cousin sat at his right hand but talked to Harry who was further down the table. Esther was next to Lord Wilmot and leant forward now to smile at Hannah.

Earlier the dressing gong had sounded while they were playing cards on mahogany loo tables in the library. Arthur had held the door for the two girls and asked Harry to pour another sherry for the two men because the dinner bell would be another hour yet and he for one did not need that long for a bath and a change of clothes. Hannah had pulled a face at him and his laugh had followed her up the wide stairs past dark oil paintings of earlier Wilmots.

Esther had her own room near Harry and had emerged at the sound of the dinner gong in a pearl-coloured dress which Hannah had not seen before. She looked quite beautiful. Hannah looked down at her own dress, pale cerise but not as low at the neck as Esther's. The table was lit by candles held by elaborate silver candelabras with discreet silk shades, though electric lights hung from the ceilings nearer the walls and illuminated more paintings, but this time they were landscapes and still life. A silver epergne held an exotic flower arrangement of orchids and ivy which trailed across the mahogany table. Hannah wanted to reach across and run her fingers over its variegated surface. It almost reached her fan, which rested on the table – mother-of-pearl and lace. Her ivory one was locked away, together with the jewellery box. Esther had wanted to borrow it to use with her pearl dress but Hannah did not want hands other than hers or Joe's to touch it though she had not said this to her cousin.

The damask napkins placed in front of each guest were folded into the shape of a mitre though Lord and Lady Wilmot's were in the shape of a fan. Hannah could see the table and guests reflected in the mirrors either side of the fireplace, which in turn picked up the reflection caught in the pier glasses between the windows, and no, she would not compare this with the rooms in which her Sunday ladies lived, not this evening, not this weekend.

The conversation was desultory; Hannah turned to one side to listen to Sir Edward Frank who lived a bare mile from Arthur.

'Should be a good day for the hunt,' he said and Hannah nodded. 'Your first time, is it?' he continued.

Hannah laughed slightly. 'Very much so, I'm afraid. My riding has been limited to Hyde Park.'

He leant forward and his breath smelled of sherry. 'Sunday morning canter, is it?'

Hannah hesitated. 'Sometimes,' she replied eventually, looking across the table at Harry, who was watching her closely. But now the servants brought in turtle soup from behind the large screen which shielded the doors leading to their entrance and the first of the five wine glasses were filled.

Dover sole followed the soup and a fine cool white wine and Arthur leant forward. 'It's been stacked in ice all day.'

Hannah nodded and smiled. The heavy smell of the candles lay over the table and the Dover sole was good and the conversation which ebbed and flowed was calm and easy.

It was good to be able to put a full stop to effort and thought, to pause a moment and regain some energy, some ideas, she thought. Everyone should have the chance – including her ladies. And so here they were again. Cutlets of lamb were served and their smell overrode the candles which flickered and rolled their heat over the guests so that the men grew hot, but the women, with their bare shoulders, were comfortable. Yes, her ladies should have the chance of a moment's peace, the chance to feel their bodies loose and relaxed as hers now was. But how could they?

Yes, how could they, Hannah thought, lifting her cool glass

and pressing it to her lips, not drinking yet but thinking. If she needed a holiday, how much more did the women who ate the buns that she and Miss Fletcher cooked; and so too their children and their men.

But now Lady Wilmot was speaking to her and Arthur was smiling as his mother talked, leaning back in his chair and drinking his wine, as Hannah pulled herself back into the room and replied.

'Yes, it really was a beautiful part of the country, though I found it a little cold around the ice store.'

She heard his laugh and looked at him, beginning to laugh too and his mother did also. Her limbs felt looser still.

She nodded as Lady Wilmot spoke again; her voice was kind, her eyes soft. She looked at the candles, at their flickering flames and then back to the flowers, the paintings, the people, and knew the value of letting go, even if it were only for two days.

And so the lamb gave way to Apple Charlotte and slowly she heard the fire crackling again and caught the smell of the candles, heard Harry laughing and Sir Edward wondering if there would be snow tomorrow and she hoped there would. Fresh and white and clean for miles and miles and she looked at Arthur again and he smiled.

'Russian caviare, my dear,' said Lady Wilmot.

The shape was sharp and strong. The grapes which were served afterwards were firm and fresh and the colour of the leaves which were budding on the pear tree. Was Mother all right, was the thought that snatched at her again.

'They're from the vine which we saw in the conservatory,' Arthur told her, his smile back, his eyes unclouded, and she turned from the swaying pear tree back to this flickering room. 'The head gardener cuts them on a long stem and leaves them for as long as needed in water and charcoal.'

He plucked one from the stem which lay on his plate. His fingers were strong and wet with juice. He sucked it and his lips were full and would taste of grapes if he kissed her now.

And then Hannah heard Esther. 'You should ask Hannah to tell you what good works she does on her Sundays.'

Hannah looked round sharply, seeing Harry turn also. Lord Wilmot was sitting back in his seat holding his claret between him and the candelabra, narrowing his eyes as he swirled the glass to catch the light. Esther was tapping his arm with her fan.

'Now, that is something I thoroughly approve of,' said Lord Wilmot, his voice emphatic, his speech slightly slurred with too much wine. 'Women going about doing their charitable duty. That's the way it's always been, that's the way it should be. A bit of charity to the deserving poor.' He stabbed his finger down the table towards Hannah. 'The deserving poor, mind you.'

Hannah smiled and nodded at him, and then at Esther. Why do you do it, Esther, Hannah wanted to ask. Leave things alone. And what do you mean by the deserving poor, she wanted to shout at the fat Lord who was busy feeding his two chins. She looked across at Harry, her anger showing until he met her gaze with a question in his eyes, and she dropped hers again.

Lord Wilmot was louder now and his wife said. 'Not now, dear.'

But he continued. 'That's the way things should be. All this change is a downright crime. Now that those damnable Liberals have had that election landslide they think they can bring in a clutch of do-gooding reforms when good little women like Hannah have been looking after things quite nicely enough for all these years. You'd think the King would put his foot down but he's too busy enjoying himself these days.'

Hannah continued to look at her plate because she knew that Harry was looking at her, willing her to meet his eyes.

'Have another glass of wine, Sir Edward,' Arthur offered, gesticulating to the butler. 'Father, would you care for one too?' He looked across at Hannah and raised his eyebrows and she shook her head. She doubted that he could distract his father.

Sir Edward spoke now. 'Just one more glass please, my boy.' Then he turned to Lord Wilmot. 'You're quite right of course, David, old boy. It is just damned nonsense to give out old age pensions and bring in National Insurance when what we need are more Dreadnoughts. It's no good launching just one, they need a fleet to compete with the one the Kaiser's building up.' He was leaning forward and Hannah could not see past him.

'Quite right,' she heard Lord Wilmot call down the table. 'Specially after that charade in Morocco when the popinjay Kaiser went parading for all the world as though he thought to challenge the French and our alliance. Damnation, that Lloyd George is a menace. Doesn't he realise we've got to show that we're up to any nonsense the Germans might care to throw our way. Anyway, the workhouse has always been quite adequate up to now.'

And Hannah sat quite still, seeing Joe at the reins of the cart, seeing Bernie at the door of his cottage, feeling the wind and the spongy moor; seeing the Sunday women who were so tired and ill and who might also go to the workhouse. But no, and she wrapped the napkin round her fingers so that it was too tight and her bones were pushed one against the other. No, she must stay calm, she must not give herself away. She kept the napkin pulled tight.

'The workhouse is not ideal,' she heard herself say, but quietly, and only Sir Edward heard and turned to her.

'But, my dear, not for you or I of course, but the poor are different. They don't feel things the way we do.' His smile was kind and his breath heavy with wine now and she wanted to lift him and drag him down to the matchmaker's room and make him see, for isn't that what Joe had done with her? But no, she must not think of him now; he was gone.

Arthur was looking at her, his eyebrows raised and a quizzical smile twisting his face. Harry had heard the conversation too but merely looked at her, his face expressionless. She turned back to Lord Wilmot who was talking, his voice loud.

'Well, if Lloyd George thinks the House of Lords is going to approve any budget which wants to tax the landowners in order to pay for his bits of nonsense, he's got another think coming. Good God, the world's going quite mad.'

The servants were removing the wine now and Lady Wilmot

was waiting to withdraw the ladies. Conversation had begun again around the loud voice of the host but again he broke in.

'And as for these Pankhurst women and the trouble they cause; it's an absolute disgrace.' He pointed his finger at Hannah again and she felt herself stiffen. 'We need more like you. Good sense of duty.'

Hannah saw Esther begin to smile and now she allowed the anger to rise in her at the opulence of this house, the ignorance of its people, at the endless handbills, the tame constitutional lobbying of the suffragists, at the government imprisoning the suffragettes on grounds of assault when they stamped on policemen's feet. Words hot and angry began to form in her mind and she wound the napkin round, tighter still. She looked up and saw Harry watching her again and as her rage seemed to leap across the space between them she saw him shake his head at her sharply and begin to speak.

Did he know what she had wanted to say? How could he know after all these years of not seeing her, not hearing her? She held the napkin tighter still but listened as he said, 'This will all seem very far away next month when I'm on the ship.' He looked back at her again. 'But there should be quite a few Cornish hard-rock miners to keep me company once I arrive.'

Hannah looked from him to Lord Wilmot, who looked confused at the turn of the conversation though Lady Wilmot took it up immediately.

'A good life-style, too, I should think.'

'Yes, indeed. All those blacks to wait on you,' Harry said, looking at Hannah. Thinking that now she could vent her anger on something that was further away from home because he was beginning to realise that the private Hannah was no different at all from the Hannah he had grown up with, and that indeed she had a secret, and one that he thought he knew.

'They're slaves,' Hannah retorted, leaping at the chance to voice an anger which was truly meant but which would not endanger her work or her hopes. 'That war was fought to give taxpaying foreigners the same rights as the Boers – but what about the natives?'

She was keeping her voice flat, her body still, but her eyes looked directly into Harry's now and he saw the anger, the fire, and he was glad.

Sir Edward shook his head, his voice kind. 'Now then, my dear, how can you have rights for people who are basically unequal? That would be mere sentimentality.'

Arthur was leaning back in his chair, his eyes lazily watching her.

'But why are they unequal? It is their land.' Hannah still kept her voice quiet and flat.

Lord Wilmot interjected now. 'Because we beat them. It's as simple as that. Think of that Darwin you young people are so fond of quoting. It's the survival of the fittest, isn't it? They weren't fit to win, therefore they deserve nothing better.'

Harry lifted his glass and drained it. He glanced at Hannah and smiled, and she knew, as the conversation started around her, that her brother had understood as he had once done and had arranged an opportunity for her to release some of her rage without doing damage to her cause, and for a moment the blank space in her was filled.

The guests arrived for the dance at eleven o'clock. Musicians had not been hired because Arthur wanted to use his new gramophone. He pulled Hannah over to the table which held the wooden box with its convolvulus horn of blue and gold. He turned the handle until he could turn it no more and Hannah watched his face as he pressed his lips together, watching his shoulders as they moved beneath his jacket. He turned the handle until there was a click and then a sound like something breathing; the black circle revolved and Arthur's steady hand placed the needle on the edge of the disc. As the music rose he took her hand and they drew together.

His arm was round her now and his breath was in her hair and on her neck and as they danced and whirled around his leg touched hers and her body sometimes swung against him.

'I'm sorry about my father,' he said. 'He is so old-fashioned and behind the times.'

She was glad he was there, for she needed someone to hold her and laugh with her and so they danced until their feet were sore and champagne was brought in silver ice-buckets. At one in the morning his parents retired, together with Sir Edward Franks and his wife. Then they danced again and this time Arthur held her tightly and as they neared the curtains which shielded the conservatory he bent and kissed her neck.

He danced her close to the curtain and then through into the dark of the cold glass room with its hanging ivy, its jasmine, which was in bud in this cold spring, and they no longer danced but kissed and the taste of grapes was no longer there.

She held his head between her hands, seeing the oat-coloured hair against her skin, the width of his shoulder, sensing the power in his back, his arms, his legs.

She felt his breath as he talked. 'I need you and love you, Hannah. You are good for me. You don't ask too much of me. We are well suited, my dear, both strong, both independent, both undemanding, and my parents do so approve of you. One day we should marry but, as you know, I cannot until I am thirty. Let's have fun while we wait.' His mouth was on her eyes, her cheeks, his lips soft, his hands holding her arms. Hannah looked out at the dark night which was dimly lit by the cold distant moon and nodded calmly. She had known somehow that this would happen and it would be good to have Arthur's easy, laughing company while she waited. And waited. And waited.

The horses had collected at the front of the house, stamping and tossing their heads, responding slowly to their red- and black-coated riders. The morning was crisp and there had been a light fall of snow in the night. Hannah sat side-saddle on her roan mare, black-coated, breathing deeply, glad to be away from the dining-room which had smelt of port and cigars from the night before. Arthur brought his hunter up close. It was arching its neck and she could hear the clink of the bit as the horse chewed and worried it.

'You'll be fine on that mare,' Arthur said, leaning down to take a glass of hot punch from the silver tray that one of the maids was bringing to each rider. His red coat made his hair seem paler.

'I hope so,' replied Hannah, taking the warm glass from

182

him, smelling the nutmeg, seeing condensation on the leather of her gloved finger.

'There are about twenty of the hunt here now. Sir Edward will be sounding the horn in a moment, so drink up. Just follow, come at your own pace.' Arthur turned and looked over the snow-covered grounds and then the distant hills. 'You won't lose us, all this red against all that white.' He laughed and pointed with his riding crop, silver-headed and stamped with the family crest.

Red against white, Hannah thought, turning her thoughts aside from the words, pushing back the flight of the fox and the hounds that were baying. Thinking instead of the red of lobster against white meat, the red of a cricket ball against Arthur's hand, the red of Joe's blood against his skin. She shook her head. No, not that.

The maid stood by her horse, her hand lifted to take the glass and Hannah drank it in two gulps, feeling the sharp heat.

'Thank you,' she said, smiling as she bent down.

Arthur was talking to Esther who was reining in to his other side, her riding crop held firmly in her gloved hand, her hair netted and glistening under the black top hat. She laughed at his words, craning forward to tell Hannah.

'He says the language should be better now that we're along. Such a shame, darling, we could have learnt a few words to scream at Miss Fletcher's children.'

Hannah laughed and Arthur put his hand on hers. 'Don't take the fences if you don't feel confident. Go round by the gates. I'd rather see that than see you hurt, my dear.'

Sir Edward was moving towards the front of the riders and the horn began to blow and the hounds to bay and they were off, trotting first, the snow deadening the sound of moving horses as they left the house and followed the drive down through to the open ground. There were riders each side of her. Arthur tipped his crop against his hat and moved forward at Sir Edward's request. Esther rode well, sitting comfortably, her face alight with excitement. She turned to Hannah.

'This is so wonderful. To be this rich, to live this life.'

Hannah nodded. 'Yes, it must be very easy.' She kept her

voice low and wished that Esther would also, because Harry was behind them and he was not rich, he could not offer Esther this life, and Hannah feared for him; but now the horses were into open country and the trot became a canter, the canter a gallop. The field stretched out and Hannah loosened the reins and let the mare have her head, feeling the wind as it rushed past, seeing the snow in drifts against the dry-stone wall, loving the speed, the freedom. Harry kept to the back of the field, holding in his hunter, not letting it get the bit between its teeth. He watched Esther as she lifted her head into the wind, following with his eyes and his heart as she took the low wall, leaning forward, urging her horse on.

He had heard her words but knew already that he could only hold her if he could offer her something like this. He looked back at the house as he cantered past the small copse which Sir Edward had first thought the fox would head towards but the hounds had swept past and were baying in the distance.

Gold had brought wealth to many, he knew that but those days were over now. The big conglomerates had created a monopoly on the gold fields but they paid well, well enough to stake a try at a diamond strike and that is what he was pinning his hopes on. The wall was close now and he dug in his heels, feeling the power of the horse as she took the jump almost in her stride. The snow was crisp and cold still, not slippery, not dangerous.

He had not told Esther that there was no hope of wealth for some while. He could not do that, she would not understand. He veered right as the hunt took a different line, heading towards the row of elms which fringed the lake where he had fished with Arthur each summer. His breath was coming quickly now as the horse cantered and pounded the ground.

But whatever happened he must make sure that he did find diamonds or there would be no future for him because life without his love was no life at all. But would she wait? Could she wait? He must make sure that she did and he looked ahead, searching for Hannah's black coat. Would Hannah help? Did she care enough about him any more? And deep within him guilt stirred at the thought of the girl in the white dress with the blue sash. Perhaps there were too many cold years between then and now; and as he rode his hunter forward he realised that he had missed his sister.

Hannah heard Harry call to her and she turned, ready to rein in, but Arthur's voice carried over her head to her brother.

'Come up, Harry, come up.'

And she saw Harry pull to the left, away from her, his face shadowed and grim. He did not look at her as he drew level and she called to him.

'Harry, shall I come up with you?'

He rode on past without looking or speaking and Hannah wondered if she had imagined his call because she wanted to hear it too much.

The hunt took two hours to close on the fox. Hannah was flushed with effort and tiredness. Her arms ached from guiding the mare onwards and over walls and gates. The sky had cleared of heavy clouds but it was still white, not blue, and the air was cold. Esther was up at the front, her black coat clearly visible as they thundered down the slope which led to a thin copse standing stark and almost black in the white air, its branches thin and hopeless without their cloak of green. Into the trees they went, and the mare cantered gently now, not fast because Hannah did not want to see the fox or hear the hounds, down the slope and then in amongst the trees which were beech, smooth and straight and not black at all but brown smudged with green moss.

There was little snow here and it was dark. She trotted the mare along stony root-bound ground. There were no birds singing here, only the baying of the hounds which was louder now and faster and higher. Hannah walked the mare, looking up into the trees and through the branches to the pale sky. The mare's breath came in quick clouds; she slipped on a root, her hoofs clinking on smooth stones and Hannah talked gently to her. Then they were out into the fields again and the light was harsh and the sounds too.

The hunt was there in front of her, gathered together, not cantering now or even walking but standing still and at the front the black jacket of Esther stood out loud against the red.

Sir Edward and Arthur were not on their horses, and neither was Harry. He stood at the side of the two men, his horse's reins lying idle in his hands. Hannah saw this and beyond them the hounds which ravaged and tore and screamed over the run-out fox, and there was red against the white snow and horror grew as she had known it would. She turned from this to Esther but she was smiling and her eyes were alight and eager as she watched and listened and now Hannah turned to Arthur and his face was the same and so was Sir Edward's as he laughed and waded into the hounds, calling them off, then bending over.

She looked at Harry and his face was not the same. It was set and enclosed, not looking at the squealing mass but above them to the hawk that circled in the air away in the distance and Hannah dismounted from the mare and moved first one step and then another in snow that was white on her black boots and along the hem of her black skirt. But before she reached him Sir Edward turned from the mêlée his knife red in his hand. There was something else in the other. Another step and another and as Harry stood still she saw Arthur take the fox's tail from Sir Edward's outstretched hand and step close to Harry and rub each cheek with the dripping fur and again there was red against white, and laughter and applause as he pushed the tail into Harry's hand before slapping his shoulder and turning back to Sir Edward.

Hannah was there now and she took the fox's tail from Harry's lifeless fingers and dropped it, not watching to see where it landed, and then tore off her blood-stained glove and bent to dig her hand into the snow, and wipe the blood from his face. But she could not wipe the look from his eyes and so she scrubbed harder as she heard Arthur's laugh. And harder still and now the blood was off and the snow dripped pink on to the ground. But still there was that look in Harry's eyes.

She dried his face with her lawn handkerchief, knowing that laughter and talking were all around and horses were being turned and hounds called to order and still there was no change in his eyes. She lifted Harry's hand, kissed it and held it to her cheek, taking his reins from the other hand, and slowly he lost the horror, the pain, and as Arthur came and threw the tail to the hounds and slapped him on the back Harry smiled at him and laughed as Esther laughed and nodded as she called, 'Blooded now, my darling. It's such fun, isn't it?'

Hannah rode back with Harry and they watched but did not see Esther and Arthur canter ahead; they watched but did not see the hounds brought to order and set off in a pack for home. They rode alone and Harry could still feel her hand on his face and the tears which had not fallen but which had filled her eyes. He could still feel the grip of her hand as she held his and the warmth of her lips, and he knew that he had missed her strength over these long years and that deep love was still there despite everything. And now tears were in his eyes and they fell, running into his mouth and her hand came again, as he knew it would, and this time it was he who held it to his lips and kissed it, feeling its cold, dragging off his glove and putting it on her hand. And now, as the day closed in and the sky darkened with perhaps more snow, they talked and Harry told her of his horror of cruelty. Was it cowardice, he asked, and she said it was not. Of his fear that Esther could not wait and of his need of her, and Hannah said she would help. Of his fear that in South Africa he would fail, and Hannah said he would not. And he told her of her picture and his beating and this time she cried and tears ran into her mouth at all the wasted years.

And now she told him of her fear of her father, her hatred, and he could only nod. And she told him of her fear for her mother and again he could only nod. She told him of her women and he said that he thought he had always known and was glad. She told him that when the waiting was over she was going to join the suffragettes and he was not surprised. And then she told him of Joe and he took her hand and said that she had her brother now, to fill the empty space.

They passed the line of elms and snow was falling lightly and they talked of many things, and as they reached the drive which led up to the house Hannah spoke again of her women and how they also needed holidays and how could she arrange it?

11 Hannah looked down on the garden from her mother's bedroom. The late spring had given way to a hot summer and the yellowed grass made the earlier snow at Arthur's seem impossible.

'Such a fine crop of pears, Hannah, my dear.' Her mother's voice was even slower today, and quiet again.

Hannah leant against the window-frame and nodded. Pears were clumped against leaves which had curled in the heat and shone pale from this distance. There were already windfalls on the grass. Hannah had seen the bees nuzzling into the soft moist fruit, heads deep into darkening holes. Bees had been all around the lavender too as she picked small bunches to put into the three vases in her mother's room.

There had been a few late roses on the bushes planted behind the neat box hedges, some with flowers tightly formed and freshly coloured and these were now in the crystal vase by the bedside. Hannah turned to her mother who sat quite still in the padded wicker chair, her head leaning back but her eyes open and looking beyond the room to the sun.

'Would you like to go back to bed now, Mother?'

Her mother smiled but did not turn her head, did not move her eyes from the blue sky and the green.

'No, my darling. There is time enough for that.'

Hannah turned again, not to the window but into the room, seeing the oak blanket chest at the foot of the bed as it had always been; the small easy chair which had been moved whenever a cradle appeared; the pictures of Cornwall which hung on stiff wire from picture rails, two on each wall except where the wardrobe stood, heavy and unyielding. Only one picture had been hung there and that was to the left of the fireplace. The scuttle was full, with coal heaped high. The fire irons stood erect in their stand.

Hannah walked past the bed to the dressing-table which

held the silver candlestick and lavender in a vase. She cupped her hand around a stem and bent her head, breathing in the heavy scent, and then rubbed a few dark blue flowers between her fingers, releasing the oil, holding her hand to her face and breathing in again. Her mother was dying. She knew that now. She had known it the day she returned from the hunting weekend and had seen her with fresh eyes. How could she have not known, she had asked Aunt Eliza, who held her hand and said that perhaps she was too close to see. Eliza had gone home now, just for a few days she had said, to arrange a few things, and Hannah was glad she'd gone because now she was alone with her mother and they could talk or not talk, touch or not touch and always be as one.

She looked at her mother's pin-boxes; the china ring-stand with her betrothal ring still on the same stem; her hat-pins which caught the light from the candle when it was lit; the pin cushions which were stabbed by bead-topped pins. It was the same today as it had been yesterday, and last year and all the years preceding. She looked into the mirror at the lines which ran down to her mouth, the circles beneath her eyes. Her eyes were not the same; they recognised that it was almost over and she turned because she could not think of that. For a moment she could not see her mother or the light which flooded into the room, or smell the late summer wind which wafted in through the open window, nor the lavender which was on the hand that she pressed against her mouth and then her eyes because there was no time for the wracking sounds of grief which pushed and tore and howled within her. There was no time now, each second was too precious. Hannah turned back to the mirror smoothing her hands down her dress, picking off pampas-grass from the drawing-room, pushing back the pain until it no longer showed and then she walked to her mother, kneeling on the faded carpet by her chair, resting her head on the pale hand which in turn lay on the arm of the wicker chair and there they sat and watched the shadows lengthen as the high sun passed over into late afternoon.

Edith Watson could feel the breeze gentle on her face, her hands, her hair, could feel it as it wafted against the cotton of her nightgown which was loosely tied at the neck and unstarched on Hannah's orders.

She smiled but her lips did not move. How Mrs Brennan had scowled at that but her Hannah did not mind. She was strong and bold and so good, so very good. Edith turned her head from the tree whose leaves were flickering as the evening brought a stronger breeze and looked at the chestnut hair of her daughter. How she loved her. Did she know how much she loved her? 'I love you, my darling child.' And she knew that her lips moved and that sound came but had it been enough? Her free hand was heavy, so very heavy. She moved it from the blanket which covered her knees and laid it against the soft warmth of Hannah's hair and she felt her daughter's hand cover hers, heard words which told of love. She turned again to the window and far away, far far away she saw two children running, running and coming closer, on through the long grass down to the wide, spreading horse-chestnut tree. She saw them laugh, watched as they swung first one and then the other round and round and round on the long thick rope. But she could not hear them though they were calling to her. She could see that they were calling and she wanted to hear; wanted so much to hear. She leant forward because there was strength in her now. 'Mother,' Hannah said. 'Lie still.'

The children faded and there was only the pear tree again and the horse-chestnut and an empty garden and then Edith felt Hannah's hands smoothing back her hair, heard her voice gently soothing and now there were sounds of carriages on the cobbles and the cries of hawkers and tradesmen, and birds as they called and collected in the branches, and her body was heavy again.

'Tell me how your holiday home is progressing, Hannah,' she whispered and listened as Hannah held her hand and told her of the concert they had planned for next Saturday, with Esther playing, of course.

'And you, Mother, in the place of honour.'

They both laughed gently together and Edith knew that Eliza would be back by then, her arrangements completed, and Harry would be there too, his departure delayed because of her illness. But Arthur was in Scotland shooting.

190

Arthur seemed a nice boy, she thought as though from a distance, and Hannah was easy with him and that gave her pleasure. It gave her father pleasure too and Edith ceased to smile for the thought of him was cold and brought her fear. But he would not come tonight. It would be just the two of them tonight and now the smile was here again.

The street noises became quieter as the shadows grew even longer and now the sun was low and the leaves of the pear tree were darker. The birds were quieter and Hannah's hand was warm on hers again and her head was on her lap and it was as it had been for these last few evenings. Edith moved her fingers slightly and felt her daughter's hair, soft and fine as it fell free of pins, brown against the faint pink of the blanket.

She looked at Hannah's profile, the wide mouth, the high cheekbones, the tiredness etched deep. Soon, very soon, Hannah's waiting would be over and Edith was satisfied that it should be so. There was so much that her daughter wanted to do, so much that she had held her back from doing, but soon, my darling, I will set you free. She felt no pain at the thought of her death, just a satisfaction that she and her daughter had found such love. She thought of Eliza and the sea which buffeted the cliffs and the moors and the cry of the gulls. She thought of Simon in that hot, parched land. She looked at the shadowed garden – the wind was brushing at the tops of the trees, rustling the leaves – and she longed to see the two children again, their strength, their joy and down through the fernery they came. Those two children running, running through the grass, swinging on the rope, round and round and round and the sun was high again and warm and now she could hear them; so clearly, so very clearly. Mama, Mama, they were calling. Come and see us, Mama; and the girl turned and her hair, her chestnut hair, trailed out behind her and her dress was white with a blue sash.

'Mama, Mama, come and play with us,' she called and held her hand towards the house. And Edith felt so strong again, so young and she stretched out her hand towards the child her daughter had once been.

'I'm coming, my darling,' she called. 'There will be no more waiting now.'

*

Hannah would not allow the curtains to be drawn across her mother's window. There was black on the door-knocker, black on the mirrors, black dresses, black crêpe on her father's hat. There had been black horses with black ostrich plumes, drawing black carriages, black veils over faces, black gloves on hands, black-edged handkerchiefs to eyes. Her mother had been light and full of love in this darkest of houses and no, she would not have the curtains shrouding the room as they shrouded every other room.

'Leave those curtains alone,' she repeated again as Mrs Brennan put her hand towards the drapes.

'You, Miss Hannah, will have to deal with your father if you insist with this impropriety.' She was dressed heavily in black and crossed her arms now, standing between Hannah and the light. Hannah sat in her mother's wicker chair.

'Move from the window, Mrs Brennan.' Her voice was measured. 'Move from the window, I can't see the tree.'

She watched as the woman turned to the garden and then back to Hannah again.

'These curtains should be drawn. You know that is the case. I would have taken it up with your father but he, poor man, has been prostrate with grief.'

'These curtains will not be drawn and the window will not be closed. Mother did not like the sun to be shut out. Now leave me alone.'

She sat quite still seeing the brightness at the side of the bulk which stood between her and the garden. Prostrate with grief, was he? Yes, he had looked the part, hadn't he, especially when the will had been read and her mother had left to her daughter a Cornish house, Penbrin, which Eliza had bought on her behalf, and enough money from the interest on her share of the Penhallon mine to run it as the holiday home she had longed for. To her son she had left the homestead that Uncle Simon had bought in the Transvaal before he died and which had come through to his sister on his death. Yes, her father had been suitably grief-stricken, hadn't he? Mrs Brennan still stood between her and the light, the curtain in her hand.

'Leave that curtain alone, Mrs Brennan. Miss Hannah does not want the curtains drawn, or did you not hear correctly?' Harry's voice was clear and calm and very cold and Hannah wondered how long he had been standing there.

Hannah watched Mrs Brennan's hand drop and her face stiffen.

'Very well, Master Harry,' she said and walked with careful strides from the room.

'It still takes a man to issue orders, doesn't it?' she murmured as Harry came over to stand beside her, his hand on her shoulder. She liked its weight and warmth and was glad he was still there.

'If you and Miss Fletcher have anything to do with it, that will soon change,' he said, pressing down with his hand, feeling the thinness which had come within the space of a few days.

'I'm lost without Mother, Harry. I love her so and she has been my whole life, day and night for so long now.' Hannah kept her voice calm. She must be calm because once she cried she feared she would never stop.

Harry stroked her cheek and they stayed together, looking out into the garden until they heard the sound of the luncheon gong.

'Come along now. Father is expected for luncheon. We should be there. It's my last time, you know.'

Hannah did know but she did not want to think of that and so she let the knowledge merge with the sun and the green leaves and the pain of it all.

She rose and walked past the bed with its fine lawn bedspread and the sheets which were freshly starched because Hannah had not ordered otherwise. But why should she? Her mother was dead so there was no need of softness. The banister was smooth and cool and the hall was dark with only the red-stained light penetrating, falling on the carpet and the silver tray which held black-edged cards. She would not look at those.

He was waiting for them, sitting at the head of the table and the gas lamps were on, hissing quietly, lighting the darkness which cloaked them as they sat behind drawn curtains.

Hannah sat opposite her brother not looking at the table but down at the table-mat, the silver knife and fork, the spoon and fork, the crystal glass, and then the tantalus on the sideboard, the stag at bay looming over them, hanging large on the wall. Then she looked at Harry and he smiled and his foot beneath the table touched hers and she knew that she could not bear the space which he had partly filled being sucked empty again as it would be when he left. How strange, she thought, to think that he only partly filled it when once it had been his entirely. How very strange. But she was too tired to think any more. She barely heard the sounds of her father intoning the grace, just saw his face, heavy-browed, thick-lipped, his moustache as neat as ever. She would not look at him but at Polly as she brought the cold meats thinly sliced.

'So, tomorrow the big adventure starts, my boy,' her father said, his knife cutting already thin cucumber, his big hands lifting it to his mouth. He did not look at Hannah. He had not looked at her since the will was read.

She listened as Harry talked, telling of the voyage, the introductions, the job which was waiting at one of the biggest gold-mines. She watched as her father nodded and smiled. She smelt the ham – 'honey-roasted' – but could not eat.

She moved as Polly took her plate and brought fruit to them all, and she watched her father as he cut away the peel of the apple, his big hands engulfing the knife and the fruit, cutting deep, taking more than just the skin in great slashing slices.

'And so it will be just you and me, my dear,' he said and Hannah did not look at him but only at the gouged apple and the peel which lay savaged on his plate. 'I feel that you will perform satisfactorily in your mother's place.'

The white of the apple was darkening now. 'And as for this nonsense of a holiday home. Well, we can put that down to the meanderings of a feeble mind. I shall instruct our solicitor, on your behalf, to sell it. It is time now that we moved out into the suburbs. Uncle Thomas is thinking of doing so and so we shall use that money more fruitfully, I think.'

The peel was brown now. Hannah remembered how Mrs Arness had dipped the peel of a cooking apple into sugar and how she and Joe had bitten one small piece at a time, hunched over the kitchen table, their faces screwing up at the tartness and then relaxing as the sweetness came through.

She felt Harry's foot on hers and he smiled and she felt tired, so tired, and she watched as he rose and nodded to her. Her apple was still green and whole on her white plate.

She looked at her father, at the smoke which was streaming from between the gaps in his teeth, at his eyes which were without light beneath his brows. They looked into hers now and were cold and hard and full of hate and so she rose and walked with Harry from the room because the meal was finished and she had not noticed its passing.

He took her across the terrace, holding her arm. It would be summer in South Africa by the time he reached the Cape and he hoped that he would have time to see his uncle's house. Eliza had told him that the homestead was barren but that Simon had loved it; the views across the plains, the isolation, and it was good to think that there was something of his own in this new land he was going to.

They moved down the steps and on to the yellow grass and he crouched and rubbed the dry soil pulling Hannah to a halt as he did so.

'It will be dusty like this only more so,' he said, shielding his face from the sun as he looked up at her, and she nodded.

'Simon told Eliza that the soil was red,' she said but her voice was flat and without interest and Harry watched as she walked from him towards the shade of the pear tree.

He rubbed his fingers in the earth again. It was hard to imagine red soil in place of this pale brown dust. He rose and brushed his hands together then followed Hannah.

It was cooler in the shade and the smell of overripe pears was pleasant.

'Will you stay with Father?' he asked, watching as Hannah picked at the bark.

'No, I shall leave tomorrow when you do.' She was still picking at the bark, trying to prise a piece away from the trunk, not looking at him.

Harry had known that she would. 'Where will you go?'

'To Miss Fletcher's.' She was still not looking at him but digging and pulling and scratching at the bark, her eyes seeing nothing else, her breath hard and fast and loud enough for him to hear. Her fingers were red now, red and bleeding, and Harry took her wrists and pulled at her hands but she fought him, straining towards the tree, her nails torn.

'No, Hannah, leave it.' He did not shout but pulled her to him holding her hands in one of his; forcing them into stillness.

'Mother liked the bark. The layers, you know.' And he heard her voice and it was as though it came from a great distance.

'She's dead, Hannah.'

'And you are leaving me too.' Now her voice was loud and she tore from his hands, and beat her fists against the trunk. 'You are leaving me too.'

And he took her again, and again she pulled from him. 'Don't go, please don't go because the empty space is coming again.'

He held her, saying, 'I can't stay. I have to go.'

He could hear the breeze now in the tree and he spoke into her hair which was tearing loose and falling on her face and he held her tighter, rocking her, hearing her words, her grief, looking out on the garden. It was so neat with its hedges, its roses, the neat alyssum and asters and there, across the lawn, were the hutches and the horse-chestnut and the rope.

So he took her now, pulling her over the close-cut grass, talking of how they had fed and nursed their pets, how they had played and thrown the balls, how they had run and run until they fell, how they had swung until the air rushed through their bodies, and as he spoke he knew it was to remind himself also because it would be years before he came this way again.

At length they sat beneath the horse-chestnut, cool in its shade, the rope knotted and dangling, frayed and old, and Hannah said that she would not let her father have her house or her money and Harry nodded. She said that when she left she would not tell her father, but just go, leaving a note with Mrs Brennan, and Harry thought it best. She said that there was much to do. She was free now to fight as other women were but there was the home too. There was work to be done at school and on Sundays. She talked on, sometimes with strength, sometimes with tiredness but Harry was pleased because now she was thinking of the future and he knew that she would survive, as she had always done.

They sat back, their heads against the tree, looking up through the branches, seeing the green, spiked cases which they had once dislodged with sticks and Hannah breathed in the scent of the summer. It was the first time that she had done so since her mother died.

Harry stood, brushing his trousers, the dust pale against the black of the cloth. She watched him as he took the rope and sawed at a strand with his pocket-knife, tucking it into his inside pocket.

'I need a reminder of all this,' he said, waving his hand down the rough garden, and she nodded but knew that she had no need of such things because all this would never leave her; and with this thought came the realisation that she was strong and she was free and her life was just beginning. But there was one more thing she had to do before her work could begin. It was something she should have done five years ago and she hoped it was not too late.

Her father found her note when he returned from taking Harry to the station. It was propped up on the drawing-room mantelshelf against the filigree miniature of his father. The white envelope stood out sharply against the black crêpe which draped the mirror. It was dark in the room and he carried the letter across to the french window, pulling a curtain to one side, brushing against the pampas-grass and picking it off as he opened the sheet of writing paper. The light was too bright and he turned to one side, wondering who had written a letter without using mourning paper, and then he read:

Dear Father,
With mother's untimely death I feel that there is no longer a reason for me to stay beneath your roof. Mrs Brennan is conversant with your needs and I have instructed her to continue until you instruct otherwise.

There is much that I need to do with my life and I cannot proceed as I would wish unless I have complete independence. I already have financial freedom owing to my teacher's salary and I have instructed your solicitor to hand over the deeds of the house and details of my financial bequest to Messrs Pain and Garrot who will in future act for me.

I will be resident with Miss Fletcher and will not be coerced into returning. I wish you a measure of peace, Father.

Your daughter,
Hannah.

John Watson stood at the window, hearing the clock, the birds in the garden, and then he turned, looking from the black-draped mirror to the tables scattered around the room, the velvet snake, the ornaments, the Indian carpet, the chairs with their white antimacassar that she, his daughter, had worked for him. He walked slowly across to the fireplace and took her letter and burnt it, holding the corner until all the rest was blackened, and then he let it fall into the hearth. He could feel the rage now, filling him, making him want to scream out that name. His breath was fast as he turned and strode to each chair, taking and tearing each antimacassar until all that was left were shreds, stark against the carpet.

Now he moved slowly towards the stairs, each step deliberate and in time with words which rolled round his head as he cursed his daughter and all those like her. Up he went, past the room where his wife had died, past his own bedroom and then on past Harry's room and up until he was there, and now he opened her door.

There was nothing left of her here; her books were gone, her photographs. He flung open the door of the wardrobe and there was only her old school coat and he could not tear that, the seams were too strong, so he took his pocket-knife and held the coat in his left hand while he slashed and cut until there was nothing left to recognise.

He moved to the bed, her bed, the one she had slept in last

night, and the smell of her was still on the sheets and he tore them once, twice, and again and again, and when he was finished he left the room, sweat falling into his eyes, and his rage still there as he strode from the house.

She is dead to me, he told his solicitor, she does not exist any more. And he walked through the park, past nannies who wheeled babies, past children who played with balls, past ducks that swam. On and on he walked until the streets grew mean and narrow and dark and he hated Hannah, her wide mouth, her brown hair, her brown eyes, the way she swung when she walked. He hated her as he had hated her mother, his mother. Oh God, he groaned deep inside his head as he came to the path that ran by the river.

The stench filled his head. How dare she neglect her filial duty, her obedience to her father. How dare she have thoughts and plans that he knew nothing of. How dare she take it upon herself to make her own decisions.

The path was dry and he kicked up dust which caught in his throat and he coughed, putting his gloved hand to his mouth. The women were here as always and he chose one with a flick of his fingers and gripped her brown hair in his gloved hand and before all thought left him he cursed Hannah once more. How dare she reject him too, he thought, and he knew that soon he would call out that word again – mother.

12 The same afternoon Hannah walked down the road in Fulham past the butcher's. She breathed in the smell from the baker's and this time there was no one heaving furniture from a shuttered shop into a large furniture dray drawn by two large horses.

The noise was different too. There were still the cries of the hawkers and the street-traders but added to the clattering horse-drawn transport was the deeper and more violent roar of motor-cars and one omnibus which passed in a cloud of dust and caused a horse to shy, spilling its load. The sounds of curses were sharp and harsh and Hannah walked quickly now, moving in and out of the stream of other walkers. Her carpet-bag was heavy and she felt the pull of muscles in her shoulder as she passed it across to her other hand.

There were no dahlias today and so she stopped and bought watercress from an old woman with a shawled head who smiled and showed blackened teeth as she wound old newspaper round the dripping, fine-haired roots.

Hannah did not need a map. She turned right and right again and the noise of the street was left behind like it had been before as the roads narrowed and the alleys converged either side. The washing-lines were still strung high and washing hung on some but did not move because there was no wind today. She passed the first public house and then the second and saw sawdust being spread across the floor and smelt the beer again. The blackened wall was on her left and the women passing in thin torn shawls looked at her hat, at her coat, but their faces did not change.

At last she reached his street. The stairs were still dark, though the child's cart no longer blocked the way. The stairs sounded hollow beneath her feet as she climbed and she did not stop, though with each step the words she had spoken when she was last here sounded louder and louder. Her bag was heavy again but she could not change hands; the watercress had soaked her glove and the newspaper ink would have run into the black cotton but it would not show, would it?

His door was closed and now she wanted to turn and leave, down those stairs, out into the street and along to the noise and bustle of anonymity. But she put down her bag and it fell to one side as she knocked.

There was no sound for a moment and she swallowed, her mouth dry, and again she knocked for he did not know she was coming; but if he did not reply this time then she could leave, run down the stairs and it would be as though she had never been there.

But the door opened and the light from the room fell on to her hand and caught the side of Joe's face, lighting the gold-red hair and the pale, freckled skin, the early smile which froze on his face and his eyes which looked blank in their surprise. She could say nothing and so she held out her hand with the dripping watercress and she knew that her face was also stiff and that no smile had come.

She looked at his face and then down because he had not spoken, and she watched as water fell on to the floor from the cress and a small pool stained the unpolished floorboards of the landing. Would he leave her standing here? Would he close the door on her without ever speaking, ever smiling? But then his hand, large and strong, took the cress and fleetingly she felt his warmth and wondered if his hands were still as hard.

'I've come to say I'm sorry, Joe.' Her voice sounded too high, too tight, and now she looked into his face and there was still no smile, no sound of his voice; she waited but the silence stretched into what seemed like hours and finally she knew it was too late. She bent and picked up her carpet-bag and turned away from the light and the marigolds which still hung on the wall behind Joe. Her footsteps were loud as she walked to the stairs and the empty space was filled with a deep ache now and she hunched her shoulders to protect herself against any further pain.

She felt his hand as she reached the stairs, a hand which caught her and pulled her round, and she could not see his face because he held her close within his arms, but she could smell the varnish which was on his clothes and the wood which clung to his shirt.

'My mother is dead and I loved her so,' she said and felt the moist heat from her own breath. 'I am so sorry I spoke to you as I did. You were right and I've missed you and Harry has gone.'

The words were tumbling now and racking sobs began which could not come before; she knew now that they had needed the comfort of his strong hands, his familiar warmth.

His voice was gentle now, not like the last time, and he talked softly as he held her. She knew that she had found her friend again and the tears went on and on until her throat was sore and his shirt was wet and still he held her and talked, though she could not hear the words.

At last the sobs became quiet tears and then just tired breathing and they walked together into his room with a silence which was not uncertain as before but full, rounded and peaceful. He helped her to a chair at the kitchen table before pouring water into the black kettle and lighting the gas burner. There were still no words as he washed thick mugs, leaving them upside-down on the wooden drainer while he held the watercress under the running tap and Hannah remembered the red-specked water as it had gushed from the cottage tap but she said nothing yet for this was a time for silence. She watched as he cut four slices from a loaf of bread which was so new that moist crumbs stuck to the knife. Did he buy it from the bakery that she had passed? His hands were deft as he placed cress between the slices and then cut the sandwiches into quarters; the green was dark against the white. He poured boiling water into the teapot, his face set in concentration, and Hannah saw new deep lines on his face which ran down to his mouth. He was drawn, thin, and there was darkness beneath his eyes. The thick-set boy was gone, the bloom of health along with it. She had seen hunger too often not to recognise it now but said nothing, only watched as he brought a newspaper from the cupboard beneath the sink and laid three sheets on the table, flattening them with his hands, blackening his palms; and it was his hands that she looked at, not his face, because he was not looking at her either.

It was only when he set the steaming mugs on the newspaper and pushed the plate of sandwiches towards her that he looked at her and smiled, and it was as though the sun had come out and the gulls wheeled and danced in the sky. He sat down at the small table opposite her.

'Have a raw colonial sandwich, Hannah,' he said. She felt the heat of her blush but laughed because there was so much in her after such a long dark time.

Without butter the bread was dry. She took a sip of tea and watched as he ate one of the sandwiches and then another.

'How is your work these days, Joe?' she asked.

'Slow, but then these things often are.' He ate another sandwich and she took a bite of hers. The cress was strong and hot.

'I had no right to talk to you as I did, Hannah. I don't know why it happened.' But he did know and he wondered as he watched her drink more tea whether Arthur was still in her life.

Hannah sat back, her gloves by her plate. She was hot and unbuttoned her coat, pulling her arms from the sleeves, shaking her head as Joe rose to help. 'It's all right, Joe, I can manage.' She turned and draped it over the chair, seeing the work-bench behind her and the two chairs of simple design beside it, partly upholstered.

'They are very beautiful,' she murmured. 'So uncluttered.' She saw for a moment her father's drawing-room, so dark, so full, but pushed the image from her because all that was over now.

'Thank you, Hannah. I wish more people thought as you do.' He rose and walked to the draining-board where the teapot stood and with his back to her he said, 'I'm so very sorry about your mother. I would find it hard to bear if mine died.'

Hannah picked up her sandwich but then put it down again for there was no hunger in her.

Joe turned, pointing to her mug, which was still half-full, but she shook her head.

'Your mother lives a different life to the one mine had to suffer, Joe. She will be with you for much longer.' Was there bitterness in her voice, she wondered, and knew that there was, and that Joe had heard it too because he came and sat down and placed his hand on her ungloved one and it was as hard as it had always been. She smiled.

'So, what have you been doing and what are your plans now?' he asked, shaking his head as she pushed the sandwiches towards him but taking another when she insisted.

He listened as she told him of her Sunday school, of the fundraising, of Esther. Of Harry and how at last they had met and talked and found one another again before he had left.

'And Arthur?' he asked.

'Arthur is in Scotland shooting deer.'

'What do you intend to do now, Hannah?' It was not what he wanted to ask and he was surprised that his voice was steady.

Hannah sat looking at the marigolds, seeing their simplicity and warmth. 'I'm free now, Joe. I have left home.' She laughed at his face, at his mouth falling open.

'My word, Cornish girl, you sure do act fast.'

Hannah registered his drawl which suddenly sounded strong.

'Listen, colonial, the British have been known to take decisions, you know.' Their laughter was soft and they were back as they had once been and Joe listened as she spoke of Miss Fletcher and the room she had been offered in the schoolhouse and he listened as she pondered aloud the difficulties which that entailed.

'If I move my allegiance from the suffragists to the suffragettes and follow the Pankhursts' militancy as I feel I must,' she explained, 'how can I live with someone who is a constitutionalist and supports Mrs Fawcett's National Union of Women's Suffrage? There is friction between the suffragettes and the suffragists already and I couldn't bear to damage the relationship I have with Miss Fletcher.' Hannah saw in her mind the calm face and soft grey dress of her Headmistress.

She was leaning forward, her finger running backwards and forwards on the newspaper, keeping level with the print, following the column lines, her face drawn in a frown, and she listened as Joe said that she must discuss it with the obvious person, the woman most involved.

Hannah looked at him. It was so good to be back with him. 'You're right, of course, and I shall, but I have another problem that needs solving first.'

She looked again at his thin face and the way his shirt hung on his body. He had finished the sandwiches now.

'How do you manage to live, Joe?'

He looked at her and laughed. 'Well, I breathe in and I breathe out and I guess that seems to work quite well.'

She did not laugh. 'Food helps,' she said and watched as his laugh died.

'Well, Hannah, better men than I have starved in a garret for the sake of their Art.' His voice was suddenly very British and he flourished his hand in a bow, his laugh returning.

Eliza had told her that Joe could barely live on the money that his craft brought him, that he would accept nothing from his father because he was too proud. He only wanted money that he had earned himself. She had said that London broke his heart with its darkness and misery, its stench and poverty.

'How is Mary?' she asked. 'Is she still making matches?'

'She died.' His answer was short and his bow died in mid-flourish as he sat back in his chair, his hands on his lap, quite still.

'Her husband too.'

'And the children?' she asked, fearing his answer, seeing their blank eyes, their thin bodies in the dark fetid room.

He shrugged. 'I don't know. They were taken to the workhouse and I could do nothing. I had nothing I could offer. I am, as you can quite obviously see, Hannah, not exactly the American success story.' This time it was his voice that was bitter.

'You saved Bernie,' Hannah said and it was her turn to put her hand on his and she felt his thumb press her fingers.

'So, we won one but lost five. It's not a good equation, teacher lady.'

Hannah sat quiet for a few moments because her next words must be just right.

'I've a problem which only you can help with.' She watched as he rubbed his thumb backwards and forwards on her fingers.

'Go on then, Hannah. You know I'll help if I can.'

'When Mother was alive I decided that if I had enjoyed my holiday so would my Sunday people, and not just them but hundreds like them. Like your Mary. I was going to try and raise funds with our Esther playing the role of musical benefactor, but from a safe distance.' They laughed because she had already told him of Esther and her fleas. Then she looked back at the marigolds and saw the flickering pear tree. 'But when Mother died she left me a house in Cornwall and money to fund the scheme.'

Joe was leaning forward now, his eyes alight, his face eager. 'Hannah, how lucky you are to be able to go back.'

She shook his hand. 'Listen to me, Joe.' Her voice was low and she found words carefully. 'I have too much to do in London. I've waited too long to fight for what I believe in. I can't go now but I want you to set up the house for me, run it as it should be run.'

Joe looked at her, hope washing over his face before dying. 'I don't like charity, Hannah.' His voice was cold.

'And neither do I.' She made her voice angry. 'I haven't time for charity. I want someone I can trust to do a job that needs doing. You will receive your salary not from me but from my solicitor who is setting up a trust.' Her voice was still angry, though there was no anger in her but rather a desperate anxiety. Would her anger work now as his had all those years before? 'I shall need someone who will care that the scheme works, who can maintain the house. We shall need to employ a cook, a gardener and a maid and I want you to find people from these streets who need work to fill the positions; the Marys of this world. I want the people we send from London to be taught by the cook, by the gardener, by you. They must come back feeling they have learnt from their stay, that they have earned their keep, that above all, they have enjoyed a holiday and possibly gained a skill to help them find work in London.'

Her throat was dry and she took a sip of tea. It was cold but she barely noticed. 'There would be the chance to do your own work of course.' She paused. 'I need you, Joe.'

And she did and it would be good to know that though he was in Cornwall he would be linked to her. He rose and walked over to the two chairs, running his hand over the smoothness of the grain. She turned, leaning her arm along the back of her chair. Oh God, he was so thin.

'Are you in love with Arthur?' Joe asked quietly, not looking at her.

Hannah felt the shock of his question. It was the one she had not yet asked herself and one that she did not want to consider, not after the hunting weekend and the look on his face as he blooded Harry but Joe was standing by the bench, his face serious, and she knew that it was time she answered both him and herself.

Thoughts were moving against one another, mingling and breaking away. Arthur's kindness, the fun they had, the ease of his company, the fact that he did not absorb her but left her free to think and plan and act. The fact that she never wished to know what he was doing. Was this love?

'I don't know what love is,' she answered.

Joe looked down at the chairs and did not speak for a few moments and then he said, 'I have another four chairs to make by December. Perhaps if the house is ready for our guests by then, they would like a lesson in furniture design?'

For he knew that she did not love Arthur or she would know and so he would wait.

He walked with Hannah to the station, taking her bag as though it weighed a bare ounce. He stood with her on the underground platform where the air was thick and sulphurous and asked if she would come often to the house.

'I have much to do,' she replied and he took her arm and held it.

'I know,' he murmured. 'But come when you can because the house will always be waiting.'

She thought of this as she left the station when her journey was over and ducked beneath the reins of the hansom cab. It was so good to have her friend back again.

'Miss Fletcher's School for Young Ladies,' she called to the driver, and watched as the lamp-lighter lit up further down the street. The school was not far from the station, not far from her house but it was not her house now, it was her father's alone. It seemed strange to be entering the schoolhouse door at this time of the day instead of Sunday morning as the church bells were ringing.

Beatrice showed her through to Miss Fletcher's drawing-room which was lit by gas lamps on the wall and a small oil lamp which was placed on the cloth-covered table at the side of the older woman's fireside chair.

Hannah smiled as Miss Fletcher rose to meet her, still in grey, and she took the chair which her Headmistress pulled up closer to the fire. She felt stiff and awkward, a visitor without a home.

'I thought we'd have some tea. I know it's a little late but dinner can always be delayed a little. Tea is so comforting, is it not?' Miss Fletcher was smiling and Hannah felt the heat from the fire sinking into her body and was tired.

'Did it go well with your father?' Miss Fletcher asked and Hannah explained that she had left a note and was relieved when the calm woman whose hair was now grey at the temples nodded.

'Perhaps it was as well under the circumstances and I'm sure we can manage should we hear from him at all.'

But Hannah knew that they would not.

The tea-kettle was simmering over the spirit lamp, rock-cakes and scones were keeping hot on a plate over a bowl filled with hot water. The butter was a liquid by now which had soaked through the scone and dripped on to Hannah's napkin which was stark white against her black dress.

Would her mother have approved of her being here, she thought, looking round the room and then at Miss Fletcher as she poured the tea, and she knew that she would, but suddenly there was a great sadness in her which could not be ignored any more. She put down her scone and looked into the fire. This was not her home, not yet, and she missed the bedroom, the wicker chair, her mother, with a pain which made her want to groan aloud.

Miss Fletcher reached across and patted her hand. 'You will grieve for a long while, Hannah, my dear. It is right that you should and you must not deny the pain and sorrow. It is important that grief should run its course.'

Hannah looked away from the fire now, down at the dog which panted on the hearthrug, then on to the rest of the room with its floor-to-ceiling bookcases down at the far end. There were bound copies of *Punch,* and the *Illustrated London News,* and standing a few feet from the shelves was a solid mahogany desk.

The hissing gas lamps lit the silver inkstand and the brass letter scales with a dull glow. Set down in meticulous order were blotters, penwipers, sticks of sealing-wax and tapers together with a snuffer. The oil lamp smelt as her mother's had done. There was silence between the two women now and Miss Fletcher's smile was one of understanding and calm.

Dinner was served in a small alcove off this room since the Sunday school had taken over what had been the dining-room.

They dined on a rosewood table without a cloth. A rose-shaded lamp was set to one side and cast a soft light into the shaded area.

Beatrice served a steak pie and Hannah thought that she would be unable to eat but she was hungry and the gravy was thick and the vegetables crisp and lightly boiled. Was Joe so lucky, she wondered and pushed the memory of his thin body to one side because it gave her too much pain.

She spoke to Miss Fletcher now of Joe and the home and was pleased when she smiled and nodded her approval. 'You are indeed fortunate to have such a friend, Hannah.'

Miss Fletcher put more steak on Hannah's plate. 'For you have become too thin, my dear, and you will need your strength.'

As they ate Hannah spoke of her plans as Joe had said she should. Miss Fletcher listened as Hannah explained that she had waited for so long to take an active part in the fight for votes but that she feared it would be destructive to the friendship that she believed existed between the two of them.

'Hannah,' Miss Fletcher said as Beatrice cleared the plates and brought fresh fruit. 'Before we discuss matters further I do feel that you should call me Frances, it is my name after all. I also feel that there is no likelihood that a difference of opinion will damage a friendship such as ours. After all, surely all women's suffrage supporters are fighting for freedom to think and speak, so surely you and I can respect one another's point of view. Our aims are the same even though perhaps our approach may differ.'

Hannah sat back in her chair. The dog was sitting by her side, her nose lifted, her ears pricked, but Frances Fletcher sent her back to the rug.

'Greedy beast,' she laughed and soon they too moved to the fire and Beatrice brought coffee which was strong and black.

'But, my dear Hannah, why do you feel you must leave the suffragists?' Frances asked as she stirred her coffee, tapping the teaspoon on the side of her cup before placing it in her saucer. 'After all the Liberal Government is one of social reform, and Mrs Pankhurst's suffragettes are campaigning against this government; against them in by-elections, and are withdrawing their support for Labour who have been staunch supporters, though they, of course, have no hope of power at the moment. Our only hope lies with the Liberals and the only hope of improved general conditions lies with them too. I am worried that if the activities of the suffragettes continue the Government will not be re-elected and reform will lapse.' She leant forward, a frown on her forehead. 'Think very carefully, my dear.'

Hannah bent to stroke the dog. 'Good girl, Bess,' she whispered before sitting up again. 'I can understand what you are saying but I feel so impatient, so angry all the time at the way in which women have been ignored, the way they have been subjugated and humiliated. Look at the women's suffrage bills, three dismissed since 1898. We have to pay tax but we have no representation. It is a crime, it is slavery.' She swallowed and rubbed her lips with her fingers. It was important that she explained herself clearly. 'The suffragettes have made our cause visible. The newspapers are writing for the first time about votes for women. Surely the Government will be forced to listen to our demands because they are just and now very public.' She laughed quietly. 'We women won't bring them down. How can we with a few demonstrations and a bit of heckling? And I agree with you that they have much to do but in time they will see that they can also give us a chance. We will convince them by being vocal, by being as difficult as they are. That there will be no peace until we have the vote.'

Frances drank the last of her coffee and looked across at Hannah's cup which was almost empty. She lifted the pot and Hannah nodded, passing her cup across. Steam rose from the cup and she did not drink yet but watched Frances stir her own cup again and give another two taps.

'I do fear, though, Hannah, that militant action will alienate those whose support the suffragists have carefully and painfully acquired both inside and outside Parliament. You know that we constitutionalists work on the basis of persuasion by example. I fear that the behaviour of the suffragettes will simply demolish what support women have so far gained.'

Hannah was impatient to answer. 'But don't you see, Frances, militancy has turned women's suffrage into a living question.'

Frances smiled ruefully. 'Yes, I do agree, Hannah. It has done that and I'm sure that we are all grateful but I am just concerned that the militancy you speak of will turn to something more. Will demonstration turn to violence and provoke general dismay among existing voters? That is counterproductive.'

Hannah was leaning forward now, her coffee cold, but she did not notice.

'But there is such an anger amongst women. There always has been and it is worse now with the imprisonments for what are, after all, simple demonstrations.' She put her hand up as she saw Frances begin to speak. 'I know that suffragettes have been charged with obstruction and assault but stamping on feet hardly constitutes that surely? I want to shout out at the unfairness of it all, the injustice, and it seems that it is only when you shout that anyone hears. Why should giving women the vote be so difficult. If we have a reforming Government, why won't they reform the voting laws. I know that they're frightened of creating a mass of female Conservative voters because of the existing property qualifications but that is no excuse. They would enlarge the franchise to universal suffrage if that were really the case.'

Frances took her cup and Hannah watched as she walked to the table by the door and brought back truffles on a plate. They were rich and soft and stuck to her teeth and she remembered with sudden clarity the chocolate on Esther's teeth the night they had danced for her father and her anger grew even more.

'You will certainly make an excellent orator, Hannah Watson, and I can hardly quibble with what you have said. The creation of Conservative voters does concern them.'

'And now you must be realistic, Frances. We have to go for what seems the most feasible and that is limited suffrage, because no government of today will agree to universal suffrage. They are scared that the undeserving poor would have a right to an opinion. Just imagine the horror if a prostitute had a vote.' She lifted her eyes and Frances laughed so loud that Bess started in her sleep. Hannah thought of all those men like her father who sat in dark pews and condemned as animals women such as these.

'No, once we have limited suffrage we will then be able to vote for universal suffrage,' she continued. 'Once we have the vote we can change so much that is unjust. We must have it. They must be made to give it to us, somehow we must make them.'

Hannah was up now, and walking backwards and forwards, her words coming quickly and loudly as she drew them in the air until Frances laughed and told her to sit down or Bess would think it was time for her nightly constitutional and then there would be a barking heckler in the room and that would really be too much.

Hannah smiled and crouched down by Bess, rubbing her ears and laughing. She felt invigorated, eager and in a hurry to join those who already spoke on platforms and challenged from the audience those who denied them their rights.

Frances spoke and she was not laughing now. 'At least, Hannah, hold back until the Pensions Bill is through. Surely that is very important, especially to the two of us because we can see just how bad things are. Then make a decision whether to stay with the non-militants or give your allegiance to the suffragettes. I'm not asking you to fight. You have been doing that for years with the suffragists but I am asking you to be responsible and not add to the Government's problems or encourage others to while they try to force this important reform through.'

Frances would not tell Hannah that she was only asking this of her because she feared that violence would indeed escalate within the ranks of the suffragettes and she wanted Hannah to be kept from it for as long as possible. After all, perhaps a miracle would occur and votes would be given, then she would never have to fight.

As Hannah stroked the dog's back and smelt her odour she saw Bernie again, watching from the cottage as they walked on to the moor, and Mary, the match-girl who was now dead, and she knew, filled with frustration though she was, that she could not on principle campaign against this government as they fought in by-elections to be re-elected. She could not make their task more difficult as they tried to steer their Pensions Bill through the house. This would be her personal acknowledgement of their worth. But she also knew that she would shout and make demands when the Pensions Bill became an Act if the government did not then turn their attention to female suffrage because they would no longer deserve support.

'I'll wait,' she said at last, taking comfort in the knowledge that it would not be long before she knew whether or not she would have to take up the struggle.

As she lay in bed that night, watching the moon through the undrawn curtains, she could not sleep in this strange bed. It was an attic room and the eaves came low as they had done in the Cornish cottage, but there was no picture in heavy oils, just prints of garden flowers.

It was a nice room, homely with pleasant furniture and a thick carpet and a fire which she had said she would look after since it was a long way up for Beatrice to come. Frances had smiled at her as she had said this. There were stocks in a vase by the bed and lavender amongst them. Their scent was not unhappy as she had feared it might be but brought her mother closer.

She felt tired now but today had been a good day; the empty space had been filled and soon she would either have the vote or would be fighting to gain it and would therefore be a person and not a thing. As she turned on her side she wondered how Harry was and when she would see him again.

And then she thought of Esther and knew that she must keep her close and too busy to forget her brother but as the clouds covered the moon she wondered how.

13 Harry sat on the *stoep* or verandah of his hotel. The voyage had left him feeling fit, he thought to himself, and he looked again at the telegram that he had received from the Ren Gold Mine, his employers.

Frank Canon would be meeting him here, or should already have met him according to the brief clipped words, and it was in this man's company that he would begin the journey into the interior. Harry looked out across the street with its trams and trees, way over to the mountains which stood at the back of this beautiful Cape Town. It was these mountains he would be passing through soon and he felt a stirring of tension, of anticipation.

He walked now to the edge of the *stoep*, hearing the cicadas, watching the butterflies, brilliant in their blues and reds, first settling then moving from the bushes of herbs which grew around the hotel, their aroma thick in the air. He moved down the steps and along the streets until he could see the blue of the South Atlantic which was visible to the south from almost any street or window. Across the miles Esther would be wondering if he had arrived, if he was safe, and he longed to feel her body pressed to his, her white skin soft beneath his hands. She had not allowed him to make love to her and that was as it should be but how he had longed for it.

He turned, impatient now to be at work, to be starting the life which would make such thoughts reality, and walked back to the hotel to sit again beneath the fan, waiting with diminishing patience for Canon.

It was not until six in the evening that he arrived and Harry was still on the *stoep* breathing in the scent of herbs which seemed to grow everywhere in this climate; a climate which was nothing short of idyllic.

Frank was keen to eat before having the first and last good sleep either of them would have for longer than he cared to think, he said, shaking hands with a firm grip, his smile broad against his tanned skin. Lines of tiredness were etched in the same red dust which coated his shoes and he cursed as he sat down on the rocking bench and motioned for Harry to join him. But Harry shook his head and chose instead the heavy wooden chair he had been sitting in when Frank had finally arrived.

'I dare say you think you have come to a slice of heaven, Harry?' Frank said, rubbing his sleeve over his forehead before removing his wide-brimmed hat and leaning his head back and closing his eyes.

Harry smiled. 'It's not what I expected, that I have to confess – and yes, it is grand.'

Frank did not open his eyes or move but murmured. 'Make the most of it, old son, for tomorrow we travel and then you forget there was ever air to breathe.'

Harry looked at him. 'It's that hot, is it?'

'It is, I'm afraid, at this time of year. January is not the best time to arrive. It's high summer for the next two months and there's been little rain on the Rand, not even the few showers that the good God sees fit to bestow normally.' He yawned and made no attempt to cover his mouth with his hand. The insects were louder now, Harry noted, and the sun had almost gone. 'You'll think you're breathing nothing but dust and you will be right.' Frank continued, dropping his head forward on to his chest for a moment and then heaving himself to his feet. 'Come on, old lad. I'll freshen up and then let's have asparagus and then some fish. Both are ambrosia though we are not yet gods. But there is time, eh?' He winked at Harry and left him in the lobby while he climbed the stairs to the room which had been booked by the company.

Later they walked together into the dining-room where the coffee-coloured maids waited to serve them. There were many tables, all of them full, but conversation was muted, elegance was all around. As they ate Harry listened while Frank talked of his days in Venezuela where he had worked in the mines before coming out here to make his fortune and, before that, his time at Eton and Oxford.

'I earn so much though that a fortune seems unnecessary. I've decided it's safer to know that there's money coming in, rather than living on nothing, hoping to find a diamond the size of an ostrich egg. I'll be able to bring my fiancée over from Britain in a few years and we'll set up house, in Cape Town, I hope. I love it here.' Frank put down his knife and fork and leant back in his chair, pouring more wine for Harry. 'They make a good wine in the Cape. What do you think of it?'

Harry smiled and lifted his glass. 'It's a bit too nice,' he said, hearing the slight slurring of his own speech, the slowness of his thoughts.

Frank laughed and his blue eyes looked less tired as he did so. He wore his brown hair longer than Harry was used to and had a beard which was darker than his hair. His movements were deft and sure as he filleted the fish. His nails were cut short and square and Harry watched as Frank clicked his fingers towards the octoroon who stood waiting by the service door, watching their quarter of the dining-room. She wore a black dress with a starched white apron and walked towards them. Frank called, 'Another bottle,' pointing to the now empty one which stood on the small trolley by their table.

Harry watched the coloured girl almost bow before walking into the kitchen. She had straight hair and fine features and there was a grace and beauty to her. He turned back and found Frank watching him, laughter in his eyes.

'You can look, but don't touch,' he grinned. 'She's what we call a Cape Coloured, a mixture of black and white.'

Harry lifted the backbone of his fish to one side of his plate, it was so fresh it tasted almost of the sea. He shook his head at Frank. 'No fear of that.'

'It's as well, it only leads to trouble,' Frank replied, patting his mouth with his starched napkin as the girl returned and placed the bottle on the table, the cork already removed. 'Too much damned mating in the early days between the whites and the natives produced the likes of her. We each keep to our own sides of the track now.' He bent his head to his meal again and Harry drank more wine.

No, there was no fear of him touching, not when Esther was

forever in his thoughts and was his whole being, his reason to live. He hoped that Hannah had remembered that she had promised to somehow make the waiting more bearable for the girl that he loved.

They left early in the morning, taking the train which chugged away from the lushness of the Cape and on through the valleys which wound between the hills which were really mountains. They separate civilisation from the interior, Frank told him, settling himself back, lifting the pink *Sporting Life*, staining the pages with the sweat from his fingers.

Once they were through the hills, which seemed to take an interminable time, Harry looked out across red arid land where few cattle grazed but where ostriches occasionally walked, the heat making even them hang their heads. Frank pointed out the dry karroo bushes which in no way covered the red terrain. He told how wool had been the chief export before gold arrived and laughed at the red-dusted sheep which huddled around the pale, parched milk-bushes. He told of the dassies; hard-rock-rabbits which would come out when evening came and it was cooler.

As Harry listened the heat made him want to die; it beat off the ground and the roof and in through the windows in spite of the shades pulled down. It took days and they slept when they could and ran water over their lips and Harry soaked his handkerchief and held it to his face and neck, listening as Frank told him of this country which was so hot and unbearable.

He told him how the Transvaal, which was where they were now heading, had been flooded by a shallow sea millions of years ago and how gold had been deposited when the sea finally ebbed. He explained how, many miles north of the river Vaal, one long ridge had been thrown up when faulting occurred; a ridge which was some sixty miles long from east to west. How, many millions of years later, Boer farmers saw streams glistening on this upland and called it the ridge of white water, the Witwatersrand.

'What we call the Rand, my son,' Frank said. 'The Mecca to all the gold hunters in the world and Johannesburg is the centre of it all.'

Gone were the sheep and cattle, he told Harry, relegated to the land which they were now passing.

Harry asked about the diamonds, for he knew that if he was to become as rich as Arthur it was these little bits of carbon which would make it possible.

'The diamonds will have to wait, Harry,' Frank said, his voice cracked and hoarse, his legs sprawled across the carriage, his boots as dusty as Harry's. 'But don't worry, we'll be going to the fields fairly soon so you'll be able to see what it's really like there. There'll be some message we have to deliver, you mark my words. I seem to spend my life running about this bloody land.

'You'll be working with the gold – at first anyway. That's where we need the engineers. It's hard rock but you'll be used to that with your Cornish roots. It's damned tough work, you know that? Especially in this heat. It's not so bad during the winters.'

He laughed at Harry's surprise. 'Yes, we have winters and they can be bloody cold, you know. The Rand is high after all and so are the diamond fields, mark my words.'

The heat in Johannesburg was greater than Harry thought could be possible; the thermometer said that it was over 140 degrees and that was inside the house which he was to share with Frank, so what would it be out in the full glare of the sun?

The small corrugated iron house with its wooden *stoep* and the thin hedge of cypress trees on three sides lay on the extreme edge of the town alongside unlit, unpaved roads. They had taken a horse-drawn tram from the station to the house and Harry had found it an extraordinary and gaudy town which looked like a circus dropped in the middle of the moon, so barren was the veld through which they had travelled. The station was on the northern edge of the town close to the post office and the telephone exchange and Harry knew now where he could post his next letter to Esther.

They had passed some substantial two-storeyed houses in brick with first-floor balconies and Frank had laughed and said they should doff their hats for these were the big bosses. They had passed through Market Square around which the town had originally grown and had continued south past stone buildings: the Stock Exchange, banks, the offices of mining companies and the Rand Club which looked as smart as anything in London. Other trams had travelled the main thoroughfares and heat had blurred the air well above the ground.

Frank had been right, he had felt as though he were breathing dust and as he lay on the bed, stifled by the heat, he felt little better. Sweat ran from him in rivulets and the bed was wet beneath him. There was no fan here just whitewashed walls with no pictures and windows with blinds so that although the sun was kept from the room so was any vestige of a breeze. But would there have been such a thing as a cooling wind? Harry knew there would not. Frank had insisted before he threw his boots to the boy, who was black and thin, with a face that was almost frightening in its strangeness, that they would go out to the mine only when the sun had gone down.

And so it was not until the evening when the worst of the heat was over and the moon had cast a white light over the land that they left the house with its sparse furniture, covered all the time with fine dust, and set out to visit the mine which held so many of his hopes and Esther's too.

The horse that Frank had produced and which would be kept further down nearer the town was sure-footed as they rode, though there was little which could have caused it to stumble; the grass was limited to tufts and the stones which lay amongst the few succulents were small and flat.

The white light of night lit a scene which was unmistakable and Harry reined in his horse and sat looking at the mines which stretched for mile upon mile while Frank rode on, his horse scraping its hoofs on the stones and clinking its bit as it jerked its head. In the centre of each mine stood the headgear, the great triangular metal box whose winding gear lowered miners below and hauled up ore.

'Low grade ore,' Frank explained as Harry caught up. They rode a few yards further and he followed the line of Frank's arm as he pointed to the left, reining in as the other man did.

'That's the start of our particular little enterprise,' Frank said as their horses snorted and changed their weight from foot to foot beneath them. 'But it's not so little of course, though at the beginning it was just a mass of small claims. The big men bought the others up, and it makes sense, because what small concerns can afford the equipment to sink shafts into the hard rock? It's not the quality of this ore which turned it into such a rich mining area but the quantity. So it's a pig for the small man.'

Harry nodded, although he already knew this from his time at the School of Mines in London. He could see the stamp batteries, which he knew had pestles weighing up to 1000lbs for crushing the ore preparatory to treatment. He knew that cyanide was now used to treat the crushed banket, which was so named because the Dutch farmers had felt that the jagged edge of the reef, dotted as it was with pebbles, resembled 'banket', almond cakes which they made. He also knew that 2000 gallons of water were needed for every ton of ore. How could they find that much water, he wondered, but knew that they conserved it in 'pans'.

And how extraordinary that cyanide of potassium precipitates gold on to zinc shavings from which the gold can be recovered and refined. He nodded to himself. Frank was right; his own supposition made while he was still in London was right. There was definitely no room for the small man in this set-up. He would have to find his fortune in diamonds.

'And the Boers? Do they own much of this?'

'No, most of them sold their land to the foreigners; the British and Germans mainly. Since the war a few farm boys work here of course. Their farms weren't worth restarting and we have room for them now that the Chinese labourers are being returned.' They rode back now slowly and from the north-west he could hear a murmuring and a chanting and he turned to Frank, a question on his face.

Frank shrugged. 'The kaffirs, you know, the native workers,' he said. 'The mining doesn't seem to make them tired enough to sleep. Maybe we need to work them harder?'

Harry was confused. 'Don't they go to their homes at night?'

'No need for that, it's best that they're kept penned up here,'

Frank said, rubbing his horse's ear with his riding crop and pointing out a dassie which was sprinting in the distance.

Harry looked over again in the direction of the sound. It had a haunting quality in the moon-bathed night. 'But don't they mind?' he queried, remembering Hannah at Arthur's dinner-table, the candles flickering, anger in her eyes.

Frank was in front now; he turned in his saddle and Harry heard the creak of the leathers as he did so. 'It's difficult for you new boys straight out of England to understand. These boys don't have feelings or needs like us. That's what makes the whole bloody thing tick, old man.' He was pointing to the mines again. 'Gold has made South Africa rich or rather the kaffirs have.' He was slapping the crop lightly in his hand as Harry rode closer, his hands leaning on the pommel of the saddle.

'How do you mean?'

'Think of Canada and its wheat. Or Australia and its cheap grazing. What are these things?' He did not wait for Harry to answer and Harry was glad for he was at a loss.

'They are the raw material which has made these countries rich,' Frank continued. 'Kaffirs or "boys" are South Africa's raw material. They work for us, dig out our gold. Their needs are less than those of the white man, far less. We pay them just as little as we can and if they are killed,' Frank shrugged, 'there is no need for compensation. They make the gold a far more profitable concern than if we were to use white miners.'

'But surely they want to go home?' Harry asked.

Frank shrugged again and laughed. 'I've told you, Harry, these boys don't have feelings like us, or wants or needs.'

'Then why do you have to keep them penned?'

'For God's sake, Harry, let it drop. You're a new boy, you must listen to what I say. Really listen, man. This is the way it is, the way it has been since the white man came and it works, it works well. We've learnt from the Boers how to treat the natives and, as I said, it works. They are just beasts, they don't expect anything else.'

They were riding forward again now and there was no breeze to carry the noise from the compound and so slowly it was left behind. Harry turned in his saddle and looked back.

'Just believe me, man, it's a good system,' Frank reiterated. 'Compounds and the pass laws work well. I'll show you the compounds at Kimberley when we go. We have more of a problem with the diamonds of course, they can be stolen as they're dug so we have to take extra measures.'

'Just slow down a moment, Frank. What are these pass laws? Is this pass something I should have?' Harry asked.

'Not you, Harry,' Frank laughed. 'The kaffirs carry passes and if they are found without one they are in great trouble, believe me. That's what I mean by learning from the Boers. They started that years ago for their slaves and servants to keep them on the job and it's a damn good idea. It stops them wandering off. Keeps them under our thumb.'

'But what if the kaffirs are working their own holdings, in the diamond fields for instance? Do they still have passes?' The lights from the town were bright now and they were drawing closer to them.

'Oh, they can't own holdings; that's a lesson we Europeans learnt early on. The way these boys work in the heat they'd have outstripped us years ago. We can't have that happening. We are white men, we have to protect our natural position, don't we?'

Harry rode on. Another dassie ran fast to the side of him.

'Are they slaves then?'

'Oh no. I told you, we pay them. They like us as masters better than the Boers. We're better to them. The British were good to them in the early days too. We abolished slavery in the Cape, you know. That's mainly why the Boers trekked inland and set up their republics in the Transvaal and the Orange Free State. The old Dutchmen didn't want to give up their free labour.'

Frank was lighting a cigarette and Harry shook his head as he offered the silver cigarette case. He watched as Frank flicked the match through the air. It was out before it hit the sand. The dust was thick in his throat but he wanted to know more about this country which was so different from his.

'So the Boers challenged the authority of the British later, did they, and tried to use our men's expertise and tax without giving them the vote?'

Frank's laugh was soft and he drew deeply on his cigarette; the end glowed a deep red. 'Perhaps that's how it seemed back home but there's many that will tell you that the mine owners didn't like the way the Boer Government was handling the supply franchises and keeping prices high for the owners. Those owners wanted a change in the power structure so that these things could be put into the hands of the British. Dynamite could then be imported more cheaply and profits would be greater. That's what it all boils down to in the end, Harry. Profits. Not honour, not the thin red line but profits.'

They were nearing the house now and Frank's voice was languid, bored. 'The Liberal Government is feeling so damn guilty about the war and the concentration camps that they are working towards self-government for the Boers again, but don't worry, the franchises are safe, thank God. The politicians are even consoling the Boers by forgetting their wonderful liberal principles and acknowledging that the kaffirs must be kept down and kept separate. Different schools, no vote, no nothing and that equals no complications so you could say the Boers won the war anyway and so did we. Couldn't be better, could it, old man?'

Harry was tired now and his head was full of a life which was stranger than he had imagined. But still, it was the way things were and he was too weary and too lonely to think about it.

For a month he worked in the office which was hot and stifling, but one morning Frank entered, took Harry's hat from the stand and threw it across to him. Harry laughed and caught it, seeing the dust shaking out on to the desk. He wiped it away with his hand, his sweat streaking the wood.

'Get your things. We're off to the diamond fields, just for a quick trip though,' Frank called.

This is what Harry had been waiting for day after day. He rose, nodding to the clerk, not waiting even to straighten the sheets of figures on his desk.

They left for Kimberley by train that day in the raging heat. His skin was already sore and burnt and his neck rubbed on his starched white collar but his sweat soon stained and softened the stiffness.

'We've to deliver some documents by hand,' Frank said, nodding at the briefcase he carried with him.

As the train jolted and rattled he told Harry how diamonds had originally been found by the Orange and the Vaal Rivers at a spot hundreds of miles from the temperate Cape across the Great Karroo, which is attractive in its own way but arid, endless, parched. Like me, Harry had thought, wondering why they had to travel as they were doing. He did not look out; the sun was too bright. He rested his head back against the seat, feeling the jarring of his neck as the train rattled along the tracks.

Frank explained that from April to August the weather was cold because the diamond diggings were at 4000 feet and from September to March it sometimes rained and when it did the great hole became a morass in which people had often drowned.

'That's the only time the dust does not seep through your clothes into your nose, your mouth, your ears,' Frank groaned.

'What great hole?' Harry asked but Frank told him to wait and see.

When he arrived he understood, and looked with awe at the man-made steps which staggered down into a great hole covering at least eight acres. It defeated any of his pre-conceived ideas. It was so deep, so busy, so vast.

'Each claim in this pipe was originally about the size of a small tennis court and those steps,' Frank pointed to steps cut into the ground, 'would take the digger down past the other claims to his own which might have been right at the bottom.'

Harry covered his mouth and nose with his handkerchief as the hot dry wind blew red dust in blasts from the surrounding veld. He narrowed his eyes to slits. The sky seemed almost yellow in the heat, the ground felt hot even through his boots.

'Keep your watch in your pocket. The dust will get in it and that will be that,' Frank warned him.

Harry knew that diamonds had been formed millions of years ago when deposits of carbon lying deep underground were squeezed by the great pressure of the ground sixty miles above them and baked by the intense heat of the inner earth so that they were changed into diamonds. He also knew that they would still have been buried deep down had not the molten interior forced its way to the surface, carrying the stones, spurting into the air and falling down again to harden and cool, forming pipes. This is what, in essence, he was now looking at.

He knew also that the weathering of years had carried diamonds far and wide from the surface of these pipes and his hope was to find in some alluvial bed the fortune which was imperative to him. This surveying is what he had been trained for and he knew it was just a question of looking. Impatience filled him but he must wait, he told himself. Just wait.

Kimberley was a dreary town with low small cottages connected by sandy tracks. There were a few thorn trees and ditches dug to drain off rain-water and Harry was glad the next day to be at the diamond mine with Frank instead of in the hot dark room of the hotel where they had stayed last night. The noises from the brothel just two dusty streets from them had screamed and laughed in his head as he had lain panting in the heat.

There were four mines at Kimberley but only one was owned by the company that employed them and while Frank stood to one side and talked to the mine manager about the documents he had delivered Harry watched the black labourers as they elbowed and bustled, crept and climbed, shovelled and sieved; working like ants in the dust bowl.

He turned as Frank shouted over the noise, waving to an area off to the west. 'That's where we keep the boys,' he said. 'They came to work here originally for dowry money and guns. Now they come to pay the poll-tax we've levied on their huts. Damn clever way of keeping 'em coming back when their spell is over.'

'I can see why they might not like it,' Harry said, coughing and choking.

'I think they prefer this to the gold. They don't like the deep mines.' Frank shook hands with the manager and so too did Harry. He felt the dust on both their hands; the dust and the sweat. Frank walked on, nodding to a white man who was issuing orders to a black team.

'Maybe we'll both be doing that bloke's job soon,' Frank murmured. 'There's a slump in the diamond market and it's affecting our conglomerate. They don't need much more surveying, here or on the Rand, but I'd quite like to work this close to the real thing. How about you?'

Harry nodded. Yes, he'd like that, it would make him feel closer to his goal. He could check out the country around here on his time off. Again he felt impatient and excited too. He wiped his mouth and then his forehead; somehow he would have to make sure that he was sent back here from the Rand.

Frank was talking again. 'Never mind, business will pick up. Bound to with industry taking off the way it is. It's not just our women who want diamonds now, thank God, but the cutting machines too; diamonds are so hard.'

With each step they kicked up dust and all around was the noise of men hacking and working. Occasionally chanting could be heard, but rising above everything was the singing of the wires which stretched taut into the base of the mine transporting the wooden boxes and the iron buckets up to the surface laden with broken rock, then back again, wheels running on wires, empty and fast now.

'You can see how this becomes a quagmire in the wet,' Frank shouted and Harry nodded. How many people did Frank say had drowned in the mud and water? He couldn't remember.

'Perpendicular shafts are being sunk too but there are still diamonds to be found in the big holes.' Frank's mouth was against his ear and Harry thought of Sam and Penhallon and it seemed so cool to him now, so measured and familiar. He thought of the moors and the sea, the river and the trap which he had driven through high-banked lanes and for a moment the heat and strangeness was shut out, but not for long. Frank took his arm.

'Come along with me,' he mouthed. 'I've had enough of this chaos.' Harry nodded and looked back again to the big hole spread over its many acres because he wanted to remember it clearly. After all, diamonds were why he was out here.

They passed high-raised boxes into which the broken ground was being deposited from aerial tramways. He listened again as the taut wires which held the wooden boxes hummed and sang as they slid down to the bottom. Could he write to Esther and tell her that the mine had sung to him? No, but he would write to Hannah. She would laugh and ask if it was high opera or a music-hall ditty. Was she all right? They passed a steam engine working a large iron bucket which was sitting empty on its wheels.

'We blast every evening when the kaffirs have been locked in for the night. You can see them now digging at the loosened soil.'

Harry nodded, they looked like ants, unreal, featureless. He walked on with Frank.

'We'll see the compound now. I don't want to come back later. We have things to do this evening, Harry.' Frank took his arm and winked. 'There's a good bar as long as you don't have too much of the Cape brandy and the ladies are kind to young men out from the old country.'

Harry smiled too but he did not want that sort of kindness, not while he was waiting for Esther. Neither did he want to see the compound, for it was not night-time as it had been at Johannesburg when darkness had thrown a blanket over harsh sights and he had made sure that during the day he had stayed in the office. The compound was some way from the four large mines and they were driven in a cart by a kaffir wearing a slouch hat and baggy jacket and trousers. As they bumped and ground their way over the rutted track Frank explained how a few big men had bought up the small diggers and had formed a cartel with a few others to prevent diamonds flooding on to the market and lowering the prices. If prices fell, as now, they would restrict the sale of stones until things improved.

The compound was behind corrugated iron fencing and they entered through the large gates. 'We have to be more careful with diamond mining,' Frank said, smoking, the dry heat causing the cigarette to burn more quickly. 'Diamonds can be hidden on or in their bodies far more easily than the gold. Kaffirs might be good labourers, good beasts, but they're

bloody shrewd and know the value of the stones they dig up.
We lock them up in here at night, six o'clock, and let 'em out
next morning to start their shift again. Before they sleep though
they are searched.' He pointed to a pole which stood between
two stands, much like Harry's school high jump. 'We make
them jump over that for a start. Then there's a body search.
Mouth and other orifices. If they are found with anything on
them they are flogged with a *jambok*.'

Harry looked away from the compound, out through the
gates, way out to the Karroo which stretched into the
distance. He seemed to breathe easier then.

'When their spell is over we lock each one up in a room over
there for God knows how many days before they can go home.'
Frank now pointed to a low corrugated iron shack with several
doors. He flicked his cigarette away through the air and lit
another. 'We purge them, we have to. You never know, they
might have swallowed a stone and it's in their intestines
waiting until they get back to their huts.'

Would one stone per labourer really break the conglomerates, Harry wondered, but pushed the thought deep down.

'And if you find a kaffir without a pass, you must always take
action, Harry. They'll get a good beating as well as a search.
We can't have any nonsense with these boys, can we? They're
like dogs, they need a firm hand.'

The room was hung with red velvet drapes, not just at the
windows but along the walls too. They were old and the dust
was in them and had dulled the sheen they once had. A girl who
sauntered past smiled at him and her teeth were yellow. She
paused in front of a man who sat near the front door and he
rose, following her up the stairs.

Harry took another drink from his balloon glass, savouring
the smell of the brandy he had poured from the silver flask
which his father had given him the night before he left
England. It was the finest Hine and there were another four
bottles in his trunk. Frank had slapped him on the back when
he had told him this and dragged him off to this house which
lay on the edge of Kimberley.

'Under this roof the lights never go out,' Frank called from the *chaise-longue* which had once been green but was now rubbed bare and almost colourless. It was set against the wall nearest to the stairs directly opposite Harry and between them was a worn rug. Frank's face was flushed and Harry raised his hand and smiled but his back was rigid. He looked down into his glass, cradling it in his hands though there was no need, for it was in fact too warm in this interminable heat. He ran his finger round his collar. Oh Christ, it was so hot. Too hot to be borne.

England was so far away with its cool green colours, its rivers flowing lazily under bridges and its punt poles dripping water back into widening ripples. He rubbed his cracked lips. Would Arthur take the girls next year? But he must not think of that, only of why he was here. But dear God, Esther was so far away and the ache of separation was a physical pain that he could not forget, could not put to the back of his mind. He felt again her lips, her hair, so soft and fine between his fingers, her eyes which looked into his and promised she would wait.

'Take your collar off, Harry,' Frank called. 'You're not amongst ladies now, you know. These girls know how to give you a good time and you'd better make the most of it because you'll be too busy when we get back to Jo'burg.'

Laughter filled the room and Harry nodded, laughing too, but not inside. A woman came and sat with Frank, her shoulders bare and her breasts barely covered. Four other men were in the room, lounging in chairs, their legs outstretched, playing poker as they waited for those upstairs to finish. Harry took a sip of brandy and the vapour captured by the glass overrode for a moment the smell from the oil lamps, the sweat from the girl and the men which hung in an almost tangible layer.

He watched as Frank wrenched at his tie, throwing it across the back of the chair, winking at Harry as he did so, his arm clasped around the woman who wore red. Her dress was tight and shiny and as she crossed her legs Harry saw that her legs were bare and he was swept back to that evening when Hannah and Esther had danced. Was this why his father had been so severe? But what would an upright churchman know of prostitutes? He shook his head, the thought was nonsense and he took another drink.

He looked again at the woman's bare legs and felt the heat rise in him, and a hunger came which made him grip his glass and lift it to his lips and he swallowed hard, and again, feeling the brandy burn his throat. He looked back at the other men. They were still playing, throwing stained cards on to the worn green baize of a table. There was no music, just the ticking of a clock which stood by the door that led into the street. Harry tapped his foot in time to it as he placed his glass on the floor, for there was no table.

'Come on, Harry, get your flask out, man,' Frank called holding out his glass, his shirt unbuttoned now and his other hand stroking the shoulder of the woman. She was kissing his ear and his mouth as he talked and Harry looked away from her, concentrating on Frank's glass as he walked across the room.

He filled his own glass as well, too full, but that was as he wanted it. He swallowed and still the men were playing, and still the clock ticked but now it was all slower, and further from him. His hands were steady as he held his glass and lifted it to his lips and he did not notice the vapour so much but saw that now Frank was stroking the woman's breast, his eyes closed, his mouth on hers.

Again Harry felt the hunger which he had fought against since he had held Esther to him. Oh yes, he had known women, but not many and he had not wanted another because he loved Esther. He poured more brandy into his glass and as he drank it spilled from his mouth on to his shirt and the heat was suddenly too much and he pulled his tie loose and tore the stud from his neck and still the players dealt their cards.

His flask was empty as Frank mounted the stairs, the girl hanging on his arm, and so Harry waved the black girl over and watched as she poured Cape brandy. He choked as it caught in his throat. Black and white. A sea of black all around them but not really visible, not really people. How strange. Red earth and great holes and blue rock. Black and white people. How strange. And he wanted to go home. To leave all this and the heat, the never-ending heat which beat against the ground and was beating in his head now, beating in time with the clock.

A woman came down the stairs now. He did not want her to come to him because he loved Esther but there was this hunger, this loneliness and he wanted to be touched, to be held. He wanted someone he could cling to, however briefly. But he loved Esther and so this woman in her blue shiny dress with shoulders plump and sweating must not come to him and smile as she was doing. She must not reach out her hand to his and he must not take it, as he was doing. The stairs were high and his legs were heavy and the room they entered was dark and he could not see this woman but saw instead the yellow hair of his love and her blue eyes. It was her breasts he kissed, not this woman's in this house. It was Esther he held to him, it was her body he stroked. It was her name he called when he could wait no longer.

The next day the train again wound across the interminable veld and Harry was glad that his head ached as though it would break because it dulled the shame of the hot dark night and the body which should have been Esther's but was not.

Frank sat opposite, smoking, his face hidden behind the pink pages of the *Sporting Life*.

'A good time was had by all then, old chap,' Frank said. The pages rustled as he lowered them.

Harry did not look at him but pushed the blind to one side, watching the miles upon miles of barren ground. 'It was fine thanks, Frank.'

He could see no houses, no farms as he looked and Frank laughed. 'Sorry we couldn't get to see that old homestead of your uncle's. Or rather yours but it's over that way somewhere. Closer to Kimberley perhaps.'

Harry leant against the window, looking back at the way they had come.

'What will you do with it?'

Harry let the blind fall and rested his head back on the seat. The train was rocking and he felt ill.

'Nothing, I expect. But one day I'd like to see it.' But it didn't seem to matter what he did with it, he felt so bloody awful. His head was worse. He wiped his face with his handkerchief. Shame was dulled by pain but it was still there. He must make up for his lapse, he must not waste more time. He had money to make. Oh God, he felt so sick.

Frank folded the paper and handed it to him. 'Have a read of the pink 'un, if you can get your eyes to focus. I told you to stay clear of the Cape brandy.'

Harry took the paper but did not read it. He sat with his eyes closed.

It took days to return to the high veld but at last the ridge was visible and Harry was glad, for up there were the mines and his future. Frank took his arm as they drew into the station and as the doors opened and they passed the carts that were waiting to take baggage and goods he held him fast and spoke low.

'South Africa will be good to you, Harry, but you know the way things are now. There are rules to be kept and questions that should not be asked. We work and we work well and so we are paid well. The kaffirs work so they can pay the poll-tax on their huts, and so the world goes round. We've done the tour, I've shown you the facts of life and what you have to remember now is that there is no place for humanity when gold and diamonds are the prize. Remember that.'

Harry looked at Frank, hearing him through the splitting head which he had been unable to overcome. He saw his broad face and long hair, his beard and his eyes which were hard. Yes, he would remember that because it was the prize he too wanted, it was the prize that would secure Esther for him and there was nothing else that was of such importance. So he nodded and Frank smiled, saying as he turned and heaved down their bags, 'There are some interesting little houses in Johannesburg too, my boy. I'll show you when we have some time.'

Though Harry nodded he hoped that he would never again visit a woman who was not Esther for the shame was too great and he had too much to do.

14 In January 1908 a deputation of non-militant suffragists were told by Asquith, the new Liberal Prime Minister, that the Government had no intention of giving women the vote.

Hannah had never seen Miss Fletcher angry before and looked up in amazement as she walked into the sitting-room and threw her hat across the room. Hannah shut the books which she had been marking beside the fire. The dog sat up and Hannah said nothing, just looked as Frances poured a glass of sherry and brought it to Hannah without a word, her face white and her lips thin.

She then turned on her heel and poured another for herself and stood, her face set, as she looked first at her drink and then at Hannah.

'Cheers, Hannah. We must drink to the start of a difficult 1908.' Then, pacing the floor, she told Hannah more about the meeting the deputation had had with Asquith.

Hannah said, 'Did he give a reason?'

'What do you think?' Frances snapped, but as Hannah flushed she said, 'Oh, I'm sorry, my dear.'

She walked over to Hannah, looking down on her. 'It is just so very frustrating. I can see more and more why the suffragettes are not content with polite requests but I can still not bring myself to work as they do.'

She sat heavily in the chair opposite Hannah. 'It's such an uphill struggle but we'll just have to go on asking, requesting, gathering support and in the end, perhaps we'll win.'

'We'll win,' Hannah assured her, drinking her sherry and leaning back in her chair. 'We'll win.' But impatience made her head ache, for still she could not join in the battle as she really wished because the Pensions Bill was not through yet. Later, when Beatrice had cleared away dinner and the fire was low in the grate, she showed Frances the letter she had received from Harry. It was short and the first he had written to her since school.

My dear Hannah,

I have just arrived and have completed a tour of the Rand and Kimberley too. It is extremely hot and there is dust everywhere and it is so very different to England. I am expected to work on the gold ridge for some while in a more direct way than I had been led to believe. I had fully expected to be out each day surveying the land for evidence of more gold-bearing ore but they have too many engineers already so I am back in the pits. I love it.

I hope to move to Kimberley in due course because the diamond mines are even better. I also hope to have a mate assigned to me soon. He will be a native or kaffir, as we call them here. I received your letter and am pleased that you are well and yes, I think that it is probably a good idea to interest Esther in your woman's movement – she will need something if she is to find this miserable waiting bearable. But, Hannah, take care of her for me. You must promise me this.

Give my regards to Miss Fletcher. I am writing to Father in a separate letter.

With love from your brother,
Harry.

As Frances finished Hannah said, 'You can see that he says nothing about the natives and their conditions. I must write to him about it; I must find out from him what is going on out there.'

Miss Fletcher passed it back, removing the spectacles which she now needed to read, rubbing the bridge of her nose. 'He doesn't give much detail of his life out there at all, does he?' she agreed. 'But he sounds happy. And do you think you will be able to keep Esther busy enough to wait for Harry?'

Hannah looked up at her. 'I don't know, but I shall have to try.'

At Easter, the King's Speech was silent on votes for women. Joe had come to London to present some furniture designs to a customer and he walked around the streets with her while Frances attended a meeting to discuss which Members of Parliament they should try and persuade to draw up yet another Female Franchise Bill. Together they handed out letters written by Frances asking for support. He held the hessian bag and talked of the home and how Eliza came to help because it was only ten miles and the trap could do it there and back in one day. Hannah's aunt had hung curtains at all the windows and the women who were staying had joined in. Sam had organised the men and the children and had cleared out the stables because there would be apples on the trees in the orchard and Joe wanted to store them in the old hay-loft.

As they walked the fog-shrouded and stinking streets, pressing against the dank wall as a drunk staggered past, she longed for the clear air, the fields, Aunt Eliza's curtains, the smell of apples which made her remember Uncle Simon. But Cornwall would have to wait because there was a battle which must be fought day in and day out before there could be that sort of peace for her.

So she knocked on the next door and handed out the letter, smiling and talking and asking for support for the suffragists' campaign for votes for women. She wanted to ask for support for the suffragette rally to be held in the Albert Hall too but she did not, for her loyalty to Frances was too strong, and she shrugged as Joe smiled and handed her another letter.

'Wait a little longer, Hannah,' he said and she nodded, taking his arm until they reached the next house because he made her feel as though it did not matter quite so much.

Joe left the next day, pleased with an order for six chairs and one table. He looked tanned and strong and well in contrast to the pallor of the people in the narrow streets, streets which still swam with a heavy fog and a cold dampness.

Hannah did not go with him to the station because Arthur was expecting her for dinner with his parents and besides, she did not want to see Joe leave the arched grey station to travel towards the lush, green, clear country. And so she had waved as he climbed into the hansom cab, making herself think not of the rolling hills and the apple-loft but of Arthur and the brilliant lights that would flood the dining-room tonight.

He had invited Esther too and she came to fetch her in Uncle Thomas's carriage, wrapped in a silk shawl which could pass through her mother's wedding ring, she told Hannah and Frances.

Hannah turned as Frances said, 'How lovely for you, Esther.' And though there was no laughter in her face or her voice Hannah knew that it was just below the surface.

During the evening they talked of Harry and the heat that he had spoken of. They talked of Arthur's work in the City. They talked of the new term in Parliament and Lord Wilmot worried about the tax that would be levied to pay for the Pensions Bill.

'Five shillings they want for everyone over seventy. It threatens the empire, you know. It's the beginning of the end.'

They did not talk of women's suffrage because Arthur felt his father would not understand. 'Though I think the suffragettes show a pleasing spirit,' he said to Hannah as he took her to see the jasmine which was growing so well in the conservatory. 'Perhaps it gives you girls something to do that's fun.' He kissed her and his lips were soft and warm.

The next week Esther and Hannah travelled to the big suffragette meeting at the Albert Hall for, reasoned Hannah, to attend meetings was not militant and could not affect the principle of no militancy until the Pensions Bill was passed. Frances had nodded but had not come.

As they entered the domed building Esther whispered in Hannah's ear, 'I wonder what Prince Albert would have said about women using his building to discuss a campaign for votes.' Hannah, forced along by the press of women behind and in front and to the side of her, said, 'He'd have looked down that long nose of his and said, "I am not amused", I should think.'

Their soft laughter sounded good to Hannah but as they entered the auditorium they both fell silent at the sight and sound of women from wall to wall; murmuring, talking, waving to one another. Hannah felt an excitement, a relief that she was here at last amongst a great mass who felt as she did. She had not known there were so many, so very many.

The suffragist meetings she had attended with Frances had been small and decorous, not crammed and vocal as this gathering was. She looked at the women in front and the large woman who stood at her side, a working woman. There was a set to her chin, a determination that the woman next to her also wore and on and on down the row. A sense of belonging took and held Hannah and there was a great peace within her because at last she was here. She wanted to be able to go home and sit by the wicker chair and tell her mother of the sights and sounds that were soaking into her with every second.

Esther took her arm. 'Look,' she said pointing towards the platform.

Hannah pushed thoughts of her mother away, back, not to her father's house, but to the home in Cornwall where Joe was sorting apples and Eliza was making curtains, for it was here that she believed her mother now lived, embodied in an idea which she had made reality. Hannah pressed the back of her hand to her mouth, making her lips hurt. To think of her mother in this way was all that made the loss endurable. She breathed deeply and listened as Esther repeated herself taking Hannah's arm and shaking it.

'Look.'

Hannah craned her head above the crowd, following Esther's hand and then she saw it. An empty chair set on the platform with a placard which read 'Mrs Pankhurst's Chair'. The speakers were entering as Hannah remembered that Emmeline Pankhurst was in prison for obstructing the police and applause filled the auditorium, wave upon wave to the very height of the dome, and it was for Mrs Pankhurst and all the other women who were deprived of their liberty because they had dared to demand their rights.

Hannah's hands ached from clapping, her throat was tight from cheering but all the time she wondered whether when the time came she would have their courage. Would she be able to carry on walking when the police called on her to stop? And would her voice be as loud when it was her turn to heckle at a meeting? She was still clapping, everyone was clapping. But could she keep on demanding until the stewards came as they always did, hurting and pushing until the police took her to the cells? Could she do it, she wondered, and her palms were damp and the noise of the women all around her could not drown the question she asked herself, one that she could not yet answer. Had she been waiting because she was afraid? It was a question which was too uncomfortable to consider.

It was the sudden hush that brought her back to Esther and to the large woman, but not before she realised that, at this moment, she was glad that the Pensions Bill still had not been passed so perhaps after all her question was answered. Fear was her enemy. A woman was standing on the platform and as she spoke Hannah rose as all the others did when they were told that the Government had released the prisoners and Mrs Pankhurst would take the chair tonight after all.

That night, when the meeting was ended, Hannah did not take a hansom cab from outside the hall but walked and walked because she was charged with energy, with excitement, with a sense of belonging and Esther was with her, her eyes alight, her cheeks flushed.

'It's all so very exciting, Hannah. Oh, to think of those women suffering imprisonment. What heroines. How glamorous.' She gripped Hannah's arm. 'It's the excitement which appeals, isn't it? Flouting the law, being seen to be brave. I must write and tell Harry what a wonderful idea it was of mine.'

Hannah's laughter was tinged with irritation at such remarks which could only have come from her cousin, but she would not allow Esther to impinge on her own elation, her own enthusiasm, and her fear was forgotten as she felt again the atmosphere and comradeship of the past few hours. It was like nothing else she had known. She would not be fighting alone and that knowledge made her feel that anything was possible, that her fear could be conquered.

The following week Hannah talked to Frances as they drank thick warm cocoa before the fire. Asquith wanted proof that there was support for women's suffrage, though, as Frances had said, what had he been seeing all these years? Her tone had been bitter. None the less the suffragists were arranging a procession to the Albert Hall and the suffragettes were marching to Hyde Park.

Frances looked at her and nodded. 'So at last you have a decision to make, Hannah. Under which banner will you march?' She stirred her cocoa and tapped the spoon twice before putting it in her saucer.

Hannah nodded, looking into the fire which leapt and spun over the dried logs which she had brought from the cellar today.

Frances continued. 'But before you do decide, just let me say that I should be hurt if you left the schoolhouse just because you chose a different path to me. I enjoy your company and want you to remain here with me.'

Hannah looked up from the fire to Frances now and felt a lightness growing within her because she had felt that to declare for the suffragettes would mean the end of all this. She looked about the room to the books, the desk, the dog, which was yelping in its sleep.

'It's just that I still feel this anger, this need to make the Government listen. They're not listening. We have to shout, to grip their collars and make them look at us while we speak the words which they must one day listen to.' She had risen and begun to pace the floor. 'They should not need proof. There are all the years of suffrage work to be seen, all the petitions, the lobbying. It is an insult.'

'Do sit down, Hannah.' Frances was laughing.

But Hannah felt restless, full of an energy that could not be released. It was as though there was something pushing and roaring against a barrier which she could not yet move aside; a barrier of waiting. She crossed her arms, her hands gripping tightly, and she made herself turn and sit in the chair, made herself take her mug between her hands, bringing it to her lips and sipping, feeling the steam on her face.

'I must choose the suffragettes,' she said, watching the face of her Headmistress, her friend.

There was a pause and she could hear the clock, and the fire as it hissed and spat.

'Of course you must. You are just confirming what we have both known for a long time,' Frances said at last, her face still calm and her voice level as it always was. There was a further pause and then Frances spoke again, her voice slow as she sought words carefully.

'But, Hannah, do be careful. It is not an easy path. The suffragettes are frequently imprisoned and that is not pleasant even in the first division which is for political prisoners. Usually it is the second division or at worst the third and that, my dear, is a true punishment.'

Frances placed her mug on the table and bent forward, using the brass poker to push a log further on to the fire. Sparks rose and some clung to the soot that coated the back of the hearth. She could not know what the women had suffered during their imprisonments but she had seen them on their release and she feared for Hannah, whom she had grown to love. This girl who was her friend and almost her child but how could one protect another? Frances shook her head. She knew it was impossible, and there would be anguish and pain for Hannah as she fought the coming battle and that would be her pain too. All she could do for now was to continue to delay the hardship for her in the hope that soon the vote would be given and Hannah need not face those things that Frances feared would break her.

'But the Pensions Bill is not through yet, Hannah.' Frances was sitting back in her chair now, her fingers steepled in front of her face. 'Do you remember what we discussed? This reform government is so important and I fear that the suffragettes will damage it. We must have social reforms, you know that.'

Hannah nodded, feeling the frustration build into a physical pain. Yes, she knew that and yes, she would wait until the Pensions Bill was through and it would not just be because Frances desired this but because she did too.

'I know and the Government won't be damaged, Frances. Women are not that strong, remember?' Her tone was ironic and Frances smiled. At least she had bought some time but would it be enough? Please God, let Asquith give us the vote.

She did not say this but tried to caution this young woman who had already faced so much.

'I know I've said this before but I worry, I suppose, in case the demonstrations, the protests become too militant. I cannot condone violence, Hannah, and it would do our cause no good, and I use "our" collectively. You see, to have the vote requires a degree of responsibility, and should the militancy escalate I fear that all that would result would be the alienation of our supporters within Parliament and that it would become almost a purposeless act. Violence for violence's sake is not healthy, neither is revenge.' Frances looked up as the clock struck eleven. 'Now I think the lecture is over, my dear, for tonight,' and as she took Hannah's cup from her she remembered herself at twenty-two, supported by two loving parents who had made everything seem possible. And so it had been until her fiancé died in India and even then the school had held her life together as, with the passing years, her father and then her mother had been 'gathered', as Hannah would say. As she held the door for Hannah to pass through she leant forward and kissed her cheek.

'You must be careful, Hannah,' she said and wanted to send her far from here, to Cornwall, where she belonged and where she would be safe with Joe. But all she could do was smile and hide the fear because had not her parents loved her enough to do that for her too?

On this warm May day in Frances's dining-room Esther was wearing cotton gloves to paint 'Votes for Women' in black furniture stain on the white calico banner while Hannah crouched beside her, her own brush heavy in her hand, her bare fingers stained with black, but it was good to see them marked like this and to feel the soreness of her palm.

She knelt upright, easing the stiffness of her back, and as she did so she saw Maureen, one of her Sunday ladies, doing the same and they smiled. The woman wore the new suffragette ribbons, white, green and purple, pinned to her bodice in the shape of a bow, and Hannah turned to look at the bag on the trestle table at the side of the room. She must remember to wear some too.

'Really, Hannah,' Esther said as she also straightened. 'I much prefer the meetings. This is all rather hard work. I do hope it isn't all too hectic on the day.' She looked across at the poles which lay by the table. 'They look a little rough and heavy to me.'

Hannah laughed. 'You'll be all right and remember, you have ordered that rather fetching dress to set off your ribbons.'

She laughed again as Esther's face broke into a smile. 'Yes, indeed, and a new hat too. One should go into these things properly, you know, Hannah. Half-measures are not the thing.'

She patted her hair into shape, and Hannah laughed again. At least she had been able to write to Harry that Esther was now very busy and working with other women, so did it matter that it was all a game to her?

'We must remember to pick up some ribbons before they're packed away,' Hannah said, stretching the calico out and painting the line of the 'T' a little thicker.

'I'll get one now,' Esther said and Hannah smiled at the speed with which her cousin threw down her brush, rose to her feet and pulled off her gloves, throwing them on to the pile of calico scraps which was growing in the centre of the room.

She sat back on her haunches and eased her neck as Esther clutched her pale blue skirt and apron close to her and wove her way between the women who were working and talking, crouched on the floor like she was. It was good to work with colleagues who had become friends. The old dining-room was transformed. The desks used on Sundays were pushed against the walls for today but they would have to be moved back before the women left.

Frances had given Hannah the remains of the stain that her suffragists had used to paint their banners when they had marched to the Albert Hall but now, Hannah thought with satisfaction, it was the turn of the suffragettes. Hannah swept the hair which fell forward on to her face back into her bun, smelling the stain again, feeling the sweep of anticipation which had been growing since news of the march had reached them. Suffragettes would be converging on London from all over the country on Midsummer's Day but before that there was all this work to do. Hannah looked around her. Everywhere in the country women would be painting and cutting and hammering their banners, their flags and their regalia. They would be gathering supporters, enlisting new members, arranging transport, determined that Asquith should never be able to say again that women's suffrage had no support in the country.

'What will Arthur say?' Esther said and Hannah looked up, startled, as her cousin dangled three ribbons in front of her. She pointed to the black marks on Hannah's hands. 'You look like some dreadful washerwoman, Hannah. It's not fair on him. He does have a position to maintain, you know.'

Hannah hushed her, looking round to see if her Sunday pupil had heard but she had not. 'Maureen is a washerwoman,' she hissed.

'But she is not about to marry a Lord's son,' Esther replied sharply.

Hannah snapped, 'And neither am I, not immediately anyway and if a bit of black stain ruins the man's prospects it doesn't say much for the position or the man.' She took the ribbons with two clean fingertips and put them in the pocket of her apron; they were smooth and cool.

'Let's leave the banner to dry for a while and then we'll attach it to the poles. Are you any good with a hammer?' she asked, enjoying the look of horror on Esther's face before pushing herself to her feet with a groan. Her knees were sore from kneeling all morning but her feet would be sorer still by the time they had walked the route of the procession. She hoped that this June would not be too hot.

It was not and the day dawned fresh and bright. The previous week Hannah had edged their white banner with purple and green once the stain had dried.

Now her group stood amongst the ranks upon ranks of women, holding their poles, which were heavy now and would be heavier still by the time they reached Hyde Park. Those who had been in prison wore white and held white pennants. Hannah tried not to hear Esther as she complained that no one could see her hat and that they must force their way to the edge

244

of the procession so that her dress could be seen. But at least she was here, where Hannah could keep her busy for Harry.

'Stand still for now,' Hannah ordered. 'We'll move across before the start.'

Sylvia Pankhurst had designed borders for some of the banners and Hannah looked up at theirs and wished that Joe could have come up after all to design hers as he had hoped to be able to do, but the house was too full, he had written, and she knew that this was true for she and Frances had sent the families down last week, chosen from the ones that came on Sundays as usual.

'There are so many here,' Esther breathed, looking round.

'It's wonderful, isn't it?' Hannah said.

'It would be, if I was on the edge,' Esther murmured and Hannah gripped her pole more firmly, wanting to tip it hard on to that perfect green hat with the purple ostrich feather. But instead she looked about her and, seeing a gap, eased a way through, pulling Esther as she went until they were at the edge of the procession.

'I do not want to hear one more word from you,' she said. 'And what if your father should see you?' she asked.

'Oh, he won't be watching but he said I was to behave myself,' Esther replied and Hannah laughed in her amazement. Uncle Thomas was quite extraordinary because not only did he not seem to object to Esther being involved in this political fight, he was in fact pleased that she was busy during the day teaching, and spending much of her other free time with Hannah and the suffragettes. Perhaps he also wanted Esther to wait for Harry, Hannah thought, and for the first time it occurred to her that Harry might indeed return with the wealth he had spoken of so often.

'The leaders are marching,' the woman in front told them, 'so we'll be ready soon.'

Hannah turned to the row behind her and passed on the message, grinning at Esther and lifting her head, not looking at the people who watched from the sidelines but aware of them. It was pride that coursed through her. Pride that women would travel from seventy towns on special trains and take part in the seven processions that were at this moment heading for Hyde Park. Pride that all these women felt as she did. How could Asquith ignore them now?

They were moving at last, the women in front hoisting their banners. She nodded at Esther and they did likewise and the seven miles did not seem long and she barely noticed the ache in her arms as she held the banner aloft. Esther changed places with a woman who waved a flag and so Hannah had a different partner and they talked of the north where she came from and the strength of feeling that was building in the provinces as well as the capital. The police directed traffic and allowed the procession to proceed without halting at any junctions. Any jeers were drowned by the louder cheers from within the spectators.

At Hyde Park they were able to drop their banners in a pile near the entrance and it was a relief to feel grass beneath their shoes instead of hard roads and to know that there was time now to walk around and listen as speakers talked of political liberty from twenty platforms. Esther clutched Hannah's arm and walked with her from platform to platform through the thousands of women who were hot, who ached, who thrilled at the sight and sound of this display of power. Hannah craned her neck watching Christabel Pankhurst but not hearing her above the noise of the crowds. She heard one woman say that there were more than a quarter of a million people here, mostly women.

As they walked beneath the trees seeking shade Hannah heard how decorated buses had been driven through the streets and steam-driven launches bearing suffragettes had halted opposite the terrace of the House of Commons to lobby MPs taking tea and she hoped they had developed indigestion.

She and Esther ate the sandwiches which Beatrice had prepared and the cucumber was moist and the bread too. They drank cold lemon tea, which Esther said should have been champagne but Hannah replied that they did not need it because the air was so full of celebration.

They talked to women without introduction. They cheered along with thousands more when the resolution was carried 'that this meeting calls upon the Government to grant votes to women without delay'. They cheered again when a letter was sent to Asquith by special messenger informing him of this resolution and asking what action his Government intended to take in response to this display of support for female suffrage. At last the women knew that he could not deny the proof of this mass meeting.

The next day he replied negatively to the letter and so votes for women were no nearer at all and Hannah could not bear the disappointment, the rejection, but she knew that she must for the Pensions Bill was not yet law. So she watched from behind with many others as a deputation of thirteen suffragettes set out ten days later to present a further plea to Asquith at the House of Commons.

She saw the police, big men in dark blue, barring the women from the House. She saw the Inspector informing them that Asquith refused to receive them. Esther was with her now. She had joined her late from a dress fitting. There were others too, many others who had met in Parliament Square and then crossed to Westminster, hearing the news of the police out in force to bar women from the place where the laws which governed women were made, and to which, in this democratic country, they were denied access.

She saw the height and the breadth of the policemen and she also saw her father in the dark of his house, his body as he loomed near her, and fear clutched at her as well as anger and, for now, the two were equal. Some women in their rage took a boat to the terrace, others entered Palace Yard by cab. Only one infiltrated the building. Arrests were made and Hannah heard the next day as she shared lunch with Frances before taking the afternoon lessons that twenty-seven women had been imprisoned.

'Do men consider us such a terrible enemy?' she asked again but aloud this time.

Frances heard the darkness in her voice and knew that it was beginning for Hannah and she fought to keep her voice level.

'It seems somehow quite absurd,' Frances said, 'and the public do seem to be appalled at such draconian measures as well. Let's hope their support continues and the Government might well change its mind.' Her knuckles were white on her fork and she hoped that Hannah had not noticed but then she saw that hers were too and that the girl was not aware of anything at this table; that her eyes were on some distant scene.

That night window-breaking began and Number 10 Downing Street was one of the first to be struck. The perpetrators received two months in prison.

Hannah fought down her fear and continued to wait for the Pensions Bill to become law.

15   Harry stood looking at the headgear in the light from the moon, knowing that after today he would not be seeing it again. He felt his horse stir beneath him and leant forward, rubbing his hand along the sleek neck. Arthur would approve of this animal; he must write and tell him. The trader had asked too much of course but after three years out here in all the squalor and the dirt, the opulence and extravagance, he had longed for something of real beauty.

'And you are that something, Kim,' he crooned softly.

Baralong, his mate, had nodded when the trader brought Kim forward from the string of animals tied to the back of his wagon, but only slightly so that Frank would not notice the movement, for there must be no friendship between black and white, must there?

Harry would not look over towards the compound, he would not allow his ears to hear the moaning which was not the wind. He would not allow himself to think of Baralong behind that fence. He looked instead over to the stamp engine clearly visible on this night which was moonlit as it had been when he had first seen the mine; colourless without the hot light of the sun but during the day there was colour. There was red and blue and black and white. Oh yes, there was black and white.

Harry turned Kim round. He was glad to be leaving the gold-field at last but they had not been wasted years, by God no, for he had learnt a great deal, mostly about himself, and he knew that the heat and the cold and the knowledge had dug lines deep into his face, and his mind would never be as empty as it had been before. He also knew that this would please Hannah even though she was in the midst of her own battles.

Would the diamond fields be different? He hoped so but he feared that they would not. Kim was walking steadily, his hoofs striking sparks on the flat stones. Yes, Harry thought as he clasped the reins loosely in his hands, not turning once to look at the mines, he was glad to be leaving, glad to be going with Baralong. Now what would Frank think of that sentiment? But, of course, he would never know because Harry knew better than to tell him.

Harry thought back over that first decadent year out here in South Africa when the excitement and anticipation he had begun to feel in Kimberley continued to burn and which now filled him with shame. How easily he had been drawn by Frank into the life enjoyed by the other management employees; how easily he had worked and talked and drunk with them through the hot dry weeks of the summer months from September to April. There had been barely any of the sudden sharp showers which the Rand usually experienced and therefore little water so that only the very rich could wash, and only then in soda water, and that in itself had drawn the young men closer together. He thought of the winter, so cold and yet so dry, and the smell of the mine; its sounds, its darkness which had thrilled him and made him feel so good, as Penhallon had done, and he had been content to let Kimberley wait as he built up his stake money and pushed aside the noise from the compounds.

He had soaked into his pores the dust from the ore, watched as the natives crouched in the upward-sloping stopes, their candles in their hats throwing a flickering light as they hunched into hand-drills which dug at the rock face. By God, it had felt so good and he had also worked in the offices and learnt much and in the evenings and weekends he had been free, and that was what Harry now remembered, sitting on Kim, looking back on the person who had once been him.

In South Africa, in that first year spent living amongst the vulgar extravagance of Johannesburg with its tasteless opulence, its noise, its excitement, he had felt free, had felt as though he were a man. There were none of the restrictions and traditions of England out here; the dreary rules of his father's people, just the excesses and pleasures of a new town which had made its own rules, its own wealth and power, and along with it had provided him with work that he loved. It had thrilled him. The conventions of his childhood were cast aside as he explored the music-halls, the clubs, the gambling, and occasionally, in spite of his promise to himself, the whores.

In the evenings when they were not out watching some show or drinking and eating at some new hotel he and Frank had sat in the nearby bar drinking warm flat beer or harsh Cape brandy talking of their own dreams of wealth, their ambitions for their future. Harry had spoken of his farm until Barry, a friend of Frank's who knew the property that Uncle Simon had bought, told him that it was good for nothing but farming ostriches, and who wore ostrich feathers these days? Frank had laughed and so too had Harry because the others had.

Barry explained that there was no river in the near vicinity and no signs of alluvial deposits of diamonds and so they had laughed again and he had not bothered to make the trip to see the broken-down house that Barry described because there was too much work to do here and besides, he had been made to feel foolish. He would visit it at some much later date.

He and Frank had always sat in the same chairs in the bar; his was maroon velvet whilst Frank's was green. Whenever Harry sipped that first beer he would drop his shoulders, savour the sourness of his drink, and look at the charcoal sketch on the opposite wall portraying the early banket of the outcrop being mined by teams of kaffirs who cut into it with picks and shovels, whilst behind them were drawn, in fainter lines, the stamp batteries crushing the ore. He would sit there, letting his body relax, letting the beer take effect, letting the conversation ebb around him as he took in each detail, knowing that the pulverised rock shown in the picture was mixed in those days with water to produce a slime which was passed over copper plates coated with mercury. The particles of gold in the slime amalgamated with the mercury which was then removed from the plates and refined, the mercury being discarded. Less than 70 per cent of the gold had been recovered in those days. It was 90 per cent now, he would think with satisfaction, downing his beer, but he was careful always not to drink the dregs.

Each evening in the bar began in this way and then he would buy another drink before joining the others to bet on how many flies would land on a piece of meat, or how many men would walk through the door in the next thirty seconds but never on which dog could kill the most rats in the pit behind the building or on the cocks which fought and died because there was too much blood and he could never laugh and call as the others did.

He sighed now in the dark as Kim jerked, startled by a dassie which ran across their path. Yes, there had been hard work in the day and hard play at night but always, too, there had been Hannah's letters and his irritation at her endless questions, her endless accusations.

What did he know of the natives, she would write. Could he not see that it was wrong to exploit them? And on and on she would go and he would drink more, smiling at Frank but silently cursing his sister because she disturbed his enjoyment of his acceptance by the other men, his enjoyment at being in a circle again, his enjoyment of friendship as he had enjoyed it at school.

Anyway, what did he know of the natives beyond the fact that they were there, like the ore or the diamonds? They had steady jobs, hadn't they? South Africa was beginning to be industrialised, wasn't it? With the coming of the mines it had made sense to use the labour force available. The natives were South Africa's raw material, just as the gold was. These were the facts of life out here, he had kept on telling himself as the beer soured his throat. After all, as Frank had said, equal rights for people who were inherently unequal was absurd. To think anything else was sheer sentimentality and Harry had nodded, looking back at the charcoal picture because after all, he had thought, this is a business world. But he had not written this to Hannah because he knew she would not understand. How could anyone who was not out here, in amongst it all, understand? It worked and that was all that anyone needed to think about, wasn't it? He had begun to drink more and more, it made him feel better, and he had not heard the noise from the compounds quite so clearly.

At Christmas he had written to her and said that he had never heard a native complain and that, as well as jobs, kaffirs had homes provided. But again he did not tell her of the compounds he had seen which were two acres or more with twenty-five kaffirs to a thirty-foot by twenty-five-foot room and perhaps 2000 to a compound. He did not tell her of the ten-foot corrugated iron fences surrounding the compounds and the passes which all the natives had to carry. She would not have agreed that it could be looked on as a way of disciplining the workforce as well as preventing pilfering and, as Frank had said, it kept them out of the town and the bars. After all, he had laughed, who wants to sit and drink next to an animal? No, he had not told Hannah much about South Africa over that year and had screwed up her harping letters and thrown them away when he had drunk enough to blur her memory.

He had written also to Esther and kept her replies, reading them every night but this had not stopped him from watching the girls who served in the bar. They had come up from the Cape eager for work, any sort of work. They would climb the stairs with you 'if you so wished', they would say with lips parted, and he had done so more than once, even though he had promised himself that he would not. At night, lying in bed, he would tell himself that men were different, that they needed a release which women did not, knowing that he still loved Esther more than life itself and missed her each hour of each day and finally he would sleep.

Harry shook his head now as he eased the reins between his hands. Would he have gone on and on in this way had it not been for that surveying ride with Baralong at the start of the second year while the summer heat still lay deep on the ground and in the air? It was a question he would never be able to answer, for he had indeed ridden across the barren land and he had indeed never been the same again.

He recaptured the stifling morning when Frank had pointed out the kaffir mate he had picked for him. As he sat astride this warm horse it was all as clear to him as the moment it had happened. Frank had stood shading his eyes against the sun, flicking his stick towards a kaffir. The shadows of the mine buildings had been sharp behind him. It's your turn to have a few days away. Go and survey the ridge and take that boy as your guide, then keep him on as your mate, Frank had said, nodding at Harry. He's a good worker and knows his job. Harry had looked towards a kaffir who stood outside the site office. He had not been able to see the kaffir's face because his hat had been pulled so low that the brim shaded his features. His rough hessian jacket had hung loose and his trousers were tied with rope. This was Baralong but he hadn't known that, not at this stage. He had merely nodded at Frank, wiping his face which was sweating again from the heat.

I could do with a break, he had said, beckoning to the kaffir, pointing to the horse which was tied to the post near the office. Bring that over, boy, he had said, and the one across the gap too, you'll ride that. I'll need a guide today. His tone had been curt and Frank had nodded, smiling into the sun and drawing on his cigarette.

You're doing all right out here, Harry, old chap. Just the sort we want, he had murmured, and Harry remembered how pleased he had felt as he smiled, but how, strangely, he could not look in the direction of the black man whom he had just treated as he would one of Arthur's hounds. After more than a year of managing native teams totally impersonally he suddenly found it different dealing with just one black man and he had been unable to understand himself.

He had walked towards the horse. It was the heat and that damnable Cape brandy. They'd stayed too long in the bar last night and there was a foul taste in his mouth. The glaring sun hurt his eyes and he had one of his headaches even though the height of the summer had passed and it was cooler than it had been last week.

He thought how good it would be to leave the office and the mine, travel easily and let this throbbing head die down but he had then looked at the long line of kaffirs trailing from the compounds to the mines, their shoulders bowed, their heads hung down and his headache had worsened, stabbing hard behind his eyes. He felt angry, impatient to be off, away from buildings, noise, people and letters, for there had been another one from Hannah that morning. He had walked quickly over to his horse. He would not think of her words, but he had determined, as he swung up into the saddle, that he must insist that she stop writing him these letters. It was too bloody much when he was out here trying to do a job, for God's sake. That was all he was trying to do, just work at a bloody job and make something of himself. And was it a crime if he tried to enjoy the experience? Damn women, he had cursed, and had heard Frank laugh as he spurred his horse from the mine, out on to the ridge. He knew his friend thought he had meant the whore in the pub last night who had taken a visitor to bed instead of him and he was happy to leave it like that, it was safer.

The ridge was over forty miles long and sufficient provisions had been packed in the saddle-bags to camp out for several nights. He remembered the heat as it had struck up from the ground, the dust as it had filled his mouth and nose, the silence between the two men, one black, one white, as they rode throughout the day across the arid terrain with the veld below and the mines in the distance. He had fought to regain the impersonal attitude he had always held towards the natives but somehow he had been unable to do so. He could see this kaffir's face and there were just the two of them out here.

With nightfall they had stopped and Harry had stood awkwardly as his new mate heated a kettle over an open fire. The coals glowed and the smoke smelt good drifting on the air, and then there was the aroma of mutton and that was good too. The kaffir handed Harry the cooked salt mutton, still in silence, before moving away from the flames which lit his black face now that his hat was tilted back. Harry saw that he was older than he had thought, at least thirty, and he was thin, but he did not want to look too closely because he might see a person where he had been told there was only a creature.

The enamel plate was hot from the meat so Harry took it by the edge and sat down on the ground, his back against his saddle. He took the tea which the kaffir then brought, wedging the mug into the crumbling earth beside his knee. The earth was losing its daytime heat.

Thank you, he had said, and the kaffir stopped as he turned away and the black eyes looked at him, then he moved on past the fire towards the horses, taking no food with him, no drink. Harry wondered why he had thanked the kaffir. He did not usually acknowledge them in any way. He had shaken his head, his headache was still there and he felt anger again. Damn Hannah.

Harry had cut at the tough salt meat, tearing it with his fingers when the knife fell to the ground. He was hungry and thirsty. It was cooler but not cold. He looked across the fire at his kaffir. The insects were sounding now, out there in the dark. Did kaffirs not feel hunger and thirst? He wiped his hands on his handkerchief but they still felt greasy and he could not spare water for washing, not until they had refilled their flasks at least. Christ, he could do with a drink. He took a quick nip of brandy from his flask, then shoved it back into his inside pocket before changing his mind and drinking from it again then settling into his blanket. It would protect him against the night chill, he told himself.

In the morning he had ridden on, still with his mate as guide, and had watched the contours of the ridge and the great plain which never changed as it swept up to its base. In the distance beyond the horizon were acres of maize which Frank said the Boers farmed now. It was good to see the sky and miles of scrub-covered earth, it made him feel cleaner somehow. He had not felt clean since he had arrived in this country, even when he had bathed. Why the hell was that?

He looked through the shimmering heat to the outlines of the mines, to the headgear which stood at the head of shafts thousands of feet deep. He looked down at the ground over which they rode, picturing the seams, the stopes which ran in all directions busy with the miners who worked with picks and hand-drills. There would be dust down there too. He had tied his handkerchief round his mouth and nose, coughing as he did so and turned back to the ridge, the plain, the shimmering heat, wanting only to see that, think of that.

That night he needed to taste something other than dust as he sat by the camp-fire so he took a cigarette from the case his father had given him and sucked the nicotine deep into his lungs. He watched as again his mate cooked salt mutton and boiled up tea and he smelt the smoke and the lamb. He watched as he brought over the plate and then took it by the edge again and when the tea came, hot and steaming in the white moonlight, he pointed to the ground opposite.

Sit down, boy, he had said, but why had he said it? He had not known. It had been some crazy sort of compulsion but he had not retracted his words. He could not.

He remembered how his mate had hesitated, his face in darkness because he stood between the light from the fire and the moon. Sit down, Harry had repeated, and this time it was an order but he did not use the voice he had used back at the mine and he watched as the kaffir did so, sitting with crossed legs, immobile and erect.

Harry's cigarette had burnt down and the heat stung his fingers and so he stubbed it out in the loose earth. The soil filled his nails and he dug it out with his nailfile, looking across at his mate. 'Are you not hungry?' he had asked, pointing to his own plate and then his mouth, for how much could this black man understand? No, boss, his mate had said, and that was all.

'Are you not thirsty?' Harry had persisted, and now, as he sat on his horse looking out over the landscape he never wished to see again, he remembered the soreness of his throat as he held out his mug of tea that evening so long ago, seeing the flask which was strung from the other's rope belt.

'I have water, boss,' the mate had replied but his eyes were slow to turn from the steaming cup and Harry pointed back to the fire.

'Get yourself some tea and some meat,' he had said and watched as the mate rose quietly and quickly, stopping to look at Harry before he turned and moved to the fire, cooking the meat and pouring tea before moving across to the horses to eat in their shadow. And still Harry did not know why he was doing any of this.

The next night Harry had ordered the mate to cook enough for them both and had ordered him to bring both plates and eat with him, and afterwards he had passed across a cigarette. Did black men smoke, he wondered.

Thank you, boss, his mate had said as he took it and the matches too. Harry watched as the flare lit up the blackness of the man's skin, the white of his eyes which seemed more pronounced somehow than during the day. Such blackness, Harry thought. It was still strange to him.

He had asked the black man if he liked being away from the city and as the thick lips drew in the smoke he had seen a smile flicker and for a moment he allowed himself to know that this was a man he was talking to, not a beast.

I do not like Igoli, the city of gold, the mate had said, and it is good to be sleeping where the eye can see no fence.

Harry tasted again the smoke he had sucked in, dragging it deep into his lungs, exhaling, and wondering if his mouth would ever feel moist again. He ran his tongue round his teeth and he felt the dust and grit that even with the tea was still in his mouth. He remembered Frank's voice, his heavy-bearded face, as he told him that these were not men, they were not beings with feelings and needs.

He wiped his mouth with his handkerchief but it was full of dust. He cursed and put it back in his pocket. I thought the kaffirs didn't mind the compound, he had said, watching the bright red glow of the cigarette as the mate sucked in again.

There was a pause as the smoke was blown towards the sky and Harry saw the mate's face as he looked upwards and heard the soft words.

We mind; all people mind filth and shame. The Boers minded too. There had been silence then and Harry had felt a confusion, and he had looked across at the fire, burning low now and he did not want to talk any more that night for this trek across the ridge was not clearing his head; the ache was back, the anger at Hannah too. They reached the limit of the ridge the next day and retraced their steps, and still there was silence between them, a closing of the space around each man. He had watched the ostriches, the dassie and the mines, which looked foreign in this landscape, their machinery too angular, their noises too loud; and there were no faults in the ground which he could report would be worth boring with the new diamond-tipped drills.

At the fire that night Harry invited the mate to sit with him and eat and drink. He did not order him. They smoked again and Harry brought his flask filled with Hine brandy from his

258

saddle-roll and offered it to the black man. His father had sent it out from England for him.

He saw his mate hesitate and so pointed to the mug. Put it in your tea, he said, for he did not want those black lips around his flask, and he saw with something he thought might be shame that the mate understood this.

Harry asked how he knew of the camps that the Boers had been in, and his mate told him that he had been a servant with a Boer farmer and had been imprisoned when the women and children had been concentrated into these camps and Kitchener had burnt their ground, destroying the crops that he and his father and his brothers had sown for their master. How those imprisoned had all starved but the blacks had starved first for they were servants, but really slaves. In his awkward English he told how both black and white had died since illness had no sight. How his father and his brothers had died; how his Boer mistress and her child had starved and died of illness; how there had been no sanitation; how the wire had stretched around the barracks; how they had been guarded day and night by the British – as they were now.

I learn your tongue in those years, the mate had said, and there had been no emotion in his voice.

Harry had felt anger at the man, at his blackness, at the further confusion that the kaffir had brought with his words. He wanted to swear at him, to beat him, to forget what he had just heard from this black man. He did not want to know that he was part of a race which fought its wars like this. He did not want to think of the compounds his people still used, of the profits they made. It was business, wasn't it? These things happened when countries progressed, didn't they? It was right, wasn't it? He did not want to have these things spoken of clearly in a moonlit sky by a man who knew the truth of what he said. No, he did not want to hear it and he would not remember it. He would make sure he did not remember. He took out Hannah's letter from his pocket and set fire to it with the stub of his cigarette. He did not want to read her words again.

He had told the kaffir to fetch more fuel for the fire and then see to the horses in the voice that he had used at the mine and

259

had turned his back and smoked until his eyes were heavy. He had lain with his back to the fire and to the black man and tried to sleep, but he kept hearing Hannah speaking to their father on New Year's Eve as the green hat slipped over their father's eye, asking how concentration camps could be justified, hearing his answer that in war all death can be justified, concentration camps included. That orders must be obeyed, whatever they are. He kept seeing the fox torn to pieces by the hounds, its cries rising above the trees.

Harry had felt the stones beneath his shoulders as he had rolled on to his back. For Christ's sake be quiet, he wanted to shout, but he could get no sleep. All through the night he had not thought of Esther once but of Hannah and her letters, her outrage, how she had always faced and fought all that which she thought was wrong. He had sat up and taken more brandy and had felt weary but still could not sleep. Each time he closed his eyes her words had rolled around his head and he could see the chandeliers in Arthur's dining-room and her face as she had talked of the rights of the black men in South Africa. Be quiet, God damn you, he shouted silently. You don't know how it has to be out here; and her face just stared at him, her chin tilted and her wide mouth firm, and he knew that he could never make her understand because he could not find words with which to argue.

In the morning Harry had not talked to the kaffir and that night he did not order him to come and sit on his side of the fire but watched as he walked without food to sit with the horses, and he was glad that the man would be hungry tonight for he had ruined the easy future he had dreamt of for so long.

All that day he had watched the mate's back as he rode before him and heard the voices of Hannah and his father and Frank chasing round in his head; he had seen her words in print, seen the compounds, heard the moans which rose in the night. Really heard them now, for drink had not covered and softened the sounds and the sights.

The voices were sometimes loud, sometimes hushed, but always the heat shimmered and the dust thickened in his throat until he felt that his mind would burst with the noise of it all and the ache which still stabbed behind his eyes. And over everything lay those moans that seemed to come from all around but which he had known must only be in his imagination. Did it matter that these men lived as they did? Did it matter that they had no rights? It was not his problem. He could change nothing, but still her face looked at him and her voice carried through his thoughts into the corners of his mind where the truth lay quiet, not wanting to be discovered. Votes, rights, these were her province, not his. Let her be quiet, for God's sake.

They set up camp for the last time that night for tomorrow they would be back in Johannesburg. Harry was tired, so bloody tired, and at last Hannah had gone, his father and Frank too but not the compounds. Would they ever go from behind his eyes, from his ears? Would they ever leave him in peace?

He watched the mate as he cooked the meat, only enough for the white man and Harry did not move, did not speak, as the mate brought it to him. He took it, and the tea and watched as he walked back, past the fire to the horses. Harry could not eat the meat but he drank his tea, feeling the steam on his face. He smoked his cigarette and ground it out in the sand half-smoked. For God's sake, Hannah, be quiet, he thought because she was back again, and he wondered for a moment if he had shouted the words.

He sat for longer, not smoking, not listening to the voice of his sister. He lay down and pulled his blanket up over his ears and buried himself in the sound of the insects but in the end they could not drown out her voice and he finally knew as he rose that it was not just her voice that he heard but his own as well, unsodden by drink, clear at last.

He walked past the fire which was low now. His feet kicked up dust and he could see it quite clearly as he walked. The horses stirred as he approached and his mate sat up, his hat still on his head, still pulled low. Harry said nothing but handed him his flask, pushing it towards him as the black man hesitated.

Take it, he had said, and watched as he drank from it, his lips dark against the silver. The mate wiped it on his sleeve and handed it back, watching as Harry also drank, not noticing the bite of the brandy as the voice faded from his head. He smiled as he brought the flask down.

My name is Harry Watson, he had said, offering his hand, and the black man rose. My name is Baralong, Smith in your tongue, he had replied, and had taken Harry's hand and in the white moonlight his grasp had been firm.

On this quiet evening Harry looked about him as he approached Johannesburg. Baralong had been his friend from that day onwards but he still lived in the compound, he was still searched before he went back to his mother's hut at the end of his spell. He still needed a pass. He could not alter that, not here anyway, but one day perhaps it would happen. One day perhaps he would try, because Hannah would want that, just as much as she wanted the rights she was fighting for in England. How could she bear to face prison, he wondered, and shuddered.

After they had returned from the ridge he had been unable to do anything openly, but he had quietly given money to the kaffir hospital to provide beds for the kaffirs so that they no longer had to sleep on the mud floor, and medicine so that perhaps they did not die of injuries and illnesses quite so readily. He had not written to tell Esther for she would not understand that his stake money was being used in this way.

He had taken the daughter of a friend of Baralong's as his servant to save her going to a Boer, something that Baralong dreaded for any of his people, and he had treated her well but he had not slept with her. He had not slept with anyone since the ride along the ridge for he no longer felt the urgent need. Neither did he drink until he could not see or hear, for he had no need to blank out the knowledge which he would not recognise. But he still drank a little with Frank in the evenings and laughed and talked, for to have altered in his behaviour would have been too dangerous.

Harry remembered the picture of the guinea-pigs and the girl in a white dress with a blue sash; the whippings with the towels when he had broken the rules once before.

Baralong had become the closest friend he had ever had but no one could know. He had remained his mate and they worked as a team, always together, and Frank said how well he had settled in. Harry rubbed his arm across his forehead frowning slightly, remembering how he had nearly given himself away.

In the two years following the ridge ride Harry had eased himself into more underground inspection since it was the atmosphere that he enjoyed the most. He felt less on edge, less exposed. And then two months ago he and Baralong had been together in the propped seams of the mine, the dust stinging their eyes from the drills and the picks, and the noise had blasted into their bodies as usual. The men had not heard them or seen them, working as they were in the light from the candles, ignoring the sweat which streamed off their faces on to the ground.

Baralong had been at his side pointing up the stopes leading off the main shaft. These are the ones we want, Boss, Baralong had said, for he called him Boss when others might hear, and they might hear if the drilling paused. Harry had been about to nod but had tensed instead as they bent down to pass beneath an overhang chiselled with lines from picks and drills, straightening when they reached the other side. Baralong had turned and looked, his face questioning beneath the candlelight, but Harry had said nothing, just stood quite still as he sensed the earth rebel, feeling that same feeling that Penhallon had brought him before the ceiling plunged down so long ago.

Harry had known it was about to happen again; it was in the air. His nerves had felt it somehow and he looked at Baralong and it was Sam he saw and he did not know whether to go back or forward. This time he could not tell. Why the hell couldn't he tell? And he knew it was because it was not his earth.

He was a stranger here and he knew it now. Baralong, he had whispered, I do not know. This time I don't know which way to go, and he had gripped the black man's arm and fear had filled the air between them, and this time it was his friend who had stood with his head to one side, his eyes looking but not seeing, his ears listening, his very being waiting, guessing, and still the men worked on around them and Harry knew it would happen but not where so he could not shout an order to leave. He could not until he knew which way they should go. Oh God, which way? And then he felt Baralong's arm around him, throwing him back, pushing him, dragging him, shouting orders which Harry could not give, and he knew that Baralong had guessed because this was his land. Then the noise came and the wind and the screams and the weight. But there had not been much weight on his legs nor on Baralong's. The weight was on the men who had been drilling further forward and had not heard the order.

As the dust cleared and the pain receded Harry had pushed the ore from his body, hating for the first time its rough edges, its size, its smell, then crawled across to Baralong and moved the splintered pit prop from his legs, coughing and choking.

They had heard the men who had been using the drills, behind the wall of rock and beneath it. It was dark though, so bloody dark, because the rush of wind had blown the candles out and filled the air with dust. After Harry had ripped his jacket and bound the cut in his right leg that would not stop bleeding he had found his matches and almost struck one, but remembered the danger of fire. Go back for help, he had instructed Baralong, scrabbling carefully to his knees, not wanting to cause sparks, and then on to his feet. And for God's sake, hurry.

Baralong had said, what of fire? His hand had gripped his sleeve and as he rode on this dark evening Harry could still feel the pressure; still feel the fear because he knew that there could indeed be fire.

Get along, Baralong. Just get along now. I'll begin. It had been an order but one that he had to give and Baralong had looked at him and though he had not spoken there was comfort in the hand that gripped his shoulder.

In the dark Harry had torn at the rocks, ripping his skin, his nails, and talking all the time. It's all right, boys, he had said again and again, we're coming, we're coming. And still he made no sparks but choked and coughed, and soon men who had been knocked off their feet by the rushing wind came to join him and Baralong brought more help, fresh miners, and Harry ordered that every man was to be brought out, dead or alive. No one was to be left in that stinking hole and they were to work quickly but carefully; oh so carefully.

. Baralong took him to the surface and the light blinded him as it had at Penhallon but this time there was no Hannah to take his hand and kiss it, though there was the black arm of his friend to steady him and support his weight, his familiar voice urging him onwards. Frank had been waiting at the top and he had brushed Baralong aside and taken Harry's weight himself.

Get along, he had said to Baralong. Back to the barracks. But Harry had called to his friend, You saved my life, and Baralong had turned. I do nothing, Boss, and there was a warning in his look and Harry nodded. His leg hurt now and his hands were throbbing and blood dripped from them on to the parched ground. Blood was on Baralong's torn jacket too. Harry had just nodded to his mate. He would not show that he cared, for he knew that Baralong was right to fear the rules which governed this small world of theirs.

Frank had taken him back to the office. There was no need for all that fuss, you know, he had said. So a few boys die? There are plenty more. We've lost time, a lot of time, Harry. I've sent down an order that the bodies are to be left beneath the rock. They are just to clear enough of the fall to be able to carry on working up the stopes.

Harry remembered the anger which had pushed back his tiredness and the feel of the wood beneath his shaking hands as he had pushed himself up from the old corner chair where Frank had placed him. Without a word he had pushed past Frank and out of that dark airless office, straight back to the head of the shaft though the pain had shot through his leg and blood flooded the torn jacket which was his bandage. He had told the white overseer that all the fallen ore was to be moved so that the equipment could be brought out, and while they were doing that they might as well bring out the bodies, they'd stink if they were left. He had raised his voice and said that if necessary he would stay here until they were finished. His voice had been strong and he had not coughed or choked but stared at the man until he sent a runner with the message, looking first over Harry's shoulder to Frank who had followed.

Frank's face had been hard but he had not rescinded Harry's instructions. Harry had gambled on that, knowing that Frank would not want it to be seen that managers were quarrelling. Harry had smiled. Makes sense, old man, he had said. There's good equipment down there, it would be a shame to waste it. We've lost time, let's not lose the drills.

Had Frank seen through him? Harry had not known then, and did not know now, but had watched as the man he lived and drank with turned and walked away, and Harry had wanted to shout after him that the drills were nothing but the men were different, and yes, they were men, who even when dead deserved some dignity. They were not beasts.

But he could not for what would this do to his mate whom he somehow hoped to drag out of this mess? So instead he said the words to himself and to Hannah whose hand he could feel kissing his own, holding it to her mouth and the wind of the moor was cool for one moment on his face.

And so he lifted his head and told her how Baralong was not a beast but a man whose forebears had lived in stone buildings as good as the one in which he and Frank lived. How he was a Sotho from the interior whose tribe had worked copper into fine wire, had smelted iron, had mined and worked gold. He told how Baralong was a man, not an animal, and how this man was his friend, and he shut his eyes to the mine and to Frank and to the injustices which comprised this world in which he lived. By now the beating heat of the sun had chased the moor and the wind away and the pain behind his eyes and in his leg surged as he turned back to the head of the shaft. He would wait until they all came out.

The house was in sight now and this evening was the last time he would approach from these God-forsaken mines. The sounds of the compound could no longer be heard. Harry's leg was still stiff but the cut had healed well. Frank had not spoken to him directly but Harry had received praise from their superiors for saving so much equipment. Harry was also informed that H. Watson Esq. was to be transferred to Kimberley and the diamond mines; to get rid of him, Harry suspected and was glad, but he had insisted that his mate went too, giving as his reason that he did not want the tedium of breaking in another kaffir.

He hoped that Kimberley would be better for them both, though he feared it would not, but it was a means to an end for during the long nights he had realised that somehow Baralong must go where there would be some peace, some dignity, but was that possible in South Africa? He doubted it and so Baralong must have money, a great deal of money to leave the country, and it was only in the region of the diamond pipes that this could happen. They had to build up enough money for a stake and then find their own diamonds as some others had recently done. It was imperative for Baralong's sake, for Esther's and for his own.

16 Months ago the Conciliation Bill dealing with female franchise reform had passed the second reading with a large majority and Hannah and Frances had cooked special cakes for Sunday morning, but now, in 1911, before it could reach the committee stage, there was talk of the Government introducing an alternative Franchise Bill which was to deal with universal male suffrage and perhaps a limited amendment concerning women, but in no way would the Government consider equal rights. All female suffrage societies were incensed. Hannah's suffragette leader assigned to her the task of reminding the politician who was to speak in her area that week that suffragettes would not be diverted from their task.

Hannah was waiting for the moment when the Cabinet Minister paused in his speech and drank from the glass which stood on the table before him. It was a good point at which to interrupt the speech, the leader of her group of suffragettes had told her.

She had not done this before, though she had marched and protested once the Pensions Act came into force in 1908, three years ago, and votes had not then been forthcoming. She had attended meetings where live rats were thrown through windows by furious men and had felt their quick lithe bodies clawing up her skirt but had not screamed and neither had the other women. She had been jeered and beaten often as she left meetings with other suffragettes; chased down alley-ways by men with sticks; stoned as they spoke on street corners.

She had earned the Holloway badge and been imprisoned for obstruction as she stood with others blocking the Ministers' cars but had only been sentenced to the first division so far. It was a holiday in comparison with the third, she had been told, for she wore her own clothes, bought her own food, read her own books and slept in good sheets, but she had hated the

268

confinement, hated high-walled cells and the way that she could scarcely breathe when the door closed behind her; she felt suffocated as though it was her father's darkness that surrounded her, his power.

She hated the way she always felt tired now; a tiredness which Frances said was born of stress and fear but which Hannah would not discuss, would not think of, because if she did, she might not go on and too many years of waiting had preceded the work she was now doing. The fear she lived with must go on being conquered.

She looked around her, at the large man sitting next to her; at the slimmer younger man in a smart suit and waistcoat on her right; at all the men and a few women who sat listening in this high-domed hall. It had not been easy to obtain tickets for tonight since the speakers were careful now and closed their meetings to the general public to avoid just the sort of action she was about to take, but somehow her leader had managed it. And she must go on doing so if their voices were to be heard questioning the Government's representatives about their attitudes to female suffrage. What would the large man do when she stood up? But no, she must not think of him pulling her down, of his hands clasped across her mouth.

She still could not see Esther who was to take up the heckling when Hannah was removed by the stewards as would inevitably happen. She should be in the middle of a row nearer the front. It had to be the middle, she had told her cousin, so that it takes longer for them to eject you. Remember that now – do not speak until I am taken. She had wanted Esther to obey her because it was the first speaker who received the harsher treatment as a rule and there was Harry to think of.

Hannah had not wanted her cousin as the second voice at all, since she must be kept safe for Harry, but Esther wanted one of the badges that suffragette prisoners were awarded by the movement, she had explained to Hannah, who sighed. Esther could see no further than the badge, of course, but perhaps just once would do her no harm. Uncle Thomas would make quite sure she received only the first division; after all Esther would be a first offender. She would not think of her own sentence.

She looked back at the stage which was hung with Liberal slogans. The Minister was still talking about the eight Dreadnoughts they were building to combat the menace of the rising German sea power, and Hannah tried to listen to his words, hoping that it would quell the fear which she was worried would weaken her voice. It was easier to be bold when friends stood with you; she was not sure if she could do this. She wanted to leave, to rise quietly and slip past the people sitting in her row and walk out of the exit and home to Frances, to cocoa and her homework-marking, her St John's teaching. She wanted to walk into the sitting-room and say, I'm back, and see the worry drop from the older woman's eyes, feel the fear ebb from her own body, for she knew that she would be hurt, that the sentence this time would be severe.

She wanted to say to Frances, don't worry, we need not arrange for another teacher to take my pay, do my job, work with you on Sundays, arrange holidays for the families at Penbrin where she had not yet visited for there had been no time. She looked back up to the stage. Still the man was on his feet, speaking, gesticulating; the audience laughed at an aside and a ripple of applause ran round the Free Trade Hall. Surely he would drink now? But he did not.

Hannah looked again for Esther's hat but she could not see it. She fingered the brooch which was in the pocket of her jacket, picturing the portcullis emblazoned with a broad arrow in suffragette colours with silver chains hanging either side. She should have given Esther this one and then she would not have come tonight. It was wrong of her to have allowed it; Harry would never forgive her if his love was hurt, but at the same time it was good to feel that she was not in the hall alone.

She would not think of anything beyond the next words of the Minister, she would not think of the men who would grab her, pull and push and hit her. And then she saw the Minister lift his glass and she took her hand from her pocket and gripped the flag which she had carried in under her jacket. All she could hear was her heart beating in her throat. It was too loud, it would stop her voice. She could not do it. She must not stand and find she had no voice. She could not stand, her legs were too weak. She watched as the Minister took another sip, smiling at the men who sat beside him on the stage, and then his glass was going down towards the table. It would be too late if she did not rise now. She was going to fail her friends; there were so many people and she was so afraid.

And then she was up and holding the flag, waving its green and white and purple colours and her voice was strong as she called on the Minister to support votes for women.

Again and again she called. 'Will you pledge your support for women's suffrage?' But there was no answer to her question. He just stood and continued with his speech while the audience turned on her and shouted her down. The hatred was all around her, in the fists that waved and the mouths that opened and shut with curses and the fear was too great to be borne, but once more she shouted across the hostile rows.

'Please will you pledge your support?'

But her voice was weaker now and the flag was torn from her hands by the large man who no longer sat at her side but stood pushing her down. She struggled free.

'Please pledge your support,' she called once more across the hostility which shocked her, frightened her, and made her think of meal-times with her father and she called on the anger she had used then to subdue the fear.

She felt a man push her from behind but she shouted once more above the noise.

'When will you consider votes for women?' Her voice was strong with anger and she said it again as the audience shouted and cheered the stewards who pushed down the row and held her, one either side, and dragged her past the people who had smiled and made way for her earlier. Now one spat in her face and as they reached the aisle she went limp as she had been instructed and so the stewards had to drag her to the exit and another glob of spittle landed wet on her face and another down her black jacket. Her hat was ripped from her head, her hair was torn from its pins. She could not hear Esther. Why had she not begun? Did it mean that she was not here, that Hannah was completely alone? And fear took the place of anger again for now the fury would be directed at her alone. But where was Esther?

As the stewards backed through the swing-doors into the lobby they threw her to the floor and her head struck the black marble tiles, but she was not aware of pain, only of the white flecks in the tiles. She would not get up so they dragged her by her arms, face down, out into the street, bumping her limp body down the steps and her knees bled from the rasping of the concrete which tore her stockings and her skin.

The police had not come yet but men had, from the hall and from the alleys where they often waited, and they pushed the stewards to one side. They loomed over her, their mufflers at their throats to keep out the Easter chill. They shut out the light from the hall, with their great bodies. Their faces were smiling but their voices were low and vicious.

She had known it would be worse not being with all her friends, being just two against the men. She turned and looked back at the entrance. Where was Esther? There were too many for just one woman. She stood now, her hands gripping her skirt, looking around for the stewards, for the police, but there was no one but these men. The same sort of men who had let in the rats, beaten them with staves.

Then one slapped her face with his open palm and she thought her neck would snap with the blow. She tasted blood and knew it coated her teeth.

She bent her head and heard the large dark man say, 'Bitch. You leave women as they be.' She felt a hand in her hair winding round and round but she would not lift her head and so he pulled harder and she screamed as he tore the roots from her scalp.

Another swung her round, driving his fist into her ribs. 'You behave like a slut, you get treated like one,' he said, and his breath was foul and then he spat full in her face and it was this that made her scream again. 'Esther, where are you?'

'The coppers are coming,' a man called and the one who held a clump of her hair in his hand laughed and threw it to the ground and Hannah turned to him and said, 'That's mine.' But her lips were too swollen to move and she looked down at

272

the long strands lying on the ground and she turned and slapped the face which grinned at her and so he knocked her to the ground and kicked her.

'Get down on the ground with it then, you troublemaker,' he snarled.

The pavement was cold; she was cold, but her hair was there, not too far away and she moved her fingers and then her hand and finally her arm and it was as though it was someone else that she watched as slowly her hand drew closer and then a boot came down. She felt no pain as she watched the studs press into her flesh and then her bones, but the police-van came and the boot was gone. Her hair was still there though, she had not reached it yet.

The stewards came out again then, just as the policeman lifted her from the ground, but he didn't understand that she had left her hair on the pavement. She turned from him, from the arm which held her, and he would not let her go but stood there listening to the steward.

'Let me go,' she said, because she could not go with him until she had picked up her hair. Didn't he understand that. 'Let me go,' she said again but perhaps it was because her lips were too swollen for him to hear and so she pushed away from him and he held her again and she fought his arms because part of her had been left there on that cold pavement.

He charged her then with assault but that did not matter because as he lifted her into the police-van and sat with her on the bench she could see nothing but that piece of herself which she had allowed that man to take.

She was offered bail, but she did not want it. Suffragettes did not accept bail and so this time she did not go to Frances to have her wounds bathed but sat in the police cell on the wooden bench which was the only furniture in the cold square room. A policeman opened the shutter and said that there was a gentleman offering to pay her bail, would she accept? She refused, banishing the thought of the warm sitting-room and Bess who panted by the hearth. Was it Arthur, she thought, but he was in Norway, salmon fishing, wasn't he?

She was unhurt, the doctor said, but swabbed her knees,

and her mouth and her bleeding scalp.

Frances was not in court the next day because she was teaching but three suffragettes were, Maureen, Ann and Sarah, and with them was Esther.

'I'm so sorry,' she mouthed to Hannah, 'but my father wanted me to stay in for a dinner-party.'

Hannah nodded. She ached too much to think or to feel. She could not smile because her lips hurt too much and her eye was black and swollen. She turned from her cousin. Esther had not meant to let her down, she never did, and what did it matter now anyway? Hannah listened as the magistrate found her guilty and sentenced her to three months in the third division. She had to grip the rail of the dock although her hand was swollen and bruised where the studs had been because she must not show that she minded, that she wanted to crouch and cry and not leave here for that place again.

She made herself lift her head, made the tears stay behind her lids because no one must see how much she was hurting.

Esther stood with her hand to her mouth, her eyes filled with horror, but Maureen smiled. 'Be brave,' she mouthed.

Hannah nodded to her and turned away and then she saw him and knew now who it was who had offered to pay her bail. His face was calm and strong. He smiled and she set her shoulders back now that Joe was here and walked upright from the dock, feeling not the plain wooden boards beneath her feet but the spongy moor. As Hannah disappeared down the steps and from the court Joe wondered how he had been able to keep his face still, his eyes calm, when Hannah had looked, for that brief moment, so broken. Her bruises were nothing compared to that.

Hannah entered through gates which were by now familiar but this time she was not with other suffragettes but alone amongst criminals. She did not go to a comfortable cell but was taken with the other women prisoners into a cold square room and together they stripped beside dark, pitted baths. She did not look at the bodies of the other women or listen to the hoarse voices or acknowledge the laughter as she removed her clothes

274

and stood naked before them. She had never seen other bodies before, nor had others seen hers. She thought of her mother's bedroom, the dressing-table, her pin-boxes, her hat-pins. How many were there? She made herself picture them all and when she was pushed towards the bath by the wardress she began again. When she was dry she thought of Frances and the chairs and the fire and the dog as she put on the thick, rough-textured, dark green dress with its heavy pleats and white arrows and then the dull blue and white checked apron with its black arrows. She tied the frayed strings of the white cap under her chin. The red and black striped stockings were rough and slipped down with each step.

She thought of the moor and the sea and Joe's apple-loft at Penbrin which he had promised to show her one day when she had the time. She collected a Bible and library book from the wardress's office and a filthy blanket before entering her dark cell, lit by one small high window, and she felt the breath tightening her chest and her father close to her as the spy-hole in the door slid shut. When would she have the time?

There was no handle on this side of the door and she sat on the plank by the wall and only now did she think of where she was. She looked at the stool and the shelf which was the table; the rolled up straw mattress at the end of the plank on which she was sitting. So this then was the bed.

There were several tins on the shelf and a wooden spoon stood up in one. It was porous and felt slimy to the touch and smelt of other mouths and old food.

That night a wardress brought round gruel and dark bread, pouring it into one of the tins. Her keys were hanging in a bundle from the chain around her waist and they rattled together as she moved. There was no expression in the prison officer's voice as she said, 'Eat this, Number 15.' The woman's face was colourless against the holland dress and dark blue bonnet.

Hannah could not use the spoon so she drank from the tin. The gruel stung her swollen mouth and she dribbled down her chin on to her dress. She rubbed at it with her hand; she had no handkerchief. She could not eat the bread, it hurt her mouth too much.

The next day she ate porridge and had to use the spoon because it was too thick to pour. She washed her tin and her spoon and scrubbed the floor on her knees and they bled again. She sat in her cell, her back against the wall, because her ribs hurt too much to lie down but she could not rest her head against the cold stone because her scalp was still tender.

Lunch was broth with a piece of meat and tea to drink. One of the girls liked being in prison, she said, when they walked round the exercise yard in the afternoon for half an hour, for at least there was food.

Hannah looked at the sky; it was blue and the clouds scudded over the prison walls and disappeared from sight. She thought of the matchgirl and looked at the woman who liked the prison. She thought she had understood poverty but she had not, she knew that now. She pulled at her dress which had rubbed her neck raw with its roughness. No, she had not understood this world at all, how arrogant to think that she had. She had not felt its roughness, only seen it. Had not tasted meagre food, only seen it. Had not known hopelessness, only seen it.

She sat for hours in her cell and all the time the dress rubbed at her skin and the high walls of the cell closed in around her.

She was allowed one library book and she chose *The History of Mr Polly* and read two pages a day but only two for it must last. So each line she read twice, memorising if she could because it made the minutes pass. She thought of these as the wardress called her out of her cell for exercise, not hearing the clink of keys above the words which she made herself repeat in her mind.

Her lips became less sore, less swollen, but her fingers grew raw and then hard from sewing thick shirts. The days turned to weeks and the weeks to one month and then two. Hannah's feet had blistered and then hardened where prison shoes which did not fit rubbed as she paced the seven steps it took from wall to wall. She walked it again and again, memorising her pages, not thinking of tomorrow, not thinking of the loneliness, the locked door, the hunger, the wooden spoon, the world outside. Not thinking of Esther who would be teaching her children, walking in the park, boating on the river. Not thinking of the fact that she should have been here too.

Again and again she thought of the matchgirl, the blank eyes, dull hair, the smell. She understood now the effect on the soul of deprivation, of poverty.

As the last month began she grew thin and silent because there were still only walls to look at, not the sky, not houses, not fields, and each morning she emptied the bucket and rolled her bedding. Each evening she drank her grey thin cocoa and would not think of Frances drinking her brown thick brew. She read the letter which came from Arthur saying that he would be thirty in 1914 and his family would like to see him married by then. She was the woman he had chosen, she knew that, he said, and he could wait for her answer, but for no more than another two years. That should give you time to work this cause from your system, he wrote. Hannah had written back saying that she would give him an answer in the summer of 1913 but she felt too tired to say more, to think more. It seemed so unimportant, so distant. Even the words in her mind seemed slow and short.

She read letters from Frances and she wrote saying that when this fight was over she wanted to start a school in the fresh country air and fund scholarships for the children of women like these. She read the letter which Frances forwarded from Harry who was now in Kimberley. She wished he would come home because she feared he would be hurt if he stayed. Someone might find out that his best friend was a black man. But she would not allow herself to think of that, only of the boy who had swung her on the rope. Did he still have that piece that he had cut on that last day?

She read a letter from Esther but she felt too silent, too tired to write. Maureen wrote and the others. She replied saying she was well.

Joe did not write but he had come, hadn't he.

On Sundays she attended the chapel, they all attended the chapel, and it was good to be with people again, to hear voices singing, and see faces in rows about her though not one face knew another.

At eight o'clock three months later she walked in her own clothes, which were too soft and too large, through the doors and gates with their large heavy bolts which the wardress pulled open as she approached and clanged shut when she had passed and then there was just the small high door into the warm July morning.

Joe was there. She had known he would be and he did not take her to the school but to the train where Frances waited.

'It's time I had a holiday, my dear. The school has broken up and so we thought perhaps you'd come. The Conciliation Bill has no hope and there is definitely to be a Manhood Suffrage Bill presented.' Frances helped her over the gap and into the train. Hannah looked out of the window. It was no surprise but she was too tired to think yet. She could see for miles and there were people in clothes and hats and there was sky and wind.

She turned to Frances. 'Yes,' she said. 'I'd like to leave London for a while. Will they mind, do you think?'

It was strange to be with those whose faces were full and touched by the weather; to be talked to, not ordered and pushed. To sit on a padded seat, to rest her head against the softness of the head rest. Comfort was something she had forgotten existed. But she was lucky, for the other women would not be coming to this. They only had the matchgirl's room. She closed her eyes. She was so tired but there was so much to do, so much to put right. She would not travel first-class again.

'Will they mind?' she repeated.

Frances was looking at Joe. 'No, my dear, they won't mind.'

Hannah was glad because she was too tired to march or to shout or heckle and she wanted to regain her strength to win the fight. She also wanted the strength to teach more women on Sunday mornings about health, about skills. To feed them all, and clothe them too.

She looked out of the window at the newsboy as he walked past the window, waving his papers. The train jolted, the whistle blew, and they began to move; past him this time and now she heard the words that he was calling in a voice which seemed just for her.

'Suffragette on hunger-strike in prison.'

She saw Frances look at Joe and looked away from them and out across the concourse which they were now leaving, but she could not leave the words behind, they were in her head; loud, too loud. She gripped the leather window-strap. I'm too tired, she protested silently, knowing now what awaited her on her return and afraid that she would be unable to bear it but knowing also that somehow she must.

The gardener, Edward, met them in the trap and Joe grinned as Hannah blushed when the man swept his hat off in a bow then helped her into the trap. The springs sagged beneath her weight. The leather of the seat was warm, the colour faded to beige.

'You're the mistress, you see,' Joe whispered as he settled himself beside her, his hands broad and tanned on his knees. 'You've done a great deal in your short life, young lady,' he drawled, smiling.

The sun was warm on her hands but it did not reach her face because the brim of her hat was too big. She reached up, her arms felt so heavy. She pulled out the pearl pin slowly and brought the grey hat on to her lap, her hand still holding the pin, her fingers too tired to release it. She lifted her face now, and closed her eyes beneath the warmth of the sun and saw the red behind her eyes as she had done when she woke that first morning at Joe's cottage when she was still a child.

'But nothing is finished yet,' she murmured.

Joe's hand was hard still, she felt the weight of it on hers, the warmth of it.

'The holiday home is, my Cornish girl. Don't forget the achievements.'

Hannah opened her eyes, lowering her head against the glare. But there was still so much to do. The luggage was on the cart now and the gardener's boy followed in this as the bay pony drew their trap through narrow lanes past hedgerows white with summer dust and thick with flowers. There was bird's foot, sorrel and montbretia; brilliant orange against the thick green of the leaves and grass. Honeysuckle reached out from the hedgerows which soon gave way to dry-stone walls.

Hannah felt safe here, tucked behind a fragrant barrier with the sky high and blue and light, with the wind blowing clean and clear.

She would not allow her thoughts to stray beyond the yellow, orange and green of the honeysuckle, the flat stones of the walls, the warmth of Joe's hand and Frances's calm eyes.

It was early evening when they arrived. The drive was not long and the gate was open so the trap did not falter but swept round the grey stone house which was fringed by oak trees and a yew hedge and then into the stable-yard at the back.

Joe took Hannah to the stone stables, not the house. He unhitched the pony first and nodded to Frances.

'Have some tea with Edward, Frances. The families will be there to welcome you. I will bring Hannah in shortly.'

His back was towards Hannah as he worked at the leather straps. She saw Frances look at him. He turned briefly to the Headmistress; he was not smiling though his face was calm. She watched as Frances put her hand on his arm and nodded before walking over the paved yard towards the half-open door of the kitchen. Hannah saw that the roof was lower this side than at the front and that ivy clung to the walls, clustered around open windows. Stocks and montbretia stood in vases on the windowsills of all the rooms.

Lavender grew outside the kitchen door in tall bushes and bees wove through the blue stems. There were smaller shrubs of thyme, heavy with pink-purple flowers beyond the old rusted pump. She walked towards the lavender.

'No. This way, Hannah,' Joe called as he pulled the pony from the shafts towards the open stable door.

She did not want to follow, she wanted to feel the lavender, smell it, hold it to her face and breathe it in and wipe away the days which had filled the endless months and years of tiredness.

'This way, Hannah,' Joe called again and now she followed as the pony's hoofs rang sharp and clear across the yard turning to a muted thud as they passed into the dark of the stable. She did not want to enter because of the dark, because of the high small windows.

'Come, Hannah,' Joe said and he was standing there, where she could see him; and so she entered and it was dark but filled with the sweet smell of hay which gleamed pale yellow. The colour of Arthur's hair, she mused. Bales of straw were stacked in the empty stall next to the pony, dry and full golden. Oil cake stood on the window-ledge and above it, light shafted down catching dust in its beam. Meal stood in containers and she could smell it from here. There was warmth in this darkness, there was light.

Joe stood by the pony watching and she turned to him and smiled. 'Yes, I should remember the achievements too.'

He nodded, moving now, across to the straw bales, pulling handfuls and passing one to her.

'Rub the pony down now, Hannah,' he said.

She shook her head; her arm was too heavy, she was so tired, still so tired but would she sleep? She never seemed to sleep, never seemed to rid her mind of fear, of plans and of prison now.

Joe came to her. 'Rub the pony, Hannah.' His drawl was pronounced and his voice loud. 'Now.'

And as though he had been a wardress she did as she was ordered and walked through the clean straw, feeling it rustle beneath her feet. The pony was damp and warm; steam rose from its flanks and it blew hot draughts of air into the feeding cradle. Her arm was still heavy as she began to work the straw backwards and forwards, rubbing slowly at the darkened sweat patches.

Joe was at her elbow and as her straw grew wet too and limp he drawled, 'Toss it down,' and she did, but he gave her more.

Again and again this happened and she rubbed and worked and the coat dried and the darkness gave way to the light of the bay coat. She moved to the other side and her arm was stronger now and she did not wait for Joe but pulled straw from the bale at the side of the stall. She rubbed hard, again and again and again, working the straw, drying up the darkness, taking it away. Taking it away all by herself. There was sweat on her face now but she didn't care. Her hair hung down across her face but there was not time to push it aside.

Joe stood leaning on the stall-post watching. She knew he watched and she wanted him there but she was glad he did not help. This must be her victory, to rub away the darkness, the thoughts, and finally it was done. Now her arm was shaking as she stood back and looked at Joe and smiled.

'Will I ever make a cowboy?' she asked.

'Too pretty,' he said, 'and not enough backside.'

She laughed and it sounded strange, it was so long since laughter had come.

That night she slept and then woke with the heat of the day. The sun was high and she washed beneath the picture of the marigolds, pouring water from the jug into the bowl, splashing her face and her body, looking out from the window over the stable to the sea beyond. She was still tired but it was not the same. She walked down the stairs past a wooden soldier lying on the blue patterned carpet. The banister was smooth, the whitewash light on the walls, the paintings were of the sea and she knew they were by Mr Arness.

The house was quiet, the dining-room cleared of plates and people. The kitchen door was open as before, throwing light across the flagstones to the stove which burnt low in the grate. There were tea-towels hanging on the airer. Hannah moved across lifting one and burying her face in its fresh boiled smell. She lifted the kettle. There was enough water in it for tea and so she put it on the range.

There was yellow soap in the sink and its scent was as fresh as the tea-towel had been. She crossed to the window and looked out at the stable-yard, half of which was in shadow, then turned and saw black beetles scuttling over the flagstoned floor.

Against the opposite wall was a pine dresser and the tea leaves were in a large tin with pictures of tea plants and Indian girls. A great stone jar was filled with demerara sugar. She found the teapot in the pantry; hanging from the ceiling were two hams with a side of bacon curing behind the door and it was these she could smell now. All she could hear was the hissing of the kettle and the sound of her own footsteps as she walked further into the pantry.

Packets of candles ranged along the shelves, with spare oil wicks since that was how the house was lit. Next to these were small candles suspended from twisted wicks for the lamp of the pony trap. She ran her finger down the cool wax before turning back into the kitchen, half sitting on the large deal table which had been freshly scrubbed but was now dry. All this was hers. She ran her hand along the grain of the table. She had come home and she had not known it was here.

She walked out through the yard to the garden at the side. Frances sat beneath a parasol in one of two wicker chairs. Yes, thought Hannah, I am home.

A hammock was strung between two trees and a swing hung from a frame which Hannah knew that Joe had made because it was simple and strong.

She walked to Frances and sat in the deck-chair alongside her. 'Would you like some tea?' she asked. 'It will be ready in ten minutes.'

She smiled as the older woman started from her sleep and turned. 'How are you Hannah?' she murmured, her eyes still heavy with sleep, her voice thick.

'I'm fine, go back to sleep,' Hannah said softly and lay back in her chair. The garden was full of flowers, Michaelmas daisies, montbretia, lavender and roses which were full-headed and alive with scent. There were daisies and buttercups in the lawn and no neat box hedges, no black patches.

'They've all gone to the sea,' Frances said. 'For a picnic. Maureen's sister is here with her family and five others.'

'Joe too?' Hannah asked.

'He's delivering some small tables to the station. He seems to be doing very well, my dear.'

Hannah closed her eyes. 'I knew he would,' she replied.

As the day passed and morning changed to afternoon she took Frances by the arm and strolled round the garden. The tightness in her body was leaving and she was less tired. She deadheaded a yellow rose-bush near to a gap in the elder hedge. The gap had been replanted with a young sumach but they did not know why.

'Joe wondered if you would like to go and see Eliza and

283

Sam?' Frances asked. 'I did write to Eliza and say that we would like to meet them again. It was so nice having them to stay for Christmas.'

Hannah nodded. The wind was rustling the tops of the trees now. 'We'll ask them here,' she said because this house was where her mother was now and where her father had never been. He had been to Eliza's.

Joe returned from the town in time for tea. He had bought Chelsea buns and they sat in the garden around the table, comfortable in their chairs and the chair-legs dug into the grass as he told them that his parents were in America where his father was exhibiting his paintings in Boston and Washington.

'They have taken some of my smaller pieces,' he said, his grin wide.

'Didn't you want to go?' asked Hannah, passing a cup to Frances. The wind was no stronger and it was still warm.

'I have work to do here,' he said. 'The rest can wait.'

Hannah looked at him, at his eyes which looked out across the garden to the distant sea, at the fulness of his face, the colour of his skin. He was so much better now but it seemed that everyone was waiting.

'You don't have to wait,' she said. 'I could always ask Eliza or Sam or someone to take over.' But she knew that there was no one else. She poured his tea, not looking at him as he took it.

'I'll wait. I'm in no hurry,' he drawled.

Still Hannah did not look at him or Frances, whom she had seen nodding at Joe.

'You must tell me if you reach the stage when you can wait no longer,' she murmured and for a while there was silence, though the birds still sang and darted from bush to shrub to tree.

He watched her face and knew that he loved her more than life itself and that he would wait for ever because one day she would know that she loved him too. Hannah took a Chelsea bun, it was dusted with sugar and coiled round and round. She eased it apart, winding the soft pastry around her finger as she used to do with his wood shavings.

'I'd slap you if you were one of the girls,' Frances said and they all laughed.

'What was in the gap where the sumach has been planted?' she asked, chewing at a piece of bun which had broken as she coiled it. It was sweet and soft and fresh.

Joe hesitated.

'What was there?' she asked again.

'A lilac,' he said and he looked not at her but at the roses which grew in the bed nearby. 'This is your home and so I took it down.'

Hannah saw the bedroom again and then felt the axe in her hands and smelt lilac so strongly suddenly that she could not believe there was none in the garden but there was not. Joe had seen to that.

Over the weeks Hannah grew strong again and the tiredness eased. They went to the sea with the brown, round children who could not believe the space after the narrow London streets. She sat on the sand and watched as the mothers paddled and held on to their husbands' hands. She held small children on her knee, kissing the softness of their arms, smelling the sweetness of their skins and laughing into their necks so that they laughed too.

Joe threw balls for small boys holding bats he had made and she laughed as he missed catches. Frances read to the children with rickets who could not run. Hannah took them in the sea and they floated and used limbs too frail to move on land.

Frances asked her if she missed Arthur and Hannah replied that she was used to being away from Arthur, it was the way they lived their lives. She did not care for shooting and hunting, Henley and Cowes, and he did not care for Cornwall.

They talked together of the school that she would one day start and Frances agreed that yes, she would help too, but when she heard that it would be down here, where the sky was wide and the wind was clear, she asked about Arthur.

Hannah shrugged and thought how far away the future seemed.

She walked in the sand with bare feet, feeling the grains

beneath her toes, she swam in the water and loved the freedom, the feel of the salt as it tightened and dried on her skin.

She cooked in the kitchen with the women; they taught her what Cook had taught them. How to cure bacon, how to baste the joint, how to make lard into small cannon-balls. She taught them how to budget, how to read, and knew that she must help them to find better jobs when they returned. She met old Sunday friends and new ones.

Esther wrote asking if she could come down but Hannah replied saying that there was no room. She did not want to see her cousin here. This was her home.

Joe made a kite and one day they took the children on the moor and Hannah ran up the slope, the breath heaving in her chest and as the children leapt down again with Joe, the wind snapping at the yellow kite, tugging at the tail, she lay on the ground and looked at them and at the moss which looked like fir trees close to.

She heard their cries and shrieks as she lay on her back on the hill and watched the kite and then she rolled over and saw that the children were paddling in the stream, their skirts tucked up in their knickers, their trousers rolled up over their knees and Joe looked and waved and climbed the hill.

His breath came in pants as he sat down beside her, the string of the kite straining in his hands. His feet were bare and his trousers rolled above the knee. He had strong legs and his hairs were thick and blond. Hannah looked away.

'Sit up, you lazy creature,' he laughed, his forehead glistening with sweat, 'and take the string. Everyone should fly a kite or they ain't worth a nickel, ma'am.'

Hannah laughed and pushed herself up on to her knees and took the string; her hair had come loose and she had put the pins in her pockets, shaking her hair free, hoping that the rootless patch had now grown over.

She sat down and felt the tug of the kite at the end of the line. Joe was close now and his hand pulled on the string. 'Keep working it, Hannah, or she'll fall to the ground.'

She turned. His face was close and his eyes followed the swoops of the kite. He laughed, his chin lifting, and he looked down at her, but she had looked from him to the moor, to the children.

There was such peace here, she thought, smelling his skin near to her, knowing that his hand was on the string, close to hers. It was good to have him close.

'I'd love to fly,' Joe said and he put his arm round her, taking the kite in both his hands. 'I'd love to be up there, feeling the air rushing through my hair, seeing so far.' His breath was in her hair and she leant back against him. Yes, it was so good to have him close.

Eliza and Sam came over the day before they left. Joe showed them their apple-loft. The slats were half-empty with wrinkled red and green apples lying along half their length and Eliza said that Hannah must write to Harry and tell him that Joe's fruit was no better than Sam's.

Eliza had lost the dark circles beneath her eyes but she had not forgotten Simon; Hannah knew that because neither had she. She had thought of him as Joe took her hand when they walked back from the moor with the kite and the children. It had made her feel warm and safe as Uncle Simon had always done.

They moved down through the stable leaving the smell of the apples behind and Hannah looked at the pony who was dry and clean and fresh. She stopped and ran her hand over his flank and Joe had stayed with her.

'I shall be sorry to go,' she said.

'Stay then,' Joe replied.

'I can't. You must know that.'

Joe did but he still wanted to make her stay though he did not try. He loved her too much.

They walked out through the yard past the bicycles, the hoops, the tops, the dolls' prams which were all collected at the side of the stable. Hannah paused looking at a doll which had fallen from the pram and lay with its head broken, displaying white eyes on metal stalks. She turned away looking from the yard out to the garden, to the flowers and the people she loved, knowing that tomorrow she would be back in London, that the time for peace was over.

17 Kimberley proved to be worse for Baralong and therefore for Harry too, though he had been pleased at first to reach the open mines, the bustle, the singing wires. Momentarily the change in his surroundings made his blood quicken, his enthusiasm stir again after being buried deep inside him by too many years in the gold-fields. He had stood and watched the endless industry inside the big hole: the men, the buckets, the pulleys, the diamonds which did not glint in this rough state but looked like children's klip-klip or jack-stones.

Baralong though was searched each day at the end of the shift, his nostrils, throat and ears examined. He had to jump the pole in the compound and almost immediately Harry lost his joy again but he could say nothing to stop it. He could only talk to his friend quietly, grip his arm as they walked to the steam engine or pulled at a bucket.

'Soon we will be away from here,' he said but it was not to be as soon as they wished for it took time for Harry to accumulate sufficient funds while still maintaining a life which allayed suspicion amongst his fellow managers. There were still the clubs and bars, still the bets, still laughter which was sour in his throat. He managed to send money to the hospital though and that helped him to sleep at night.

Baralong did not go to his homeland at the end of his spell of work. He stayed and worked another period because he could not stand the thought of the days in the locked room, naked with only leather fingerless gloves to wear, sitting amongst his own excrement while this was searched for the diamonds that he might have stolen. He sent his money back to his village through another worker.

Harry took no leave either but worked as his mate did and no one thought it strange for they knew he longed to be back with Esther but needed that all important handful of money first

288

and, after two long years, they had almost enough. He had written to Esther saying that it would not be long now and she had replied that 1913 was such fun at the moment, she could easily wait. Hannah had given her a badge and the suffragettes were in the newspapers all the time; such excitement, darling, she had written. Harry had smiled and put the letter with all the others that he kept in the locked medicine chest, along with the rope he had cut from the horse-chestnut tree. Its green leaves seemed an impossible dream out here.

He was at the rim on the day when Frank rode up, the day he was never to forget. The men were working deep in the hole, the wires were singing, the buckets were travelling up and down, up and down. His eyes were sore from the limestone and cement of the ridge and he had been rubbing them, not looking at the team working nearest to him. He had pulled his hat low over his eyes and thought of the wagon he had bought and furtively stored in the old zinc-covered shed down from the house which he had rented. It was full now of picks, shovels, sieves, pots and pans. He had one kettle and four sheepskins because he did not know whether Simon's homestead would have furniture or not, for it was to his own property he had decided they must travel when the time came. He nodded to himself, a sheepskin was comfortable but took little room in the wagon.

He would take a barrel of salted pork or mutton, mealie, potatoes, tea and sugar but he had not collected them yet. They still had two weeks until Baralong had finished his stint but somehow they must leave before he could be put through the indignity of the search and it was of this he was thinking when he heard Frank's voice.

'Harry, do you know where your mate is?' Frank called. He was on horseback and sweat stained his shirt but he still looked a gentleman in his cravat and jacket. It was summer weather although it was the start of the South African winter, Harry thought as he turned to look down the track. It was April 1913 and everywhere was parched after the hot season. He hoped there would be rain soon, even if it was only a light shower. He looked to the sky and then past Frank to the track.

No, he thought. He did not know where Baralong was. He should be back by now. There was no point in checking the watch his father had given him, it had become clogged with dust months ago. He checked the sun again. Well past midday. Where was he?

Harry shaded his face with his hand and looked up at Frank. They had barely spoken since Frank had arrived last year, sent across from the Rand to work here for two years; there was too much that Harry wanted to hide, too much that he thought Frank already suspected. The other man's beard was full of dust. Harry was still clean-shaven except for his moustache.

'He went for tools from the store for me,' he shrugged. 'Sometime this morning.'

Frank leant forward, his arm on his pommel as he flicked at flies with his crop.

'Went without his pass, didn't he, old man.'

The words dropped slowly into Harry's head. He watched the crop, the end was slashed into many fronds and then he moved. Gripping the crop, pulling it from Frank's grasp.

'He never goes without his pass.' He was close to the man now, close to his laughing mouth and he wanted to put his boot into that face. He could not hear the noise of the mine or see it, though it was there all around him. All he could see was Baralong's pass, his bloody pass. He couldn't have gone without the bloody pass, he wanted to shout.

Frank pulled back from his grasp, smoothing his coat where Harry had creased it with his hand. 'Well, he didn't have it this time, old man. He's back at the compound. If you hurry you might be in time to see the whipping.'

He reined his horse round, spurring him into a gallop and his dust blew into Harry's mouth and eyes but he didn't notice for he was already running, back to the office past black men who stared at this boss who ran. Bosses never ran in this heat. The black men ran for them.

Kim was in the shade of the wooden shed and was unsaddled and Harry cursed as he heaved the saddle on and strained and pulled at the girth as Kim shifted, blowing out his stomach. Harry cursed again and slapped the animal and he pulled again and this time he secured the buckle and dragged the horse out into the sunlight, heaving himself up on the stirrup, throwing his leg over and spurring the horse on before he was seated. The fool, how could he have forgotten? But even as he thought this Harry knew that Baralong would never have done something as stupid as that. He must have lost it. Oh God.

He could not see the compound from the rim but he wasn't looking, he was too busy riding. He galloped the horse past columns of kaffirs, white foremen, sheds and carts. He dug in his heels, leaning forward, breathing in the dust which was thrown up, tugging Kim to one side as the manager stepped from his office on to the dry track but he did not stop. The manager of the mine called.

'For Christ's sake, Harry, where are you going?' But he did not answer, just dragged his cravat up round his face knowing he would ride the man down if necessary but it wasn't. The mine manager stepped back, his hands up, alarm on his face as he watched Harry ride on past without checking his speed.

'Get on, Kim, get on,' he shouted, leaving the man behind. Down the tracks leading down the mines, past wagons and trolleys, past more labourers hunched beneath their loads and still he could not see the compound and now he was looking.

'Please let me be in time,' he said. 'Let me be in time.' His cravat became wet from his words but as he saw the fence and the horse which Frank had ridden, as he reined in at the entrance, as he leapt down and did not hobble Kim he saw that he was not in time and it was as though the scene was frozen, as though no one moved and there seemed to be silence.

Across the bare cracked earth, through the gate, he could see that Baralong was still tied to the wagon wheel. His back was wet with blood which did not show as the fox's had shown against the white snow. It had dripped to the ground which was now stained with dull red patches. There was movement now; he saw Baralong's head lift slightly and the men turn as they heard him pass through the gates, but then they looked back to his mate again and now he heard the murmur of their voices. Harry walked faster now, breathing rapidly from the ride, from disgust and rage. He pushed Frank aside and the men who ringed the wheel. Flies were on Baralong's back, he could see them moving, hear their hum and he wanted to vomit.

He walked to his friends and his legs were steady and so was his voice as he said to the white man who wore a slouch hat and no jacket and still panted as he held the whip, 'I'll take over now.' He took the whip and laid it against the wagon, gently so that it would not fall and now there really was silence from the crowd. He must be careful, he knew that. Harry undid the leather thongs which tied the black hands wide to the rim of the wheel and he said nothing but worked in time with the gasping breath of Baralong, seeing the fish as it lay on the bank and his father's dark hands as he crushed its head.

As Baralong slid face forward to the ground Harry picked up his shirt, his jacket, and slung them over his shoulder and then he took his friend's warm wet body. He scarcely felt the weight as he heaved him over his shoulder too, but he did not touch his back. He was very careful not to touch his back. He was very careful with these men too.

He moved through the crowd until Frank stood in front of him and there was dislike in his face and a strange excitement.

'Where are you going with your mate, Harry?' he challenged.

Harry stopped and turned. 'Nobody beats my mate but me,' he said. 'I can do it better. That's where I'm going now.'

He pushed past Frank, past his disappointment and his eyes which spoke to him. He listened to the cheers as he eased Baralong over Kim's saddle and he walked now along the track, away from the fence which was beating back the heat, away from the men and the system. Away from Frank whose eyes had told him that he wanted to kill this white man who was breaking the rules, for Harry knew now that Frank had, for that brief moment, seen into his mind. The ground was hot beneath his feet and he felt stones sharp through the leather. Out of sight of the men he stopped and tried to move Baralong so that he was sitting in the saddle but he groaned and said, 'No, Harry.'

So Harry left him as he was, hanging over the saddle, his

292

head limp, blood running through his hair and falling to the ground, the flies in a cloud on and above his back. Harry did not stop until he reached the zinc shed; neither did he speak, for what could he say? He put Baralong on a sheepskin in the triple canvassed wagon which was still in the shed. He bathed his back with salt water and the gasps turned to whimpers.

'Lie still,' Harry said. 'We leave tonight.' For he knew that he could not stay one more day in this place, with these people.

Baralong lay on his stomach but now lifted his head, his lips moving, his words a mere whisper.

'We cannot. They will come after us.'

Harry shook his head, pressing his friend's arm. Christ, he hoped not.

When the moon came up Harry tied Kim to the tailboard of the wagon and Baralong's horse too. He had spent money today on a spare team of horses so he tied them at the back too. He packed the medicine chest which held his letters and his rope, dropping it in his haste, taking a deep breath, calming himself before he packed guns for shooting game, provisions he had collected before the sun went down and many cans of water and then urged in the dog he had bought a year ago. He looked again at the route which Sam had sent for Simon's homestead. Once he was there he would be able to think more clearly about his next step.

'They will follow, Harry. I have not been searched,' Baralong whispered again, pulling Harry close so that he could hear the words.

'Perhaps they won't,' Harry answered, his voice calm. 'And how will they know where we are?' His fists were clenched and his nails dug into the palms of his hands.

Nothing mattered now but leaving here, taking his friend before they did any more to him. Anger was still deep within him but he knew that fear was there too and he looked at the guns.

Rain came that night but just enough to damp down the dust, not enough to bog the wheels in mud, and Harry could have wept with relief for now it would not be so easy for anyone to follow them. They travelled all night and all the next day, switching the teams around, then resting during the following night, though Harry did not rest much but listened and looked. They did not light a fire. They did the same for the next three days, two of which were wet and so still the dust was laid.

On the fourth day they saw a Karroo *dorp* in the distance but skirted the tin-roofed houses, not wanting the Boers of the township to see them, not wanting them to tell those who came after them; if anyone did come after them.

'They probably won't come anyway,' Harry called through to Baralong but he did not know if his friend was conscious yet. He looked again at the letter from Sam and it was good to have in his hand paper that had come from somewhere other than this place. It was good to see his uncle's handwriting. It made him seem less lonely, less frightened.

And so on and on they travelled and Harry could see no one behind them. On the fifteenth day he felt the tension begin to ease in his shoulders and that night he slept for four hours at a stretch and did not start at every sound, even laughing when the dog barked at a dassie instead of straining every nerve, listening for horses approaching. By the nineteenth day Baralong's back was beginning to heal and on the twentieth Harry saw in the distance the kopje, the raised mound which Sam had remembered Simon writing about. It lay just to the south of the homestead, the letter said, and he felt excitement and relief surge as they drew closer. He could see the pile of round stones which stood high against the flat green and red landscape. Short grass sprouted amongst the earth, rejuvenated by the rains. Baralong came out on to the seat when he called.

Baralong looked at the kopje. 'A man in the compound says that to the east of this kopje lies the Orange River, some days away by foot. If the rains come it will fill and take boat. If men come we can go there.'

'They haven't come though, Baralong. Surely they won't now?' Harry said, looking over his shoulder.

Baralong said nothing, just looked back the way they had come. Harry felt Sam's map in his hand. No, they would not come. Not now. They didn't know where he was, did they?

Frank wouldn't remember the existence of the homestead, let alone the direction, and why would he think Harry would make for it anyway? The dry winds would have hidden their tracks by now, wouldn't they? He shook his head. No, they wouldn't come now. He felt safer somehow now that he was near a place that had known his uncle; that now belonged to him.

He drew a deep breath and pointed to the map which Sam had drawn. 'We should be just north of this.'

It was another day before Harry saw the homestead but it was not until the sun had moved across the sky and it was afternoon that they were close enough to see the stone-walled sheep-*kraals* and the kaffir huts, broken with the thatch half-gone. Harry drove the horses on towards the square red-bricked building with the thatched roof and he pulled his hat down to protect his eyes from the fierce light which was reflected from the walls. He was tired, his arms ached and his hands were blistered from the reins but he was here at last, on property which he owned.

He tied the reins to the brake and jumped down on to his land. He turned and took Baralong's arm, taking his weight, easing him to the ground so that his back did not bleed again. When night came they had already housed the wagon in the zinc-roofed wagon shed and emptied the pots and the kettle into the main room of the house. The noise of cicada insects had filled the daylight hours and Harry realised that this had been the only sound. There was no wire singing, no men chanting, no engines steam hauling, and it felt good.

Inside there were blackened beams and hanging from these were old bits of harness; there was a pile of mealie sacks in one corner but that was all. They brewed up the kettle in the fireplace. A ladder led up to an old loft but Harry threw down the sheepskins on the mud floor. He felt less trapped down here. Baralong picked his up and took it to the door and began to walk across to a kaffir hut.

'Come back, you sleep here. We are partners now,' Harry called. He threw two potatoes on the fire and the smell of their cooking filled the room. He cooked up salted mutton, brewing the tea when the kettle boiled and brought it to Baralong who sat cross-legged on a sheepskin.

'Thank you, Harry,' he said.

Harry nodded and turned to get his own.

'Thank you for saving me from the search,' Baralong continued, but Harry did not want to listen for that had been easy. He should have stayed and faced them, changed them, stood up for what he believed in but he had not.

That night he put the dog by the door to sleep for she had good ears and Baralong still feared that they would come. He looked at the guns by the door but would he ever use one? There had been so much brutality, it made him feel sick.

They rode the homestead land the next day where sheep had once grazed and Baralong shot a dassie and so they had rabbit that night.

In the morning Harry rode back along the boundaries and sat on Kim looking at the land, at its flat, scrubbed earth, and over to the east where the Orange would run if the rains came. Kim shifted beneath him, snorting and easing his weight from foot to foot. Had Simon ridden here, Harry thought, looking to the west and back behind him. He rode on, round the western boundary, past well-fleshed thorn milk-bushes revitalised by the sparse rain which had fallen. He quartered the area until darkness fell because he had decided that here was as good a place as anywhere to start his search for diamonds, despite Barry's words in the Johannesburg bar so long ago about the farm being good only for ostriches. After all, it gave them a respite, gave Baralong's back a chance to grow strong again. The next three days he quartered the western section and then as more days passed he covered the land to the south and the north. There had been no sign so far of alluvial beds.

'So perhaps Barry was right,' he said to Baralong that night as they sat wrapped up in the sheepskins before the dying fire in the hearth. 'But it's worth trying the last section, though so far I haven't found any evidence to indicate diamonds. I just have a feeling somehow, and besides, we can move on soon if necessary.'

He watched as Baralong nodded, rising with an easy

296

movement, holding the sheepskin round him as he checked the window again. Harry looked at the dog but there had been no sign from her of danger, she lay quietly, her head on her forelegs, eyes watching as Baralong returned, her tail thumping on the hard earth floor.

'Try and relax, Baralong. The mining company has more important things to think of, like profits and day-to-day running of the mines.' But he wasn't sure whether or not he believed his own words. He knew he must hurry with his surveying and move soon if there was really no hope here.

In the morning he approached the house from the east, standing up in his stirrups, traversing the ground with shaded eyes. Up and down he rode seeing it from one angle and then another and as morning turned to noon he at last saw the marginally lower fall of the land this side as it ran on well beyond the house. Drawing closer he saw a strip which just might once, long ago, have been a dried-up stream and if it was it meant an alluvial bed; it meant decomposed yellow ground; it meant diamonds.

Harry pulled in Kim and looked again. He turned in his saddle shading his eyes, looking to where the Orange must be, far away over the horizon, tree-lined and dug out by early diggers. Then back again to the house, to the land and that strip of sunken earth which could only be seen from where he was now positioned. He felt the reins in his hands, worn, sweat-stiffened and looked again. He couldn't be sure, that was the devil of it but by God, maybe there was a change. He tightened his hands on the leather, dug his heels into Kim's sides, feeling the excitement which he hardly dared voice because he could be wrong. He rode back then, quickly, urging Kim on, calling to Baralong and as he reached the house Baralong came out, throwing a gun at Harry, running to his horse.

'Where are men?' he called and his voice was loud and fierce.

For a few moments Harry had forgotten that they were perhaps the hunted and he shouted, 'It's all right, Baralong, it's not them.' He laughed as his friend turned, his face puzzled. 'It's the land. I think there's an old water course, an old sloot.'

Baralong walked back, his face still confused.

'Alluvial plains hold diamonds. Look at the banks of the Orange, the first diggers staked their claims along its banks. Come on, man.' He pointed back to Baralong's horse. 'We'll go and see.' He had kept his voice calm, he sounded in control, but inside he was not for this was so important to them both.

They dug in the sandy soil for at least a month at the point which Harry thought most likely and now it was colder and their fingers were stiff as they shovelled gravel and earth which was yellow and decomposed as alluvial ground should be but which so far held no diamonds. How long should they try? This was the question which Harry asked himself endlessly. How much time could they afford to waste? It was June now, the middle of winter and they had to find gems before their provisions ran out. They had to find them if either of them were to have a future. They had to find them before the men came, if they came.

They worked until Harry thought his back would break and his hands would never heal. He thought of the kaffirs toiling in the great hole, hour upon hour and then sleeping behind fences, and knew that his hardship could never be as great. After all, this was their piece of land, for it was Baralong's as much as his now, and so his hands hardened with the unaccustomed labour. Sometimes it rained and the coolness of winter made each day easier than it might have been. But at the end of another two weeks they had found no diamonds.

'It's no good,' he said at last, resting on his shovel. 'Maybe I was wrong.'

Baralong stood and looked at him. 'You not wrong, Harry. I feel it. I know it. They are here, somewhere. They are here.'

Harry threw his shovel down, looking at his friend. 'But where, for Christ's sake, where?' He wiped his hands on his dust-caked trousers. Yes, he knew they should be here. All the signs pointed to it but the damn stones did not seem to exist. Time was passing too fast. They'd have to decide whether to move on and try nearer the Orange; maybe some of the old diggings weren't worked out yet. He'd talk to Baralong tonight. They'd have to decide.

That afternoon he walked the course of the stream again leaving Baralong to shoot a springbox or dassie for later. Backwards and forwards looking at the contours, the stones, the boulders. Knowing that somewhere in this soil there should be diamonds which had been deposited when the pipes were new and the elements had violently weathered and dispersed the crystallised carbon.

'They should be here,' he said to himself, sitting down, his arms on his knees, his face running with the sweat of tiredness, of panic. He lifted his arm and wiped his forehead on the rough torn sleeve of his shirt. Looking towards the homestead he could see the empty sheep-*kraals*, zinc-roofed outhouses, the kaffir huts, but not Baralong. He knew though that he would be out there somewhere on his horse hunting, but all the while watching the trail from Kimberley. He rose again. As he walked, looked and kicked with his boots he decided that they could only give themselves another two months here, that was all the time they could afford. Apart from anything else it would be time for Frank's spring leave soon. Perhaps he would come then.

He walked again and felt the stones through his worn boot soles; earth ran in through the split uppers. His neck ached from looking down, from seeing the earth so red, and then so brown when the rain fell as it now began to do. Baralong called him as the sun went down and dark shrouded the land. He unhitched Kim from the milk-bush, riding slowly back in the darkness, seeing no light from the red-bricked house for they had hung the mealie bags in front of the windows to keep in the dull candle glow. They wanted no beacon shining out from their house.

He was up at first light and rode out again on Kim but further along this time, and as he did so he looked down the course of the dry bed to a rise in the land where perhaps the bank would have been. That is where they would try next, he decided.

An hour later they brought their guns to the rise, along with the sieves, the shovels, the buckets. It took two trips.

'We need one diamond per fifteen buckets,' Harry said and Baralong laughed for Harry called this across to him every morning. They sank their shovels into the sand and stones and the horses pawed the ground and mouthed their bits, the clinking and snuffling reaching the men, but they took no notice. In the distance the dog sniffed around the house.

Baralong laughed. 'You are sure, Harry?'

Harry nodded and smiled. In spite of his conviction that the hunters would come Baralong looked younger now, the drawn lines around his mouth had gone and there was a looseness in his walk, a set to his shoulders which had not been there before they had reached Bloemfon, for that is what Simon had called this place. Baralong's back had healed well but it was not that which had made him different. Harry knew that it was freedom.

Harry dug and filled the buckets while Baralong hoisted them up and poured them through the sieve. After fifteen there were still no diamonds but they did not stop digging, just moved along about ten feet. How many hundred feet had they covered in this way, Harry wondered, stamping his foot on the shovel, lifting the earth, dropping it into the bucket and again and again. As he worked, he did not think, just counted as he did every day and then Baralong called.

'Harry, you right. You bloody right, man.' His voice was high, fast, more of a song than speech.

Harry did not understand at first.

'Harry, Harry.' This time the words were more of a scream and now Harry turned, dropping the shovel. He ran to his friend and looked at the sieve where two dull glassy pebbles lay amongst the stones and earth.

He held the edge of the sieve with Baralong and together they lowered it to the ground as though fearful that the diamonds would slip through the holes – but how could they, they were too damn big. Baralong's hand was shaking as he picked one up. It soaked up the colour of his skin as he held it in his palm. He took it between his finger and thumb and held it to the sky.

Harry touched the other that still lay in the sieve. It was cool and still and held no beauty yet but when facets had been cut it would flash and live with a vividness which would hurt. He lifted it now, holding it to the sky as Baralong was doing. This would be for Esther.

As he stood there it was as though a great dam had burst within him and he turned to Baralong. 'These are five carats each, Baralong. Five damn carats. We've done it, we've bloody done it.'

He was dancing now, the diamond clasped in his hand, and he hugged his friend whose cheeks were wet and he knew his were too. They hugged and wept and danced and sang and then dug again and sieved and as night fell they brought their diamonds back. Some small, some large, but not as big as the first two that they had found. Harry cooked salt mutton as Baralong stripped the fleece off one of the sheepskins, using Harry's knife to cut large circles.

'We'll carry the diamonds in these pouches all the time,' Baralong said, making holes and threading strips of hide through, knotting them and drawing them tight. He divided up the diamonds and threw a pouch to Harry.

'In case they come, Harry,' Baralong said.

Harry put down the plates which he had been about to bring across to where Baralong was working. For a moment he had forgotten Frank's spring leave. He must not do that again for now they were so very close to all that they both needed.

He tied the pouch to his belt, and the two empty ones which Baralong also threw across to him. He lifted the plates again. The fat had congealed on the enamel and the potatoes were charred where they had lain on the ashes and he was not hungry but he knew that they must eat for they had much work to do before they could leave, before they could escape.

The next day they took up boards from the loft, wrenching them up from the beams, bending the long, strong nails as they tore them free. They carried them to the dig and they both shovelled, both sieved and when their arms ached with the sideways motion they emptied the buckets on to the boards and sorted with a wooden scraper.

When it rained the earth grew sticky and Harry's back

strained with the effort of lifting the shovel, but the water washed the earth from the diamonds and so they were easier to find. Baralong lifted his face to the rain and grinned. 'The Orange river will be filling up with this rainfall, Harry. If they come the river will take a boat now. It would not have done before. Spring is a good time.'

'It's not spring yet,' Harry grunted but he knew that in six weeks it would be.

They worked all the daylight hours for the next three weeks, stopping to shoot a dassie or a springbok, stopping every half-hour to check that there were no riders coming past the kopje though Harry felt they were safe until the spring. When they each had one full pouch they had a day of rest and sat in the house as the rain came down heavy for once and drank the brandy which Harry had saved for the day they found their fortune.

'How we sell stones?' Baralong asked. 'Dealers here, in South Africa, report us for not using cartel, for bad dealing.'

Harry threw across the flask. 'Have a little, my friend,' he said and he knew his voice was slurred. He had not been drunk since Johannesburg.

'As to that problem', he said, wagging his finger at Baralong who took a long swallow at the brandy before screwing on the top and tossing it back to Harry. 'We shall go to Antwerp. I have come across a name while I've been out here. It belongs to someone who likes fine white diamonds and is not fussy where they come from. The slump is over and quality is always desirable anyway, Baralong.'

He stood up and moved unsteadily to the window, lifting back the mealie bag one inch and peering out but he knew there was no one there because the dog had not barked. He just liked to make sure from time to time. Did other people feel fear as he did? He wanted to ask Baralong, but how could he, for if his friend did not fear as he did then he could not bear the truth.

'Yes,' he repeated, dropping the mealie bag and turning. 'We shall go to Antwerp and then I shall take you to my home. You will be safe there, Baralong.'

Baralong was sitting cross-legged, his arms loose on his

knees, his head back against his saddle. The fireplace was blackened and the coals were almost dead.

'No, I not come with you. I stay.'

Harry did not move towards Baralong but stood leaning against the wall as he had been doing. The candle's glow did not reach into the corners of the room; there was just Baralong in its circle of light. It seemed very quiet suddenly and Harry could not find the words to say that he could not bear the thought of being without his friend for he had never known anyone as he knew this man, anyone that is except for Hannah.

'Why must you stay?' was all he said but he wanted to shout at him. Don't stay, I need a friend I love. He still did not move but the dog did. She pricked up her ears and looked at him. Did she sense the pain behind the words?

'There much to do in South Africa. They take the rights of my people in the Cape too. Now, things get worse everywhere. In Cape Town are natives who see this, who come together to stop it. I want be with them.'

Baralong's head was tilted back, his eyes were shut. 'I have love for you, my friend,' Baralong said, 'but I have love for country too.'

Harry could still not say to Baralong the words which he was forming in his head and so he just nodded. 'Yes, I can see that you would feel that you must stay. I will go to Holland, Baralong, and send you back your money.'

He moved back to sit opposite, resting against his saddle now, hoping that his face was in shade and that night they finished the brandy and the next day began work late. They rode their horses down to the sloot and dug and sieved again and it was warmer today.

By late afternoon they had found one of the largest diamonds Harry had ever seen. It was about seven carats and lay heavy in his hand. They had half-filled a pouch with smaller ones and Baralong said that they must put this in the last pouch on its own, for it was of almost too great a value to be borne.

They did not hear the dog barking until it was almost too late and then Harry stopped as he was pulling the pouch tight and held out his hand to Baralong. They stood quite still as they listened and Harry felt cold and he could see that his hand had begun to shake. They eased their way slowly up the bank that had been formed as they dug but pressed themselves in close. Harry could smell the earth, so close to his face.

The men were at the house, four of them on horses and Harry saw Frank as he flicked his cigarette outwards on to the ground.

'Our guns by the rise,' Baralong whispered. They would be seen if they moved to fetch them and Harry was glad for he was sick of violence.

'If the dog doesn't come towards us, maybe we'll be all right,' Harry said, feeling the sand beneath his hands and in his nails. As he talked it puffed up into his face. He could still smell it, see it, each minute grain.

The horses were tethered in the sloot, would they be seen from the house? Harry dug his fingers in deep and lay flat against the rising ground. He could only hear the breath in his throat. There was no more barking from the dog. Please God, let it stay that way. He looked again, carefully, and saw Frank pat and stroke it and then it barked, loudly and turned towards the sloot bounding towards its masters. Harry felt the shaking in his hands and saw the rod which he had held years ago, heard his father's voice, so vicious. You took the rod too far back, the line wasn't damn well straight. He dragged his mind back. For God's sake, there was no time for that. He took Baralong's arm. 'Get the horses, ride for the bloody river. It's all we can do. Ride for the Orange. There are trees, houses and it will be dark before we get there.' His voice was jagged as he ran but he heard Baralong with him, slipping as he was on the earth and pebbles.

He snatched at the reins, scrambling into the saddle and dug his heels into Kim, turning, checking that Baralong was close. He heard the men shouting, saw Frank leap into his saddle, saw him draw his rifle from near his bedroll.

They did not stir up sand as they rode, for the rain had been heavy yesterday. Their horses were away quickly, and he could hear and feel the thudding of their hoofs and the barking of the dog and soon they were clear of the property and he did not even turn for one last look. Were they following? He didn't know but was glad that the sand was wet and there would be no dust for the men to follow. He dug his heels into Kim.

'Come on, boy,' he yelled, hearing Baralong with him.

But because there was no dust kicked there was a clear view for the marksman as he fired. As he galloped past a thorn bush Harry felt a blow in his back, a thud as though he had been hit by the flat of a shovel, the pain did not come until a few minutes later and then it tore and wrenched at his body. They rode on, not stopping, and after three hours the men were still after them but not quite so close for their horses were tired after their ride across the veld.

Kim was sweating now, Harry could see it, stained dark at the base of his neck beneath his mane. It would be wet, and his lips were dry. He wanted to rest his head on that strong neck, lay his mouth against the smooth wetness. Yes, that's what he would do and then maybe the pain would ease, but with each galloped stride it jerked again through his body. Why was he riding like this? He would stop. It was absurd. He would stop and sit. His father must let him rest for a moment. He would ask him. He turned and it was not his father but Baralong and he was glad. Baralong came close to him now and he saw that the sun was going down and soon it would be dark. Please God, soon it would be dark, for now he remembered why he could not stop.

'Can you ride more, Harry,' Baralong said close to him and Harry nodded.

I'm fine, he wanted to say, but he could not open his mouth for if he did he was afraid that he would scream. He wanted to turn his head but he could not bear the thought of any more movement.

Baralong looked though and Harry could hear his panting as he said, 'We make it to river but they close now. It getting dark, Harry, and it not far. Hang on. Hang on, my friend.'

Harry gripped the reins and the saddle too and his back felt on fire and he wanted to fall from his horse and lie on the ground where it was still. But he heard the gun again and felt the fear and then there were boys' voices and the bag was heavy on his shoulder, though he had emptied the paper long ago.

The boys were close as he ran down the hill, his legs were heavy and his breath hurt in his chest and he turned and saw Arthur, his pale hair close but not close enough. Or was he? He must try harder, he must win. Just this once he must beat Arthur. His father would be pleased, and so he ran on again and there was white paper behind and about him, blowing in his face, blurring his vision. But there was the finishing line, he could see it and the people cheering. Would he make it? But he was too tired, they were too close and he was alone.

But then he heard his friend. 'There's the river, Harry.'

He looked but it was dark and then he saw it, gleaming like a ribbon in the moonlight and there was Hannah over by the tree, by the rope. But he had left his rope behind, with his letters. He'd have to tell his friend Baralong that they would have to go back for the rope. But his horse was slithering down the bank now into the water and he watched as Baralong reached and took the reins.

'Get down, Harry. Into the water.' It was an order, and Harry stroked the sleek sweated neck of Kim and lifted his leg, which was too heavy, over and into the water. He watched as Baralong came wading to his side, the reins of the horses in his hand. It was cold, so cold as they stood there, but only up to their knees and he was shaking again, but this time throughout the length of his body.

'We send off horses, they follow those. We swim, float, find boat but get away, we must get away or they kill us.'

Harry knew they would for he and his friend had broken the rules. He had loved a painting done by his sister and so they would kill him, drown him and so he would tear it up and then he could lift himself from the water.

He told Baralong but his friend took his arm and pulled him and so he went with him and this time the water did not surge into his face as it had once done, it did not cut the breath from his body and there were arms round him, holding him up as the water cooled his back. He was not alone any more.

'Harry.' Baralong's voice was a whisper. 'Let me take you. Trust me. Float, say nothing for they ride along bank.'

Harry did not know who was riding along the bank because

all his friends were laughing at the picture his sister had drawn, but he did as he was told because it was his friend who told him.

'I have love for you also, Baralong, my friend, and I will miss you,' he whispered into the dark night. He looked up into the sky, floating clear of the pain, seeing Uncle Simon and Hannah as they walked across the moor. Was he going to die out here as well?

18 Hannah looked out at the endless fog which swirled dark and yellow over the rhododendrons and the roses which hung limp and discoloured from their stems. They would have to prune them next week when September 1913 gave way to October. There was a smell of burning on the air and she shut the window. Frances was walking the dog and would be coughing into her cashmere scarf when she returned but for now she wasn't here and so there should have been a relief from the tension which had been growing between them as the militancy of the suffragettes escalated and filled the newspapers, the prisons and the air with smoke and had done since January when the Speaker had ruled that no women's suffrage amendment could be added to the current Reform Bill.

Hannah drew the curtains and turned to face the room. But there had been a different tension here this afternoon. The fire was bright in the grate after the matt colour of the garden. The teapot was empty now on the table near her chair; the scone on Esther's plate was half-eaten, the once melted butter lay dark yellow where it had reset on the plate. Her gold-rimmed cup and saucer lay next to the crumpled napkin. Yes, a different tension. Hannah looked away, to the books which gleamed around the desk and the silver paper-knife which shone in the light of the gas lamp, cold against the dull, stained paper of the blotter. She moved towards it, picking it up, feeling its weight, its smooth coolness, but her own anger was still burning inside, the air still felt as though it would suffocate her.

Esther had just left, her cloak pulled over her head, droplets of mist forming on the fur edging as soon as she stepped on to the path. She remembered Esther's words, her thin smile.

Thank you so much, darling, for the tea. So kind. And remember, Hannah, you owe it to him, she had said and there had been a frown on her forehead, a coldness in the deep violet of her eyes. Hannah put down the knife. Yes, she knew she did.

It was September 1913, and Arthur was still waiting for her acceptance of his proposal.

She turned away from books, so many, too many to ever read. There was no time. Couldn't Arthur understand that? There was no time to read, no time for marriage. Did he never listen to her? Couldn't he understand that after Asquith had dismissed the possibility of women's franchise as an improbable hypothesis last year during the second reading of the Reform Bill there had been so much more to do and then there had been no ruling over the amendment. She threw the knife down on to the desk. The vote was as far away as ever.

She moved again to the window, lifting the curtain, wiping away the condensation, but she could see nothing. Where was Frances? Where was she? Perhaps they could talk again as they had once been able to. Impatience was making her back tense and her shoulders rigid.

Did marriage and the thought of it always make you feel as though you were dying in thin air, trapped by unseen bars but strong and immoveable none the less? Why did Arthur crowd so closely, why did Esther remind her of duty? Why couldn't they leave her in peace to live her life? She wanted to go to Joe, to talk to him, tell him, see his hands, so still and strong. He would understand but somehow she could not speak to him of Arthur, of marriage, and he would only say of her suffrage work that the choice was hers.

She dropped the curtain and stood by the fire, feeling its warmth on her face and her hands. She reached out and gripped the mantelshelf. The wood was warm and smooth and dark. It was solid and the same today as it had been yesterday. She gripped it harder. She wished that she was solid, that there was no room for thoughts and feelings and fear and despair and at that word she looked up into the mirror which hung above the clock.

For there was such despair in her, such darkness, such conflict and she did not understand herself any longer. She was tired but there had been nothing to tax her this year. She had stayed in the headquarters of their suffrage group. She had painted posters, sorted leaflets, made tea. She had taught her class in school and it was a good class. She and Frances were pleased with the girls. She had extended the Sunday school to take in a kindergarten for children too. It had been an easy year because she had not joined in the arson campaign of the suffragettes, yet. She had not slashed paintings of beauty in art galleries, not burnt the homes of Cabinet Ministers or derelict churches or halls.

No, she had done none of these things and today Esther had asked why, her voice edged with contempt, swiftly replaced by an excitement which filled not just her voice but her eyes as well as she had spoken of the thrill of it all, the sheer joy of replacing the boredom of her life with destructive actions which daily filled the newspapers for all to see; and still her family did not know and that appeared to Hannah to be part of the attraction of it all. What a child Esther still was. A dangerous selfish child but so far all this activity had kept her faithful to Harry and so she should not object.

Hannah looked now into the mirror. And neither should she be so tired. Why were her eyes tight and set deep in her face, why were there lines around her mouth? Why was there such despair? She gripped the wood more tightly still. The heat from the fire was too hot on her wrist but she did not move.

She thought of the satisfaction which always burned on her cousin's face when she returned with empty paraffin cans, of the penknife which she had borrowed from her brother George's drawer and which was covered now with cracked oil paint. She thought of how there had been no answering exhilaration in her, no feeling of moving forwards just distaste for the violence, the destruction, the criticism of the movement which was now being voiced. The criticism that asked whether women deserved the vote. But the Government would not listen, and they must be made to, mustn't they?

Hannah heard the front door and then the sitting-room door but she didn't want to turn because she was working her way at last towards something which she could not yet see clearly but which was forming out of her confusion. It was too important to lose; she must grasp and face it for it was the root of her despair and the knowledge was close now.

'This really is the end, Hannah,' she heard Frances say, her voice loud, but Hannah did not want to listen, it drew her from inside her head. 'Your fellow suffragettes have burnt down another building.'

'Ssh,' Hannah said, her fingers white from gripping the wood. It was close now, almost . . . here.

But Frances's hand was on her shoulder, pulling her round away from the centre of her mind and she had been so close, so very close and anger flared, harsh and ugly because something important had been about to crystallise. She lifted her head and Frances was close, her face tight and cold.

'They have burnt Benson House. It was beautiful. I use the tense with great care, Hannah.' Hannah could feel her breath and still the older woman's hand held her shoulder. 'It is a disgrace. An absolute disgrace and to think that you are involved with this behaviour. Can none of you see the damage which has been inflicted not just on property and works of art which have been an expression of a man or woman's genius but on the suffrage movement?'

She took Hannah's arm, and pushed her to the window, drawing back the curtains, opening the casement. 'Take a deep breath, Hannah. Can you smell it, can you picture the flames, hear the crackle of the wood, the rush as the bricks fall in?' Frances was shouting now and Hannah had never heard her do so before; had never seen this usually calm face distorted with anger, with frustration. 'We women should be asking for the vote as responsible people who deserve it,' Frances said, through lips that were thin.

Hannah watched as Frances walked from her towards the desk. She tried to snatch back the thoughts and the decision which had been nearly within her grasp. In her desperation she wanted to cry, 'For God's sake, be quiet.'

From the sudden turn of her friend's head she realised that the words had indeed struck across the room. Frances paled; her mouth slackened for a moment and then her lips grew tight again and though she did not shout there was a chill to her voice, to her body.

'No, Hannah, the time for being quiet is over. Yes, the

suffragettes have made us visible. Yes, Asquith is making our task difficult. But no to this behaviour.'

'But who are you to say no to anything?' Hannah wanted to know. She really wanted to know if Frances could produce a reason to say no, for her, for everyone, because for any one person to have such authority would make her life so simple. There need be no thought, no decision taken, it would all be so easy, but after all, wasn't that the right she was fighting for; the right to decide her own life? But there were too many things to decide about. Too many.

'Who are you to say no?' And this time her voice was more than a shout, it was a howl of rage. Her hands were bunched into fists, the dog came into the room and whined, looking from one to another knowing that there was too much tension, too much feeling and she left to lie by the front door.

Frances did not answer her question but clasped her hands beneath her chin and spoke quickly, almost without drawing breath. Her grey dress was wet at the hem and smelt of smoke. The white lace at the neck was spotless though. She stood straight, looking at Hannah, her back to the fire.

'Violence becomes a way of life, the aim is forgotten, our influential friends are alienated. The work of years has been ruined. Women are being sentenced to long terms of imprisonment. The Cat and Mouse Act has been introduced to overcome hunger striking. Women are released when they are too weak to survive and then re-arrested to continue their sentence. Some have died as a result. One of them could be you. It is all madness. The vote is no nearer, damage and violence are everywhere. I cannot condone it. I cannot condone this senseless suffering and damage or anyone who subscribes to it.'

'But remember what Asquith said,' Hannah shouted now, wanting to push everyone away. They were all too close, all pulling at her, wanting her to go in their direction. Arson or lobbying, which should it be? Marriage or not? There were too many loyalties tearing her apart.

'Yes, but what have the suffragettes really achieved? Have you been given the vote? No. There is just a great deal of suffering for the rank and file whilst Christabel Pankhurst has exiled herself to France and directs you all from there, out of reach of imprisonment and hunger strikes. Can any member put forward an opposing point of view within the organisation, Hannah? Can you object and argue if you don't agree?' Frances was pointing her finger now, her head shook with each word. 'No, of course you can't. You have no democracy in the WSPU, have you? Even Sylvia Pankhurst has left to start campaigning on her own for universal suffrage because there is no room for dissent. Others are leaving. You are in disarray. Think, Hannah, about where this is leading.'

Hannah could not think, there was too much noise. Esther, Maureen and Ann had not left, they still fought on. How could she leave them? And what about Arthur? Frances was still making too much noise.

'You do not deserve the vote if you hurt others and it could come to that. Do your campaigning in the constitutional way, Hannah.' Frances's voice was quieter now and she sounded tired suddenly. She moved towards Hannah. 'Let the Government handle the Irish Question, the Reforms, the arms race. Let them keep our country free from war. Come back with us. Lobby constitutionally. Violence is never justified.'

Her hand was on Hannah's arm now and her smell of lavender eau de cologne was faint on the air between them. It would be so easy but Esther's contempt was sharp in Hannah's mind and Arthur was there too, pulling at her, demanding her life. She felt Frances's hand guiding her towards the chair, pulling her as the others were doing and she stopped and moved her arm from the grasp of her Headmistress.

Her face was still, her mind also. There were no clear thoughts; nothing was there at all but a need to breathe. The books were closing in on her, the people were dragging at her clothes, the gas lamps were hissing too loudly. The oil lamp smelt too strong. She must get away from them all, leave so that she could think and breathe. That is what she must do and quickly, before she drowned beneath them all. Why had she not seen it before?

'I shall leave in the morning, Frances,' she said and there

was no anger in her but a great certainty. 'We cannot go on living together while we are so very different.'

There was red now on the other woman's cheeks and her hands came to her lips. There was silence for a moment. The gas lamp threw her face into shadow and Hannah turned to look at the mantel, blue and yellow.

'Very well,' Frances said and her voice was calm now but it was high and Hannah knew she would speak again and she did not want to hear any more words. She just wanted to go to her room and pack her clothes, quickly. Some into her trunk, some into the valise. She wanted to go to a room like Joe's and sit in the quiet and try to find the thought which Frances had chased away earlier.

'Hannah, please listen.' Frances was struggling to keep her voice level but she wanted to reach out for this girl who was now a woman, hold her, not let her go, but she knew that during the last year a darkness had settled on Hannah, a tension which had distanced them and she, Frances Fletcher, had not helped at all. Was it Arthur? Was it the arson? She did not know, but now Hannah must be allowed to find out for no one could help her, least of all her; or Joe. But somehow contact must be kept. Frances ran her hand over her forehead, watching Hannah as she moved towards the door. She must speak but she must be calm and clear and without emotion for Frances suspected that there was already too much emotion tearing at Hannah.

'I shall expect you to continue in my employment. It is not good for the girls to be subjected to an abrupt change in teacher. Please also continue to come on a Sunday. You cannot desert your women and children, you know.'

She smiled. Somehow she had to keep hold of Hannah until she had come to a decision but if she turned towards violence, then Frances knew that there would be no understanding left between them, no future for their friendship, and that thought broke her heart.

Hannah had wanted to rent Joe's old room but it was too far and there was already a tenant. She walked down the street,

314

passing the grey washing rigid with frost and an old man had answered her knock, shaking his head and pointing to the matchgirl's room. It was empty, he had said, but Hannah had wanted only Joe's room.

She looked around the one she had moved into two months ago. The bed was in the corner as Joe's had been and there was a grate with a small fire which had not yet warmed the room for school had only finished two hours ago. Books for marking were piled high on the small table and the single gas lamp on the wall by the sink gave off a light which did not in any way illuminate the walls; it was as well, she thought, for they were spotted with mould and the plaster had crumpled near the ceiling and floor. She only noticed the smell of damp when she first entered the room and what did it matter anyway? Mary, the matchgirl had not had any light and neither did many of her Sunday ladies; they only had rickets and consumption and would take no money from her.

She had no mirror to see whether the cream shot silk dress she wore was creased so she smoothed it with her hands. There was a mug of tea on the table but it had cooled. She sat on the upright chair and shrugged on her working coat around her shoulders. She was cold but not hungry. She was never hungry at the moment and her thoughts were no clearer. There was always too much noise in her head to think. She picked up the ivory fan that Joe had made when the sun seemed to shine and they were little more than children and her mother was alive.

What would Lady Wilmot have planned for dinner, she wondered, drawing her coat closer. Arthur was going to Europe for four months and she knew he would require the answer which she had promised before he left and she would not think of love because she still did not know what it meant.

She heard his footsteps on the stairs and he did not knock but walked in. His silver-tipped cane was tucked under his arm and his pale hair flopped across his forehead. His cloak was heavy with beaded moisture and she rose as he walked to her and kissed her with cold lips.

'I hate this place, Hannah,' he said against her mouth. His

315

breath was scented with champagne but she did not wish to know where he had been.

'Sit down while I fetch my cloak,' she said and walked to the hook behind the door. She had taken it from the bed earlier since she did not want to draw his eyes to where she slept though she did not know why. When would he ask her and what would she say? She still did not know. The cloak caught on the hook so he came to her and took it, taking the old coat from her shoulders and throwing it over the chair. He drew the cloak around her and the satin lining felt cold on her bare neck. She felt his lips on her hair, her skin and knew that he was beautiful, but he took away her air, made her feel as though she would never breathe again, never fly free.

'I've been patient, Hannah,' he said, his voice muffled by her skin. His arms were round her now, pulling her close to him. 'Marry me. Say you will. I need a good wife, someone to bear my children. My family have accepted you and I can take you away from all this. You and I understand one another, you don't cling, you let me live my life.'

His arms were tight around her and she could not breathe. She was tired and he was pulling at her again and Esther had said that she owed it to him. He kissed her again, talking into her neck, and her head ached with his words and perhaps if she answered he would stop. And so she said, 'Yes, Arthur.'

His lips were not soft as he kissed her now and his hands were pulling her tight. She still could not breathe.

On Tuesday morning four days later Hannah arrived at school. Arthur had left for Switzerland and he had agreed that they would not announce the engagement, for they were not to be married until December 1914 and it seemed a long way away and that made the air clearer. She did not want anyone to know before Harry, she had said, and wondered again where her brother was.

She walked across the black and white tiled entrance porch and then the assembly hall towards Frances's study at the end of the dark passage-way remembering how she had bought glucose sweets from the Emporium for Esther when they were children. Now they barely spoke.

Frances did not answer her knock and so Hannah walked in. Her Headmistress was not there and the room seemed dead without her. Hannah looked at the letters unopened on the blotter. She looked at her watch; school would start in half an hour. She ran her fingers along the polished desk. The fire was not lit and the dog was not lying on the rug.

Hannah left and walked past the wall where once Queen Victoria had hung and then her son. It was now King George V but she did not notice. She used to curtsy and Frances would laugh but that no longer happened and still she had come to no decision. She walked through the shrubbery towards the house. The leaves were deep on the ground but not crisp because the air was so damp.

As she rang the house-bell it chimed deep in the hall and when Beatrice did not answer her knock she walked into the house and called. She moved into the sitting-room and the curtains were still drawn. Was Frances ill? Now she hurried down towards the kitchen. Cook would know, but Frances had been well yesterday. No, she couldn't be ill and for a moment she saw the pear tree, the weak hand of her mother, but pushed it away. No, Frances could not be ill.

She knocked, not waiting for a reply but entering. Cook was sitting at the table, her cap as white and starched as always, her overalls too and she turned, her plump arms crossed, her hands gripping her flesh tightly.

'I'm glad you came, Miss Hannah. I've just sent Beatrice round to fetch you. Did you see her?' Her eyes were red and Hannah shook her head. She could not ask why Cook was crying, she did not want to know. She stood by the door. It was light in the kitchen and warm. The fire was red in the grate of the bread oven. No, she would not ask why. So she stood and looked and did not want to listen as Cook told her how Frances had been attacked as she had walked home from a suffragist meeting and was in hospital.

'They thought she was one of them suffragettes, like you, Miss. Them girls had fired another house, you see.'

Hannah did not move, she could not. Neither could she

speak. All she could see and hear was Frances as she stood grey against the fire, her hands clasped as she spoke out for moderation.

Cook gave her tea. It was sweet and she did not like sweet tea but it tasted good and the fire was warm and the chair she sat on was firm and familiar but Frances was waiting; she knew she would be waiting.

She did not wait to tell Esther where she was but told Cook to ask her to run two classes together until she returned. She waited all morning in the hospital passage. It was tiled and the nurses' shoes seemed loud on the floor and the light was too bright.

'Miss Fletcher will survive,' they told her, 'but she is very poorly. They struck her rather hard on the head and one arm is cracked, the other badly cut.'

Hannah was glad it was cold in the passage and that her back ached for she deserved no less. She would not leave to eat or to drink, though Maureen came and sat and held her hand and said she was sorry and perhaps it had all gone too far.

At three o'clock they let her into the ward and pointed to the bed nearest the long green curtains which cut off the ward from the annexe. The bed was surrounded by screens and Hannah did not want to part them because she was afraid of what she would see. She lifted her hand and took the heavy iron frame which was flaking and uneven beneath her hand and moved it back just enough to pass through.

Frances lay with a bandage round her head. It was stained with blood, so red against the white. Her face was almost blue and her breathing was light and rapid. She looked older than her years as Hannah sat down and laid her hand lightly on that of her Headmistress. She did not hold it because there were bandages down both arms and the fingers of both hands were swollen. Yes, she thought it has gone too far, and she knew that at last her decision had been made.

She sat there all afternoon and into the evening, watching and waiting. At eight o'clock Frances lifted her eyes and smiled and Hannah said, 'I'm so very sorry.'

There were no words from the blue lips but Frances smiled

318

again and Hannah bent and kissed her cheek for now she had to go. It was perhaps too late already.

Maureen had told her that Esther had planned the fire at the old Methodist church for this evening but did not know whether it was nine o'clock or nine-thirty. Hannah ran through the fog, hearing the clink of the horses drawing the hansom cabs carefully through the gloom. She had forbidden Maureen to come too. Her hair was wet and her breath hurt in her throat for it was cold.

She knew she had to turn right past the park, but was the road clear to cross? She listened but did not know how close the car was that she could hear, and the old cart which was rattling somewhere in the fog. Did she have time? She lifted her skirt and ran and the car horn was loud as it braked to avoid her headlong rush but she was across and unhurt. She did not stop when the driver stopped and called for she must reach Esther. This must all be stopped.

She walked as she drew near the church because she did not want to draw attention. People were passing now because it was busy here and there were houses either side of the street with soft light dissipating in the mist before it could reach her. She turned down the alley which ran beside and then behind the church. There was not even the dim glow of the fog-bound gas lamps here and she put her hands to the wall which was slimy and cold, hearing her own breath coming in sharp pants. She had to stop them. She reached the railings at the bottom and followed them round to the rear of the church.

Esther was there, heaving at the petrol can in the light of a shaded hurricane lamp before pouring the fuel over old rags. She whirled round when she heard Hannah and then laughed, her face eager and welcoming.

'Where are the others?' Hannah asked quietly.

'They wouldn't come. Too scared.' Esther was pouring more petrol and the smell was strong in the heavy air. 'They think someone's tipped the police off. Stupid fools. Oh, Hannah, I'm so glad you're here, that we're together again. Mother thinks I'm marking homework, she believes me every time.' She was panting. 'It's so glorious, isn't it?'

She turned as Hannah wrenched the can from her. The handle was cold and jagged and cut Hannah's hand. The can was heavy and clanged against the park railing which divided the park from the church.

'Go home, Esther. This is not a game. Frances has been hurt because she was mistaken for one of us. This has all gone too far. She has been right all along.'

Esther pulled back at the can, her shadowed face contorted with effort and rage. 'Hannah, you are the most miserable woman I've ever known. I'm having fun, I'm leading people and all you want to do is spoil it.'

Hannah slapped her then, the noise flat in the night air, her hand stinging from the blow. Esther put her hand to her face. Her mouth opened but she was silent. Her necklace had broken and the amber beads lay around their feet.

'Go home, Esther. This is not a game. I got you into this and I will get you out. This is not the way to win the vote.'

'I want to do it.' Esther was not talking quietly now. She slapped at Hannah and pulled at the can. 'I want some fun.'

As they struggled they did not hear the running feet, it was only the whistle which pierced the fog and the sound of their harsh breathing. Esther spun round then, dropping the can so that the petrol spilt on Hannah's skirt and shoes. The smell was acrid and sharp.

'Oh my God,' Esther whispered, her face wiped of its exhilaration, an animal fear taking its place. Hannah felt her own mouth run dry. Oh God, oh God, not this again. Please God, no. She turned, putting her hand to Esther's mouth, looking down towards the alley which led eventually towards the street. She could see nothing but she could hear them. They would soon be here and the passage-way they now stood in led only to a brick wall. There was no way out for them.

Hannah's breathing had slowed as she fought to think, think hard and fast. She looked out over the park. The railings were broken but one of them could escape if the other lifted them over. She listened and the steps were nearer. She looked again at Esther. Harry loved her so and she had promised that she would look after her, hadn't she? There was no other choice. She pushed her cousin to the railings.

'Put your foot in my hand,' she breathed. She clasped her hands together and as she took the weight of Esther's body and lifted her it seemed as though her arms would be wrenched from her shoulders. The pain tore at her but she needed to lift her even higher because Esther could still not scale the railings. They could hear the police now in the alley. Soon they would turn into the passage-way.

'Higher, for God's sake, Hannah,' Esther sobbed and Hannah made one last effort and at last Esther was nearly over.

'Don't run, move over to the tree and lie still until they've gone,' Hannah breathed as Esther fell to the other side, 'or they will catch you too.'

Her hands were scored from the buckles which had caught as Esther had jumped to the other side and her arms were shaking as she sagged against the bars and saw her cousin disappear into the fog. She did not once look round and neither had she spoken, even to say goodbye. Would the police believe that she had not intended to fire the church? Hannah turned now as they entered the passage and could smell and feel the wet petrol on her clothes and her foot kicked against the can which lay on its side. She bent down and blew out the hurricane lamp. She preferred to wait in the dark.

The sentence was six months in the third division and now Hannah filed with other prisoners through the blocks, hearing the echoes of their feet, but not their voices, for speaking was forbidden. She walked up the same flights of black iron steps as before, climbing from one landing to another and then another She looked at the black netting strung between the landings of the first floor to prevent death by suicide and then back again to her own level, to the rows of doors. Inside these she knew would be the darkness again.

As she entered the one which the wardress pointed to she saw that it could have been the same cell as last time. There were the same tins, the Bible, the bucket, the rolled mattress and the sheets which she had collected from the office along with the other prisoners. There was one other suffragette but she did not know her.

'Courage, my friend,' the other said as the door closed on Hannah.

The clothes were as rough as last time and the wooden spoon smelt as it had done before. Hannah put it back in the tin mug and sat down on the bare wooden bunk feeling the ceiling and the walls pressing in on her already and the darkness sucking at her breath. She looked again at the spoon.

'Well,' she said quietly. 'At least you and I need not bother to renew our acquaintance this time,' and she smiled to think that already she was talking to herself.

They brought her gruel and dark bread but she left it on the tray. Bedboards, hairbrush, shelves, bars, windows, sky. She listed them again and again, not looking at the food, not looking at the drink.

The wardress unlocked the door. 'Not you too, Number 9? Hunger striking is foolish and gives me more work,' she said, her blue dress and bonnet as severe as her colourless face. She had a faint moustache, Hannah saw.

'I'm not hungry, thank you,' she said, not looking as the gruel was taken away.

She slept that night between coarse sheets and in the morning rolled up her bedding and scrubbed the floor and looked and listed the items as before when the porridge and tea of breakfast filled the cell with their smell. She did not watch the vapour rise from the mug and bowl just listed the bowls and then the girls in her class and the shows that were on in London. Again and again. On the third day the wardress looked at the uneaten gruel. Hannah was sitting on the bunk; her head was aching, her tongue was swollen and dry and there was a foul taste in her mouth. She had scrubbed the floor this morning but it had taken two hours because the brush was so heavy and when she had stood the walls had rushed in on her and she had fallen to the floor. Her cheek was bruised.

'If you do not eat tonight, you know what will happen, don't you, Number 9?'

Hannah did not nod, her head ached too much to move. The pain was bulging out of her skull and into the room. In and out, in and out and the wooden spoon was moving in its mug. She just sat, feeling the two letters she had received this morning. What did it matter what happened tomorrow, could it be worse than this hunger, this thirst, the pain in her head and eyes, the pain in her chest which had lodged when she had read the letter from Frances that had come this morning?

She held it in her hand now, carefully folded into square upon square. She had done it so carefully, squeezing the folds tight and straight. They must be straight because Frances was a schoolteacher and she was angry at slovenly habits. She opened her hand when the wardress had gone and the thick squares were rounded into the shape of her palm. She must fold it again.

Hannah bent her head but it seemed too full of pain and sank on to her chest. She forced herself to lift her head again and slowly her fingers opened the letter, smoothed it flat against her knees. She did not want to read it again but the words were written in strong black ink and as she smoothed and smoothed it she read again.

Dear Hannah,
I understand from Esther that you have been imprisoned for arson. I think then that you have taken the decision to end our friendship.
Yours,
Frances Fletcher.

It seemed so strange, Hannah thought as she folded the paper, hiding the words behind folds too tight for them to escape, that she should lose her friend. So strange. Esther had written too. Her letter was in the bucket in the corner but Hannah remembered each word.

Dear Hannah,
Father is taking me away for the winter, he thinks I need to build myself up a little to cope with such a long engagement. I have not told him that you slapped me, he would never forgive you. I have not told him anything that happened. I think it best,

don't you, since I will not be returning to the suffragettes. It's no fun any longer. My father wrote to Miss Fletcher explaining that I needed a long holiday in the sun. I hope she is better, I have not been in touch at all.

I will see you in the spring when perhaps Harry will be back too.

Your cousin,
Esther.

She had felt anger before she had become so tired but she must not feel that for the woman her brother loved, so instead she had torn the letter into smaller and smaller pieces so that she could not picture her cousin, not at the moment anyway and Arthur was in Switzerland so she need not think of him either.

In the morning she lay on her bunk. Her head hurt too much to move now, the door was too loud when the wardress opened it. Her keys jangled too close to Hannah's head as she walked to the uneaten porridge and cold tea. She did not open her eyes as the woman stood over her.

'You know what this means, Number 9? I shall be back later.'

Was the sky blue, Hannah wondered, as blue as it had been in Cornwall? But no, it was winter, and there would be fog, and belching chimneys and stench from the slowly flowing river. She wished it was the spring and she could walk across the fields through the daffodils and the primroses. She could feel the spongy moss, Joe's hard hand and she wanted to laugh but it did not squeeze past her swollen throat. He was there though, Joe was there, and they were walking with the wind in their hair and the kite was flying now, the string taut in her hand, jerking and pulling and soaring high.

The scream pierced her mind and she opened her eyes but did not move her head. The scream came again and the rattle and jangle of trolley and keys.

'No, no.' It was the suffragette who had called to her as she entered her cell.

Hannah clenched her hands to her ears and pulled back into

her head, to the kite, to the tail which whipped in the wind but soon they came for her and the kite flew far away.

There were four wardresses and the doctor and the cell was not big enough, they were too close to her. You should go away, she wanted to say. You are taking my air, my light, my life. They stripped off her bedding and pulled her into a chair which one of them had brought.

'Eat this,' the doctor said, showing her a light stew. She did not shake her head because it was about to burst.

'No thank you,' she said through parched lips and did not recognise the cracked husk as her own voice.

Her head seemed too heavy for her neck and she wanted to lie down again but the doctor was holding two long tubes made from rubber joined by a glass junction and the wardress who gripped her head and smelt of sweat would not let her.

She could not move her arms now, or her legs either because four other wardresses held them.

'Open your mouth, Number 9,' the doctor said. He did not look at her eyes, just her mouth. How strange to be just a number. My name is Hannah, she wanted to say, but did not for he would push that tube down if she did.

'It is easier, less painful to use the mouth,' the doctor told her. His breath smelt of cigarettes and his teeth were yellow and the pores were open on his skin. She shook her head and so he took a wooden gag and tried to force it in between her teeth but he could not and so then he took a steel one but it squeezed the skin between her teeth and his steel, his ice cold steel, and she tasted blood in her mouth and it was moist, so wonderfully moist. The tube was then forced down her nose, her throat and at last her stomach, burning and tearing into her, shutting off her breath. It reached her breastbone. She was suffocating but she could not say anything, only watch, as the doctor raised the funnel end of the tube and poured brown liquid into it. She could not breathe, only feel the tube, enormous in her and the liquid bulging into her stomach. A worse pain gripped at her throat, her stomach, her chest as the tube was withdrawn and she retched then, spraying the doctor and the wardresses with her vomit and she was glad.

The next day a letter arrived from Maureen and Hannah was glad but her eyes ached too much to read it more than once.

> Dear Hannah,
> I'm sorry I didn't help. I should have done. Be strong. I've left the militants. It's all going nowhere.
> love,
> Maureen.

They came as she folded it and the next day too but then she did not know any longer how many days passed, how many times this tube was thrust into her body by this hand which was large and had black hairs and tasted of nicotine. How often it was forced past swollen and cracked membranes.

As she lay on her bunk on the day when the doctor had sworn at her she could see through swollen lids that her hands were thin with raised blue veins and she could smell lavender. She turned her head. Mother, she called, but made no sound, Mother. And her mother stayed with her, even when she had to be lifted into the chair because her legs were too weak to support her weight.

Oh Mother, I miss you, she called as the tube was passed down each time and she no longer smelt the rubber or the nicotine but only the scent of lavender.

Neither did she stay on her bunk for the long days and nights but sat by the window in the wicker chair and watched the pear tree with her mother. The sun was always flickering on the leaves and then Joe came and he flew his kite in the garden and there were no black patches on the grass only hundreds upon hundreds of daisies.

They let her out three days before Christmas. They helped her down the steps and through the doors but each step made her want to lie down, each step jarred the pain inside her head, in her throat, in her stomach. They held her arms as she reached the small door on to the outside world.

'But there is no one there for me,' she said, for her mother had gone and Frances had gone and Harry and Esther and Arthur too and Joe was where the kite was flying.

The wardress unlocked the door. 'You will be re-arrested when you are strong enough,' she said.

Hannah climbed through the door. It was cold, so cold, and she could not stand alone but he was there. She should have known he would be there.

She felt his hands take her arms and then lift her, holding her close so that she breathed only warm air which was trapped between them both.

'Is Mother with you, Joe?' she whispered.

Joe nursed her in the small room with the solitary gas lamp. He carried her from the cab and up the stairs but she did not know this or that Maureen brought food back each day and so too did Ann.

Joe sat each night at her bed and all through each day and she knew he was there as she played on the rope with Harry and sat by the window with her mother.

She felt his arm around her as he spooned light broth through her lips which were still cracked and swollen and she felt it travel down the bruised gullet and into the stomach. He bathed and sponged her and she did not mind that he saw her body because he was her friend. At last the pain in her head drifted and died and as dawn came one morning she finally awoke.

'It's January,' Joe drawled and laughed. 'That's one way of avoiding the Christmas festivities.'

She looked at his face, the blond-red hair, the wide grin, the few freckles on his nose. Joe never changed and she was so glad. She looked about the room, it was different now with two of them here. It seemed lighter somehow, warmer. Joe had brought his tools and there was a smell of wood-shavings which were swept into a pile near his camp bed. Above the sink hung the marigold picture and she moved her hand and held his.

'Joe, how can I . . .'

'No more talking now,' he said, smoothing her hair off her face, and she wanted to sleep again.

They walked in the park the following week and she clung to his arm because it made her feel safer. They ate scones in a corner house but she could not tolerate the butter. He built up the fire each evening and they sat by it and talked.

Joe wanted to write to Frances and tell her what had happened but Hannah felt too ashamed. He asked if she would like Arthur to be told but she told him that he was in Switzerland and what was the point?

The police came for her the following week. She heard them climbing the stairs and she clung to Joe, just for a moment, before they knocked. He was so strong, so dear, and she did not want to be alone again and she was not sure that her mother would come back when the tubes were brought.

His arms were tight around her and he breathed in her hair. 'Just serve your sentence, my Cornish girl, don't go through all this again.' He held her away and his eyes were as full of tears as hers were. There was the same fear in them that she knew was in her own and then his head came down towards her lips and she wanted to feel their softness and their warmth, to taste his breath, and then they knocked and she spun round. She did not want them in here, in the room which she and Joe had shared.

'I must go,' she said and knew that she must starve again because this was the only way she could leave the suffragettes. She must suffer as others had if she was to live with herself and her breach of loyalty.

It was March before she was released again and this time Joe took her home to Cornwall because they would not be re-arresting her. The prison doctor said she was too weak, too ill to withstand any further forcible feeding or starvation.

She did not remember anything of the journey but as she lay in the bed Eliza came and she and Joe nursed her. Sometimes she knew this but the pain was so great and the fever climbed so high that one night she could bear it no more. Joe sat by the bed and she felt his hand on hers and she left her mother for a moment in the garden and turned to him. Her head was heavy and she wanted to close her eyes again but her friend was here and she wanted to say goodbye.

'Joe,' she whispered. 'I'm going now with my mother. I'm so tired.'

He did not stir, his head was on his chest, his eyes were asleep, his blond moustache was barely visible in the moonlight. She wanted to bring his hand to her lips and kiss it but she could not even lift her own and so she looked at him once more and then closed her eyes, looking for her mother again.

She was there, over by the tree where the rope was swinging in the breeze. Her mother looked young again, her hair shining and loose. She looked at Hannah and smiled, then began to walk away. Mother, Hannah called, wait for me. I'm coming and she ran, she could feel the air pumping in and out of her chest and the pain was leaving and the tiredness. She was closer now but her mother was still walking. Mother, she called, wait for me. Her hand was stretching out and now her mother turned. Go back, Hannah, go back. I love you but go back. She walked down into the fernery and Hannah was left and the pain came back and she groaned and wept. Joe woke and saw the tears running from her eyes on to the pillow and he called Eliza though it was only three in the morning. Together they sponged her down, held a hand and wondered if they dare hope that somehow she would live. She did.

Eliza went back to Penhallon in April and Joe took Hannah on a short walk across the moors. They read the letter that arrived the next day together and Hannah wondered how Frances had come to know the truth and Joe explained that Eliza had written. Hannah sat in the deck-chair and smiled as she read.

Dearest Hannah,
Forgive me, I should have known. It all seems to have been such a dark time of struggle and stress. Forgive me and come back.
Frances.

She passed it to Joe who read and nodded and then returned the letter to the envelope. They both sat back and let the sun wash over their faces. Joe looked tired, there was blue around his eyes and he slept as she slept all that day.

The families who were staying took the jingle to the sea the next day. It was too cold to bathe but one of the children had consumption and the fresh air would be good, Hannah had said.

'Shall I write to Arthur now?' Joe asked as they watched the wagon disappear. Hannah picked at the tartan blanket which covered her legs; her hand was still white and blue veins still stood out, but not so much. She did not want to think of Arthur, only of the myrtle which she was watching Edward planting out in the borders and the thyme which was growing well now. Arthur was London, not home. Arthur did not belong here, when she was ill and her hair was dull and her flesh hanging on her bones.

'No, he thinks I have measles, let's leave it at that. He doesn't want to come out in spots. The club wouldn't like it.' She grinned.

She still hadn't told Joe that the marriage would be at the end of the year for it was 1914 now but he had not asked of her future plans and she could not tell him.

Each day they walked further and picked early violets and Hannah breathed in the scent and Joe too. Soon there was colour in her cheeks and she could eat a little butter on her bread, and melt it on her scones. There was still no word from Harry though and she did not think of Esther. Joe would not talk of her either because it made his cheeks burn with anger.

As the sun warmed the earth and the birds nested and sat on eggs Hannah walked in the sea with the families, feeling the salt water stinging her legs as she lifted her skirts, laughing as Joe splashed her, throwing seaweed as he came closer. He rolled his trousers up above his knees and the children screamed as he swung them high and skimmed their toes in the cold water while the gulls screamed above them.

Eliza came with Sam and they had not heard from Harry either. 'We would have heard if there was something wrong,' Sam said and Hannah nodded. Yes, of course they would, and she wanted to push the shadow away because there had been so much darkness and now it was light and the sky was clear and the air was fresh. She could breathe; at last she could breathe. Sam and Hannah played jacks with the children and Eliza baked Chelsea buns and Hannah wound hers and showed the children how to make pastry rings on their fingers.

When they had gone Hannah and Joe walked to the hill and as she gulped in great breaths of air he laughed at her, but said that it was putting roses in her cheeks and they talked then of asking Edward to grow some ramblers up the stable wall, of replacing the conservatory glass, broken in the winter gales, of painting the outside of the house and it was good to talk of domestic things, of tomorrow.

Her legs felt strong as they walked round the lower slopes of the hill and Joe ran on, throwing up his yellow kite, feeding out the line until it was snatched by the wind and soared above them. The moss was damp with rain and everywhere was green and fresh. Hannah let her hair hang loose now and it swirled about her face. They walked down to the stream and sat there to eat their pasty. They shared just one and the crumbs fell on to her skirt and his trousers and Joe still held the string of the kite in his right hand, playing it, pulling it back and forwards.

'I'd love to fly,' he said, his mouth full.

'Don't be disgusting,' Hannah said. 'Wait until you've finished your mouthful, what would the children say?'

'There aren't any here,' Joe said, his mouth still full. 'You are the only one and you're doing enough nagging for a regiment.' He was grinning and Hannah laughed.

'You're thirty, old enough to know better, Joe.'

She picked at the moss, it came away in a bunch. 'Your father said that there was an aerodrome nearby where you could start lessons.'

Mr and Mrs Arness had come over for lunch last week. They did so every month, Joe said, and his father taught painting to the visitors.

'I know. Maybe I'll try one day.' He brushed himself down, throwing the crumbs into the stream which rushed over boulders and scythed into the bank, taking earth with it. 'When there's time to spare.'

'No trout to tickle here,' he said quietly and Hannah looked at him and nodded. She had remembered that day too. How old they both were now and somehow she could not believe that so much time had passed. She looked across the moor; the stunted trees, the fresh grass growing amongst the bright heather. A few ponies were grazing amongst the sheep. Across to the west there were clouds building up and a wind. She threw the moss into the air and it was caught and blown three feet away. The kite was jerking as though fighting to leave the string and race instead with the blackening clouds.

'We'd better go,' Hannah said, for she knew that though she was stronger she could not run if the rains came.

Joe rose and pulled her to her feet before hauling in the kite, his tongue between his lips as he wound the string around the wooden frame he had made. Once it was free of the wind it plummeted down, helpless without the force of air and was no longer graceful but clumsy as he carried it under his arm, the tail hanging limp.

'You're too old for a kite,' she laughed and he nodded.

'Oh I know,' he agreed. 'I just do it to amuse the children and I have to practise to keep my hand in.'

'Liar,' she murmured and they both laughed as he nodded.

He took her arm and they talked of London and of the arms race and the Kaiser who had threatened France and Morocco. Joe said that perhaps there would be a war and Hannah thought of Uncle Simon and was glad that she knew no soldiers. They talked of the vote and she told him that she would work with the suffragists now, constitutionally lobbying. It seemed that Labour were supportive now.

The clouds grew heavier and the rain began but they were back in the fields which were enclosed by dry-stone walls and were near a stone-built shelter which housed hay for the cattle in the winter. Joe dragged her in and she sat hunched on a hay bale and watched the rain as it lashed across the moor in great waves. It was not cold and she felt safe, as she did when she lay warm in bed and heard the rain beating on the panes.

There were no bars here on the moor with Joe, no sense of anyone pulling at her, there was just peace and they sat in silence watching the stunted trees bend before the rain and the wind and the cows turning their backs or laying down.

Her back ached now and Joe moved nearer. 'Lean on me,' he

said and she did, feeling his warmth, smelling his skin. The rain sprayed into the entrance as the wind veered and the scent of wet hay reached her.

'I never want to leave here,' she murmured.

'Stay then, Hannah,' he whispered.

She wanted to, how she wanted to stay, and as they walked back when the rain had stopped and she felt her dress soak up the water from the grass she could hardly bear to look at all this around her. She loved it all so much. Neither could she look at the man who walked beside her, his arm on hers.

'Stay with me, Hannah,' Joe said as he held open the gate into the drive. The trees were dripping on to the sodden grass, and the sun was already heating the ground so that there was the sweet smell of warm soil.

She put her hand near his, the wood was soft with the wet and the grain stood sharp and she could feel it with her fingers. She looked not at him but at the land which ran to the sea and then at the grey stone house surrounded by daffodils and tissue-sheathed crocus and then at the drive, at her hand, his hand. So firm, so strong, so familiar.

And then at his face which was always ready to smile and laugh, which seemed to bring the sun and air into every room, at his eyes which were normally so blue but were now dark.

Why did she want to stay so much? Was it just for the peace of the place or was it . . . ?

'Hannah, Miss Hannah.' It was Edward, running down the drive, his leggings flapping, water splashing from the puddles which he ran straight through.

'A telegram, Miss Hannah.' He was breathing hard. The yellow telegram was wet and limp in his hand.

'It came two hours ago but we didn't know where you were,' Edward panted to Joe while Hannah tore open the envelope and read.

Hannah,
Your brother is back Stop He is very ill Stop
I will allow you to return to house for purposes of
nursing Stop
                    Father.

19 Hannah climbed the steps to her father's house and rang the bell. She had no key now; she was merely a visitor and did not want to enter, but Harry was here and so she must. Was he very ill? But she must not think of that, she must push it away until he was with her.

It was not Polly who answered but Beaky, her nose still sniffing the air for bad odours. Well, this particular nasty smell has risen to haunt you, hasn't it, thought Hannah, and smiled to think that her return would discomfort this woman, grateful too that she could focus on this old antagonism while she stepped in through the door of her father's house.

'Good afternoon, Mrs Brennan,' she said. 'I'm expected.'

Peppermint still wafted on Beaky's breath as she walked into the dark hall and it was as it had always been, but smaller somehow. Red still shafted in from the two side windows set in either side of the doors. The wire cage on the back of the door held no letters and there were no visiting cards in the bowl standing on the carved rug-chest but then there was no lady of the house any more, was there? She wanted to go straight up the stairs to Harry but the darkness dragged at her, slowing her.

She put down her valise. 'My trunk will be arriving shortly. Perhaps you could make sure that it is sent up to my mother's room.' She was pulling off her gloves as she talked, and now she climbed the stairs. She could not run and it was not just that she did not feel strong enough. The banister was smooth and shining beneath her hand.

'Your room, you mean, Miss Hannah, on the top floor,' Beaky said, standing at the foot of the stairs, clothed in black with her white apron stiffly starched.

'My mother's room,' Hannah insisted without stopping, for that room was the only place in the house that held the warmth of past memories.

'Harry is in his old room next to Mother's?' she asked turning as she reached the half-landing. She watched for Beaky's nod but did not falter in her stride. Up past the half-landing on to the dark red patterned carpet which ran down the length of the landing. The dark varnished floorboards either side were dusty and the glass fronting the prints which hung on the walls was cloudy. It was so quiet, Hannah thought, and did not pause outside her mother's room but in time with each step she took ran the words. 'He's not here. Thank God Father's not here.' His hat and stick had not been in the hall.

She was nearly there now, nearly at Harry's door. She opened it and there was the thick smell of fetid air and the darkness of drawn curtains. She left the door open and moved, not to the bed but to the curtains and drew them back letting the sun flood in, and then she heaved at the sash windows, pulling the bottom one up and the top one down. She felt the air on her face and knew that soon the draught would have cleansed the room and only now did she turn to the bed. Harry was there; his eyes were open and he smiled as she came towards him, lifting his hand, which she took. It was trembling and thin but brown from his years in the sun.

She bent and kissed his forehead. 'So, you've come home, Harry,' she said quietly moving her hand to his wrist. His pulse was weak. She kissed him again and sat down on the upright chair by the bed. Thank God he was home. She had missed him so much. His face was too thin, the lines ran deep and there were so many. She lifted his hand and kissed his palm and Harry knew that he was safe. His voice was dry as he said, 'Oh Hannah.'

She poured water from the muslin-covered jug into the glass but could tell it was not fresh; there were bubbles clinging to the sides. She gave him a sip and another and listened as he told her of Baralong, Frank and the diamonds, the Rand and how they had floated through the night, rested in the day and then had found a cart which took them to the station. There they had taken a train to Cape Town with the money which Harry had on him.

'I left him there,' Harry said. 'He wouldn't come, it is his home, you see. That hot land where he is less than the dirt is his home and I did nothing to alter the system. I left him there.'

His voice faltered and Hannah hushed him, checking his wound which had now been cleaned but was still infected; his body was hot with the fever of it.

'I sent him money, half the money from Amsterdam. He says he will use it to fight, but there's been so much brutality, Hannah. Too much.' His voice was fading and Hannah poured water on to her handkerchief and laid it on his forehead.

'Sleep now,' she said but he opened his eyes.

'I'm rich, Hannah, very rich so I can have her now, can't I?'

Hannah took his hand again and nodded. 'Yes, my dear, you can have her now.'

His eyes closed and he looked so ill and so very tired. Hannah sat until his breathing was deeper, steadier, and then looked around at the dark mahogany furniture, the chest of drawers, the shoe-stand, the wardrobe which stood against the wall. There was a layer of dust on all of them and a mustiness to the room which had nothing to do with illness. The framed prints of Hastings and Dover were also filmed with dust.

She checked Harry again and then walked down to the kitchen where Beaky was drinking tea with the cook and the maid.

Hannah told them that if there was not fresh drinking water in Harry's room every two hours they would no longer be employed in this establishment. She leant on the scrubbed wooden table and told them that every room in the house was to be cleaned by the end of tomorrow but that she would do Master Harry's room because absolute quiet must be maintained. She stared at Beaky as she said that Master Harry was not to have his windows closed, was not to have his curtains drawn.

She addressed them all when she repeated that there was to be cool water brought in a washing jug every two hours night and day for the next three days. There were to be clean strips of sheeting supplied also torn from the best linen in the laundry cupboard if necessary. The sheeting was to be ironed so that it was sterile; it was to be picked up only by the edges with washed hands and placed on the steel tray which must be heated in the oven and untouched except at the handles.

She then told Beaky to send for the doctor and would expect him to arrive within the hour. She ignored the heavy frown, the crossed arms which clenched heavy breasts.

The doctor arrived within half an hour and checked the wound again and explained that the bullet had been left in the body too long. It had apparently not been removed until Harry had arrived in Amsterdam and he had then wanted only to get home so that there had been no time for recovery.

'Will he recover now?' Hannah asked as the doctor packed away his stethoscope. His hat was on the dark side table next to the oil lamp which Hannah would need throughout the night. The lavender she had picked after speaking to the staff was in the vase on the dresser, next to Harry's hairbrush and comb and the scent soothed her.

The man looked up; he was dressed in a dark frock coat and his side whiskers were as grey as his hair.

'Yes, in time he will be restored to health. Whether it is full health remains to be seen.'

Hannah nodded and looked again at her brother who was sleeping now, his face flushed from the pain of the examination and the fever.

'I wonder if it was worth it?' she murmured, and shook her head as the doctor looked up at her. 'I'm sorry,' she said. 'I'm just thinking aloud.'

She arranged that he would come every day and that no nurse would be necessary because she was back in her father's house again. It was not until seven-thirty that her father came home. She heard the dinner gong and left Harry who was sleeping. She drew her hand from his but for a moment he tightened his hold and groaned, then relaxed and slept again. She was not hungry, for he was there, downstairs, waiting for her but he must be faced. There was no choice.

The dining-room door was open and she made herself breathe slowly as she entered. The table was laid with a white cloth and her father was sitting in his mahogany carver chair at the end of the table as he had always done. Beaky had laid her place halfway down the table as though no time had elapsed since her mother had died.

Hannah moved to her chair aware that her father continued to read from the book which rested on the bookrest at his left side as though she did not exist. He was older, his black hair had streaks of grey and his moustache too; his skin was sallow and dry and hung loose around his neck.

The room was dark, though behind the drawn curtains Hannah knew the evening was still light. The gas lamps hissed as they lit the moulded sideboard and the picture of the stag at bay. It did not seem as large as memory had made it. The tantalus still held whisky and brandy, the same amount as always. Did he ever drink any?

The silence between them was heavy and Hannah wanted to leave now, go up to Harry and stay where she felt needed, but no, that would mean this man had won and she could not allow him that victory.

'Good evening, Father,' she said, her voice loud in the stillness.

He turned from his book now, his eyes still dark beneath his brows, still empty and cold.

'Good evening, Hannah. How is my son tonight?'

Before she could answer Beaky brought in the haddock. It was Friday, Hannah remembered, and looked at the small white fish on the gold-rimmed plate. Would he still have salmon?

'Harry is stable,' she replied, watching as salmon was brought to her father. 'How is the Vicar?' she asked as the salmon was placed before her father.

He did not answer. As Beaky walked from the room she turned and called her back.

'I would like salmon too, please, Mrs Brennan.' Hannah picked up her plate and handed it to the woman who flushed and looked beyond Hannah to her father.

Hannah turned to him. 'If I am to nurse your son, I will need an adequate diet.' She pointed to her plate. 'This is not adequate, as you obviously realise since you prefer salmon.'

She looked at him, at his face, his eyes, and hers were steady for she realised that the fear was gone, and the anger also, both washed away by the years which had passed and the life she had led. What was left was a knowledge that this man could no longer hurt her. Her mother was dead, what could he do?

That night sitting beside Harry's window she wrote to Esther asking her to call; telling her that Harry was home and longed to see her. She wrote that she hoped they could be friends again and as she gave it to the maid to post she knew that, for Harry's sake, she had had to write those words.

She also wrote to Joe telling him that his furniture was beautiful, because the heavy darkness of her father's house had made all that her friend created seem even more a meeting of simplicity and style. Was it any wonder his work was in such demand? She told him that she would be seeing Frances on Sunday when she would leave Harry with Esther and begin her school again. She told him too that she would be working as a suffragist beside Frances. Hannah paused now, her pen drying in her hand as she looked out across the garden which was colourless in the moonlight. She still could not find the words to tell him of her engagement to Arthur because marriage seemed so far away, and when she did think of it the bars closed round her and the air grew thin. But tomorrow Arthur would be here and now she signed off her letter to Joe and moved to sit by Harry, to hold his hand and nurse him throughout the night, and as the moon rose high and Harry stirred she smiled and nodded. Arthur must be made to understand that there could be no marriage until her brother was completely better.

April turned to May and May to June and the summer of 1914 was warm and glorious and the shadows were sharp and Esther wore a large diamond ring and kissed and stroked Harry and he laughed and smiled and grew stronger.

Hannah brought him down to the garden in July and they set up the wicker chairs on the terrace and Arthur and Esther ate cucumber sandwiches and drank tea with them and played charades as Harry could now stand and move, but carefully.

Arthur's hair bleached in the sun and became lighter than the colour of hay. He seemed to have matured since his stay in Switzerland and he understood that Hannah wanted to wait, and so he enjoyed the garden and the soft summer air and Harry's return to health.

When Arthur and Esther could not come Hannah walked with Harry in the garden and one day they strolled to their old play area and pulled at the long grass, clearing the weeds, feeling the heat on their backs. Hannah wore a broad straw hat and Harry his old school boater. They stacked up the old guinea-pig hutches, one on top of the other, talking of something and nothing. Harry hammered in nails so that the frames were once again firm and strong and said that she should give them to her Sunday ladies, the ones with children.

They walked on then to the swing and Hannah held the rope while Harry tied a loop and she saw that his hands were broader now, not so thin, and though his fingers worked slowly they were stronger. She put her foot in the loop and hauled herself up feeling the rope as it gripped tightly round her shoe and she hung on as Harry pulled her back and let her go. She leant back, dropping her head and seeing red through her closed lids as the air rushed through her body, and she could hardly breathe for laughing. Again and again he pushed her until she begged for him to stop and as she jumped down he chased her slowly across the lawn and round and round they ran until they sank to the ground and her face was amongst the fresh green grass. She could see the ants as they wove in and out and smell the earth and the sweet scent of fleshy stems and feel his arm across her back.

I never want this moment to stop, she thought, because she was back in her childhood with her brother.

That afternoon he spoke of his plans, his money. How he would buy a grand house in the country and another in London. How he would use his money to buy shares and live off the interest. He would take Esther around the world, dress her in the finest clothes, adore her. Hannah smiled. Yes, Esther would make him happy if he could give her this.

She and Esther had not spoken of the petrol cans or the prison sentence but her blonde cousin was kind to her brother and made him flourish and for this Hannah was grateful and so she laughed and talked as though there was no shadow on their friendship. Each day Harry grew stronger and the weather hotter. They would be harvesting in the fields which ran beside the railway line down to Cornwall. The corn would be golden, the carts stacked high with bales on the roads and Hannah looked at how the grass in the garden was browning and the roses growing limp almost before they burst from bud. The air seemed to hang motionless, heavy with sun and scent.

Harry could bear the heat more easily than Hannah and they all sat on the terrace when he did but sheltered beneath the large parasols. In mid-July they watched the gardener trim the low neat box hedges and cut back the neat aubretia. Would the stocks be sprawling across the garden in Penbrin? Would the delphiniums still be staked or would they have become limp with each passing day, Hannah wondered.

Esther sat back and sighed. 'To think, my darling,' she said, 'we can spend our winters abroad from now on. We need never feel the cold again. I'm so glad we're marrying before Christmas. Let's go to France, the south, and spend Christmas there and New Year.'

Hannah watched as Harry touched her hand.

'Of course we'll go,' he replied and Hannah hoped that his health would continue to improve and that he would be well enough. But if he was, then she would also have to marry. The heat was too much suddenly and she fanned herself with the newspaper, seeing the large black letters and feeling anger coming from nowhere. She shook out the paper, wanting to think of something beyond their own small lives, wanting to read about something which did not affect them.

Where was Serbia, anyway, and how sad that some poor Archduke had been assassinated. Yes, she would think of that, not of tomorrow, or next week or next year. She would think of something too far away to matter.

'What about you, Hannah, what are your plans?' Harry was shading his face against the sun, the skin of his wrist was dark against the white cuff and beige stripes of his blazer.

Hannah looked out at the lavender which was woody now. It really needed to be replaced. She folded the paper and put it down on the terrace. Beaky would be bringing tea soon and the table should be clear or the frown would come and the breasts would be thrust forward in indignation. One day they would burst, she thought.

Esther said, 'Yes, what are your plans, Hannah?' She was looking at her, her face shaded by the parasol, her eyes cold.

Hannah paused and then said, 'I want women to have the vote and I will work for it with the suffragists.' She saw Esther flush and look away for Esther was not now involved in the struggle in any way. The excitement was no longer there.

'I want to start a school and take children from the dark mean streets and let them live and run in the country. I want their parents to have houses in the grounds where they can come and stay. I want children from our class to come to my school too and mix with my children so that with time and education poverty will not be allowed to exist because those with money will not feel comfortable knowing that there are those without.'

She turned to Harry. 'I want to give some children a chance.'

Harry looked out over the garden, tapping his finger on his white slacks. 'Will Arthur let you, do you think?'

Esther turned to Hannah now, her eyes wide, a set sweet smile on her face. 'The lifestyle of the wife of a Lord's son will be different, Hannah, even if he is only a second son. You should be grateful, you know, and make his life easier.'

Hannah brushed away the fly which flew in front of her face and wished that it was the smile that she was wiping from that perfect face. She tucked up the hair which was hanging limp across her forehead.

She was too hot; far too hot to stay out here. She rose. 'I'm going in, Harry, to find some shade.'

He turned. 'You can't keep running away from this, you know,' he murmured, leaning towards her so that Esther should not hear.

Hannah stopped and ran her hand round the top of the wicker chair. It was smooth and hot. She wanted to talk of the difficulty in breathing, the bars when marriage was talked of, but how could she? Harry was so happy and besides, Esther was here and Hannah did not want her cousin to know anything of how she felt any more. She smoothed down her dress, shut the parasol and watched an ant climb up the wicker slats.

'I'm not running away, Harry,' she whispered and smiled. 'The decision is made, it is just a question of when.'

Arthur came for tea at least twice a week and he and Esther played desultory tennis without a net and not enough space, and once Arthur trampled on the neat box hedge but her father did not object when he came in from his club. He patted Arthur on the shoulder and called him 'my boy', and Arthur laughed, bronzed against his white and red striped blazer.

They played croquet too, all four of them and Harry could handle the mallet easily now, even though the effort of chasing Hannah that day in the garden had jogged his wound and caused pain for several nights; but only slight pain. He was very much better. It had been worth it, he had said as they drank tea when Esther and Arthur had returned to their homes one day at the end of July. Hannah turned the page of her newspaper. It was between her and the sun and cast a pleasant shade. She read of the Balkan conflict. The ink came off on her fingers and she wiped them on her napkin, making dark smears.

'How will poor little Serbia survive now that Austria-Hungary has declared war on them and all for the death of an Archduke in Sarajevo?' she asked as the long warm evening of 28 July drifted into night.

'They won't,' said Harry shortly. He did not want to think of brutality and suffering. How was Baralong, he wondered. He had not heard from his friend at all. And why in Britain was there talk of war when there had been crises before in the Balkans? It was nonsense and too far away to bother with.

On 30 July, the Russians mobilised against Austria-Hungary in support of their fellow Slavs in Serbia and Arthur was delighted.

'Perhaps we might get a little bit of excitement,' he told Hannah, sucking on his cigarette as they sat on in the garden and watched as Esther and Harry merged into the shadows which led to the fernery. 'Life is so damn boring but with this alliance system we may well be in the fighting, if there is any.'

343

Hannah looked at his boater, his blazer, his gold watch which glinted on his wrist. She had known him for so long but knew nothing of him really and what did he know of her? He had not seen her yellow, ragged and vomiting, only glittering and laughing. Would he ever let her run a school, or write letters to MPs when she was his wife? She looked away from him as he read the paper, fanning herself with her hand. But Harry was not well enough yet, was he? Or was it that she could not admit the truth to herself? She looked as Harry stopped and kissed Esther. He did indeed look very well. She shaded her eyes; the sun glinted on his watch too, the one her father had bought him now that his hunter was at the bottom of the Orange River.

He spoke less and less of South Africa now and he did not call out in the night as often as he used to but she wished that Baralong would write to him because her brother grieved for the loss of his friend and she wondered how she would feel if she never saw or heard from Joe again.

'Yes, a bit of a tussle would be pretty good,' Arthur repeated. 'But that old fool Grey is trying to make sure war never reaches these shores, more's the pity. He's rushing around Europe acting as peacemaker. Silly old fool, there's such a thing as honour, you know.'

Hannah looked again at Arthur. His lips were pursed as he blew out smoke which hung on the windless air. Would her women think war was exciting? Did they think life was boring? She sighed. You are the fool, Arthur, she thought. Look around you and see who has time to be bored between rearing children, working in factories, nursing children who die of rickets and diphtheria, putting one foot in front of the other until they also die, too old for their years. And what about the strikes, the unemployment, the starvation? Is that boring too? But she said nothing. It was too hot, the air was too thin.

The next day was just as hot and it was lamb for dinner and Harry smiled at Hannah as Beaky brought it through. The steam was rising from the joint and Hannah raised her eyes at the sight. Could they never have anything cold? Harry's foot touched hers and he wiped his forehead and they laughed but not so that their father could see. They had picked mint in the garden and Hannah could still smell it on her hands.

Her father did not read when Harry ate with them but neatly and regularly lifted and chewed one hot greasy mouthful after another and throughout the meal he talked of the latest news in the European war arena. He stabbed his finger at Harry and said how the Huns had been building more and more warships. How all this social reform of the bloody Liberals had held back the British Navy. How the Kaiser had waited until the Kiel canal was widened before declaring war on Russia in support of her ally, Austria. Did he never think of anything but this war which was nowhere near England, Hannah thought.

'Clever, that little swine,' he said. 'You have to give him that. He's always wanted to give them another thrashing. 1870 was just the beginning. You mark my words, they'll be next.'"

Hannah could see the lamb in his mouth as he spoke and she thought of Joe and his pasty but she had not found that distasteful.

Harry did not answer but he could not finish his meal. He felt too tired. And he was too tired also to think of war even though Uncle Thomas had said it would spread from Europe to Britain. Harry prayed that it would not. The brutality and degradation of violence was something that he could no longer support. He thought of the long nights when he still woke sweating and groaning with the pictures of the compounds, the whippings, the shooting and knew that he could never associate himself with the taking of life or the inflicting of pain.

'If Grey doesn't keep Great Britain out of this, we'll make a soldier of you yet, my boy,' his father said and smoke streamed through the gaps in his teeth.

On 1 August the Germans declared war on France and his father poured champagne because he had been correct. Harry was thankful that in Sir Edward Grey Britain had a peace-maker, not a warmonger but he did not say as much. He just drank the sweet cool wine and saw the bloodied back of Baralong again and the look of bloodlust on the faces of Frank and his friends.

On 2 August the Germans demanded free passage through Belgium to reach France. Belgium refused. Great Britain had not wanted to become involved in the Balkan quarrel but, on 4 August, by 11 a.m. England knew it was at war with Germany.

It was hot on that day and Hannah and Harry sat in the garden after a lunch they could not eat. Today Harry was pale and Hannah wondered what the war would mean and how many men would die a senseless death as Uncle Simon had done. She thanked God that she knew no soldiers for it was only soldiers who fought wars. Would they hear the guns from here? It had happened so quickly really, all so quickly and it had been such a glorious summer. It couldn't be serious. There would have been more of a fuss. More in the papers, more talk in the streets. More steps to prevent it. No one wanted war surely, not after the Boer War? Had everyone forgotten that death came too often in war? It was not a game. Couldn't they see it was not a game?

At four o'clock Esther came and her dress was white cotton and trimmed with lace and her eyes flashed as she swirled across the terrace, her hat shading her face, her parasol held in her left hand. She bent and kissed Harry and Hannah saw his eyes light for the first time today and he snatched at Esther's hand and kissed it, holding it to his lips as though he feared he would never touch her again if he let her go.

Esther laughed and sat next to him. 'Arthur's just coming,' she said. 'George has come home. He has volunteered of course and Arthur is to join the Blues. Such excitement and at the end of a perfect summer too. Isn't it all quite marvellous?'

Hannah turned as Arthur came through the french windows. His boater was in his hand and his hair shone almost white in the brilliant sun. His smile was wide. He was a beautiful man, she thought, and smiled as he stooped and kissed her hand. His fingers were still long and thin and his skin soft and unmarked by work. He was like some unreal doll whom she did not know at all. He threw his straw boater at Harry who caught it and held it in his hands which were still tanned from the sun. Arthur had tied a red, white and blue ribbon around the crown.

'Bloody marvellous, isn't it, Harry? It'll be like the Volunteer Rifles again. My father has arranged the Blues for me. What about you, old lad?'

Hannah watched as he walked past her to Harry, standing with his back to the sun, casting shade over her brother. He rocked back on his heels, his hands in his trouser pockets.

'It won't be like the Volunteer Rifles,' Harry replied, his voice quiet. 'Don't be a fool.'

Hannah looked at him.

Arthur laughed. 'Don't be so serious. It'll be live ammunition, that's the only difference.'

'And deaths,' Harry said, his hand shading his face, his legs crossed one over the other. 'Hasn't it occurred to you, Arthur, that there must be another way of solving this? The politicians could still talk. You could pressure your father.'

The air hung motionless, the leaves were curled on the pear tree and the sun burnt Hannah's hands as she sat and watched and listened. Esther was looking at samples of curtain material for the London house just off Eaton Square which they would live in when they were married.

'Don't be such an old woman, Harry.' Arthur was impatient now and no longer smiling. 'Just join the regiment with me. It'll be good fun.'

In the silence that followed Hannah watched the ants run in and out and over the terrace cracks, the moss, her feet.

'I won't be volunteering,' she heard Harry say.

'I mean when you're better, old lad.' Arthur smiled. Esther was holding up the samples to the light. Hannah knew that she could not decide whether it should be white or cream for the bedroom. 'Come on, you old misery, surely it will be the Blues.' Arthur kicked Harry's boot.

Harry handed Arthur back his boater and Hannah saw that his hands were trembling. 'I've just told you, I won't be volunteering and it has nothing to do with my health. I really am quite fit now, as you can all see. It is simply that I can't agree with violence.'

Hannah watched as her brother sat looking up at Arthur, and the lines were deep to his mouth again; and then she rose,

347

walking behind the table, moving to stand behind her brother. She put her hands on his shoulders for she had immediately realised what this meant.

'I will not be fighting at all. I will not be a party to this war. I will not kill anyone, fight anyone. I have seen too much.'

Arthur stood there, quite still, his face puzzled, as though he could not understand the words he was hearing.

Hannah was gripping her brother's shoulders now. Though Harry sat quite still she could feel the trembling throughout his body and was glad that it did not show because he was so very brave. Did he know what this would mean? And then she remembered how he had held Esther's hand. Yes, he knew. She saw that the bees were rising from the lavender. They moved to the thyme which she had planted in the late spring.

Arthur was still standing, quite still, looking at Harry, and as the meaning sank and gripped him he flushed and turned away. Hannah looked at Esther. The samples lay on her lap and her face was turned to Harry as astonishment changed to contempt, and she recognised the look which her cousin had once bestowed upon her and she wanted to stop everything now; to somehow wipe away the last few minutes, the last few days and change the world and the words but she could say nothing. She could only watch and it all seemed so slow but so inevitable as Esther rose. The bees had settled into the pink flowers of the thyme and could no longer be seen.

'Harry, you can't mean this. Where is your sense of honour, of duty?' Esther's voice was cold. The samples fell from her lap to the floor as she rose to her feet. Her parasol was still in her left hand and Hannah saw that her hand was gripping the handle so that white showed on her knuckles.

Harry stood now and reached for Esther's hands but she pulled back, her eyes large and dark. Hannah wanted him to sit again so that she could hold him, steady him for he was so thin.

'Try and understand, my love. I cannot take a life. I just cannot hurt anyone, not now, not after Baralong.' He tried to take her hands again and Hannah flinched as Esther backed from him striking his hands from her, her face contorted with rage and disgust.

348

'What has a negro got to do with courage? It is natural to keep a dog in order. These are white men and Britain needs to fight. You are a coward, Harry, hiding behind this nonsense of principle.'

Her face was flushed and Harry turned from her. He could not watch as she walked away as he knew she would. He loved her and he hated her, for Baralong was not a dog.

Arthur looked at Hannah who walked from the sun, into the sitting-room where it seemed as dark as night. She followed Esther who did not stop to say goodbye but walked out through the hall and the front door. She did not close it behind her. Hannah walked past the empty silver tray on the rug-chest and watched as Esther turned into the avenue and disappeared from sight.

Arthur stood opposite her, his boater in his hand, his cheeks red, his top lip tight and she leant against the banister, feeling it solid against her back. Once before she had wanted to be as solid as the wood she held and now she wished it again. She put her hands behind her and held it. So much had happened out of nowhere. She could not speak. Thoughts fled in and out of the shadows in her mind, she did not know what was right or wrong. She could only feel the pain that Harry was feeling.

Arthur put his hand in his pocket while all the time the red light from the small window shafted through and stained his hay-coloured hair. Red on white, Hannah thought and looked away from him. This was all so unreal, like a dream. She would wake and there would be no war, no heartbreak for Harry, no decision to be made. But she did not wake and there would have to be one, she knew that.

She looked at Arthur again. 'He is right and brave. If he feels as he does, then he has courage to say it.'

Her voice was without emotion and Arthur looked at her and there was the contempt that she had seen on Esther's face but this time it was for her.

'You realise that you will be dishonoured if you support your brother.'

'There is nothing that Harry could do that would ever make

349

me feel anything but honoured,' she replied and still there was the red on white and the tautness of his face.

'Your brother, madam, is a coward. If you insist on supporting him, I withdraw my offer of marriage.' His face was so cold, his lips thin and his voice clipped.

Had they ever laughed together, Hannah thought, had they ever stood by the ice pit, danced in the conservatory, kissed with soft, cool lips? She held the banister tighter, feeling her shoulders drawing back.

'I wish you well, Arthur.' It was all she could reply for there was nothing left to say and nothing more between them. She was glad when he moved from the house into the sunshine for then the red left him and shafted, harmless now, to the carpet.

She did not watch him turn into the street but moved through the shaded sitting-room and out again to the terrace but Harry was not there. She saw him by the horse-chestnut tree. There were young conkers clustered in the parched leaves and as she approached he sat on the ground and wept, his head down on his knees. She knelt and held him and heard him say:

'You understand, don't you, Hannah?'

'Of course. You must have the courage of your convictions. You have a right to your own opinion, Harry.' She feared for him because the course he was taking meant that he was breaking the rules and he had done that before; in South Africa, at school. Because of her knowledge of this she held him tighter, wanting to keep him here safe from everyone. The birds were scrabbling on the branches, a fly clung to the bark. She watched it jerk and then fly to the ground. Her mouth felt dry. She did not think of Arthur but was aware that she could breathe again; she was free.

When afternoon had turned to evening and they had talked until they were merely repeating words a letter arrived from Esther and Beaky brought it through to the terrace on the silver tray. Harry took it but did not open it until the housekeeper had entered the house again. The paper was parchment but the white feather was from a fan of Esther's. Hannah recognised it.

'She has broken the engagement,' Harry said, but they had both known that already.

Hannah took the feather from him and put it back in the envelope. She hated her cousin now and hoped never to see or hear from her again.

Harry just sat and looked out across the garden. The croquet hoops were still in the lawn; she must ask the gardener to remove them, Hannah thought as she walked into the sitting-room. She was tired, very tired but this was only the beginning.

She took matches from the silver filigree box on the mantelshelf and, drawing up her pale yellow dress, knelt before the unlit fire drawing out the feather from the envelope. It was so soft with a cold, hard spine. Hannah would not think of Esther or the pain which Harry was now feeling, she would just strike the match and watch the feather flare and become nothing. The first match would not light and so she threw it on to the crushed newspaper in the grate and then took another from the box.

She had not heard him come in. The front door must have been left open; had she not closed it, she thought, as she lifted her head and his darkness towered above her. She had thought that he could no longer frighten her but his hand as he reached for her arm was so big and his nails so long beneath the black gloves that they dug into her flesh.

He dragged her up, bruising her arm, and even when she stood he was still so very big. Her father took the feather between his thumb and forefinger and the white was shocking against the black of his leather gloves. He still gripped her arm and the pain was harsh.

'Thomas has told me,' he said, crushing the feather in his hand. Hannah watched as he dropped it to the floor. The spine was broken, the fronds twisted and coiled together. Dear God, what will he do to him, she thought, and her throat was taut with fear. But it was her face he bent towards; her face he whispered into.

'It's all your fault. You bitch,' he said through lips that hardly moved. 'You came here and filled him with your poison.' His eyes were not blank now but filled with the hatred that she had seen before.

His grip tightened on her arm and she could not speak as he began to shake her.

'Bitch, bitch,' he said and then brought his hand up and slapped her face but she did not cry out as the blood from her lips flooded her mouth and now he shook her again and still she would not cry out or let her eyes fill with tears for him to see.

'Bitch,' he ground out and she could smell the nicotine and Scotch on his breath.

She closed her eyes so that she could not see his face. Her hair had fallen loose and she felt him grip it and force back her head and it was like the men outside the meeting again. His breath was heavy now and closer, in her nostrils, her mouth. She opened her eyes and his were close and were filled with hatred and something else and his lips were full and too close to her mouth and his breath was rapid. It was as he kissed her that she screamed but his mouth absorbed the sound and now she beat him with her arms and her hands, pushing his panting face from her and thrusting against the hand that gripped her hair.

She screamed again and thought the sound would never stop rising from the terror which tore inside her. Everything was darkness and there was no air, just her father, and she could not fight him, he was too strong, but suddenly, dear God at last, he was gone and there was air to breathe and Harry's voice.

'Leave her alone, you bloody bastard.'

She fell to her knees and she was weeping but she must not weep, not when he could see her and so she held her hand to her mouth, smothering the sobs, brushing at the tears. Harry had pushed him up against the fireplace, their faces were close and Hannah's blood was on her father's mouth. She heard Harry's voice again.

'Leave her. Are you mad? She's your daughter, your daughter, your daughter, your . . .'

'Harry,' she shouted, dragging herself to her feet. 'Harry, leave him, leave him.'

She went to her brother who turned to her and cried, 'I should hit him but I can't. I can't, Hannah.'

352

She pulled him away from the man who had struck her, whose mouth had been on hers but she must not let herself remember what she had seen in her father's face, what she had felt in his body. She would not look at him. She would never look at him again because she would never be without fear of him now and hate.

She wiped her mouth and her hand was bloody and so she wiped it down her pale yellow dress but still pulled at Harry who struggled to reach the man again but she would not let him. No, they must leave. They must go from here to somewhere where they could find some peace to think. Where she could wash, where there was water, cool clean water to wash her mouth. Where Harry could think of the rules he was breaking. Yes, he must, for this was just the start and she was weeping again but she must not. This was not the time. War had been declared and this was not the time. She pulled at Harry until they were outside the room and then she felt her strength ebb and now it was Harry who held her, summoning a cab, talking to her and holding her hand, blaming himself as he left their father's house for ever. She told him the only fault lay with the man who used to be her father.

John Watson did not watch them go. He wiped the sweat from his face with his handkerchief instead and sat in his chair by the fire until it grew dark and then he walked through the streets until he reached the narrow alleys that led to the river.

He found a girl, not the right one but what did it matter and as she screamed when he tore into her and gripped her breasts and felt the surge of his passion he called 'Mother' and hated her again for leaving him that day when she had looked so beautiful in her pale yellow dress. He hated her for kissing him goodbye with tears that wet his cheeks too. He had not known she was never coming back. Had she writhed beneath her lover as this girl did, he wondered? Did she ever regret that she had never seen her son again?

20   The October cold hung heavy beyond the window; the leaves were limp on the trees, dark red and brown. Some had already fallen and lay dull and damp on the grass; they should have been swept and burnt but the gardener had left for Flanders. Hannah put down her toast. The marmalade seemed too sweet this morning.

Frances poured more tea and passed a cup to Hannah. Harry shook his head and looked at the war news in the paper again. His face was thinner, his hands nervous. Hannah looked at Frances who smiled and mouthed, 'Don't worry.'

Hannah wiped her hands on her linen napkin before rolling it up and placing it in the silver ring. 'Perhaps you would rake up the leaves this morning, Harry?' she asked.

He lowered his paper and looked out of the window and then back at her. 'Of course. I thought I'd stack the desks up in the loft as well. If that's all right with you, Frances?' He turned now to the Headmistress who nodded.

'Thank you, Harry. I don't know what we'd do without you.' She rose and walked to the desk, lifting the paper-knife and then replacing it.

Hannah watched and knew how Frances was feeling. There was no hurry any more. The school had closed because so many pupils had been withdrawn since the start of the war three months ago. They had been taken to the country because there might be zeppelin raids, their parents had said, but was that the real reason? She looked at the newly puttied window which had been broken by a stone thrown at the conchie's house, the coward's home. Did Frances regret taking them in, she wondered, looking at the woman who was thinner now too.

But no, Frances had said after she had bathed Hannah's face the day war broke out, the day her father had . . . She stopped her memory. She would not think of that but thought instead of Frances sending Harry for more damp cloths, the feeling as

Frances had rubbed her hands, the comfort of the familiar sitting-room which was where they were now. Frances had said then that Harry was braver than those rushing in a fever to enlist; violence was wrong. Hannah shook her head. She did not know what was right or wrong, she only knew that she loved Harry and must support him for now it seemed that it would be a long struggle, both for the men who fought and for those like Harry. She looked at the paper which her brother had laid on the table. A map was drawn of the trenches which ran from Switzerland to the North Sea. She sighed; big pushes led to small advantages at the cost of many lives and it was clear that this was not going to be a quick war.

Last week they had heard that Arthur's elder brother had been killed at a salient on the Somme. Did Esther know yet? For that would make Arthur the first son, the heir.

She stacked up the plates, watching as Harry left the room; at least he was safe and Joe too, for Americans would not be fighting in the European war, or so Harry had said.

She moved to the window and watched as Harry took the besom and swept the leaves from beneath the lime tree. Once they would have laughed at the sight of that broom and the thought of Beaky sitting astride it, old witch that she was, but now he was too full of grief for Esther, though that was not what bowed his shoulders and made his movements those of an old man. It was the guilt connected with the war. She had heard him in the night, walking up and down, up and down and still the casualty lists came in and he was not amongst them. But he would not weaken, she knew that. He would never take life after South Africa, he had said again and again, even if it meant losing the only woman he had loved.

'It's no good, we must do something, Hannah. This idleness is not good for any of us.' Frances was walking over to the fire, lighting it with a long taper, watching the crumpled newspaper burn blue and then yellow the kindling darken and then burst into flame. She stooped and pulled at the dog's ears. Bess had died last year and this was Molly, a new liver-and-white spaniel.

'I know,' Hannah replied. Without the school there was no

355

haste in the morning and there was no suffrage work because the suffragists and suffragettes had suspended all work for the duration of the war. But she had been active, even though Harry and Frances had not, and there was something that she needed to talk to them about, and was relieved that her Headmistress had now approached her.

She thought with gratitude of the Sunday ladies who had kept her busy with their problems because she did not want even a minute of her day to be free for thoughts of her father, of men at all. She looked at the pile of correspondence on the cabinet at the side of the desk and could still hear the cracked and broken voices of the women as their men had enlisted and the separation allowances had been delayed, if they came at all.

She had written letters, walked to Town Halls, talked to the authorities and sometimes been able to help, but did Frances realise the scale of the problem, did Harry?

Sitting on the arm of her chair, she told Frances that the local factory had closed because its goods had been exported to Germany and there was now no market. Women had lost their jobs. There were no others because other workshops were closing also but prices were rising all the time; coal and flour were expensive. The Poor Relief was worse than inadequate. People were starving.

'Did you know,' she asked, 'that the separation allowance for those whose husbands have enlisted is only one shilling and one penny a day with twopence for each child? Rent is usually about six shillings a week'. The husbands can make an allotment up to half of their pay but more often than not it doesn't come through and a soldier's pay is far less than his previous wage. With the factories closing more men are going. It's a vicious circle. My women are starving. Those who are nursing babies are dry.' She dug at the rug with her toe. 'They need milk and albumen water for the babies. They need food; at least one meal a day but they don't want charity. They've been forgotten by the politicians, who are too busy to realise that there's a home front which needs to survive too, somehow. I think that's where our fight is.'

Frances sat down opposite, smoothing her skirt then leaning

forward, her hand under her chin, her eyes calm. The fire was smoking slightly and Hannah stooped and used the bellows.

'You want to feed them, to use our school kitchens but charge a very small rate, say one penny a meal?' Frances asked.

Hannah smiled, still working the bellows, watching as the coals began to glow red. The fire irons were glinting and the gas lamp was hissing, giving out enough light to warm the room on this dull day. 'So you have been thinking too?'

'Yes, I have seen you rushing in and out, writing long letters, swearing under your breath.' Frances smiled. 'Not at all ladylike but very understandable.'

Hannah put the bellows down on the hearth and rubbed her hands before sitting back in her chair. 'Well, what do you think? Can we do it? I thought we could employ the women to cook and pay them. That solves more than one problem for it feeds them but they keep their self-respect.'

Frances sat back, her eyes on Hannah. 'But with what do we pay them, dear Hannah?' she chanted.

Hannah looked from her to the window, to Harry brushing at the leaves. Were there leaves or trees left where the guns were firing, she wondered? She picked at her dress.

'I'm going to ask Harry. He is rich and has nothing on which to concentrate but I want him to help us organise as well as fund it. He must be kept busy, Frances, or he will go mad. Another feather came in the post today. Anonymously, of course.' Her voice was bitter.

Frances touched her hand. Her voice was low as she said, 'You're not a stranger to persecution so don't let this affect you.'

Hannah looked at her and nodded but it was hard when the persecuted was someone you loved. But now was not the time to think of this. She rose, taking a pencil from the mantelshelf, pulling out a notebook from her apron pocket. Her voice became brisk as she sat down again. The mirror above the mantelshelf was picking up the colour of the fire and the prints on the opposite walls were alive with the reflected glow.

'We'll need to arrange for someone to look after the children of the workers too. I thought I could do that. If you are

357

agreeable?' She sucked the pencil, the lead was bitter and the paint flaked off in her mouth. She picked it from her tongue and threw it on the fire. She looked up and smiled as Frances nodded. 'I also think that we could use some of the classrooms as workrooms. Just because there is a war on doesn't mean people no longer need clothes. Could we not start some sort of a sewing workshop, employ more women? If Harry will let us have the capital of course.'

She listened as Frances suggested that they use the toys which the smaller pupils had used on wet days, that Cook should teach the women how to cook in large quantities. 'And us too.' She laughed. Hannah suggested they toss to see who should peel the potatoes. She looked out into the fog again; Harry was coughing and the leaves were gathered into two piles. He was scooping them up and carrying them to the old wooden wheelbarrow. His hands were white with cold but he would not wear gloves or allow himself any form of comfort; it was as though he needed to suffer.

Hannah walked quickly to the window and knocked on the glass, beckoning to him. He straightened but pointed to the leaves and it was only when he had finished that he returned to the house, wearing only socks when he came into the sitting-room because his boots were clogged with mud.

He would not sit near the fire which was burning strongly by now but sat well back in a dark green chair near to the bookcase. Hannah wanted to bring him nearer; to rub his hands and bring some warmth to his thin body. He nodded as she talked to him but his face did not change, his eyes still saw something other than this room; his ears something other than her voice, but he did agree and so they began that day after he had talked to his solicitor and secured the funds.

Hannah wrote to Joe to tell him but the letter was brief and spoke only of her scheme because she would not think of men any more, not yet. She and Frances flung on coats and scarves and ran panting to their Sunday ladies and brought them back to the house. She peeled potatoes with Irene whose husband had been killed in the first month and their hair became limp from the steam of their cooking. Frances went out with Beatrice and they posted letters through doors and stuck posters on walls. Harry brought down toys from the loft, pushed desks back against the walls so that there was room for the children to play. He dragged tables into the assembly hall and helped the Sunday ladies to lay out the tables. Not many came that day but as the week wore on more and more arrived, Maureen too. Hannah hugged her, glad to have her friend with her again. Harry bought machines for the sewing workshop and paid the women eighteen shillings a week, but still his face did not change or his voice become more than a monotone and so Hannah brought him into the kindergarten with her. She showed him the children as they broke each toy, systematically and brutally. He watched with her as their faces and eyes did not change during their activities.

'It's the war,' she said and he nodded, turning from the room, and she wanted to run after him, drag him back, make him come alive again but instead she knelt by a girl with curls and a dirty face and held her close, taking the broken doll from her, hiding the rolling eyes, the cracked skull, seeing again the doll at Penbrin. She held the child and talked and told her of the giant who lived in the clouds and watered his garden and made it rain on the world so that flowers grew and colours filled the gardens but still there was no expression in those eyes or in any of the others that now looked and listened as she told them of the mermaid and the prince.

Harry came in again. He had wood and nails, a saw and a plane, and he took the boys, and the girls too, and showed them how they were going to mend the toys and look after them carefully. He told them how they were going to make a house and sweep it and keep it clean; how they were going to play games and look after one another and his voice was alive now and he listened to the voices which spoke to him and heard them rather than the sound of his own guilt, his own grief, and so it was the children who brought back some life into her brother and in turn he made the children's eyes light up and their actions became gentle, building not breaking.

The stones still came through the window and the feathers in the post but he just worked harder. Hannah asked him to help

359

move beds into the classrooms on the top floor because the hospitals were full of war-wounded so that there was no room for the civilian sick, but that did not mean that they did not exist, and they had space here to take them, hadn't they?

The doctors began to send their patients to the school and Harry and Hannah nursed them and Frances helped and so did the women Hannah had taught on Sunday mornings. She moved amongst the beds, bathing, soothing and comforting. Helping with the birth of babies; with depression because a telegram had been received to say that a husband or a son or a brother was dead; with illness caused by deprivation.

She talked to the doctor who had cared for Harry and he agreed to call each day and the rooms smelt of lavender and oil lamps and there was a peace growing within her and slowly her father was being sponged from her mind as she washed down the women and the children.

Beatrice helped in the kindergarten and Cook taught the women in the kitchens and Hannah and Frances worked until they dropped into bed at night and Harry worked even harder but still she heard him walking in his room and knew that peace was far from him, as distant as it was for the rest of the world.

By Christmas more husbands and sons were posted as missing or dead but a few returned and were full of gas, or had no feet, or arms or no legs and there were no provisions for them to improve and then find work. Her feet ached from walking from office to office seeking pensions and allowances and so she wrote to Joe, asking if these men could come down to Penbrin with their women too and their children because they needed good air and freedom from the war.

When she received his reply she stopped rushing and sat down and read the words again on a cold morning when frost had crisped the leafless tree and petrified the grass. Her toast lay uneaten and her tea grew cold. Frances looked at Harry and they waited in the silent room.

Dear Hannah,
I'm so glad you have written and I think it is a swell

idea but Harry will have to come and run Penbrin. I have enlisted in the Royal Flying Corps. Eliza has said she will help Harry. It might be as well to get him away from London before the casualty lists get longer and bitterness grows. I don't know where I'll be, Hannah, but write to me if you would like to hear from me. The waiting has proved to be very long.
With love from Joe.

She felt tired, sitting in the chair. Her hair hung lank on her forehead, her apron was clean but not starched. She ran her hands down it, smoothing the creases, smoothing the paper too. How could he go? He was American. She looked up as Frances came and Harry.

'How can Joe go, he's American?' She knew her voice was rising as she thrust the letter at the grey-haired woman, watching her as she read it, seeing the calm eyes lifting to face her.

'His mother was English. Had you forgotten?' Frances asked.

Hannah slumped back into the chair. Yes, she had forgotten but how could she? And how could he go and leave her? Didn't he know that she loved him, that he did not need to wait any longer? Why hadn't she stopped long enough to know? The endless days and nights, the sickness, the need had pushed him away, and her father, but it was there, all there. She knew that now and he should have known too. He knew her better than she knew herself, didn't he?

She felt her finger rub her lips and she repeated the words to herself. She loved him even though she had never told him, never told herself. She wanted to scream the words. He knew that, surely he knew that. She looked out at the grey cold again. Was it too late to tell him?

She looked up at Frances and took the letter back. With love from Joe, he said. Did he mean it? She thought of the men without feet, hands, eyes, those who were dead, and he was amongst that now. For a moment she wanted to scream at Harry, 'But you're not, are you? It's Joe who'll die.' But it was panic saying those things. She knew that and she turned her head away from him so that he could not see her eyes. She saw the books, dark on the shelves and then the desk and moved, running to it, taking pen and paper and writing.

Dearest Joe,
Don't go. I love you. I need you. Stay with me, Joe.

She folded the letter once, twice and put it in the envelope, licking the flap, the stamp and running out of the room, out of the house and down the road to the post office. He would receive it tomorrow. He wouldn't have gone by then, would he? He mustn't go, not yet.

Eliza wrote saying that Joe had left the day he wrote to Hannah but she had forwarded the letter, though mail was difficult for the troops, she added, so it might be held up. You must be patient. Could Harry come at once with the first batch of wounded because Sam had his nurse's cap on and looked lovely in his frock. Don't worry about Joe, he's a good pilot, he's been taking lessons at the aerodrome as you suggested.

The next day Hannah folded linen for the men and rolled the bandages for Eliza and packed them into the second valise that Harry would carry and decided she would not think of the death-rate for the aviators. She would not think of the guns, the anti-aircraft fire, the German aces, or she would go mad. As she packed the men into the taxi with the women and the children she decided she would not think of his wide grin, his red-blond hair.

She turned back into the house, her coat drawn about her and found that Harry was ready and she held him, drawing him to her, holding his face in her hands and told him to look after the men, but she meant look after yourself and he understood.

At the station she gripped his arm as they pushed through the khaki throng and sheltered him from a woman who shouted, 'You should be ashamed of yourself.' But she could tell from his face that he had heard.

Frances wheeled the man with no feet and Harry lifted him into the train, helping the others, holding the smallest child, and as the whistle blew he turned to Hannah. It was all going too fast for her and somewhere Joe would be wearing khaki like all these men and she wanted to hold on to Harry, on to someone she loved who was alive and whom she could feel, here, next to her.

'Thank you, Hannah, for all you've done.' He bent to kiss her and she took his other hand. Veins were raised on the still tanned skin. She kissed his palm. It was cold.

'I love you, Harry,' she murmured and he pulled her to him again.

'And I love you, my dear,' he said and turned, stepping up into the train, not looking back as he stepped over the legs of those already sitting. She wanted to pull him back, keep him with her, hear his footsteps throughout the night but she slammed the door, feeling the milling and pushing around her, hearing the whistles, the feet.

'Come back,' she called, running now along the platform, tearing from Frances's grasp. 'Come back.' He was at the window now but she could not see his face. He was too far away and the train was too fast, people were in the way and her breath was rasping in her throat. The train was grunting and gasping past her and now he was gone and she had not been brave enough to tell him that this morning she had heard from Uncle Thomas, that Esther and Arthur had been married last week.

The crocuses and snowdrops had forced themselves through the grass beneath the lime tree and the sky was blue. 1915 was proving to be an expensive year for Arthur's bit of excitement, she thought ironically. There had been another zeppelin raid last night; twenty killed. She had taken the children to the cellars and left them with Frances and had returned to sit with the women who were too sick to be moved from their beds. They had heard the growling of the engines and then the thud of the bombs which had not been close enough this time to knock the plaster from the walls or the shouts from their mouths. The fear had surged though, and she had gripped the sheet of the woman in labour and tears had run as the ground shook and the woman screamed. Was there no end to the war?

Maureen's husband had been killed at a place called Ypres but Maureen hadn't cried yet and she must, Hannah knew that she must, for she had been through it with so many of them. As the sun warmed the morning she took the children out into the fresh air and walked them in a crocodile past lamp-posts which had the glass painted to dim the glow.

The children bet with one another a farthing that on this walk they would see a policeman riding with a placard on his back warning them all to take cover and Hannah smiled as they laughed when one did pass on his bicycle with his helmet strap above his chin whistling and wobbling but not warning them of an air raid. Scarborough and Whitley Bay had been bombarded by the German Navy and on a fine day it was said that the guns of France could be heard on the south coast. Would that be from the Somme where Matthew's father had been killed?

She looked down at the boy who held her hand. He was smiling and she was glad that he could now do so. They walked back to the house, into the room which was hung with children's paintings. Some were of flowers; the purple, white and yellow crocuses, the blue cornflowers which had bloomed in the meadows last summer. Some were of families and one included the father. Some were of sausage-shaped zeppelins.

Hannah gave them milk and biscuits which Cook and the women had made but they were not sweet for sugar was scarce again. They sat on two layers of carpet; the top one was an Indian rug with an irregular pattern and she ran her finger round its edge. The children were quiet while they ate and drank and she sat with them, wondering whether Joe would ever write, and if he did, would he say he loved her?

Why hadn't he written? It was six months now. He couldn't be dead because there had been no knock and no buff telegram. Perhaps, after all, he did not love her but then she remembered his arm about her as they flew the kite, his face as he had said over the gate, 'Stay with me.' His face as he had said the same words all those years ago in the storm on the moor. But why hasn't he written, she asked herself again.

Milk lay on the children's upper lips and she wiped each mouth and one child, Naomi, put her arm up, drew her head down and kissed her. Hannah stroked her hair. It was soft, short and fine and there were no nits any more.

She settled back on the carpet in front of the children, leaning her arm on a chair because her back ached these days and listened as they took it in turns to tell a story. It had been a successful idea because fear and anger and loneliness was put into words and Hannah wished that she could have a similar outlet. Amy told of a rabbit who lived in a hole but a big growling fox came and stamped on the warren and the plaster fell in and so the rabbit took the baby rabbits down into the cellar and they were all safe.

Matthew told of a day by the river when the sun was hot and his daddy picked him up and hugged him and hugged him.

David sat up and said that he had once been to the sea and the waves had knocked him over and when he had laughed the water had run into his mouth and it was sharp and salty and his mummy had told him he would be sick. But he hadn't been, he told them proudly.

Naomi told of the little doll who got lost in the woods and couldn't find her mummy or her daddy and so a nice lady had come down from her house on the hill and taken her hand and said that she could come and live in her house, because she liked dolls.

While the children's voices ran on Hannah looked at Naomi and knew that if she did not keep this girl she would go to an orphanage because both her parents were dead. She looked out again at the trees, at the sky and missed Joe. She picked at the raffia seat of the chair she leant against. It was always warm, she thought, running her fingers down its smooth strands and as the children ceased to talk she turned to them, seeing their faces not looking at her but away, over to the door and there was a draught which was not there before and so she too turned and looked.

He was standing there, in khaki. Solid and strong with his red-gold hair and she did not feel herself rise or run to him but only saw his face, his eyes and then his arms around her and

365

she was safe at last. His uniform was rough against her cheek and his hands hard as he lifted her face.

'I've only just received your letter,' he whispered. 'I love you more than any man loved any woman.'

His lips were soft as they kissed hers, soft as they covered her face and her hands. His skin was rough as hers touched him, again and again and then he held her away and nodded to the children.

'I'll just sit until you have finished. This is their time.'

He turned her round and walked over to the chair which leant against the wall by the door, putting his cap on the floor, undoing his buttons as he sat. God almighty, he was tired, so bloody tired.

He watched as she walked back, turning to look at him as she did so, smiling, and he felt again her mouth on his and wanted to pull her back and hold her, love her as he had longed to do since the first moment he had met her. And she was the only one who could wipe the war from him, for a moment at least.

She joined the children on the floor. They were giggling now and he liked the sound. It seemed a long time since he had heard it and seen small faces, clean and round. He listened as one by one they continued with their stories but could hear beyond them the noise of the war and still found it hard to believe how quickly death and chaos could become the same as breathing; that the clear Cornish air could be the same that swept over the choked battlefield, the dangerous sky.

He looked at Hannah, her face which was lined now and tired, but still so beautiful. The wide mouth, the brown eyes and at last they had looked at him with love. He watched as she leant on the chair, her body curving. How he loved her, dreamt of her, thought of her each minute of every day. How he had longed to feel her in his arms as he had just done, her lips on his, her eyes full of love. He wanted to sweep her away, hold her again, breathe in her scent but part of him was still with the war and he wanted to come to her free of its contamination. He shook his head but still it hung upon him and so he listened as the small dark boy spoke of teddy bears and picnics and

366

wondered at the quietness of it all. It should be so normal but it was not any more.

He pushed his shoulders back against the wall, fighting to stay with this woman and these children. He made himself remember how good it had been to be back in England where he had been given Hannah's letter. How he had travelled from the aerodrome in Oxford through rich countryside full of shades of green and had felt that he was coming home after the unhedged empty chalk landscape of France. How he had looked out on winding roads which now took the place of the straight poplar-edged thoroughfares of France along which solid-tyred lorries had bumped and rattled round pot-holes.

He looked at Hannah again, drinking in the sight of her, of the children. There were children in France and Belgium too but not amongst the grinding of gears, the rattle of equipment and the shouted orders and snatches of songs as transport was moved under cover of darkness away from the prying eyes of the German observation balloons 6000 feet high.

He looked from the children to the window and did not see the lime tree, it was not strong enough to hold him, but saw instead the baskets which hung beneath the balloons and held observers using telescopes and wirelesses to convey information direct to the gunpits while low-flying two-seater aircraft equipped also with radio and protected by fighters flew in lazy figures of eight filling in gaps left by the balloons.

He had never been able to get close enough to take them out and he knew that the men on the ground could not forgive the airmen for that, and who could blame them?

He looked back from the window to the children who were singing *Oranges and Lemons* and ducking beneath the arms of two who waited to chop off their heads. He looked at Hannah as she clapped and laughed. He leant his head back against the wall watching the children again, watching her, seeing the young men he had enlisted and trained with at Oxford. They were dead now, though he, the old man, was still alive. Harry was right. It was senseless. He was tired but he did not want to shut his eyes because he saw too much then and so he looked at the children again, fighting to stay with them. He listened to

Hannah laughing and wondered how long he would enjoy her love, how long he would live.

When would it be his turn to see the enemy too late, to feel the thud of bullets fired between the turning propellers, hear the silence as his engine died and the struts became unpinned in the spin and the wings collapsed? When would it be his turn to feel the air as it rushed past him as he dived helpless, like his kite without a tail?

Would he feel the pain? Would he hear the sound of wood breaking into a thousand fragments; the spruce ash and linen becoming one mass of flame or was the sound just reserved for those who were onlookers as he had been, too often?

He felt a hand on his knee and looked down from the window. The girl had short fine hair and a solemn smile.

'Naomi wondered if you would like to come and join us?' Hannah called.

Joe took the small hand in his and stood looking first at her small face, then at Hannah and behind her to the other children. The war had no place in this room and he finally managed to push it aside and was glad of the respite as he walked towards his love and held her hand and sang *Old MacDonald had a Farm.*

They ate with Frances that night and then took an underground train into the centre of a darkened London. They walked to the Haymarket and he made her laugh when he told her that the War Office preferred to recruit gentlemen to fly their planes for 'the powers that be' felt that flying was much like riding a horse, only more comfortable because you had a proper seat. Joe added that they were having to take other ranks now and they were excellent airmen but he did not say that this recruitment was because the life expectancy was only five weeks. He told her instead how he had to pick out strands of different coloured wools before he was pronounced medically fit to fly.

They went to a show at the Haymarket and there was too much khaki walking along the streets, too many women laughing up into strained faces but there was no light coming from windows, no lamps from the cars or carriages to guide in

368

the zeppelins. They passed a hot-chestnut man, his brazier hidden beneath a canopy and they bought some, and they were hot in their hands and the smell was nutty and sweet.

As they walked they saw a Royal Flying Corps NCO being pushed out of a theatre entrance by four officer cadets who insisted, as Joe intervened, that all NCOs should use the side door because they were not gentlemen. It did not matter that this was a fellow pilot. They had young faces, clipped voices, and Hannah watched along with others as Joe grabbed one by the collar.

'You will call me Major,' he drawled. 'And leave this theatre at once. I will be seeing your Commanding Officer tomorrow.'

She felt proud as he apologised to the NCO and accompanied him into the theatre. They sat with Sergeant Thomas and sang along with Gilbert and Sullivan though the words were too fast for Joe's drawl and Hannah laughed until she cried and then she could not stop the tears.

Later, over cocoa in front of the fire when Frances had left for bed, he explained to Hannah how NCOs could not claim their kills for themselves as the gentlemen did, but must attribute them to the squadrons. How they were despised but were frequently the best because they were there on merit, not class.

'Strange, ain't it, Hannah,' he drawled. 'Mighty bloody strange way to fight a war.' His voice was bitter.

She watched as he sipped his cocoa, his large body slumped in the chair, one leg lifted over the other and she knew that she wanted him because he was good and kind and beautiful and so she banked the fire with ash and went to him and took the mug and placed her hand in his, feeling the cocoa warmth still there.

'I love you, Joe. Come with me, we have waited too long already.' He did not move but his face was tense as he turned to her.

'Marry me,' he said.

She nodded. 'Yes, but I can't wait for that any more. We have so little time.'

She pulled his hand and he came with her, pausing at the door, pulling her to him.

'But you still haven't got the vote,' he teased. 'Weren't we supposed to wait for that, my Cornish girl?' He was smiling but his voice was shaking and his hands were moving over her body. The room was dark behind them, the mugs were on the table where they had left them.

Hannah took his face between her hands. 'Don't you worry. That's on its way. The women will have earned it by the end of this stupid mess.' She kissed him then, hard, before leading him from the room and up the stairs.

Her room was dark and she did not light the lamp because to do so would mean drawing the blackout blind and she wanted to watch the moonlit sky and the stars which were vivid and seemed so close tonight. She stood at the window and felt his arm around her, his breath on her hair and it was quiet and calm as she turned and lifted her face to his. This time their kisses were not soft but urgent.

His fingers were quick as he undid her buttons and carried her to the bed, where she lay and stroked his hair as he took her clothes from her body and kissed her breasts and shoulders and lips. As he stood and unbuttoned his uniform his body was white in the moonlight and big and strong as he moved towards her, sitting on the bed and running his finger along the line of neck and cheek, and chin, drawing her loose hair gently into his hand, bending his head to kiss it, breathe in its scent.

'Are you sure, my darling?' he asked and his voice was unsteady though hers was level and sure as she took his hand and kissed it.

'Yes, I'm sure, my love, my darling love.'

He held her then, close to his body and he was warm, his hands were sure as he stroked her and she felt the wind on the moor and the sound of the gulls and then he brought his mouth down to hers but for a moment it was not his face she saw but the dark one of her father with his nicotine-laden breath. She made her eyes close and her body stay loose as Joe's mouth touched hers gently, then harder now and with the taste of him came enough power and strength to take the other face, and push it from her.

I will not allow you to destroy this moment or any part of my life ever again, she told the echoes of his darkness, and now she

let her body rise to Joe and banished her father from her life for
ever. It was only Joe who would fill her body, her mind and her
life and she cried out and clung to him, calling, 'Stay with me,
Joe.'

He replied, 'I always will, my love.'

21   Harry sat in the garden at Penbrin. It was 1915 and the September sun was warm and the sumach glowed rich red in the gap in the elder hedge. Its bark was as smooth as the fur of the guinea-pigs which he had bought for the children who stayed here. He looked again at the letter he was writing to Hannah. He wrote of the gardener's boy who had been killed at Ypres, of the guinea-pigs who had borne more young and, at last, of the fact that he could not stay out of the war any longer but would still not bear arms. I've written to Uncle Thomas, he continued, and he's arranged that I should enlist as a medical orderly. So you see, Hannah, my days with you have helped to prepare me for my war. Don't worry about Penbrin and the convalescents here because Eliza and Sam are stepping in. Keep sending those who need to come because they can spill over into Penhallon. Mrs Arness will keep things going over there.

If anything should happen to me I have lodged my will with my solicitor and you are the sole beneficiary. If I come back I thought we could start your school together, perhaps enlarge Penbrin. Joe would like that too. If something happens, go on with the idea anyway. I shall be here, all around you.

He sat back and the wicker chair creaked and then settled. He would not write of Esther, she was not allowed outside his head now. The larks were soaring in the distance, carving clean clear lines against the blue of the sky. Would she be wearing his ring as she slept with Arthur?

He heaved himself out of the chair, walking across the dried grass, pulling at the overblown roses and the bursting seeds of the marigolds, scooping up straw which had blown across from the hutches. The children were shrieking there, playing touch-tag around the hutches, their hair flicking as they ran. One boy sat on the back step and played jacks. Harry heard the click-click of the stones and for a moment felt the stronger heat of the South African sun, saw the flat veld and Baralong. He had never heard from his friend and he missed him.

He turned and looked back at the house, at the open windows and the sweet peas, lemon balm and lilac which filled the vases in each room. He could hear the coughing of the gassed fusilier and then his squeaky voice as he talked to his wife. Don's lungs were damaged, they all knew that, but they did not know whether he would live. Harry doubted it. He looked out again across the moor. Would there be such beauty where he was going? He doubted that too.

A late October sun was shining when he disembarked at Le Havre from the troopship as a non-combatant. He was directed to a long low shed where he threw down his kitbag along with the others before lining up at the cooker with his mess tin and spoon. The guns were pounding dimly in the distance and before they slept they unloaded stores from the ships and brushed aside the small boys who pimped for their sisters.

The next day he was glad to move up the line, travelling in the troop train whose forty-five carriages carried nothing but khaki-clad men; singing, sleeping, grunting, cursing. At Bethune he was attached to a platoon as stretcher-bearer because he had asked to be sent to the front, not assigned to hospital duty. He listened as the men and boys talked and laughed marching from the village to the Cambrin trenches through the unlit streets, nudging at the flashes of gunfire which lit the sky and shook the earth, wincing at the noise which rolled like thunder over and through them. The cobbles of the village roads turned their ankles and now the mud of the dirt tracks dragged at their legs and talk died as they saw the real nature of war.

Flares rose from the front and curved over trenches, yellow and green and the noise grew too loud to talk. They passed the batteries and ducked as their own shells whizzed over their heads. He and Bob, the other stretcher-bearer, did not carry guns but a rolled-up stretcher, morphine and water bottles.

He looked at the lurching batteries as they pounded the

enemy and heard the hissing shells overhead as they marched forward and west to the trenches, away from the belching guns. He saw the red flash, heard the hollow bangs and tried not to think of the German husbands, sons, brothers they had crushed and destroyed. One private turned to him.

'How about that then, Harry?' His face was filled with fear, his voice with the bravado of his eighteen years. Harry felt old.

'Makes a lot of noise,' he said. 'It'll frighten away the burglars.' Tim laughed and turned back to his mate.

They marched until they reached a village with its broken trees standing like rotted teeth.

'There are no birds any more,' an old woman said to Harry, clutching his arm.

It was not dawn yet and so the only chorus was the guns. Was she right? Would no bird sing as the sun lifted in the east? He looked around. The buildings were half-ruined, the church spire was jagged and incomplete and, of course, there were the dismembered trees.

They were given respirators and field dressings as they queued outside an old doctor's surgery, and Harry's legs felt tired, his calves ached from the marching, his shoulders from the knapsack, his ears and head from the noise. The sergeant handed him a gauze pad filled with chemically treated cotton waste.

'Should sort that gas out, eh?' said Bob and Harry nodded but he heard Don's cough again, his squeaky voice and knew that he had been wearing the mask when gas filled the trench and lay heavy within its sides. So it would not sort the gas out, would it? But he said nothing.

They moved on again now, clinking and stamping from the village along the straight, crowded road, bypassing lorries and horses before entering the trenches which ran for what seemed like miles. As he walked in the darkness his feet slipped on mice and frogs which had fallen down the sides and could now find no way out. With the dawn came the light and he saw that the earth was dull red and that duckboards lay along the bottom of the trench, nudged by the water which lapped at its sides.

Still they marched and in front of him Tim changed his rifle to his other shoulder, and ahead Harry could hear their guide calling out the warnings. 'Hole here!'

They flattened themselves into the sides and eased round the sump pit which was supposed to drain the trench but did not.

'Wire low!'

'Wire high!'

They eased themselves over or under the field telephone wires whose pinioning staples had dropped from the damp crumbling mud of the trench walls. The gunfire was closer but they hardly noticed any more. Can one become attuned so swiftly, Harry thought.

The trench was not so deep now and they kept their heads low, only Tim forgot and a bullet tore into his throat. Harry caught him as he sagged and his blood spurted on to the man in front and all over Harry's hand and face. He wanted to rub it from him, this wet sticky mess, and then run and run but instead he called Bob and they put the gurgling boy on a stretcher and returned over and under the wires, round the sump pits, ignoring the frogs and mice until they reached the dressing station where they left Timmy, but he was dead and it was only then that Harry began to shake.

The rain was falling on the canvas of the Red Cross tent as Harry at last washed off the blood, watching as stained water filled the enamel bowl. He lifted his head to the drizzle which was now falling, and it was welcome on his face. He lifted it to the noise which he now knew never stopped. Dear God, what had he come to, what had they all come to? The rain was soaking his clothes now but he did not feel cold as they returned to the trench. They passed men huddled over a brazier and their clothes were steaming in its heat. The coals glowed through the holes and he thought of hot chestnuts and London with its theatres, its restaurants, its noise of trams and cars and horses, not this thump and thud of guns.

The walk back along the trenches seemed longer now without the other men and their boots sounded hollow on the mud-stained boards. He and Bob did not speak and Harry looked up at the sky and wished he could talk in the open, away from the smell of wet earth, excrement and blood, away from the blinkered trench. A fatigue party approached carrying bundles of sandbags and lengths of timber and Harry put out his arm pressing Bob against the side of the trench. Wet earth fell down his neck. As the party passed the rifle of one caught Harry's cheek and the blow knocked his head to one side; blood trickled to his chin.

'Serve you right, you bloody conchie,' the sergeant said, and Harry felt cold but returned the man's stare. He had a moustache like the father who had disowned him.

'Yellow, that's what you are,' hissed another, his face too close, his teeth rotten like the trees.

Harry did not look at Bob nor Bob at him. They waited until the party had passed and then moved forward, quickly now because their own platoon no longer said that to them any more. Harry knew that Bob's family did not speak to him because he was a non-combatant, that his father had thrown his clothes out in the street but he knew nothing else. One did not ask other conchies about the paths they had taken, the blows they had received.

As autumn turned to winter the rain continued and they were never dry and this was noticed more by the officers because they had only known comfort and ease. Sometimes the frost cracked on their khaki as they moved and Harry's hands could not feel the stretcher as they carried those wounded by sniper fire. The battalion frontage was 500 yards long and casualties were many, usually head injuries. The men froze and longed for a 'push' which might give them a 'blighty', a wound that would be their ticket home, though it would more likely bring them death as it had done to the soldiers at Neuve Chapelle in March, to the 50,000 French at Champagne in February, to the 60,000 dead at St Mihiel, the 120,000 at Arras in May, the thousands and thousands and thousands at Ypres in April and May, at Loos in November. And on and on and on it went and there was no advance, no victory, no sense to any of it, just the slaughter.

It was a crisp cold night when their sergeant forgot to duck below a wire as he followed Harry down the trench on

Christmas Eve, and a sniper took off the top of his head. Harry barely noticed the blood which splashed his face. There had been too much of it.

'Stretcher-bearer,' he called and Bob came and together they took him back past working parties who were filling sandbags with earth, piling them up like bricks, headers and stretchers alternating. As Harry passed he heard the thud of the spades as they patted the bags flat. He was sorry the sergeant was dead, they had shared cigarettes together and joked about the weather; but slowly he was learning not to like people too much for in time they died and he was too tired anyway.

Sentries stood on the fire-steps, stamping their feet and blowing on their hands. It was only the new men now who ground out the word 'coward' into their faces for the others had been through two pushes with them and had seen Harry ease out over the top and bring back the men long before dusk because he could not bear to hear their cries.

Bob slipped on the duckboards and the sergeant's arm flopped nearly to the ground but he was dead and so it did not matter. The dressing station was full as always and Harry wiped his mouth and leant against a lorry with mud-covered wheels while Bob talked to the doctor. Dusk was drawing near but the ground still shook as shells plunged to the ground as they did each day. He lifted his head and enjoyed the air, the sky, the horizon but knew that in a moment he must return to the claustrophobia of the trench network.

The water was high as they eased around the sump holes and up and over the wires, flattening against the sides as a platoon passed followed by their captain who stopped in front of Harry, his bulk blanking out what little light there was. The rain and the noise had restricted Harry's senses to the inside of his head; it was where he preferred to stay these days and so, for a moment, he did not recognise the officer but stood to attention, dragging his eyes back to the present and then he saw the face as well as the uniform.

'I knew you were here,' Frank said. Harry did not move but he looked at the man he had last seen in South Africa. There was the familiar smile now as he said, 'Breaking rules again, eh? Yellow as a hottentot, you are. I'll be watching for you, Harry, but the war will get you, I won't have to.'

He slapped his swagger-stick in his hand and laughed before he pushed Harry against the sodden side and walked on past. Harry did not look at Bob but pushed on, quickly now, wanting to leave that voice far behind and the guilt stirred. He should not have left, he should have stayed with Baralong and changed the structure which people like Frank had created and for once he was glad of the guns which reached a crescendo and blotted out his own thoughts.

That week he used his two days' leave to travel to the South African native contingent which the new sergeant had said was stationed up the line. None knew of his Baralong though and they shouldered their spades and looked strangely at the white man who wanted to speak to one of their own.

The sergeant told Harry on his return that the natives were not allowed to bear arms. They were there only for fatigue duties. Were the whites afraid that they would learn too much about slaughter, Harry wondered, as he drew on his cigarette that night. He had just begun to smoke again and it was not the noise or the stench but Frank.

In June when frost was only a memory they were moved along the line and a machine-gunner removed his boot and sock and pulled the trigger of his rifle with his toe. The muzzle was in his mouth and Harry and Bob carried him back as they had done for so many and Harry wondered why the young machine-gunner had not seen the meadow blooming between the two front lines and the deep blue cornflowers that were the colour of Esther's eyes blowing in the breeze? Had he not seen the red poppies glowing amongst the long green grass? Did he not know that pleasure could be gained by the smallest of things, that sanity could be retained by a skylark's song? Perhaps though he had not been able to forget that the shell-holes were still there beneath the meadow's beauty and it was not the dew but barbed wire glinting in the fresh new sun.

At the end of June Harry looked from a safe vantage point at

378

the village behind the German lines, opposite their new emplacement. It was built of red brick and lay beside a pit-head and two small slag-heaps. He thought of Penhallon and the primroses, the hedges and the pain he would feel if he saw them churned up by guns and gas. No wonder the old women in the villages wrung their hands and wept. Could war continue with the spring, he wondered. Could this fresh beauty that he was looking at now be turned to mud and blood like the rest of the line? He knew it could for a push had begun two days ago further down the line and it would be their turn tomorrow but now it was mail call and he took the letter which Hannah had sent and as the day ended and dusk was falling he leant against the trench and read the words from home.

Dearest Harry,
We are all well here. There is still a great deal of work to do of course and I am trying to sort out the pensions which are still delayed. The women need them so badly but I will not go on too much about that. Joe and I have adopted Naomi, Kate and Annie, all from separate families, all of whom we love. I feel less alone and so do they, I think.

The lime tree is so fresh in the garden and young Matthew helps me with the planting of new seeds. He is growing well but his mother is very sick. She has been working in the munitions factory since the shell crisis at Neuve Chapelle.

At least women are proving that they are the equal of men and even Asquith has said that he does not see how we can be refused the vote when the next reform is enacted. But don't hold your breath, Harry, and I can't help feeling that this war is too high a price to pay.

Joe writes regularly but the letters get held up and so come in batches after a long empty period. Frances is better now; she is less tired because more of the women are able to take over in the sick-rooms.

How are you, Harry? Do write a little more often since I worry so much. Penbrin is waiting for you.

Try to believe that you did all you could in South Africa. One man cannot change a whole system and you showed that black and white are equal. It is not your fault that no one was watching.

With my love,
Hannah.

PS Arthur was killed last month. Esther is expecting a child.

Harry read those last words again and again. He still loved Esther, she still filled his thoughts each night when he could not sleep. He could feel no sadness for Arthur's death only hope that perhaps now Esther might consider him again. He would write to her when the big push was over.

He looked over at the dim scene, at the observer balloons which hung motionless and he wondered how long Joe would survive. A plane had fallen from the sky yesterday and the pilot had plummeted with it. The War Office would not allow parachutes because they were too heavy. The Germans carried them.

And why no children of their own? How strange, just all these waifs and strays. Was it too hard for Hannah to forget their mother, he wondered. He would write soon and ask her, life was too short to let fear ruin it. He heard the sound of footsteps now and pushed the letter into his pocket.

'Get some sleep now, Watson,' his sergeant said. 'Busy day tomorrow.'

He smiled but there was no humour in his eyes because they both remembered the last two pushes. The others would not though because they were replacements for the dead of that battle. Even Bob was dead, killed by a sniper's bullet.

Harry nodded and moved along in the dark to the dug-out, feeling for the steps with his feet, holding his hands in front of his face. He felt the Wilson canvas which was hung across the passage and pushed it to one side but it fell back and rasped across his cheek, then a piece of torn blanket brushed into his face as he pushed on past, into the dug-out.

He struck a match and lit a cigarette once the glow could not be seen from outside. The air was fetid and he lit the candle which was already stuck by its own grease on to the lid of a tobacco tin. The flame wavered as the barrage, which always preceded a push, began. In the dim light he saw that Ted, Bob's replacement, was already asleep, rolled up in the blanket on the floor. He took out the letter again and reread it, holding the paper to the light. Would she take him back, he wondered? He took a pencil from his pocket, it was merely a stub and he wrote out a short letter. He could not wait until the guns and the push were tired and spent.

> Dear Esther,
> I still love you so much. Can you look more kindly on me now?
> > Yours,
> > Harry.

And one to Hannah telling her that this month the cornflowers had been vivid and the poppies too and that there was hope in him again. And that perhaps somehow he should have made the Franks of South Africa see.

He placed them both in the silver cigarette case which his father had given him. He seldom thought of the man now, not after his brute strength had fought against him as he tried to reach Hannah. He did not wish to think of him for if he did he had to face the thought of what his father had done.

Harry opened his hands, looking at the calluses which now marked his fingers, his palms. His shoulders no longer ached so much from the weight of the stretchers but his wound still pulled as he edged along the trenches, his back straining to take the weight of countless men. He had taken three cigarettes from his case and he lit one now, looking at Ted, wondering how he could sleep when they both knew what tomorrow would bring to others and what it might bring to them.

He drew in the vapour and then exhaled, watching the

smoke drift up until it dispersed beyond the range of the candle's glow. There had been so many candles at Arthur's parties, flickering and illuminating even the very highest corner. How he and Esther had danced, her eyes so full of life, her lips so close to his. How they had laughed and clung close to one another and waved to Arthur and Hannah as they sipped champagne and listened to the orchestra. But he had never known her body and now he ached to do so and perhaps, one day, he might. He smiled and breathed in the taste of the cigarette, savouring its flavour.

He looked round the dug-out. The guns were pounding harder now and he shook his head. It was a different sound now, wasn't it, Arthur, but perhaps you no longer hear it where you are, my old friend; though the men say the ghosts do not go, will not go until this crazy war is ended.

He held the old table as a whizz-bang landed short and dirt fell from the ceiling. The blanket hanging this side of the canvas billowed and he looked at his hands which had begun to shake as they always did the night before the push.

The Germans were sending their shells over now and the bangs merged into one endless assault. Harry did not sleep but lit the second of his cigarettes at two in the morning and allowed himself to think of Penbrin and the roses; full-headed and heavy with scent, of the children who played with soft-coated guinea-pigs. At four in the morning he lit the third of his cigarettes and thought now of the girl who had stroked guinea-pigs when they were young, of the rope which he had swung for her, of the Penhallon rock-fall and her face as she had watched him emerge safely, her eyes as she had held his hand and then kissed it.

At five, when the gas was discharged he thought of Baralong guessing correctly in the dark long stope, felt his arm pushing him to safety, saw him saying goodbye at the Cape Town docks and then he thought of Esther and the ring on her finger, her blonde hair, her blue eyes and he felt almost young again.

Ted woke as dawn came and as he groaned and ran his hand over his chin Harry moved out. An observation balloon, sausage-shaped, hung swaying in the air.

'Come on, Joe, shoot the bloody thing down,' he groaned, seeing the smoke of anti-aircraft shells exploding near the aeroplanes which darted like silverfish above and below it.

'Cushy job,' Ted said as he came up the steps and stood beside Harry.

Harry shook his head. He knew the wastage rate. The lice were itching again but he did not scratch, he was too used to them. He rubbed his chin and wished he could shave; that was all. If only he had the time and the hot water, he would love a shave.

Rain was falling but it was not cold. He moved now, towards the rest of the platoon but slipped on the duckboard and felt Ted's arm as he caught him.

'You could drown in that,' Ted said. 'The mud's as thick as the sergeant's head under that water.'

Harry looked at his watch – five-forty. The bombardment that always followed the gas would begin now and so it did, shaking the earth and filling their heads with noise. Neither spoke as they walked and slipped and kept their heads low until they reached the fire-step. Would the poppies still be standing, would the cornflowers survive the day?

The ground shuddered and a machine-gun rattled. A private stumbled on the duckboard and swore and Harry was glad to hear a human voice above the noise of the guns. A sergeant motioned the private into the fire-bay. A sniper had their range and as Harry looked a bullet thudded past, scoring his neck. He ducked and the graze stung but before he had been forced down he had been able to see that the wire was cut, ready for the division to go over the top.

Shells were passing over. One landed very short and earth dropped on to his helmet, his shoulders. Ted swore and dropped his stretcher. He was only twenty and frightened and Harry touched his shoulder but the lad shrugged him off, flushing and ashamed. The trench smelt of mud and sweat and Harry took out his jackknife and scraped at his trousers, removing the red wet earth. Krupp high-angle howitzer shells tore into the earth close to them and now the air was thick and choking with its fumes. He could not stand the waiting.

He looked along the trench at the men who were drinking a tot of rum, smoking a cigarette. Some talked, some just stood, leaning back on the trench wall. How could they stand it, those men who went over the top in the first wave? Why did they not break ranks and run? Perhaps they were too tired, too numbed by the great machine of war. He looked at their faces and though they were new and young they had the same deep lines as he and the sergeant and hands that shook.

Runners were passing through the centre of the trench, not pausing if men were slow to move but pushing them to one side, cursing and shouting. Their sergeant came from the captain's dug-out to warn them, the corporals took their places at the ladders and when the whistle blew they climbed up and over the top and one by one the others followed, some with their cigarettes still in their mouths, some throwing them, arching through the air to hiss into the water.

He and Ted remained in the empty trench but the cries and rattle of guns filled it almost before the men had gone and Harry climbed the ladder because he could not wait for dusk but fear dried his mouth as it always did and his legs shook. Shells were landing and machine-guns were tearing at the men, some of whom were past the wire now and then he heard,

'Stretcher-bearer, for Christ's sake, it's the major.'

Smoke was all around and the thick long grass was now churned and stinking mud and no cornflowers or poppies remained. Harry could see the corporal who was calling now, his own arm bloodied and limp. He leapt over the top of the trench but turned as Ted started up the ladder behind him.

'Stay there, I'll carry him back,' he called because Ted was crying.

The major was wounded and lying twenty yards out. His leg was torn off but Harry could not see much blood as he stooped and gave the man morphine, but he wouldn't, it would have been soaked up by the earth. He dragged the unconscious man back and a bullet plucked at his sleeve and another dislodged his helmet so that it fell over his eyes and he could not see. He had to lay the major down and tip his helmet back and then he saw Ted take the officer's other arm and they dragged him back together, Ted taking the weight as Harry lowered him down into the trench.

They ran the major back down the trench, round corners widened to take the stretchers. The breath was hurting in his chest when they reached the dressing station but they did not pause for there was no time for rest.

They struggled back through others bringing their loads of groaning men and the corporal passed them, leaning on a man whose other arm was hurt.

The corporal gripped Harry's arm. 'The sergeant's in the shell-hole, the one the other side of the wire. I couldn't get him, Harry.'

Harry nodded and on they went and up the ladder again. The rain was still falling and the machine-gun was still stuttering, the shells still pounding and the smoke lay thick around them. The shell-hole was off to the right and Harry turned to Ted and said, 'Stay here,' but Ted was lying on the ground with a hole through his chest and his eyes wide open. The rain fell in them and clods of earth from a nearby shell but nothing could hurt the boy now. Harry turned to the front again. He threw the stretcher down and, ducking, ran towards the hole. He slipped and fell in the mud but pushed himself to his feet and ran on, into the shell-hole, falling and rolling down the sides. The sergeant could not speak but he smiled and Harry took him on his back and clawed up the sides, his fingers slipping in the mud, his mouth cursing, his feet digging in and forcing his weighted body upwards. He ran then, back to the trench, but he needed another stretcher-bearer.

'Stretcher-bearer, quickly,' he called and one came and together they forced their way to the dressing station again and now his legs were shaking but they would be worse if he stopped, so he staggered back to the trench, fear still drying his mouth, exhaustion tugging at his arms. His old wound was hurting. The call came again and the noise was louder now and his legs felt weak as he climbed the ladder again. The man was over beyond the shell-hole and it was so far and suddenly he was very afraid. He ran slower this time and when he reached him, all life had fled and Harry left the body until it could be retrieved at dusk. The groans he heard as he ran back came from a boy ten yards to his left. He turned and ran.

'Coming, I'm coming,' he called but knew the boy could not hear his panting call against the fury of the battle and as he reached him a Krupp howitzer drove into the ground too close to them both. He felt a thud, and the mud was soft as he fell; then the pain came, tearing and coursing through him and he could not hear the noise of battle just the screaming, and he realised it was himself. He tried to crawl but he could not move his legs and he felt so very cold.

The mud was soft, too soft, and it was drawing him down but he should be helping the boy who was lying looking at him with eyes which never blinked.

'I'm coming,' Harry said but his mouth was full of blood and the words drowned before they could reach the air. He dug with his fingers, dragging himself towards the boy who had blond hair like Esther but the mud was too possessive, it wanted him too much. Had he wanted Esther too much? He coughed and there was blood on his hand, like the hunters' jackets against the snow, like the fox's tail against his skin; red on white.

He was tired now and he could not fight the mud or the weight of his body which was pinning him deeper into the softness. They were tearing up his picture now and pouring water in through his mouth, his nose and he could not breathe and Frank was there, his face twisted as he shouted, 'You should not break the rules.' And then Frank faded away as the sun lit up Penbrin and the children stroked the guinea-pigs but he could not hear their laughter for it was so quiet. So very quiet. Hannah would like this peace, he thought, and he did not move again.

When Hannah received the telegram informing her of Harry's death she wrote to her father. He sent back a message from his solicitor. I have no son.

22 Hannah's eyes ached but there were only three more lavender bags to sew for the Christmas stockings. In a few days it would be 1918 but would that make any difference? Would it bring an end to the horror that was the war?

She pushed the needle through, breathing in the oily scent, feeling the lavender and its leaves in the centre of the bag, grown from Penbrin cuttings which she had brought up from Cornwall after Harry had died. The fire did not blaze but burnt steadily; ash had settled on the top of the coals and soon she would bank it up with more from the ash pan, to keep the core alight until the morning. Frances and she had cut down the lime last year and that had helped to supplement the coal rationing but nothing blazed these days, inside her body or outside. Not since Harry had died. No, not since then.

'Drink your cocoa, Hannah,' Frances said, peering over her spectacles, her pile of camomile bags toppling as she reached over them for her own drink. The dog stirred on the rug. Hannah's hand felt stiff and she flexed her fingers, easing her shoulders.

'Good idea, Frances.' She laid the bag on her lap and reached for her mug, holding it between two hands, dropping her head to the drink. The steam flooded into her face and she closed her eyes wanting to shut out memories, feelings, just for one moment, but it did not work because Esther was there, behind the darkened lids, looking as she had done this afternoon – cool, smart and no older. No, she would not think of her cousin and she opened her eyes, focusing on the bubbles which clung to the edge of the mug, counting them, one two three four and then one burst. Esther had gone again. For now.

When she sipped the drink it was strong and dark and she thought of Joe's letter which had arrived today and was folded again and again in the pocket of her apron; bulky so that she could feel it all the time. He had been safe up to the time his pen had finished on the paper. So far he was not dead like Harry, like Maureen's Edward, like the gardener, like Arthur, like his brother, like George. But no, that was enough. She must stop. It was Christmas after all and Joe was still not dead but the war was not over. When would that be? When would that damn well be? How many more Sommes, Ypres, how many more Passchendaeles, Arras, Vimy Ridges? How many more Cambrai's could they bear and would there be any men left at the end of it all?

She lifted her head and looked at Frances. The Chinese lanterns were hung across the room and tonight Father Christmas would visit the children and tomorrow there would be geese from Penbrin and potatoes and sprouts. Crackers would be pulled, but not by her for she still did not like the crack and the smell. Would the guns stop? Would Joe sit in his mess and think of her? She had to believe that he would, that he had not yet plunged from the sky, that as her lips were touching the mug, sipping the cocoa, tasting, swallowing, he was still breathing, was still warm, was still alive. To accept anything else was to die herself. But Hannah shook her head. She must stop this. She must make herself stop.

Frances crossed her legs and picked up the last of the camomile bags, sewing rhythmically, the needle passing in and out. She wore socks and slippers because the shorter fashions were too cold she had said and Hannah had grinned and told her that this vision in knitted red socks would not cause men's hearts to flutter. Frances had laughed and said that she had come to the conclusion that her heart was housed in her feet and socks were a better insulator than a bit of flutter.

Hannah picked up her own sewing, eased by the memory. Her hand ached and her finger was sore but she could still not use a thimble. Was Beaky sewing comforts for the troops, she wondered, and were needle-makers still dying as the house-keeper had once told her or had the war solved their problems as it had for so many others? But no, she must stop this. Death must not keep intruding.

In and out went the needle and the lavender was strong again and with it came the memory of Esther, standing,

388

watching, dressed in warm brown velvet as Hannah had stripped the flowers from the stems this afternoon and she knew that she must face the scene again for there would be no release from the anger until she had.

It had been late in the afternoon when her cousin had called, had sent in her card and not given Hannah time to refuse her admittance, sweeping in on the heels of Maureen's daughter. Hannah could still feel the engraved card as she had returned it without speaking to this blonde woman whom she had once loved, whom her brother had loved up to the end. As she sat her by the fire she remembered sending the children from the room, remembered scooping up the naked stems and tipping them into the bin, turning her back on Esther while she forced her face into a calm mask for there had been no love in her any more.

She had turned as Esther spoke and waved her hand towards the chair that Frances was now sitting in. It had been heaped with hessian bags filled with the puppets which Hannah and Frances had made for all the children and Hannah had not moved to help her cousin lift them from the chair on to the ground, but had watched the distaste on that unlined face for the flecks of hemp that clung to her skirt as she sat and then she had asked her cousin why she had come, not moving from the table where the lavender was collected in small piles, but leaning back against it, her hands gripping the edge, her voice tight.

She had watched as Esther had turned, her hat matching perfectly the material of her dress, and Hannah had listened as that voice, so clear and untouched, had called her darling and asked to be friends again.

Hannah had looked at this woman, so straight-backed, hands pale and smooth holding brown gloves. Had they ever been friends, she wondered, thinking of the fight for votes, the school, the apologies she had always had to make for her cousin. But then she had thought of the nursery at Uncle Thomas's, the puzzles they had finished together, the warm afternoons when they had sat while her mother was ill, the dance they had performed together, bare-legged, red-lipped, and she had paused a moment, watching as the dog lifted her head before sleeping again.

But then Esther had spoken again and the memories had been reduced to nothing as she said, looking with her violet eyes at the fire which barely glowed, that as Harry and Arthur were dead any differences should die with them and that they were both rich women now, equals as it were. She had laughed, Hannah could hear it now, and had not looked at Hannah but around the room where the carpet was fraying and the furniture was worn.

Hannah looked around now in the dull glow of the oil lamp, seeing again her cousin, but tasting the cocoa which she made herself drink. Hearing Esther as she had gone on to ask if Hannah would take her son into her school because Lord Sanders would marry her tomorrow but he did not like children. And so there it had been, out in the open, and Hannah knew then and now as she sat by the fire that Esther had not changed at all, even the war could not change this particular woman.

She remembered looking at her, thinking that Harry was better off dead on the battlefield than destroyed by Esther. She had said no, of course. Had said that the school was still just an idea, Esther's son was too young, but Esther had risen, stroking the velvet of her skirt, picking at the hessian, smiling and saying that she was not thinking of now, but in two years time, when he could join the kindergarten. Again Hannah had refused because she did not want to have to see her cousin ever again. She remembered looking at the lavender and the clock. There was too much to do to waste time talking to Esther.

Then Esther had said, just think, there would be no need then to bear Joe a child, for you would have the son of your ex-lover. It would be quite perfect, wouldn't it?

Sitting here, opposite Frances, Hannah felt the table as she had gripped it, feeling the rage which had broken then, wanting to hurl Esther against the wall, see her break as she had broken Harry, as she was now breaking her and Arthur's child.

Get out, she had shouted and the noise of her heart had been loud in her chest. The dog had barked and the room had been dark with the coming of dusk but still Esther had not left and again Hannah had called. Get out, and this time Esther had moved, her face flushed and hard as she gathered up her skirt and strode to the door. Her hand had been on the brass doorknob when she had paused, turning her head to look over her shoulder at Hannah, saying in words that Hannah could remember exactly even now.

'I thought I would offer you the consolation prize, after all you are behaving like the old woman who lived in the shoe, busying yourself with other people's problems and stray dirty children, always too frightened to stop and think, stop and bear your own child because of your mother.'

She had left then and Hannah had stayed at the table for too long, until her neck had ached and her hands grown as numb as the table she clutched, hating her cousin, trying to forget what she had said. Wishing she had not come out of the past as she had done. Glad that she was gone and need never be seen or heard again. Now in the soft light with the books on the shelves behind her chair, the silver paper-knife on the desk which she could not see, she could still not forget.

Her hands were still aching, her neck too, and she felt that words must have burst from her again because she had told Frances over supper but all was quiet and the dog was still asleep so she had not cried 'get out' though her throat felt as tight as though she had. She looked down at the lavender bag. It was finished. Her hands had been working whilst her mind tore back over words she should forget. Must forget. There was blood on her apron from her finger. Red on white. She brushed at it, licked her finger and rubbed and rubbed.

'You'll need cold water for that,' Frances said, coming across, disturbing Molly. 'Or you won't lift the stain. But my dear,' and she took the needle from Hannah's hand. 'You will need more than that to rub away Esther's words.' She picked up the two remaining lavender bags and the cotton and Hannah wondered how Frances had known the thoughts which had filled the last few moments.

'Go to bed, Hannah. I will finish these and at two we'll take round the stockings to the children. I'll come and wake you.'

Frances touched her face and Hannah leant into the thin hand, wanting the warmth of someone who loved her.

'My dearest Hannah,' Frances said and her voice was gentle. 'My dearest girl, think carefully about your cousin's words. Perhaps they are true. Perhaps you cannot forget your mother.'

As Hannah rose, picking up the hessian sacks which contained the puppets and left without a word, tiredness dragged at Frances. She did not like Esther but was glad that she had come. Frances banked up the fire, leaning away from the ash as it floated into the air. She stroked the dog, hoping that Hannah would face up to the fear that Frances now realised was there. If she did not, then a darkness would settle in her and Frances could not bear to think of more anguish for this woman that she loved as her own daughter. Yes, Hannah must face it.

Hannah's bedroom was cold but she did not mind. She doused the oil lamp and drew back the curtains, looking out over the city which was in darkness leaving only the rivers to guide in the zeppelins and the aircraft though there had been no more raids for a long time now. She liked the nights for she could not see then that the buildings were scarred with shot and bomb damage and that blinds still covered shop windows and paint dulled the glass of lampposts. She leant her head on the cold pane. At night, up here, you could almost believe that there was no war, no pounding guns, no frenzied dancing in shuttered bars, no desperation showing on the faces of the men as they attempted to compress into a few days what should have been years of life. No anguish on the faces of the women who snatched at a moment of love, frightened that there would be no more for the rest of their long lives. Hannah rubbed at the pane. When would Joe come? It was six months since she had seen him and now they had Matthew as well because his mother had died and he was all alone.

She pushed away Esther and thought only of Matthew's

mother and the other women, yellowed and ill from the munitions work which had sucked in so many since the battle at Neuve Chapelle had shown the grim necessity for more shells.

She thought of the women in the classrooms which were now wards, yellow from liver failure and the babies they bore which were the same. She had visited one factory, had seen how the TNT was brought into the factory in powder, then heated and mixed with a nitrate and poured into the shells in liquid form. She had seen how the powder blew about the factory to be breathed in and how the hot liquid fumes had caused her to feel nauseous and giddy. Was it any wonder, she thought as she rubbed at the glass to clear the condensation, that women working there day after day were so ill?

She leant on the sill. Of course objections had been made once it was realised that the TNT attacked the red corpuscles of the blood causing the liver to shrink and death to occur. Masks had been issued but still women died because the masks were not that efficient and there was no other work around here. Hannah sighed. When the women came with their children for the Christmas lunch she would look for the early signs; the lips that went blue-grey, the strained eyes which hid a headache and that way some would be saved.

She felt anger towards Esther again. Did she not realise what was going on in this dark country? She looked towards Henson Terrace, craning her neck to see, feeling guilt because she still had not managed to obtain even a tiny pension for Maureen's sister whose fusilier husband had been killed falling off a lorry. She had been refused a pension because he had not been blown apart by a German shell.

And there was Joyce whose husband was back from the front, too disabled to work. Their separation allowance had ceased but no pension had been paid. Hannah had written but the authorities said no arrangements had been made on his discharge, they would just have to wait. Did they live on air in the meantime, Hannah thought, these thousands of families which starved and wept? No, she would not think of Esther. She would think of Albert, not Esther. Albert who used to scrub potatoes here and the leg he had lost at the Somme. He had been awarded twelve shillings a week and told by the authorities to go out and earn the rest.

Hannah looked up into the clouded sky, dark without the moon and stars. Tonight was Christmas Eve and tomorrow morning all the children would have their stockings, but her own four, Naomi, Kate, Annie and now Matthew, would also have a Christmas card drawn by Joe and signed by them both, with all their love. No, she would not think of Esther.

She looked away from the window now, to the bed, big and empty. His letter was still folded and lay on the bedside table. It would stay with her until his next one arrived and only then would it go in the box with the others. She walked to the bed in her thick nightgown, her hair plaited and heavy down her back. She sat on the edge, feeling the letter, knowing the words. Knowing too that life expectancy was three weeks now for the pilots leaving England and that Joe had lived a very long time.

She looked at the hessian bags which she had carried from the sitting-room, they were full of the stockings, bright and colourful and full of promise. She thought of the flecks of hessian clinging to the rich brown velvet.

Get out, she shrieked inside her head, but it was no use and now she was forced to listen as tiredness allowed the words past the images of war, of want. She listened again and again and again, flinching as the layers within her head were lifted and the words pried at forgotten feelings, memories, and dug at the darkness and at last she knew that Esther had spoken a truth out of spite and Hannah should be grateful. As though it were the calm after high screaming winds she saw the fear which she had not allowed herself, Mrs Hannah Arness, to recognise or even seek, but which had ruled her life for ever and ever and ever.

Now she sat in the darkness and let it come and cover her. She remembered the days when her mother had breathed in the foul air, and the cradle had been removed, empty. When her father had set his face against the failure and her mother had wept and grown thin and ill; how she had died too young, too defeated. The cold clung to Hannah as she sat on the bed and frost lined the windows but she only saw the pear tree, felt the bark under her fingers, smelt lavender all around and then she reached for the folded letter. It was firm and smooth and had been held by Joe. His words of love were written by hands that had stroked and loved her, held her and held the children and she knew now that he would never let her die, or her babies, and she wept because too much time had passed and she did not know when she would see him again. But she would because she loved him more than any woman had ever loved any man and no God could be cruel enough to take him from her.

Joe came when Christmas was over and the New Year of 1918 was pounding into being. It was cold on the day he walked in through the front door and Hannah held his shivering body close to her, breathing in the chill which still clung to his damp coat, his skin, his hair.

'I love you, I love you,' she whispered and kissed his lips, his cheeks, his hands and then the children came and caught at him, pulling his coat and laughing, dragging him through into the room where Hannah had been reading to the class. Joe nodded to Hannah, his eyes tired but full of love, and as she read he sat back against the wall as he had done each time and made the transition from machine to human being.

Matthew had grown, he thought as the boy moved from the group and came towards him, his brown hair hanging across his forehead, his eyes questioning. Joe raised his hand, beckoned, and Matthew came to him then, leaning first against his leg and then climbing up and on to his knee. Joe held him close, his face pressed deep into the boy's hair, breathing in the smell of chalk and youth and innocence.

'I'm glad you're home, Dad,' Matthew whispered.

'I'm glad too, Matthew. I've missed you all, so much.' So much, so much, his mind echoed as they clung to one another and Joe hoped that Matthew would not notice the shaking of his hands, the eyelid that quivered and drooped.

The room was rich with paintings and colour and Hannah. Her presence was everywhere, in the lavender and rose-leaves which lay in bowls on table-tops, in the square wooden pit which stood in the corner and held Penbrin sand, in the kites which hung from the ceiling. He listened as she told the children of the robin who wanted a yellow breast, of the fish who wanted legs and he watched the faces, heard the laughter and slowly, in the midst of such life and light he left the noise, the guns, the death.

That night they lay in the light from the cold white moon and Hannah held his hands which could not stop shaking and kissed and held them to her breasts, kissing his mouth, his eyes, every inch of his skin because by covering him with her love, she would make him inviolate.

'I want a child, Joe,' she said as he stroked her body and he drew her closer then.

'We have four, my darling.'

She could feel his breath on her hair, his strength against her.

'I want one that is half you and half me.'

She could not feel the shaking of his hard, gentle hands as they held her face.

'Are you sure, Hannah? What about your mother, your fear?' His eyes were dark and shadowed in the half-light, his eyelid quivered, his lips were full.

She kissed him and clung close because all this time he had known, though she had not and had waited and she couldn't bear the thought of such love leaving her in just a few more days.

'Don't go back,' she cried and tears were wet on her cheeks and in her mouth and they were salty but as he kissed her and the moonlight touched his red-gold hair she felt the strength of his body against her and wanted him too much to wait any longer.

Later Joe held her, watched her steady sleeping breath but would not sleep himself. He must not because his screams might wake her and she must never know the man he had become. He would think of Penbrin, his workshop, his soft, smooth, warm wood. He would think of the school that he and Hannah would run, the children they would teach, the child which might already be stirring in her body.

What had happened, he wondered, to make her suddenly put aside the thoughts of her mother which he had always known dragged at her and blocked all thoughts of pregnancy? But then he paused. Did it matter as long as she was free now of the past and they could go forward? Please God, let him live so that they could go forward. He felt the shaking begin in his hands again and so he made himself think again of Penbrin, the wind, the moors, the cry of the gulls. He would take the children to the hill and fly the kite. But no, he would not think of a kite, not a bloody kite. Not something that flew then plunged.

Joe looked around the room, fixing his eyes on the chair, the print on the wall. Hannah's clothes, flung impatiently across the chair, his own next to hers; dishevelled, normal, not like those he wore where the air was thick with noise and fear. But no, he must try not to think of the fear or let the war inside this room, and so he held Hannah close and she murmured and turned her face into his shoulder.

But it was not enough, he knew it would not be, for the war never left anyone in peace, and he could feel it dragging him back, like a greedy lover but he must not close his eyes, he told himself. As long as he did not close his eyes it was he who would dictate the path his memory took through the sounds and sights and feel of the war.

He stared out at the sky. While he was with Hannah he would think of routine; ordinary, manageable. He would think of patterns and then the nightmares would not be able to take hold, this insatiable lover would not drag him to the depths again, so he pictured the dawn on the air-station, so fresh and clean and his walk across mist-covered ground to the dressing hut; checking the wind strength and direction, evaluating the humidity and cloud type. Could he ever fly a kite again, he wondered, ever walk in the open air without humidity, cloud, wind strength ticking themselves off inside his head?

The hut would be dark and cold, the silk underwear cool and light at first, the looser woollen underwear making him warmer, the cellular vest and the silk undershirt warmer still. Then the khaki shirt, one and then two pullovers. He would be

397

hot now but there was still the gaberdine Sidcot suit lined with lambswool, the musk-rat-lined gauntlets with silk inners, fur-lined goggles with triplex glass, thigh boots, also fur-lined. Silk scarf to stop the air getting into the flying suit. Must not allow that. No, too cold, too cold. Then the whale oil smeared into every pore on the face, the balaclava helmet, the dog skin of wolverine-fur face mask to further protect the skin but what for the lips? Nothing worked, they always cracked.

Then there would be the walk to the CO's hut over frost-starched ground, stumbling, cursing. The filling of the boxes with all he held dear. The form, black on yellow. I swear on my honour that I do not have on my person or my machine any letters or papers of use to the enemy. His signature, jagged, shaky. The walk out across the grass again, the cold catching in the throat, warm skin beneath the layers. Riggers and armourers near each machine. Morning, Sir, they would say to him. He would hold the Very pistol in his hand and fire the flare; the signal which means 'Into machines'. Up now on to the petrol tank, the fuel that explodes and burns and kills. But don't think of that. Just climb forward, into the cockpit, slide into seat, ducking head below upper wing. Don't think of the fear. Mustn't think of the fear.

Think of the cushion on the wicker seat, slide feet under hoops of rubber. He couldn't breathe. He looked at Hannah but she couldn't drag him back, nothing could now, the greedy lover had come again. But try, he must try to think of routine, of patterns, not fear, not flames.

Think of the safety harness, the four separate straps for the shoulder and thighs, each one twelve inches wide and a quarter of an inch thick which come together over a large diameter central conical pin held down by a spring clip so that you can't get out now. They have pinned you into their web. But no, don't think of that. Think of the checks.

Rudder, bar, control column, throttle, instruments. All fine, damn it, all bloody fine. Look round now for the raised arms indicating readiness. Poor young fools.

Good luck, says the mechanic. The nod, the order to start up. His voice is quite clear. How strange.

The mechanic is moving the propeller, his face is strained as the clonk, clonk, clonkety clonk begins.

'Contact, sir.'

Contact, damn it, flick ignition, push choke right back, open throttle halfway as mechanic swings the propeller hard against the compression. One jerk is enough this time. Blue smoke jets and the slipstream flattens the grass for fifty yards behind. The nutty smell is here again. All around. The lubricant is burning but that is as it should be. Nothing is wrong. Keep calm. A mechanic is holding each wing and a third is across the tail fuselage in front of the tail plane.

Chocks are away. Don't let me go. Don't let me go up there again, but they do and the machine is there at the cinder runway and at one-minute intervals we're up, up into the air.

It's cold up here, I always forget how cold it is and lighter than the ground. The line is crossed at 1500 feet, always at that height and always there are the artillery flashes. Now patches of white mist lie in hollows and steadily the light is seeping from the east. Lighting hills, dispersing the mists, blinding pilots for a moment but now there is so much soft colour either side of the grey roads, the railway winding threads, the woods which merge with ploughed fields. How strange that people still farm in this hell.

Over Ypres, looking like broken teeth. Beyond it, in the far distance gleams the white of the Dover cliffs. Let me go home. But they won't, they won't. It must be peaceful over there by the cliffs and in that convoy of ships. The curve of the earth is the same as it always is and we are just trivia after all.

But then the anti-aircraft shells burst and deafen, jerking the machine about in the air. Metal fragments cut the face, the machine, and now we're in the fighter zone, behind the German lines and I can't hear the planes because my own is so noisy. I can't hear them, Hannah, and so I don't know if I'm going to be shot from the sky. Can you hear my heart, Hannah, it's so loud, my breath is slow, sweat is trickling in runnels down the whale oil, fear is foul in my mouth.

And then they're here and I must dive, take a breath, stick forward, feeling crushed, the left hand on the throttle, the right on the stick. Two fingers slightly on the gun buttons, and now I must slow, Hannah, to eliminate vibration and let the target fill the whole Aldis screen. I must take my right hand from the stick, stretch out slowly and fire in one- or two-second bursts until I kill another man, Hannah. Another bloody man but it might have been me, you see.

And I can't stop hearing the screams of my pupil as they took him out of the plane. He was a flamer, you see, and he didn't jump out. I would jump. I couldn't burn, but he burnt. He was blind and burnt and they gave him morphine and he died, thank God. But someone's coming again. I must dive, Hannah, feel the pressure, I'm diving, diving, diving.

His screams tore into her sleep and she gripped him, held him and talked and kissed until the dawn came but she knew that she could not take the thoughts from inside his head, or the war from around his body and they both knew that Harry had been right and nothing was worth this slaughter.

In January propertied women over thirty were given the vote because they had shown their true value, it was said. Hannah drank wine with Frances and they were glad but the children had the influenza which was sweeping Europe and so had some of the women and Joe had gone and she could not forget his screams.

Only two women had died and no children and Frances said that they had been lucky and Hannah nodded because she knew it was true. In April the buds were forcing through the ground and Hannah no longer felt sick each morning but was tired and sat with Naomi and Kate to listen to their reading and Annie and Matthew wrote their words for her. And the other children too. Frances would no longer let her sit up for night duty in the wards and in May Hannah took the bus to the station with the four children because Frances said that Eliza needed help at Penbrin but Hannah knew it was because her baby was growing and she was too tired.

The spring turned to summer and there was talk of peace perhaps but Joe did not come because he could get no more leave. Hannah watched the children in the sea and the men who coughed the gas remains from their chest and laughed as they laughed, smiled as they smiled, and slept as they slept, with a measure of peace, for Joe's screams had faded as the baby grew.

In the evening, with Eliza and Sam she talked of the school and they decided that she should buy Penhallon which was bigger and no longer spoiled by her father's past presence. She sat in the warm evening air, breathing in the thyme, watching as Sam, so broad, so grey now, smoked his pipe and swatted at the mosquitoes and decided that she would write to Esther and take her son, because she owed that to her cousin. She felt the baby move within her and smiled. It was strong and she was well and ready for the birth which was due in two weeks, at the end of September, and tomorrow she was taking the children on the moor but not far, for she was too heavy – like a great cow, Matthew had said.

'Are you all right, Hannah?' Eliza asked, leaning forward and pulling at the cushion behind Hannah who smiled, for how many times had she done this for her mother but she was strong and this was Joe's child and nothing could go wrong, not now.

The next day was cooler but still they went out on the moor with Kate and Naomi carrying the kite and Matthew the picnic. Annie held her hand and pulled at her dress which was too tight, she said.

Gulls wheeled over them and gorse flashed yellow against dark green. Primroses were pale yellow and violets vivid blue. The heather was purple and white and Kate picked some and brought it to her.

'This is good luck, Mother.' Her blonde hair lay in curls about her face, her wide mouth smiled as she tucked the heather into Hannah's bodice, and as Hannah kissed her she could smell the soft sun on her skin and hoped that Kate's mother could see her child. They ate pasties and the children ran down the hill to the brook and Hannah flew the kite, feeling the string taut around her hand as the wind snatched and pulled. She sat on her jacket and could hear the bees amongst the heather. She was tired but the air was good and clean and the children were laughing and splashing.

'When Daddy is home he will show you how to tickle trout,'

she called, pulling in the kite, watching it flop and plummet as it dropped beneath the cushion of wind.

Was it really so long ago that Joe and she had lain on the bank, their hands growing numb as they caught trout without lines and flies? She knew that it was an eternity.

'My oil lamp is smoking,' Naomi said as they walked back to Penbrin when the wind grew chill and that scent of late summer seemed stronger in the air.

'Bring it to the kitchen when we get in,' Hannah said. 'I'll clean it. I quite enjoy that job for some reason.'

The men were still at the beach with their families so Hannah sat on the kitchen chair and eased her back, feeling the baby kicking, longing to see and hold it. Was it a girl or a boy? Did it look like Joe, red-gold and blue-eyed or like her, dark-haired, dark-eyed? Naomi brought the lamp and then Hannah heard the knock at the door but knew that Eliza would answer. She stood, stretching her back, her shoulders, and drained the bowl of the lamp into the tin which she always used. The smell was the same, thick and rich.

Eliza came in and Hannah looked and her face was pinched and her lips were strange, thin and pressed hard together and her hand was reaching for Hannah.

'Sit down, my dear.'

But Hannah knew she must not for there was a telegram in her aunt's hand, a buff telegram, the same as the one they had sent for Harry and if she sat down she would have to read it, and she would not do that because she was cleaning the lamp. It needed cleaning.

'I must clean this lamp,' she said but her voice was dead.

'Hannah, you must read this.' Her aunt was shaking now and came round the table and took Hannah's hand.

'I won't read it. If I don't read it it can't be true.' She took the rag which lay on the table and wiped round the bowl again and again because it must be quite clean, quite dry. Naomi would like that. She would not listen to the rustle of the paper as Eliza lifted the flap. She would not listen to the words which said in Eliza's voice. 'Regret to inform you that Major Joe Arness is missing, believed killed.'

No, she would not listen. She had too much to do.

'Hannah, please stop. Please sit down.' Her aunt was crying now but she, Mrs Joe Arness, would not, because she had not heard, would not listen.

She poured fresh oil into the bowl and put a clean white wick into the burner.

'It should fit exactly,' she told her aunt. 'But must be able to move up and down easily and yet not loosely.'

She would not listen to the soft crying but to the hiss of the fire, the sound of her voice, 'It must be soft and not too tightly plaited.'

Her fingers were shaking. How absurd. She could not ease the wick through the burner. She must not talk while she tried again. Her neck was hurting, she must get close, so that she could see the gap, not the yellow telegram.

She shrugged off her aunt's hand. 'Don't you realise I must concentrate,' she said. 'Of course there are candles if this lamp doesn't work.' The shelves were full of them, wax built up on twisted wicks, the smell would be the same as that which had oozed across the table at Arthur's party. But he was gone now, wasn't he? There would be no more candles for Arthur, for Harry, but the wick was through now.

'To put out the lamp it should not be turned down so far that the charred wick can fall into the bowl of the lamp. You must tell Naomi to blow out the flame, turn down the wick very low and leave the glowing end to go out of its own accord.'

Hannah stood now and turned to her aunt. 'Tell Naomi please, Eliza. I have to go and check the apples.'

She walked past her aunt and now she took the telegram and Eliza put her hand on her arm but she walked on alone, out across the courtyard and up the stable-loft steps.

Moss had dried dull green on the wood and it was cracked and needed staining, but it was smooth and warm and the air inside the loft was full of motes caught in shafts of light and apple scent. The apples were fresh and full and firm and juice would fill her mouth, she knew that.

She picked one up, so red and green and held it to her cheek, remembering the feel of Simon's hand, the touch of Harry's as she had kissed it, the pale thin blue veins of her mother's, the red glint on Arthur's hair, and Joe, the gentle hardness of Joe who was her life.

And now she read the words, so black on the paper, and heard his screams. How could they have faded? And the tears came, not silent but loud, and howls too. The floor was hard as she dropped to it and beat her hands, harder and harder and harder until the splinters dug into her skin and she bled, red on white.

The baby was born that night, a girl, Edith, with red-gold hair and dark eyes and six weeks later the war ended on the eleventh hour of the eleventh day of the eleventh month and Sam went up to London and traced the remains of Joe's squadron but they could tell him nothing.

In December Hannah received a letter from a customer of Joe's commissioning another table. She put it with the other two which had arrived for him to read when he came home.

She told Frances, who had come down to stay, that he would come back. He had said 'Stay with me', and so she would. He would not leave her, would he? Would he? Would he? And she cried again and held the baby close and Frances made her cocoa and they sat by the fire and sewed puppets and lavender bags and talked of the school they would begin but it was all so empty now. During the day her thoughts were never still, at night her sleep was never sound.

Winter passed and the tears still came and there was no peace for her anywhere, though Eliza and Frances said that somehow she must find some. Edith grew well and plump and Matthew carved a rattle which Naomi, Annie and Kate rubbed down and painted. They were brown from the mild winter, the bright spring, when Hannah walked them on the moor again in May, wrapping the cloak around herself, feeling tired as they turned and waved to Frances who held Edith, white-shawled in her arms.

She did not bring the kite. There was not enough wind, she told the children, watching as it flicked the hair about their faces. The primroses were soft yellow again in the green fields which led to the moor and the violets vivid blue, the heather purple and white. The calves were out grazing and the children walked cautiously through the herd.

Hannah listened to their talk, their laughter, for they could laugh again now and that was good. She drew the cloak tighter. She wanted to reach out and hold their hands but they were running on, their heads lifted to the pale blue sky.

They ate sandwiches down by the stream and Hannah lifted her skirt and walked on the rounded pebbles, feeling the water cold and strong, tugging at her feet, rolling the stones across her toes. She felt it but not inside. Nothing touched her inside any more. She sat on the bank, and picked at the grass, holding a stem between her thumbs and blowing, the piercing whistle startling the children, making them laugh. When the sun had passed above them Hannah rose, eager to be walking, unable to stay in any one place for long because he was not here, her love, her love.

'Let's go home now.'

She did not turn as the children groaned but walked back the way she had come, knowing that they would follow and they did, picking primroses for Frances and Eliza and violets, which they gave to her, and she wished they had not, for it was violets she had given to Joe.

Hannah looked at the house as they walked down the sloping field; its grey stone, the Virginia creeper, the windows filled with flowers, the driveway which swept up and round the house, the white stones which lined it. The white clouds moved across the sky behind it, changing shape from swans to ships to billowing sheets on a washing-line but the house never changed and she was grateful for its certainty.

Frances was at the gate. Her hands were white where she gripped the bar, she pulled the children to her, her eyes red.

'Joe's home, Hannah. He's come home,' Frances said. 'Sam's just picked him up in the jingle.'

Hannah looked at the house, at the garden, at Frances. 'Where, where?' she cried, starting to run up the drive.

'The stable, my dear, but . . .'

Hannah did not wait to hear but ran up the rutted drive, her ankles turning; she did not notice or care and there was no breath left to spare to call his name and so she ran across the stable yard past the thyme to the open door.

He was there, dressed in an old tweed suit, rubbing the pony down, round and round with straw which fell from the hook where his left hand had been. She watched as he stooped and picked up the straw again with his right hand and pushed it between the two curved metal prongs and rubbed at the pony's damp flanks again but still it fell and now she watched as he leant his head on nis arm and cried.

She held on to the door, feeling the solid wood beneath her hand, seeing the pony that shifted from foot to foot; the bale of straw, the oats in the sack and knew she must not cry, not yet, not now. She gripped the door again and drew a breath.

'Do it again, Joe,' she said, because she must do for him what he had done for her so long ago.

He turned and she moved towards him, holding him as he wept, smelling the violets which were crushed between them, feeling the gentle hardness of his hand on her face, hearing his voice speaking of his love, his fear, his despair. The flames, the prison, and now the search for peace.

'Do it again, my love,' she said at last, breaking free of him and placing straw in the cold metal, forcing herself not to help as he wound it round the hook and rubbed at the damp flank until some of his memories were wiped away and Hannah watched, knowing that life could go on now, for them at least.

Also available in Arrow

Somewhere Over England

Margaret Graham

War will not break her spirit...

In England in the 1930s, eighteen-year-old Helen Carstairs braves the prejudice of friends and family to marry Heine, a young German photographer who had fled the growing horror of the Nazis.

But the storm clouds are gathering in Europe. When fighting breaks out, Heine is interned, their small son is evacuated and Helen is left to face the Blitz alone.

And the agony of war threatens to divide a family already tormented by conflicting passions of loyalty, shame, betrayal – and love.

Previously published as *A Fragment of Time*

arrow books

Also available in Arrow

After the Storm

Margaret Graham

War can end more than one life, and break more than one heart.

'I am in despair too, but I want to go on living, fighting, getting out of here to something better.'

Born into hardship in a Northumbrian mining village, it takes all Annie Manon's spirit to survive the bleak years following the First World War. As her family fractures around her, she longs to make something of her life.

Through hard work and determination she eventually leaves the poverty and despair of her childhood behind her. But then war breaks out once more, taking her further away from her dreams and those she loves most. And it is all she can do to keep hope alive.

Previously published as *Only the Wind is Free*

arrow books